D1206888

ISABEL THE FAIR

The historical novels of Margaret Campbell Barnes

THE PASSIONATE BROOD
(first published as *Like Us They Lived*)
MY LADY OF CLEVES
WITHIN THE HOLLOW CROWN
BRIEF GAUDY HOUR
WITH ALL MY HEART
MARY OF CARISBROOKE
THE TUDOR ROSE
KING'S FOOL
THE KING'S BED
LADY ON THE COIN
(with Hebe Elsna)

MARGARET CAMPBELL BARNES

Isabel
The Fair

MACDONALD and JANE'S · LONDON

First published, *1957*
Reprinted, *1971*
This impression, *1974*

Copyright © *Margaret Campbell Barnes, 1957*

ISBN *0 356 01754 0*

Published by
Macdonald and Janes (Macdonald & Co. (Publishers) Ltd),
St. Giles House,
49–50 Poland Street,
London W1
Printed in Great Britain by
Redwood Burn Limited
Trowbridge & Esher

For

MICHAEL

"Je maintiendrai"

—"She has a lovely face;
God in His mercy lend her grace."

The Lady of Shalott,
ALFRED, LORD TENNYSON

AUTHOR'S NOTE

I would like to remind readers that contemporary information about events described in this book is to be found mostly in chronicles kept by monks, in the accounts of household stewards, or in the letters of King Edward the Second and various people of his time, all of which are written in Latin or old French. Also that in this pre-Chaucerian age the Court language of England was Norman French. In consequence all dialogue, whether authentic or imaginary, is necessarily a translation of the characters' thoughts into modern English.

For the purposes of my story I have used the incident of the masked lady riding into Westminster Hall as if it happened during the hey-day of Piers Gaveston, but it is generally believed that it occurred a few years later when Hugh le Despenser was the royal favourite.

MARGARET CAMPBELL BARNES

Yarmouth,
Isle of Wight

CHAPTER 1

THEY had finished dressing the bride at last. Her excited women had bathed her in rose-water and settled the folds of her wedding gown and bound her cloud of long fair hair with pearls. And now they stood aside or knelt back on their heels to regard the result of their handiwork. Each woman, whether she loved her young mistress or not, sighed with satisfaction. And the King of France's daughter herself, seeing the radiant reflection in the mirror which they held for her, knew with a fierce inward joy why men called her Isabel the Fair.

"In a few hours I shall be Queen of England!" she proclaimed, lifting her bejewelled skirts and letting her little feet dance to the excitement that stirred her blood.

"It will mean leaving your family," the old Countess de Bringnencourt, who had been her nurse, reminded her sadly.

Sixteen-year-old Isabel Capet, who always lived for the moment, pushed that inevitable spectre of home-sickness to the back of her vivacious mind. "Not for weeks yet, Bringnette," she said. "It is not like the time when my poor Aunt Marguerite had to cross the Channel to be old Edward the First's second wife. *His* son has come to fetch *me*, and as you all know we are going to spend our honeymoon here in Boulogne. And after that," she added a little wistfully, "perhaps I shall not mind quite so much."

Royal etiquette demanded that the second Edward should come to fetch his bride because both of Isabel's parents were reigning sovereigns, and like any young girl she thrilled to the report that he had hurried away from his wars in Scotland to make sure of their marriage. Of course, his eagerness might have been prompted by some dull political issue, but she hoped that he had heard how many important people had foretold that she would grow up to be one of the most beautiful women in Europe.

9

From the apartments so sumptuously prepared for her in Boulogne castle she could see the fine fleet of ships flying the Plantagenet leopards down in the harbour, and the place-at-arms where shining tents had sprung up like a spread of mushrooms to accommodate the English. And yesterday there had been a great deal of ceremonial pother in the great hall when Edward had paid homage to her father for Guienne and Ponthieu, the lands which he had inherited through his ancestress, Eleanor of Aquitaine. He could not have enjoyed doing that, she supposed. No son of the all-conquering Edward Longshanks could have. But it had been part of the price which he was willing to pay for her, and her brothers admitted that he had done it with pleasant grace. She herself had not been allowed to go down and watch. It would have been unpropitious, people said, to meet her bridegroom before the wedding. But to-day was *her* day. He would be in the great cathedral-church of Boulogne waiting for her, and judging by the sudden commotion down in the courtyard the bridal procession must be forming now.

"I *must* see what he looks like!" she cried, pushing aside the two girls who held her mirror and running impetuously to a window.

To their consternation the heavy Florentine mirror was swept from their hands to shatter in fragments on the stone-flagged floor. "Merciful Mother of God, it means seven years bad luck!" cried Ghislaine, the younger one, swooping down upon it with outstretched hands.

"Misfortune to your Grace's marriage!" shrilled the elder, who envied the Springtime of the bride's beauty.

But Isabel Capet scarcely heard them. Half screened by a solid Norman pillar she was gazing down into the courtyard, hands pressed to heart. "Oh, but he is handsome!" she was murmuring ecstatically.

At three-and-twenty Edward the Second of England was certainly good to look upon.

Scarcely less eager than their mistress, all the women in the room crowded forward to see him for themselves—all except fond, foolish Ghislaine du Bois who still crouched tearfully over the broken fragments of glass, trying to fit them together as desperately as though she were mending the pattern of her beloved Princess's life.

Like a scene in some bright, unfaded tapestry they saw the distinguished company forming themselves into a procession in pale January sunshine. Silks and velvets made splashes of vivid colour against old stone walls, bringing an extravagant breath of Paris to the grim utility of a busy port. The men from across the Channel were well enough made, but not half so modish as the Dauphin and his suite, decided the watching Frenchwomen. They spoke disparagingly of short *cote-hardies* and the cut of woollen hose. But with the tall, splendid bridegroom himself, even they could find no flaw. If he lacked the commanding, warlike aspect associated with his renowned father, his supple limbs had strength and grace, and his fair-skinned, sensitive face was undeniably beautiful. The sun shone becomingly on his golden crown and bright brown hair. Though Isabel had been betrothed to him since she was a child of seven, this was the first time she had ever set eyes on him; and, Heaven be praised, he looked the kind of husband she had always longed for! His easy charm would fulfil the secret dreams of any romantically-minded girl. Though whether that was a blessing to be entirely thankful for she was not, on second thoughts, entirely sure.

"Tell me quickly what rumours you have heard," she whispered, catching at the sleeve of a worldly-wise countess who had but recently returned from England.

"Rumours?" The Countess looked both embarrassed and alarmed, so that Isabel's heart sank.

"I am not a child," she insisted, her voice sharp as it was apt to be in moments of anxiety. "I realize that with so handsome a bachelor king there must have been other women."

"Other *women*?" The Countess's brows shot up, her reply came more glibly. "Oh no, Madam. I was over there in the Dowager-Queen Marguerite's suite for months, and never heard of any. I do assure your Grace that there will be no need for unhappiness on that score."

Isabel's heart soared high again. The carefully picked words pleased her even more than they must have relieved the embarrassed Countess. She was too inexperienced to perceive their sting. And in any case her old nurse broke abruptly into the whispered conversation, deliberately distracting her attention. "Look, my lady, there is your Aunt Marguerite. The tall crowned one in the lovely furs. She seems to have acquired more poise and grace during these past few years. So strange to think that you were betrothed to *your* Edward on the same day that she married his father!"

"It was all part of France's foreign policy. I remember how everybody in Paris went about crying after she left."

"Every night I thank the blessed saints that she will be over there in England to advise you. She is so sensible. Although she had to take the place of that legendary Queen Eleanor of Castile whom the first Edward loved so dearly, they say she never made an enemy of anyone. And see with what affectionate courtesy her step-son leads her forward to your lady mother."

"When he turns and smiles like that he is *ravissan*!" murmured Isabel, looking forward to the time when all his most intimate smiles would be for her.

But there was no more time for dreaming. "The bridegroom's procession is leaving the Castle, and the moment arrives for Madame la Princesse to descend!" announced the resonant voice of the Master of Ceremonies. And down in the great hall King Philip of France, the handsome father from whom Isabel inherited her beauty, was waiting to take her to the church so that her young body might set a further seal upon the alliance which he had planned.

No daughter of the house of Capet had ever been given a more splendid wedding. For was not her mother Queen of Navarre, and were there not several reigning sovereigns and half the nobility of the land scintillating among the guests? Formally and obediently, and with a touching effort at composure, Isabel moved through the ceremonial pattern of the day. She strove to please her parents, who were watching her with fond pride— a pride in the dignity of their royal line in which she fully shared. Her youthful craving for importance was satisfied by the grandeur they had provided, her vanity fed by finding herself so suddenly blossoming from the schoolroom to become the magnet for all men's admiring eyes. But most of all she hoped, with childish uncertainty, that the tall bridegroom by her side admired her too.

Because she was eager and impressionable it was the sacrament of marriage inside the vast church which moved her even more than the pomp of the public ceremony enacted upon the steps for all to see. Long after the thrill of fanfares had faded she would remember the hush that followed cheering, the solemn chanting, the tall candles on the altar, and the sudden sense of irrevocable reality as she and Edward approached the golden haze of light. Because he held her hand all her vows to love and cherish were made with willing gladness. A new awareness of spiritual values informed her, temporarily swamping all tawdry pride. In a brief moment of maturity she glimpsed those elements in marriage which lie beyond the lure of physical attraction. It was as though she and Edward were setting out from that hallowed place upon a hazardous journey. They were both young and had so far to go—so much to learn about each other. There would, she felt, be such alarming need of patience. And she was not a patient person. "To have and to hold until Death us do part," she heard the Archbishop say in sonorous Latin. She looked up from beneath the priceless lace of her veil and Edward Plantagenet looked down. He smiled, and she hoped that Death would be a very long way off for both of them.

Afterwards, highborn guests and the crowds still cheering in the streets were all in agreement that it had been the most gorgeous wedding they had ever seen, and that no royal pair had ever looked so attractive.

"God send that it was worth it!" muttered Philip le Bel, thinking of the depleted state of his Exchequer.

"It will be worth any price, dear Philip, if it ensures a lasting peace between our two countries!" said his sister, the Queen-Dowager Marguerite of England, who only nine years ago had been called upon to give her youth to an elderly widower in the same cause.

The day was by no means over. Back at the castle bride and groom must welcome their guests, graciously acknowledging gifts and congratulations. The representatives of each royal house must be received according to rank and with an eye to existing political relations. At sixteen, decided Isabel, it is difficult to be sure of saying the right and tactful thing, particularly when one's head is beginning to ache beneath an unaccustomed veil of priceless old lace. But, by the grace of God, she now had a husband—a pleasant-voiced young man who good-naturedly took most of the conversational burden from her. Whether *he* said the right thing or not seemed to matter much less since he was a foreigner and remarkably adroit at shearing away from any profound or controversial topic. "How do you manage to speak French so fluently?" she asked with gratitude, between receiving one batch of guests and the next.

"We are not quite savages," he said, laughing without offence. "Although we speak English with the people, French is the language of my Court."

"I should have remembered," said Isabel abashed. "But you have no accent like most of the people in your suite. Or if you have it is not at all Norman, but rather—of the South, I should say?"

"Scarcely surprising, my little sage, since my best friend is of Gascon lineage." He seemed quite pleased that she should have detected it and, rising from the double throne they shared, held out an inviting hand. "And now that we appear to have done our duty by all those pompous people let me give myself the pleasure of taking you to talk with the May Queen."

"The May Queen?"

"My stepmother. The people always call her that—possibly because they associate her with the kind of happiness they feel on May Day. Or maybe my Gascon friend invented it. He has a nickname for everyone."

"I hope he will not invent one for me." Isabel Capet was on her dignity. Most of the people he had alluded to as pompous were her grandest relatives. She was tired and hungry, and not a little piqued by his obvious devotion to the May Queen. He had even called his stately new ship after her, whereas Isabel had hoped to find her own name on the prow. The easy comradeship they shared made her feel like a child. While talking respectfully enough to this widowed aunt of hers, she decided that although the Dowager-Queen of England might be kind and full of common sense, as old Bringnette had said, yet she looked far too young to be a grown man's stepmother. Having always had to give place to her three brothers, Isabel's besetting sin was jealousy. She took stock of Marguerite's frank, serene face and caught herself thinking reprehensibly, "Well, at least she is not as beautiful as I am."

She knew that she was being cat-like and falling away from that grace she had felt in church; but she wanted Edward to smile down at her like that. "To-morrow, dear Aunt Marguerite, we must have a long gossip together and you must tell me what it is like living in England," she said, to make amends.

Heralds were summoning the wedding-party to supper and when bride and bridegroom were seated side by side beneath a golden canopy at the dais table, they contrived to further their acquaintance a little.

"My parents have made me learn English for years. Ever since they arranged for me to marry you," Isabel told him.

"That was very wise of them. It should help you to feel at home, being able to talk to your grooms and falconers and such."

"It is very difficult because you have so many words which mean the same thing," pouted Isabel, who had no particular desire to do so.

"That must be because we are mongrels, with a language made up of Latin, Norse, Saxon and Norman."

"But *you* are a Plantagenet," reproved Isabel, a little shocked.

The King of Sicily claimed her attention for a while and Edward was being polite to the Archduke of Austria, but while the roast peacock was being brought in they were able to snatch another moment to themselves. "Does it not tire you talking to so many people?" whispered Isabel.

The idea appeared to surprise him. "Tire me? No. I suppose I am very strong."

"So am I, really. But I could sleep and sleep. Perhaps it is the hours they spent dressing me and having to act for hours on end as if one were part of a pageant."

"It must be worse for the bride, whom everyone stares at," he allowed kindly. "And perhaps I am more accustomed to all this ceremony. I endured hours of it only yesterday when I had to do homage to your father." And King of England though he was, he made such a comical grimace and spoke so boyishly that, in spite of his six years seniority, his little bride ceased to stand in very much awe of him. "I wanted to come and watch, but they would not let me," she told him.

"If you had I am afraid you would have found it very dull. But your father was most generous. He gave me some splendid presents in return, including the loveliest sorrel mare."

"Oh, I am glad!"

After a polite conversation about mural paintings with the Archbishop, Edward returned eagerly to the subject of the well-chosen gift. "She has a white star on her forehead and one white hind fetlock. Nothing will ever make me part with that animal."

Isabel laughed at his enthusiasm. Hounds and horses, she had always understood, were an obsession with the English.

"I hope nothing will make you part with *anything* my father has given you——"

Edward turned and grinned at her. "Including the bride!" they both said in merry unison.

The main courses were over. The board was being cleared and the best wines of France were circulating freely. Jugglers and mountebanks and mummers were beginning to entertain the company. "My mother has had some wonderful dresses made for me to bring to England. My women say they will give the ladies of your Court something to talk about for the rest of the winter," confided Isabel. But Edward was laughing at the antics of a clever little dwarf and did not hear her. "Do you always have such clever jugglers in this country?" he was asking of her father. His naïve delight in them was flattering to his host. Wine and candlelight had brought a flush to his fair skin, and his laugh rang out spontaneously. He was so engagingly ready to be entertained.

"Some of the new dresses I am bringing to England are rose red. It is supposed to suit me," persisted Isabel.

The mummers had begun declaiming a dull classic oration. Edward's swiftly darting mind was suddenly interested in her again and she was delighted to find him far more knowledgeable about dresses than were her brothers. "Deep rose red by candlelight, with a touch of that silvery stuff, should be enchanting," he agreed, discussing the problem as earnestly as any woman. "But the blue and white of your lovely fleur-de-lys by sunlight, I think, so as to bring out the gold in your hair."

Isabel felt pleasantly important and grown-up again. "Do you think they will like me at West-min-stair?" she asked, attempting a sideways glance from beneath lowered lashes such as she had often seen her father's favourite mistress make use of very effectively.

"How could anyone help liking my new Queen when she is so young and beautiful?" Edward disengaged her fingers from the half-filled goblet she had been toying with and lifted them gallantly to his lips. Sentimentally approving smiles settled foolishly on the faces surrounding them. His manners were certainly exquisite, but Isabel felt sure that half his attention was back on the slick movements of the mummers. And she hated having him think of her as someone too young for passionate attention.

There were more entertainers and bursts of laughter and interchanges of compliments, and before supper was over King Philip delighted with his new son-in-law's appreciation, had given him the amusing little dwarf to take back to England.

"In case you should be bored with your immature wife!" said Isabel, jabbing at a manchet of bread with the jewelled fork which her favourite brother had given her. Her little spurt of laughter made a jest of the words, but there were tears in her eyes.

While all the fine company danced in the hall Isabel's ladies prepared her for bed. She shivered, listening to their broadly jesting advice, and could not tell whether it was from excitement or fear. When the hilarious laughter was at its height she was borne along in yet another procession—the final procession of the day which must end in the bridal chamber. With downcast eyes she swept a good-night curtsy to her father when he released her hand at the door. People crowded about her, holding torches high above their heads. "God send an heir for England!" they cried, when the Archbishop blessed the great damasked bed. She dared not lift her eyes to the other side of it where Edward stood in unaccustomed silence.

At a sign from her father the room began to empty. They were all going away at last. Her mother was kissing her as fervently as though she were going on a journey—the first stage of that journey which was marriage, presumably. Bringnette was undressing her by the warmth of the brazier. Taking off her jewelled slippers and her fur-lined wrap, Isabel pulled the thick cloud of her hair about her slender breasts. At the last moment she clung to the old lady's loving hands. "There, there, my sweet!" comforted Bringnette. "There is no going back to virgin modesty now." And Isabel, to whom fate had given a personable husband, was woman enough to know that she did not really want to.

At last she was lying naked between the sheets. The curtains had been drawn and for the first time a man lay beside her. Together they listened for the click of the latch, the dying away of laughter down the tower stairs. All the lights had been snuffed out save the little night-lamp which shone through the richness of the bed hangings like a wavering yellow star. Tense and helpless as some small wild creature caught in a snare, Isabel stared at the comforting star, waiting for initiation into the reality from which sprang all the half-understood jests and sniggerings she had heard.

She felt Edward reach for her hand. Heard him mutter something about hoping the whole inquisitive rabble would break their pestilential necks on the stairs, and then, with a spurt of high-pitched laughter, begin to tell some fantastic story about a prying page who had hidden himself under some English duchess's bridal bed. Gradually it dawned upon her that her new husband, whom she had thought of as so mature and experienced, was as nervous as herself. A tender concern informed her, making her forgetful of self. She sat up in the great bed, clasping her hands about her knees as she did when telling legends to her younger cousin, Philip of Valois. Guided by her growing maturity she began discussing the events of the day, touching lightly upon this moment or that, criticizing each guest with clever mimicry, striving to set handsome Edward Plantagenet at ease. He enjoyed her pungent comments, the same things amused them both and soon they were laughing together uncontrollably. Until Isabel, becoming breathless, pressed both hands to her brow and moaned through the remnants of her mirth: "Oh, my poor head!"

Edward was all concern at once.

"I do suffer from these devastating headaches. Whenever I am emotionally upset, the doctors say," she explained. "But surely only the cruellest spite of witchcraft could have sent me one to-night!"

"My poor sweet!"

"It will pass," Isabel assured him with desperate optimism. "But my women waked me at dawn and now——"

"Now it is long past midnight. And you must be cold perched up there hugging your knees." He pulled her down into his arms and began kissing her until her senses stirred deliciously. Eager for his embraces, she lay mute until, too soon, his lips released her. "In truth you are tired to death, you sweet child," he whispered with compunction, not guessing at the strength of her awakening desire.

The charcoal in the brazier had burned low. He lay back and yawned, holding her gently against him as though she were indeed a child. It was warm and dark in the bridal bed, his shoulder made a comfortable resting-place and the hot spiced wine of their loving-cup had made her sleepy. Gradually the waves of pain in her forehead quietened. Desire gave place to drowsiness, and Isabel fell asleep.

When she waked sunlight lay bright upon her eyes. The damask hangings had been drawn back and Edward, resplendent in his scarlet bed wrap, was standing by the open window. "It is a hunting morning with no frost," he was saying as she began to stir, "and I must ride my new sorrel."

"I am married. I am Queen of England," remembered Isabel almost automatically. Then, as she pushed back the golden weight of her hair and came slowly into the day's consciousness, her mind plunged back to review her wedding night. "And I must face my chattering women and my fondly probing mother and—worst of all—the concern in Bringnette's eyes," she thought, "and tell them all that my handsome bridegroom has been— kind."

CHAPTER 2

FOR Isabel the days that followed were an almost bewildering succession of excitements. Tournaments and pageants followed each other, each more gorgeous than the last. Every meal was a merry feast, each night brought masques and dancing. All the delights which a young girl could dream of were packed into the short, sunny space of her honeymoon. And she herself was always the centre of attraction, reigning as Queen of Beauty over it all.

"Small wonder if it turns her head!" complained wise old Bringnette, who had to bear with Isabel's over-wrought tantrums whenever some detail of her toilette displeased her. "How will she ever come down to the level of everyday living in that rough, fog-bound island over there?"

Isabel, hasty tempered but swiftly repentant, would remember to save the old lady some special dainty from the high table next day, or delight young Ghislaine, whom she had slapped, with a gay tournament ribbon. If her lovely crowned head were turned, at least her heart remained constant. She drank in the compliments of French and foreign knights with equal avidity, but it was her English husband who filled her bravely widening world.

Newly awakened to the lusty urges in her own nature, she

sometimes wished that he were less gentle and more passionate. Lack of experience prevented her from realizing that he was by no means in love with her. She found him good company, and all the more amusing to talk to because he was less hemmed about with formality than were her own relatives. Because he looked so splendid on a charger she was proud to see him wear her favour in the lists, and clapped her hands with joy when he broke the lance of her uncle Louis of Clermont. And because he had all the visible attributes of an athlete even those spectators who bore no love towards England backed him as a probable champion. But Edward, unlike the rest, was by no means fiercely competitive. He enjoyed his sport indolently, mostly for the pleasure it gave him to use well-trained eye and muscle. And when, to the momentary dismay of his hosts, his brother-in-law the Duke of Brabant unhorsed him in the second bout, his backers were surprised to see the Plantagenet pick himself up smiling. He was quite cheerful and ungrudging about his defeat, and seemed content to sit beside the Queen of Beauty to watch his erstwhile opponent charge on to further triumphs.

"Do you *really* not mind?" asked Isabel, trying to hide her own disappointment.

"Why should I? It is very pleasant sitting here with you beside a cheerful brazier and watching the other fellows hacking bits out of each other," said Edward, flinching a little as she insisted in the best tradition upon binding up a slight gash on his wrist.

"My brothers and my uncles are for ever practising new thrusts, and laying bets and comparing their chances. Did you not *want* to win?"

Edward removed his stifling steel helmet, with its famous sprig of *plante de genista*, and laid it aside. He smoothed back his rumpled hair with obvious relief. "When one has been brought up among men who live, think, eat and frequently sleep in full armour——" he began, with an apologetic shrug.

Having finished her romantic bandaging, Isabel handed back napkin and bowl to a waiting page. She looked around at her Father's banner-encircled lists which up to that moment had seemed so bravely fine, and recalled how her husband's father had gone crusading. "You mean," she faltered, "that all this seems to you merely child's play?"

That had not been Edward's exact meaning, but he let it

pass. "I would sooner go hawking, or play some game of chance or listen to good music."

"But you went to war with the great King Edward."

"Oh yes. He saw to that."

Isabel stared, uncomprehending. She was surprised that he did not seem proud of the fact, and still more surprised to sense some antipathy towards that great soldier. But Edward only laughed at her shocked perplexity. He pulled the coveted broom flower from his helmet and stuck it coquettishly in the folds of her wimple where its golden sweetness vied with the golden lights in her brown eyes. "My dear Isabel," he said, "whatever you and your ladies may imagine, I do assure you there is nothing particularly glamorous about war. One of my sisters was born in the middle of a Crusade—and I myself was born in a beleaguered Welsh castle, so I should know!"

"Did—did your poor mother get enough to eat?"

"I am quite sure she did. My father would have seen to that too, even though she bore me in a small, bare room with men-at-arms tramping about outside the door. It was at Caernarvon. And actually he had just taken the castle from our unruly Welsh and they were still outside the gates, shouting for a ruler of their own. The Welsh can be as pertinacious as they are brave, and my father was all for consolidating his realm. So as soon as my mother's women had clothed my puling nakedness he carried me out on to the battlements in the hollow of his shield and showed me to them. 'Here is your Prince,' he shouted in that far-carrying voice of his. 'Cannot speak a word of English, and born on Welsh soil. Edward, my firstborn.' They were quite pleased, I believe. And that is how I came to be Prince of Wales. Until my father died hurrying to lay siege to some other castle up in Scotland. He had been widowed, and eight years married to your aunt by then."

"Did each of his Queens always have to go campaigning with him?"

"He expected it of them. You would not like *your* marriage to be like that, would you?"

"N-no," admitted Isabel, who was beginning to suspect that some of the unpleasant things her ladies had told her about the country across *La Manche* might be true. "But I should like to be adored as your own mother was. The name of Eleanor of Castile is a by-word here for a woman who enjoys a long and happy married love. Was it true what my brother Philip heard about the thirteen crosses?"

"Quite true. She was travelling up north to join my father as usual when she caught a dangerous fever. And he, whom nothing could ever deflect from his military purposes, left off battering the Scots and travelled down day and night to reach her. But she died, God assoil her, before he came. It must have been terrible for him. We brought her body home to Westminster. The journey took thirteen days. And in his agony of grief my father had a stone cross of exquisite craftsmanship erected in every place where her coffin had rested. The one nearest my palace I often pass on my way to the City of London. It stands in a thriving little hamlet beside the Thames. *Chère Reine*, the villagers call it now, because of his dear Queen's cross."

Isabel listened to him enthralled. With her vivid imagination, strengthened by all the romances which she loved to read, she saw herself as a second *Chère Reine*. She imagined the people strewing roses in her path, a handsome devoted husband standing by her side and the legend of their marital life going down to history.

But truth to tell, here in France—although they had been married only a few days—her husband was *not* always at her side. He liked to go off hunting or horse-racing with the younger men of the company. He grew restless sometimes and talked of going back to England, urging her to have her baggage packed in good time while the wind served.

"Why, *mon cher*, when my father has turned his kingdom upside down to provide us with so much happiness here?" asked Isabel, who had not yet come to know the difference between happiness and pleasure.

"You forget that I, too, have a kingdom to attend to," Edward would remind her.

"But only yesterday I heard you boasting to that odious Duke of Austria that you had been able to leave it in the hands of a capable Regent. Do you not trust him?"

"As myself. In fact, he is much more capable than I," said Edward, with a diffidence which she found so endearing that she was prepared to give up her own way to please him. Even though he added a warning that once they were back at Westminster there would be all manner of State business to attend to and he might often have to leave her to her own devices.

During the second week of her honeymoon Isabel found herself already looking round for company. She was no horsewoman, and it was while Edward was out hunting in the forests around Boulogne that she really came to know and love his step-mother. Although Marguerite was an out-door sort of person who would sooner have been out hunting too, Isabel would coax her to sit by the fire and tell her about the country in which all her own future would have to be passed—a future which now seemed to be looming very close. "Tell me, Madame, do you really like living in England?"

"It is good to be back on a visit to France," admitted the tall Dowager-Queen. "But please call me Marguerite, my dear, and do not look so depressed. I assure you the English have been very good to me."

"The people, do you mean? Or the nobles?"

"I was really thinking of the people, who are much less subservient than ours over here. The great barons—men like Lancaster and Warwick and Pembroke—each keep a standing army of retainers and are very jealous and quarrelsome. But it seems to me that it is usually the town burghers and the rich wool merchants who have the last word about things which concern the country as a whole."

Isabel smoothed the rolled-back flaps of her becoming headdress and stretched her daintily shod toes to the blaze. "Will they like me, do you suppose?"

The older woman surveyed her with admiring amusement. It would have been easy to say, as Edward had, that the English were bound to like their new little Queen because she was beautiful. But, although incapable of jealousy, Marguerite did not. "You will do wisely to *win* their love," she advised soberly. "As long as you act kindly they will protect you."

"Protect me?" Up went Isabel's short, haughty little nose. "Do you, in that crazy country, look for protection from a lot of unwashed peasants? Have I not a husband who is their King?"

It occurred to Marguerite that even kings who persisted in annoying their nobles might be glad of the protection of their people. Though never, of course, the kind of king her own husband had been. "The wealth of England lies on the backs of her sheep," she murmured, with a kind of contemplative irrelevance. "And her farmers and merchants have a strong sense of fair play."

A discussion about a lot of foreign rustics and shopkeepers seemed tedious to Isabel after all the colourful excitement of minstrels and tournaments. At the back of her mind she was deciding to wheedle as many lovely table appointments and tapestries as she could out of her parents so as to keep her Court in this benighted new country as French as possible. "You have two sons of your own, have you not?" she asked, politely turning the conversation.

"Thomas, who is seven, and little Edmund. They were too young to come."

"And you adore them," said Isabel gently, observing the lovely smile of motherhood that warmed her companion's face. "Yet you bear no grudge to Edward for inheriting everything. Nor to me, I think, because my dower is to be made up partly of your property."

"That was agreed to, was it not, at the time when I married the late King and you were betrothed to his son? Besides, I prefer to live simply. The effect of so much camping among my husband's soldiers, perhaps."

Isabel got up and kissed her impulsively. "I think you must be the most unself-seeking person I have ever met," she decided laughingly, "and we are both fortunate to have you. Edward must love you very much to have named his fine new ship after you."

"He had not met you then, and I had been able to—to smooth things over sometimes between him and his father."

"Then I was right in thinking that they did not get on very well?"

"They did not always see eye to eye."

By the humorous quirk at the corners of the Dowager-Queen's mouth her niece guessed this to be a wild understatement. "What did they disagree about?" she asked, with eager interest.

But Marguerite had heard the clatter of horses down in the courtyard and made it an excuse to go over to the window. "Oh, a variety of things. They were so utterly different in temperament," she answered, with calculated carelessness. "Look, the hunt is back already, and judging by the spattered state they are in they must have had a very good day."

Servants were already hurrying to and fro past the door of the solar where the two Queens sat, laying out fresh linen for King Edward and filling the great wooden tub with steaming water for his bath. While Marguerite slipped tactfully away, Isabel ran out to the stairs to meet him. But, hot and dusty as he was, he lingered by the great window in the hall reading a letter which a messenger had brought from England. He looked inordinately pleased as he read, and once or twice he laughed aloud as though the writer had been anything but dull. Isabel saw him refold the letter and thrust it into the unbuttoned front of his tunic, and make some answer to the waiting messenger. Then he came running up the shallow, curving stairs as blithely as a boy. "We are going home the day after to-morrow," he shouted, seeing Isabel waiting at the top. He tilted up her chin and kissed her briefly in passing. "The Earl of Cornwall has it all arranged. My Regent, you know. There will be a fine welcome for us at Dover, and I have sent word to him to have Roger Bigod's wife and the Countess of Hereford there to attend you on our journey to Westminster."

Isabel stiffened with anger. She stood immobile beneath his carelessly planted kiss. "And what will my parents feel about such curtailment of their hospitality?" she enquired coldly.

He halted in his tracks towards his waiting servants and the bath-tub. Clearly the thought had not occurred to him. He was not very clever, she thought, about other people's feelings. Yet as he stood there halfway across the solar like a chidden boy whose pleasure has been spoiled, there was something so attractive to her even about his backview that she forgot her hurt family pride and ran to him. "Let us stay a little longer," she entreated, reaching appealing fingers up his arm until they inadvertently touched upon the crackling stiffness of the letter which seemed to have spurred him to such curt decision. "What is another week when it will be years before I see my home again!"

He looked down at her as if seeing her only through the haze of some pleasant preoccupation of his own. His lips were smiling, though their amused tenderness, she felt, was not for her. He detached her fingers gently, kissed the tips of them with absent kindliness. But he shook his head. To Isabel he suddenly seemed to be all of twenty-three and terribly remote. "No, no, it is all arranged," he said irritably. "Tell that good old Bringnette, of yours to see that the other women pack your gear."

"And my parents?" repeated Isabel, in the small voice of a stricken child.

"I will explain to them."

What or how to explain he did not know. It was just that he could no longer stay away. But soon she heard him recounting to his servants some ludicrous incident of the chase and, in the midst of their hilarious laughter, splashing and singing in his bath.

"Why is he so absurdly anxious to get back just when we were all enjoying ourselves here?" she demanded tearfully of her aunt.

"Why was *my* husband always crazy to go to war when the roses were in bud at Sheen or I had just become pregnant?" countered Marguerite, with a comical grimace.

"It is too bad!" raged Isabel.

"Yet if we women can bring ourselves to come or go at our husband's bidding it is never *quite* so bad. At least *one* person is happy," said Marguerite.

Isabel saw the sense of it, and betook herself to the castle chapel to pray. "I have a vile temper and I am often jealous," she whispered. "But, oh, Mother of God, he is so good to look upon! And more than anything I want a wonderful love affair which will last me all my life, so that I never glance sideways at any other man and my husband sets up thirteen crosses when I die!"

Prayer helped, and as usual Marguerite was right. By entering gaily into Edward's eager preparations instead of sulking, Isabel was able to accept their going as a part of the splendid marital adventure. And Edward was so pleased with her that he allowed her to bring Bringnette and Ghislaine and several of her people, and when she said goodbye to her family, he promised that he himself would one day bring her back to visit them.

The sun still shone and even the Channel was calm. Her three young uncles and quite an entourage of French nobles were coming for the Coronation. The whole gay company set off in high spirits. The only people who had any private misgivings were Ghislaine, who could not forget the broken mirror, and the Dowager-Queen of England, who had refrained from telling her niece quite everything about the kind of life awaiting her there.

With a light breeze in their sails, they made the crossing in a few hours. Before Boulogne was out of sight they could see the white cliffs of Dover. Isabel stood at the poop rail hand in hand with Edward while he gladly pointed out the coastline of his land. All his thoughts seemed to be projected there before him. "And see, Isabel, it is just as I promised you. As usual my friend has carried out my wishes. *Là voilà, ma chère.* The crowd to welcome us on Dover quay."

White cliffs and crowd seemed to be rushing to meet them. The *Marguerite* was gliding to her mooring. Sails were being furled. Isabel could distinguish the faces of the waving people. Above the shouts of the crew and the shrill call of gulls she could hear them cheering. Something of Edward's enthusiasm caught her. She would play her part right royally to please him. "I am Queen Isabel of England," she told herself, "and in a few minutes I shall be talking for the first time to some of my subjects."

She tried over a gracious phrase or two in their tongue. She would say all the right things, just as she had tried to do on her wedding day. She would surprise Edward. He would be watching her, a little anxiously perhaps, and she would see to it that he had good cause to be proud of her.

But first she must be quite sure about their names. "It pays to remember people's names," her astute father had often told her. There would be the powerful Earl of Lancaster, who was her uncle. Guy Beauchamp, Earl of Warwick, and Aymer de Valence, Earl of Pembroke. And her two new ladies. Alicia Bigod, wasn't it? And the Countess of Hereford. And then there would be the Regent, of course.

Standing beneath the great blazoned standards of England and France, with a glittering suite grouped behind her, Isabel secretly ticked off the names on her little jewelled fingers. "Your friend the Regent will be one of the first to be presented to me, I suppose. But except that he is Earl of Cornwall I do not think that you have ever told me how he is called," she whispered to Edward in a last-minute flutter of nervousness, as the anchor chain began to rattle down. "What *is* his name, Edward?"

"Piers," said Edward, his eyes searching eagerly among the crowd on shore. "Piers Gaveston."

CHAPTER 3

With perfect sense of staging Isabel stopped on the raised steps leading down from the sea wall, knowing well that the moored ship's standards formed an effective background. Because she was not very tall she calculated that this would be the best place in which to stand so that all the assembled company could see her. And, more important still perhaps, it was a good vantage point from which to take a quick pre-view of them, since inevitably much of her life would be determined by the kind of people they were. While Edward was formally handing her ashore she gave his fingers a purposeful little tug so that he, too, should stop.

But to her surprise he did not. As she was still taking rapid stock of the nobles and ladies drawn up to receive her, he let go of her hand and ran lightly down the steps and across the quay as though impatient to greet someone. The mighty Earl of Lancaster perhaps, or one of those other grim-looking English barons grouped around a bollard. But he was making in an altogether different direction and, like them, she turned to stare after him. It was then that she noticed the tall, dark young man in the gaily chequered *cote-hardie* with the modishly high-cut collar. He stood there so nonchalantly and was so flamboyantly attractive that he was unlikely to be overlooked in any crowd.

Important as he might be by virtue of some office he held, it was not for him to press forward before a cluster of middle-aged earls, most of them connected with the blood royal. Indeed, no one could accuse him of moving at all. He just stood there, carelessly arrogant, and let the King of England come to him. And even when he could have bent a respectful knee Edward stayed him, seizing his hand and flinging an affectionate arm about his shoulders. And then the two of them, laughing into each other's eyes, began talking in short, glad sentences as though they had not met for months and were completely oblivious of all others who had travelled equally far and still waited.

Isabel gazed in bewilderment at the spontaneous intriguing little episode, for once entirely forgetful of the effect which she herself was making. She stood there all alone on her impromptu dais, her pale face slowly reddening with annoyance. She was aware of inquisitive muttering from her own people newly disembarked behind her, and of an unexplained fury harshening English faces. She knew that Marguerite moved to her side, trying to cover the awkwardness of the moment, and found the tall, martial-looking man whom she guessed to be Lancaster taking advantage of his high lineage to waive the neglected formality of presentation. "I am proud to welcome a kinswoman to these shores," he said, trying to set her at ease.

"Your mother was my maternal grandmother," recalled Isabel, gratefully suffering his bear-like embrace. His hasty intervention only served to emphasize the King's lapse, for Edward, realizing his remissness, had already returned to her, with his friend following leisurely at his heels. "I have been acknowledging the care with which Piers Gaveston, Earl of Cornwall, has conducted the Regency of our realm during our absence," he began, with all the pomposity which ceremonial occasions demanded. "And it will be our immediate pleasure to present him to your Grace."

But Isabel was not a Capet for nothing. Fortified by a sympathetic relative on either side, she allowed her glance to rest on the Regent of England as briefly and witheringly as though he were some ill-favoured lackey. "It will be my pleasure, too," she said coolly, "as soon as these noble lords who are waiting have been presented to me and to my uncles."

Her clear young voice had a way of carrying further than she intended, and she was quick to notice that the scowl on some of the noble lords' faces softened to an ill-concealed grin and that two beardless young Lancastrian knights, who were standing in the rear, spluttered with delight behind their betters.

Piers Gaveston, far from resenting the snub, stood watching her with indulgent amusement, rather as though he were observing the tantrums of a spoiled child. He was even handsomer than Edward, and Isabel hated him at sight.

To the satisfaction of most people present the King paid heed to his wife's stricture. Guy Beauchamp of Warwick, a stocky, weather-beaten man with high-coloured cheeks, was presented to her. The tall, lean Earl of Pembroke kissed her hand and looked at her approvingly. There was Lancaster's heir, Henry of Lincoln, and a pleasant, red-headed youth called Gilbert de Clare,

Earl of Gloucester, who, as far as she could make out, was the son of Edward's sister. Then, in his proper turn, Isabel received Gaveston, who knelt to her with an exaggerated reverence and who, she suspected, was already coining some unflattering nickname for her. Finally, her new English ladies were brought to her, and while they admired her garments and made kind enquiries about her journey, French and English began to mingle, exchanging polite speeches with bluff welcome.

Presently they all went up to Dover Castle, which stood like a grim grey sentinel guarding the fair white cliffs. And to the annoyance of everyone except Edward and his young nephew, Gilbert of Gloucester, this Piers Gaveston, who had planned the occasion, acted as host. But they were all hungry after the crossing and it was impossible not to enjoy his entertainment. Undoubtedly he had a flair for such things and, prejudice apart, it did not seem unwise of the King to have assigned to him the planning of the forthcoming Coronation. After supper he unrolled a long parchment upon which his scribe had set down lists of names and duties, and, impervious to the jealous looks of his fellow subjects, began discussing the arrangements. "The Archbishop of Canterbury being abroad, I supposed your Grace would wish the Bishop of Winchester to celebrate," he said, in a pleasant voice flavoured with a faint Gascon accent. "The London Guilds are providing the usual banquet when we get back to the palace, of course. And in honour of the youth and beauty of our new Queen may we not, Sir, break with custom and ask each peer and knight to bring his lady to the Abbey?"

"Their colourful dresses would certainly enhance the scene," agreed Edward, who shared his interest in stage-craft.

"And while our guests are with us I propose to arrange a tournament on the scale of the one we all enjoyed so much at Wallingford last year."

Gaveston grinned round jocundly at his fellow peers, most of whom were still sore from the memory of how easily he had unseated them. But in spite of their glum looks and her instinctive resentment against the man Isabel could not but listen enthralled to the picture he went on to draw so expertly of the projected ceremony which had for so long been a highlight of her dreams.

"If you will tell us what you intend to wear, *ma petite*, we can create an effective colour scheme for the procession through

London," suggested Edward, who, for all his informal tastes, loved the rich trappings of pageantry.

"I have a lovely taffeta, stiff as fine Venice glass with silver threads and golden fleurs-de-lys. And I shall wear all the handsomest jewellery my parents sent," said Isabel, eagerly entering into their plans. "You, I know, must wear your velvet of royal purple, Edward. And what will our Master of Ceremonies himself be wearing?"

"I have not yet decided," Gaveston told her negligently. He had rolled up his parchment again and had just blown a grape through it so that it hit the King's jester on the nose, sending the ebullient young Gloucester into gales of laughter. "Something peacefully frivolous I think, Madam, the better to set off the warlike aspect of my lord Warwick. Though I fear it will be but idle to try to compete with the elegance of your Grace's entourage," he added, with a courteous little bow in the direction of her dignified relatives.

They had discussed their plans for the Coronation with only an occasional grunt of grudging agreement from the solid-looking English barons and a few helpful suggestions from the French Chamberlain and Aymer de Valence, Earl of Pembroke. And as soon as the cloth was drawn Edward had the dwarf whom Philip had given him brought in by way of diversion. He insisted upon a bout of wrestling between the droll little fellow and Robert the Jester, with a table as their stage, urging his guests to lay wagers and then tossing them double or quits on their winnings.

It had been a long day of travelling and Isabel, looking round at so many unfamiliar faces, found it difficult to believe that only that morning she had been in France. Most of the company were sleepy with good food and sea air and were thankful when the King arose and took himself off, leaving them free to seek their beds. "Come, Piers, and see the fine sorrel mare my father-in-law has given me," he invited in high good humour.

The two tireless young men sauntered towards the door together, with arms linked and laughter in their voices, and the two weeks bride was left behind. Everyone in the hall stood still to watch them go. Gaveston turned in the doorway to grin back at them all deridingly, and as one of the servants flung about his fine shoulders a cloak more gorgeous than the King's, the jewelled clasp of it sparkled almost blindingly.

"Look, I implore you!" cried Isabel, suddenly clutching at her aunt's arm. "The Gascon is wearing the famous clasp which my father gave to Edward on our wedding day."

"The blood-red rubies re-set from great Charlemagne's ring," echoed her uncle Thomas of Lancaster, starting forward in fury, hand on sword.

"Which was part of my dowry," cried Isabel.

"And should have gone to your eldest son," said Marguerite.

But priceless clasp and the two young men had disappeared. And since one of them was the seething Frenchman's royal host no one dared strike a blow. The sound of careless laughter came up from the courtyard, following in the wake of a bobbing lantern.

The new Queen of England sank down on a stool, covering her face with both hands to hide her tears. Inquisitive faces peered at her, but Lancaster and Warwick were quick to clear the hall of servants. Gilbert, the King's nephew, had hurried away. Perhaps, she reflected bitterly, to make a jest to Gaveston of the jealous bride's distress. Pembroke tactfully persuaded guests from the lower tables to retire. Then, together with her outraged relatives and the closest of her ladies, they gathered protectingly about her. Indignation seemed to have welded them into one common cause.

"I cannot believe it—that Edward would have *given* it to him. . . . Almost as soon as it was in his hands, and knowing what store I set by it," stammered Isabel, trying to recover herself. "Uncle of Lancaster, can *nothing* be done to get my jewels back?"

"Since the King himself has made the gift——" murmured Marguerite, putting a soothing hand upon her niece's shoulder.

"Who *is* this low-born fellow?" demanded Isabel's younger uncle, Louis of Evreux, haughtily.

"He is not low-born," defended the Dowager-Queen dispassionately. "His father, Sir Arnald de Gaveston, fought valiantly for my late husband, and when Sir Arnald was killed King Edward had his motherless son Piers placed in his own son's household. They were brought up together."

"And apparently conceived for each other a most inordinate affection," sneered the Count of Clermont.

"The Earl of Cornwall is besotted with him," corroborated Pembroke.

"Earl of Cornwall!" repeated Guy Beauchamp of Warwick, almost foaming at the mouth in his exasperation.

Isabel was becoming confused. That the royal favourite should have been given the most precious of the Capet wedding presents was surely *her* grievance—and an insult to *her* family. That the man was unpopular was evident. But that all these men should be shouting and raging round her betokened something more personal than chivalrous sympathy. Particularly when one considered how far from chivalrous some of them looked. "What is wrong with the title 'Earl of Cornwall'?" she ventured to ask.

"Everything, in this case, Madam, because it is usually reserved for a member of our royal house," explained Aymer de Valence of Pembroke. "If it is to be bestowed upon anyone but the King's son there are some of us here who have Plantagenet blood in our veins. But when your Grace blesses our country with an heir the unfortunate matter will be settled, and we can only regret that here on your first night in England you should have suffered such an unnecessary affront."

Although Pembroke spoke to her gently Isabel could hear the others still muttering among themselves. "Some such *betise* was bound to happen with that upstart in the saddle," she overheard someone saying apologetically to the Countess of Bringnencourt. And then caught odd scraps of conversation like "offending the French" and "He may have a play-acting sense of colour, but certainly no tact". To be summed up by someone less tolerant, "Tact, my dear fellow! When we all know that it was done purposely. To flaunt his favour at us."

Isabel sighed deeply and stood up. "Tell me, my lords, why do you all hate him so?" she asked straight out.

There was no lack of answers.

"In truth, he is the King's evil genius, Madam," Lancaster told her seriously. "Only a year ago he was sent out of the country for it. And last summer before the first Edward died— God rest his upright, valorous soul—he made me, his cousin, swear by all I held most sacred that I would not allow Piers Gaveston to return unless the people themselves wished it."

Warwick was prowling up and down before the fire looking, Isabel thought, as fierce as the wild boar on his quarterings. "He makes your husband lily-handed," he said, "stuffing his thoughts with frivolities and turning them from his promise to pursue his father's wars."

Aymer de Valence, standing tall and dignified beneath a torch which lighted the clever, semitic lines of his face, settled his belted, fur-lined gown more gracefully about him. He would have made a very effective Regent himself during the King's brief absence, and was well aware of it. "Every honour in the country which should be ours goes to that Gascon," he said, voicing his opinion quite as fervently as his fellows.

"And now the distribution of all the most coveted duties at the Coronation lies in his hands," complained the Earl of Lincoln who, as Lancaster's heir, was jealous for the family privileges.

"If there *is* a Coronation," muttered Warwick.

Isabel looked up quickly. How could there not be a Coronation, since that was what so many of her friends and relatives had come for? Yet she shivered at sight of Warwick's dark and vengeful looks. Remembering that, what with marching on Scotland and crossing to France to fetch a bride, Edward had not yet had time to get *himself* crowned, she suddenly felt insecure. She began to wish that she had not inflamed his fierce barons' grievances still further by stressing her own. Annoyed as she was with Edward, she had no desire to be disloyal to him or to do him any harm, and her aunt's serious looks made her uncomfortably aware that she had been behaving like a spoiled child. Realizing that Bringnette was anxious to get her to bed, Isabel allowed Ghislaine to put her sable wrap about her so that she could pass in comfort through the draughty passages. All the men present bowed and stood aside for her to pass. "I shall write to my father about the ruby clasp," she said, with her pert little nose high in the air.

"There is nothing they would like better," remarked Marguerite sadly, following her from the hall.

"You mean you think I should not?" snapped Isabel.

But the King's practical step-mother seldom preached. She stooped to kiss Isabel at the door of her room, and the compassionate spontaneity of the gesture suggested her rare genius for comprehending other people's pain. "If you must, let the letter go privately," she advised.

As Isabel was about to enter the firelit room, a young man stepped forward from the shadows outside her door. He appeared to have been waiting there on duty, and could not have helped overhearing them. He bowed respectfully to both Queens, but the elder he had often seen before. His eyes were bright with approval as they rested upon his new young mistress. "If your Grace wishes a letter sent to France I myself will row out to the *Felicité* and give it into the hands of her captain. He has orders to weigh anchor at dawn so that he may take King Philip news of your Grace's safe arrival."

Isabel looked up in pleased surprise.

"He is Sir Robert le Messager, whom Edward has appointed your Master-of-Horse," explained Marguerite at parting.

"My messenger, just when I need one," punned Isabel, with the first light-hearted laugh that had passed her lips since supper.

"It will be my heart's happiness to serve your Grace in all things."

Isabel regarded him with relief as he knelt on one knee before her. He was young and impulsive like herself, and as well as being able to make pretty speeches, he appeared to be moved by a genuine desire to help her rather than by personal interest as the barons had been. She had suffered unaccustomed humiliation, and in the midst of her bewilderment in this strange country she allowed her hurt pride to salve itself for a moment or two in the admiration manifest in his eyes. "I pray you have someone bring me pen and paper," she said, momentarily forgetful of her bitterness. "Then wait outside my door, Sir Robert, and one of my ladies will bring you the letter as soon as it is done."

By the light of a single tall candle she poured out her heart to her people at home. She guessed that women like Marguerite kept their griefs and disappointments to themselves, but the Almighty had not made her in that mould. She was Isabel the Fair whom no man should slight, and when she suffered she must speak or suffocate. If her father should think she was making a mountain from a molehill, or upsetting the political situation, at least her youngest brother Charles would understand. She had always been able to coax dear Charles to her way of thinking. And it was cruel—cruel—for a husband whom she adored to neglect her for some self-assured young man on her first night in England, and to offend her uncles and to give away the Charlemagne jewels. The scratching of her angrily moving quill and the occasional plop of wood-ash from the fire were the only sounds in the room. The embroidered coverlet had long since been turned down and the bed curtains pulled invitingly back. She started when Ghislaine, moving softly on slippered feet, touched her warningly on the shoulder. "It is getting late, Madam. If the King should come on you unawares and see what you are at——" she whispered, with a scared glance towards the door.

"What do I care? It would do him good to read what people think of his odious friend," thought Isabel, and went on writing.

"The King must surely be coming any moment now," warned Bringnette, an hour later.

And in the end Ghislaine had fallen asleep and had to be wakened to take the letter to Robert le Messager who was still stationed faithfully outside. By the time the two women had undressed her both fire and candle had burned low. Isabel dismissed them repentantly and stood for a moment or two alone by the window. Only a horse whinnying down in the stables and the distant tramp of a sentry's feet somewhere out on the battlements broke the Kentish silence. Castle, town and shipping all seemed to be asleep. Dawn was breaking in the east but still the King had not come. "I am Queen of England," Isabel told herself sternly, and climbed shivering into her empty marriage bed to cry into her pillow like a broken-hearted child.

CHAPTER 4

IN A room in the Tower of London Bringnette and Ghislaine had laid out the Queen's Coronation finery ready for the morrow, and because she appreciated her husband's taste in such matters Isabel had made him promise to come for a preview of the gold and silver dress. He had kept his promise, but seemed unusually morose. As the late February evening closed in, fog had drifted up the Thames, obscuring what little light the thickness of the walls allowed, so that his sullen gaze fell first upon her jewels glittering out of the gloom as they lay upon her table.

"But why two crowns?" he enquired, picking up one of them and twirling it round on his fingers. "To emphasize that the Capets are more important than the Plantagenets?"

She had meant to tell him the fascinating history of each and to ask which she should wear, but his manner goaded her into a spiteful retort. "Perhaps my father was afraid you might give one of them away before the Coronation."

Edward put down the golden thing as though it had bitten him, and went to stare out at the murky river. "If there *is* a Coronation," he said.

Isabel looked up at him sharply and dismissed her women with a gesture. "I have heard someone say that before," she recalled uneasily.

"Guy of Warwick, probably. Or Lancaster. It was the monotonous burden of their argument at the Council Meeting last night."

Isabel was pleased to learn that it had been a meeting, and not Piers Gaveston, who had kept him from her bed until the early hours of the morning. But the thought of having all their splendid plans for the Coronation spoiled was alarming. She crossed the little room and stood beside him. "You mean they want to postpone it?"

"No. To prevent it. As you very well know."

"I?" Isabel stared at him in amazement as he swung round on her accusingly.

"All your precious relatives turned up in strength to back them. Otherwise I scarcely think even Warwick would have dared to give me his orders." Edward began to tramp angrily up and down the room. "They want me to send Piers Gaveston away again."

Although her hopes soared high at the thought, she did not want anything to happen which would diminish her husband's power. "But how can they? How can mere subjects dictate what you do? I had supposed you were popular—their lionized Longshanks' son. Do they not want you for their king?"

"Oh, yes, as far as I know. They certainly have no one else in mind," answered Edward wearily. "But the devil of it is they have not yet taken their oaths of allegiance. I was always up in Scotland, or somewhere. And should they refuse to do so tomorrow some of them may feel free to band together with their cursed private armies and force me to do whatever they want."

"You have your standing army. You could fight them."

"And plunge the whole country into civil war?" He slumped down into her high-backed chair and ran distracted fingers through the perfumed smoothness of his hair. "Ever since my father's death they have been growing more domineering. Now they have had the impudence to give me an ultimatum—no exile for Gaveston, no Coronation," he said dramatically.

To Isabel, who knew nothing of the horrors of civil war, the natural answer was to fight. She could have wished that his anger sounded a little more determined, and less petulant. But, close as her wishes ran to those of his barons, her instinctive desire was to comfort him. She knelt beside him, her hands outstretched across his knees. "My dear, I swear I know nothing of this. I knew they were angry and offended, yes. A little sorry for me perhaps that first day we landed at Dover—if such self-important-looking men *can* be sorry for other people's hurts. But since I share your throne, whatever they may do that undermines your power will be against my own interests too. How can you suppose that I would have tried to stir up trouble against you?"

"Not intentionally, perhaps. But you must have written home complaining of this and that. Your father, who so lately seemed to be my generous friend, now writes subjecting me to unwarrantable questioning about my private life." Edward moved impatiently, shifting her arms from his knees. "I am getting tired of your childish jealousy, which makes you look for slights where none were intended."

Isabel sprang to her feet. She could scarcely refrain from hitting him. "You have no right to be always speaking of me as though I were a child!" she cried. "Am I not your wife? And, if it comes to that, have I no cause for complaint, left alone while you spend most of your time talking and laughing with Gaveston?"

"A pretty gratitude, I must say, when we are planning to return French hospitality with the most splendid Coronation——"

But Isabel cut recklessly across his indignant self-justification. "And giving him half my father's gifts! Your barons were furious, and even Marguerite was shocked."

Infatuated with Gaveston as he was, Edward knew that his foolish generosity had been indefensible. He rose with a sigh and, taking her by the shoulders, tried to turn her passionate face towards him. "Oh, my dear, I am sorry—talking to you like that," he apologized, with the sweetness which made his most intimate attendants and servants love him. "But, to tell the truth, I am worried sick." Restlessly, he wandered back towards the window. "They are calling another meeting early to-morrow morning, when they will hold this ultimatum to my head, and I shall have to answer."

The frightening urgency of the matter shook Isabel out of her self-pity. "But surely they could not stop our Coronation *now*—just a few hours before the procession starts? With the streets all decorated and packed with people, and the Bishop waiting in your Abbey?"

"That is where they are so clever. Forcing my hand at the last moment. Pembroke's idea, probably. Although he is less pugnacious, he is cleverer than all the pack of them put together."

Isabel's whole heart cried soundlessly, "Oh, my love, send Piers Gaveston away, as they want. As I want. We could be so happy. Soon, without his brilliance always there blinding you, you might come to love me. Left alone, we like each other. You know we do. Except for your everlasting dogs and horses, we enjoy the same things." But she hated the too true taunt of jealousy, and was trying to learn to leash her tongue. "What will you tell them to-morrow?" she asked soberly.

"That I will call a Parliament directly I am crowned. That I will abide by whatever Parliament decides—when the time comes."

"You will really promise them that?"

It was as if all the fine hopes which had enraptured her during their wedding service had been given back to her. She scarcely noticed that Edward did not really answer. "I am sorry about all this, dear Isabel," he repeated. "I do not forget that it is your Coronation too, and I had wanted it to be a happy day for you."

She was quick to respond. She coaxed him back into her chair and perched on the arm of it, leaning, relaxed and sweet, against his shoulder. "I know I am often jealous. I was even jealous of my brothers sometimes at home because a girl always has to take a secondary sort of place," she admitted, fondling his freshly-shaven cheek.

He took her marauding fingers and held them in his own. "I do not want my wife to take a secondary sort of place. But I do wish she could bring herself to like my friends a little," he said, with a rueful laugh. "Life would be so much more entertaining for us all."

"Indeed I will try," she promised, feeling that it should be easy enough to like the rest of them once Gaveston was gone.

"Now that it may be too late," sighed Edward.

"You seem to depend upon this Gaveston so much. Have you known him long?"

"Since I was fourteen. Although I had several friends of my own age it seems to me, when looking back, that I was always lonely until he came. You must know yourself, Isabel, how 'set apart' one always feels being 'royalty'. The others never really treated me as one of themselves, although I longed to be treated so. But Piers always did."

"But why were you lonely when you had good parents?" asked Isabel, thinking of her own united family.

"My father was always away campaigning, and my mother was so often with him that I scarcely remember her. He gave me a household of my own when I was far too young—only ten. To make a man of me, he said. Though probably it was because it left him free to attend to things which interested him more. In his mind—and in the minds of the people, no doubt—I was always that Prince offered to them almost from the day of my birth as the stalwart successor to carry on my father's work. Edward of Caernarvon. Someone who would grow up with all his fine administrative ability and aptitude for war." The less warlike Edward turned and smiled into her eyes with a self-deprecating appeal for understanding. He seemed to have forgotten that he looked upon her as a child whenever it suited him. "You know, Isabel, it is not easy to be a hero's son."

"I *can* imagine that it is not, although so many thoughtlessly envy you." She took his hand and held it comfortingly in her lap. "But it was natural, was it not, that your parents should be ambitious for you? After all, when we have a son you would want him to be a trained soldier and ruler, would you not?"

"I hope to God he will be! If only for his own sake."

Isabel was both surprised and pleased by the vehemence of his reply. Her proud upbringing had been such that she could not picture any son of hers preferring to idle away his time. "And did Piers come to live in your household when you were fourteen?" she prompted.

"Yes. He was a year or two older than I. The other fellows made fun of him at first because, coming from our possessions overseas, he seemed to them like a foreigner, and was poor. His father had lost almost everything in my father's wars. Poor Piers did not even have a tutor like the rest of us. Only a devoted oddity of a servant called Dragon."

"What an apt and lovely name!" laughed Isabel.

"If it really was his name. Piers may have invented it. He

invented so many pleasant things. Life suddenly became gay and took on new meaning after he came. I—grew to love him——"

"And the others?"

"Oh, they did not sneer at him for long. He always took it in good part up to a certain point. And then he would hit them—just once, and hard." Edward stretched his long legs before him and laughed pleasurably at the recollection. "After that they left him alone. They found it was pleasanter to join in the entertainments he created than to sulk alone. Jealous as they were, he never bore them ill-will, and it made it easier that he and I were usually winners at the quintain or first home in the hunting field. And then, of course, young Gilbert, my sister's son, always imitated him in everything."

"The sister who was born in the middle of a Crusade?"

"Yes, Joanna of Acre. And Gilbert's infatuation was another thing which irritated my father. When he came home to Westminster after his massacre of Berwick he had time on his hands for once. Time to poke into the expenses of my household, to find out that I was not made in his mould. He sent Piers away to his family estates in Guienne. Said he had a bad influence over me. So I know what life will be like if he is forced to go again."

Isabel was regarding him with a puzzled frown. She was learning yet more—and discomforting—facets of the man she had married. But Edward was so tortured by the thought of separation from his friend that he did not notice. "Life will be empty without him," he said, staring before him as he had done in the desolating gloom of the Tower.

In his circumstances Isabel would have drawn upon her courage. "Could you not fill it with the absorbing interest of ruling your people—and making your own decisions?" she asked without conscious irony. "After all, you will still have Marguerite —and me."

Although everything that he had told her had puzzled or hurt her, she was glad that he had confided in her. It must surely bring them nearer together, she thought. The unhappiness he was so obviously enduring brought out that maternal element in her which had prompted her to ease his strange embarrassment with frivolous conversation on their wedding night, and her wish to comfort him brought with it a sense of union which went beyond the warmth of passion. Sitting there within the shelter of her husband's arm and with her lovely Coronation clothes spread before them Isabel hoped that the worst of her troubles were over, and began to feel a little ashamed of having complained to her father. After all, she had thoroughly enjoyed the journey from Dover with the people in each town turning out to cheer them and Edward explaining so knowledgeably about the heaths and farmsteads, and watermills, and how the quaint little strips of land were divided between master and peasants at each manor they came to. Their short stay at Eltham Palace had been pleasant too, and that, she had to admit, had been largely due to Gaveston's entertainments. And to-morrow, after so much preparation, promised to be yet another wonderful day. Once more she would be the centre of attraction in a becoming dress and jewels. Riding through London she would taste again that sweet, heady draught of public admiration. Admiration which, each day in private, she read more clearly in Robert le Messager's dark eyes, and which had helped to revive her self-esteem in moments of depression. But now that Gaveston was going, sorry as she was for Edward, she would not be depressed any more. Once she could get out of this grim old place she would strive to make their marriage all important to him. She would unpack her lovely French furnishings and arrange some masques and music herself. "I am glad we do not have to spend more than one night here," she said, looking round with distaste at the untapestried stone walls. "I am sure it is damp. And that there are ghosts."

"I know. But it is one of our foolish hidebound traditions that all sovereigns of this country must lie here the night before they are crowned."

"Well, at least let us retire early and lie in comfort," laughed Isabel. "For without a doubt we shall both have to be up early in the morning. And do not, I beg of you, Edward, leave me long alone for your Tower of London makes my flesh creep."

Edward withdrew his arm from her and sat hunched forward, with hands clasped between his knees. "It is the weight of all the unhappiness that has gone on here," he said. "Ever since Norman William built it countless men have lain here condemned to die. When I was brought here as a boy to see the lions down by the gates, I scarcely enjoyed them for thinking of all the prisoners who had languished here through the ages. I used to dream about it sometimes and wake my nurse with my screaming. I wondered how men bore it. Sometimes, when I was alone, I could almost put myself in their place, hearing the clang of a dungeon door which would shut out the sunshine for ever, and being dragged out to be killed or left to rot."

Isabel shivered and clutched at his arm. "Stop, Edward!" she beseeched. "You are staring before you as if you could see— and feel—it all. You have far to vivid an imagination. It is not for you to pity every poor caitiff in your realm. You are their king. At least it could never happen to you."

"No, I suppose not," agreed Edward, shaking himself out of his morbid imaginings with a half-shamed laugh. "Let us talk of something more cheerful until supper time. Our homecoming, for instance. I think you will like living at Westminster."

"Is that old, too?"

"Parts of it. But the part of the palace where we shall live was burned down and I have had it rebuilt. Ready for my bride."

"Oh, I am glad!" Isabel began to glow with happy antici-pation. "Is there a garden?"

"A lovely rose garden. I have re-turfed it and put new trellises, and had the fish ponds cleaned out. And we have built out a stone pier for your barge."

"You make it sound as if you did it all yourself."

"I did. Together with my gardeners and masons. I would sooner dig rose beds or build a beautiful house any day than go to war or preside over some stuffy council meeting. What are you looking so bemused about, my sweet? There is nothing shameful in preferring beautiful things. I planed the oak for your bunk aboard the *Marguerite* with my own hands, and helped design those clothes cupboards which you liked so much. Being a king does not prevent me from being able to do things as well as my own servants."

Isabel felt that she was seeing a surprising and lovable side of him at which she had never guessed. And that this coming to understand each other was, perhaps, one of the most rewarding things about marriage. But to-morrow he would look far removed from any mason, in his crown and purple velvet. And that was a subject they were bound to come back to at the moment.

"Now call your women and let me see you in this marvellous dress the Queen of Navarre had made for you," he urged. "Even in this dark room it shines, so it should be breathtaking among all the lighted candles in the Abbey. I am sure it will outshine all of us."

But to her intense mortification Isabel did not outshine everybody. And neither did Edward. The Earl of Cornwall, who had spoken as if he would have little time to think about his own choice of clothes, appeared in purple velvet, too, and decked in jewels which rivalled his royal master's. Being taller and stronger, he seemed to over-shadow even the handsome Plantagenet. And if the men in the crowd were openly admiring Isabel, most of the women spent more time gazing at Gaveston than at her glittering gown. And many, even while they resented every breath the Gascon drew, could not refrain from staring at such amazing and impervious insolence.

It was Piers Gaveston who bore the King's crown, while Thomas Plantagenet, Earl of Lancaster, who had expected to do so, had to walk behind him bearing the Sword of Mercy. The Princes of France, arrayed like a field of golden lilies, would never forgive the slight of sartorial eclipse. The barons' hands were never far from their swords, and Isabel, watching them anxiously from behind her illuminated missal, felt sure that but for her presence and the holiness of the place, Piers Gaveston would never have come out of the Abbey alive.

And in spite of all his carefully-thought-out plans everything seemed to go wrong that day. Carpenters, officials and cooks might well have been bribed to clumsy inefficiency by their betters, or—more likely still—might have agreed among themselves with grim Cockney humour to do everything possible to discredit the hated favourite. Although King and Queen each walked beneath a beautiful silken canopy held over them by the barons of the Cinque Ports, although a splendid carpet stretched all the way from Palace to Abbey, although the ancient crowning stone which Edward Longshanks had taken from the Scots stood ready, the very insistence upon such magnificence served to lengthen the proceeding so that the ceremony was not over before mid-afternoon. By that time the tormented barons, who had breakfasted early on account of their meeting, were ravenous as famished wolves, while several of their wives, admitted for the first time to the ceremony, fainted and had to be carried out. It was almost dark before any of them got anything to eat, and even then for some reason or other the Queen's table was served last.

Accidents which normally might have been accepted with good humour were all blamed upon Gaveston. It was true enough, what Edward had said, that all of them were looking for insults because they were consumed by jealousy. But it was not until long afterwards that Isabel and some of the more tolerant among them came to realize this. At the time the annoyances which excited their anger seemed too flagrant to be borne. And a final blight was cast over the whole unpropitious day by the news that a highly esteemed knight, Sir John Bakewell, while helping a fainting lady from the Abbey, had been heartlessly trodden underfoot by the ill-controlled crowd, and crushed to death.

After the Coronation life could have been pleasant at Westminster, but Isabel's relations prepared to sail home in dudgeon and most of her husband's barons could scarcely wait for the opening of the promised Parliament when they would have a chance to voice their long-repressed grievances.

"The King is doing his best to postpone it until after Easter," his brother-in-law, de Bohun of Hereford, told them.

"At least there will be the Coronation tournament," said young Fitzalan of Arundel, who had been diligently perfecting a cunning thrust with which he optimistically hoped to unhorse the Gascon.

"And what good will that do us?" growled Warwick, whose buttocks still ached in damp weather from the fall he had taken at Wallingford.

Although the Dowager-Queen had warned her niece against complaining in their presence or allowing them to make her a focal point of their discontent, Isabel and her ladies were often to be found sitting at their embroidery in the same room. It was certainly more entertaining than a stroll in the rose garden in a March wind. "How aggravating it must be for them to have to swallow all these slights which they grumble about from milord Gaveston, and not be able to unhorse him in the lists!' giggled Ghislaine, who secretly admired him.

"One could almost bear that," murmured Pembroke, whose sharp ears had overheard her, "if he were not so unwarrantably funny about it afterwards."

CHAPTER 5

"You cantered well, Madam, in spite of the slippery mud along the Strand," encouraged the Queen's Master-of-Horse. "A little straighter in the saddle and you will have all our English ladies envious."

"You flatter me, Sir Robert," laughed Isabel, pulling up breathlessly. "You know very well that though I might plague you to instruct me from now till Doomsday I should never be half as good a horsewoman as your May Queen."

"She has far more experience. She rode everywhere with the late King."

"And now goes hunting with the present one. That is what *I* want to do."

"But only the other evening, when you were learning one of our card games from the Lady Alicia Bigod, you said that you detested hunting."

"How you do remember every small, foolish thing I say! And even if I did say it, are there not sometimes reasons why one should make oneself do even those things which are detested most?"

"You are anxious to improve your riding only because you think it will please the King if you go hunting," said Robert le Messager, staring glumly between his horse's ears because he had entertained a wild hope that it might have been an excuse to enjoy his own company.

"He will be lonely if the Earl of Cornwall goes," said Isabel softly.

Her companion did not answer, and presently she called to him to stop. It was one of those mornings of early spring which stir undefined longings and whisper of immortality. From London to Westminster the Thames curved beside them, her golden rushes rustling in the shallows. Soft willow catkins delicately fringed the banks, and here and there against a cottage wall a lilac bush was tipped with hopeful green. Before them, stately against a pale blue sky, rose Palace roofs and Abbey towers. "Let us look at the Chère Reine cross," said Isabel, riding up close to examine it. She liked to linger there because it was a memorial to Edward's mother, and because for her it would always be a symbol of the ideally happy marriage of her dreams. But, being Isabel the Fair, she had to improve the occasion with a little mild coquetry. "It is a lovely thing," she said, reaching out a small gloved hand to touch the stone and glancing sideways at her enamoured escort. "Fit to express a man's undying love for a woman, do you not think?"

For a Master-of-Horse le Messager seemed to be having a great deal of trouble with some buckle on his harness. "I would express mine in some warmer medium—heart's blood, not stone," she understood him to say.

"Dear Robert!" she murmured reprehensibly. And they rode on to Westminster with the sap of springtime rising in their blood and the song of mating thrushes in their ears.

In the courtyard he waved aside the grooms and lifted her down himself, and, inspired by the songbirds and the springtime, and partly, perhaps, by pique, because she had scarcely seen her husband all day, Isabel invited him into her private apartments to drink a cup of wine.

Before going to spend a few quiet moments in the Queen's private chapel Bringnette had flung wide the window to let in the warm sunshine which her mistress loved; but it was no fault of hers that two gardeners were talking carelessly down in the rose garden below. It was the sort of thing which was bound to happen sooner or later. Not expecting the riders back so soon, the good woman had left only Ghislaine in attendance; and Isabel, with an exclamation of pleasure, had crossed the room immediately, wine goblet in hand, to enjoy the informal hour and the sunlit prospect. The homely thud of spades on earth reminded her how anxious Edward was to make her garden beautiful and although she could not see the men she guessed that he had sent them because they were specially clever with roses. Even her foreign ears could detect the difference in their voices, the one with the cockney twang of a regular Palace gardener, the other with an unfamiliar rustic burr. "Should be a fair sight cum zummertime," he was saying. "An' a place for the Queen to sit in, God bless 'er! All they blooms we planted afore Christmas'll just be at their best, I reckon, when her time comes to rest 'ere, big with child."

The speaker chuckled kindly, and the listening Queen smiled because she liked to have the common people's love. The sound of digging had ceased and she could imagine the old fellow pushing back his hat and scratching his sweating brow while he pictured how his handiwork would look when come to perfection.

But the other man's words struck her cold. "If she ever manages to get a child," he said, with an angry sniff.

"Aw, cum now, Job. I do allow 'er be but a tiddy little lass. But still, cum zummertime——"

"It is neither her Grace's stature nor her age that threatens fertility."

There was a shocked kind of silence down among the rose bushes.

"You never mean to tell me the King be impotent? Lord save us, not the lusty Longshanks' son!"

"It is easy to see you are up from the country, Jacques. It is not the King's virility that is in question, but we all know that he'll have little desire to spare for *her* with the cursed Gascon's fine body at hand."

Isabel stood motionless, the red wine slowly spilling down the folds of her riding habit. Her young, unlined face seemed to grow sharp and old with understanding. Her golden-brown eyes were full of hurt and horror.

Too late, Robert had created a noisy diversion with an overturned stool. Too late, Ghislaine had moved in front of her and slammed the casement shut. With its closing, an unhappy silence hung in the room, so lately filled with the glad scents and sounds of spring. "Only this morning I was so young—so ridiculously young and unthinking!" The words formed themselves somewhere within the lonely waste of Isabel's consciousness, but no sound came. She recalled with new understanding the strange tone in which the worldly-wise Countess in Bologne had said, "Other *women*? Oh no, I never heard of any." She was quite unaware of her companions. But she must speak aloud to someone—someone of her own whose judgments had no roots in this strange, disappointing land. Someone who could tell her if she had overheard aright, or—overhearing—rightly understood. Instinctively as a scalded child, she roused herself to find Marguerite. The empty goblet dropped from her hand as she turned, to shatter among the scented rushes on the floor.

Young Ghislaine, bewildered as herself, cowered against the stone window seat, staring down at the fragments as though they were in some way a part of the mirror broken on her mistress's wedding day.

Before Isabel could reach the door Robert le Messenger had

waylaid her, daring to grip her shoulders with both hands. "Parliament is not likely to fail in their insistence upon Gaveston's exile," he said. "But lest they should, though the King kills me for it, I will make sure that the Gascon goes."

Outraged by his passionate sympathy, Isabel struck him and shook herself free. She could not bear that he should know— that men should talk of it. She could have sent Ghislaine to ask her aunt to come to her, but she had to get away from that room, from those who had shared the hearing of such lewd humiliation. She ran, light as thistledown, along the passages to the old part of the palace where the May Queen lived, and Marguerite rose instantly from her book at sight of her.

Isabel banged the heavy oak door behind her and sagged back against it, hugely relieved to find her aunt alone. "Is it true, what they say about Edward and Piers Gaveston?" she asked.

Marguerite stood and looked at her with pained compassion. To have asked "And what do they say?" would have been a useless offence against integrity.

"Oh, yes, I see by your face! Of course it is true." Coming further into the room, Isabel stormily answered her own question. "Anyone but a fool must have seen it. Everybody has always known, I suppose. Even the very gardeners. Everybody except innocents like me and poor Ghislaine. How right Edward was to treat me like a child!"

"How did you—come to realize?"

"I told you. Or did I? Two gardeners were talking. Just now, under my window. Even my Master-of-Horse had the impertinence to pity me."

"You poor child!"

Isabel scarcely heard her. "You must have known," she accused. "Why did you not tell me? At Boulogne, when I asked you about England?"

"What good would it have done?"

"I would not have come!" flared Isabel, almost hating her aunt's still composure.

Wrung by the whiteness of her face, Marguerite pushed her gently into her own vacated chair. "My dear, you know that we women are only pawns in this game of politics. Your father is probably furious, having now heard what my other brothers— your uncles—have to report upon their return to Paris. But an alliance depends upon years of foreign policy, not upon individual morals or a bride's happiness."

"I could have appealed to the Dauphin—or to my favourite brother Charles who has always listened to me."

"The most that either of them will do is to back the English barons in their determination to get Piers Gaveston out of the country. "

Isabel sat in silence for a while, reviewing her wrongs. "So however Edward blamed me, there really *was* nothing unreasonable about my jealousy," she said slowly. "Many a woman is jealous of her husband's friends, knowing full well that he still has need of her. But Edward has no need of me. When I am wild with happiness because he comes to my bed, for him it is just a duty. I have nothing—nothing—which Piers Gaveston cannot give him. 'No desire left for her' that wretched gardener dared to say!" Overwhelmed by a flood of bitterness, Isabel buried her face in her hands. "Oh, Marguerite, *ma chère*, to think that once I used to pity you!" she sobbed. "Just for going young to an upright, warlike man of sixty!"

"You had no cause to, I assure you." But married life had not been a ready-made Heaven for Marguerite of France either. She too had had need to school her young desires, and learn. She seated herself on a low stool and, if only to quieten her niece's sobs, spoke of it for once. "It was frightening, at first, taking the place of the beloved wife of more than half a lifetime. But my husband was just in all his dealings. He saw to it that being a second wife and step-mother made no difference to my status. He was pleased when the people showed me even more love than they had shown to his Castilian wife. He trusted me in all things, and there was never anything I did for him which he did not reward with affection and appreciation. And he gave me sons."

"He has certainly become a difficult legend to live up to!" agreed Isabel, borrowing some of her husband's bitterness.

"Perhaps. But it is not only I who speak of him so. Consider those hard-bitten barons. When he died I saw many of them weep. And even those who did not love him feared him with respect. His memory remains with them, as a pattern and way of life for this country. They are bewildered and disappointed because they have not the same guidance from his son. Isabel, you must not form a picture of England's finest Plantagenet King from the twisted things young Edward says of him."

Isabel had got a hold on herself and sat up very straight in the high-backed chair. "Yet you are fond of—young Edward, as you call him?" In spite of her disillusionment—or perhaps because of it—the words were almost a plea.

"I have always found it easy to love him, Isabel, because of a certain sweetness in his disposition. For all his insolence and frivolity, he would never willingly be unkind. See how he inspired love in you. And those of us whom he loves, he loves with singular loyalty. His tragedy is that he was born heir to a throne. I always think he would have made such an admirable lord of the manor, getting on well with his neighbours and knowledgeably farming his land!"

"And Gaveston?" asked Isabel, after a pause.

Marguerite rose with a sigh and moved back to the desk where her book still lay open. She turned over the thick illuminated pages unseeingly. "I know that what I say can only be offensive to you, suffering as you at are this moment. But even Gaveston I do not find all bad. I have known him since he was a lad. His father, a good man if ever there was one, died worn out and impoverished with fighting for his country. It seems there was no money left for a good conscientious tutor for Piers. Oh, I am not making excuses for him! But at least he is seldom boring and has courage." Seeing the set look on her niece's face she shrugged and closed the idly fingered book. "But there," she admitted, with a reminiscent smile, "probably I am prejudiced because among all the people at Court whom he flays with his wit I am perhaps the only one towards whom his teasing is softened by tenderness. I have even gone so far as to wonder at times whether there is anything about me which could possibly remind him of his mother."

"Is it to her that he sends so much of Edward's money?" asked Isabel harshly. "Milord Pembroke was saying only the other day that half my dowry has gone to Gascony."

"His mother died years ago, I believe. He never speaks of her. But there is no doubt that he spends money like water, that most of it comes through the royal Exchequer and that a good deal of it goes to his Guienne estates and his impoverished relatives."

Isabel gathered herself up wearily from her aunt's chair. She felt far more exhausted than the morning's canter warranted. "I used to think that the barons were too harsh, and was often sorry for Edward. But now I shall pray nightly that they exile his—

minion—for life." Halfway to the door she stopped, remembering something else she had wondered about. "Why was he sent away before? Was it because of this same thing?"

"Yes. And their senseless extravagances. When his father came home from Scotland, he had more time to look into his son's household accounts and to hear how things were. He ordered them not to see each other, but it seemed that so long as they were in the same country nothing could keep them apart. Edward begged me to intercede with his father to let him keep Gaveston—ask 'in the most conciliatory manner you are able', he wrote, with good reason. I did what I could, but the two of them broke into the Bishop of Chester's park and then asked that good old soldier, Hugh le Despenser, who was leading an army up to the border, to excuse them because they preferred to tilt at a tournament. After that the King was adamant. But even when Gaveston was forced to take ship from Dover he made a kind of carnival of the journey and half Edward's fiddlers and servants were sent to accompany him. And then Edward must needs enrage the King still further by asking him to give Piers Guienne. He must have been mad, I think."

"He never does understand very well about other people's feelings. What did my father-in-law do?"

"Flew into one of the famous Plantagenet rages. I do not suppose you will ever have to encounter one with his son. Perhaps it is as well that that terrible family inheritance seems to have been left out of him."

"I would sooner he had it. I would not mind if he beat me—so long as he were strong and passionate!" cried Isabel, with closed eyes and clenched hands. "You do not know how humiliating it is to have a husband who is never stirred to be anything more than—kind and gentle."

"It could have its advantages," pointed out Marguerite drily. "They say that mine shook yours so violently on that unfortunate occasion that he tore out a lock of his perfumed hair! And then had the guards put him out of the room." She crossed the room and kissed the overwrought girl with real kindness. "Take comfort, dear Isabel, for Lancaster and Warwick and the rest are sure to get their way, and life here at court should be very different after Gaveston is gone."

"Yes. Edward will sulk and mope all the time," said Isabel unresponsively.

"And you will have all the time there is in which to make him love you more than he already does. To make him need you. You know that it is his nature to depend upon someone."

"His thoughts will still be with Gaveston, and Gaveston gives him all he needs."

"Oh, come, pull your resources together. There is one thing Gaveston *cannot* give him. Perhaps if you were to bear Edward a son——"

Isabel turned like an angry cat, one hand already on the door latch. "You say that! And you a Capet!" she cried. "Of a truth this pernicious country must have worn away your pride. You do not suppose that, with my foolishness at last informed, I will ever again have him in my bed?"

"But no man would endure that."

"No *man*!" agreed Isabel bitterly.

Marguerite hid a smile for her untried arrogance. "I do not think you are the type of which nuns are made, with their life-long vows of chastity. You would be very lonely, would you not, in your big empty bed? And the nights, when one is lonely, can seem very long."

Isabel resented her rallying tone. In her hurt pride she found her thoughts straying to Robert le Messager, remembering how recklessly he had held her. He would always be there. Edward had appointed him to her household, just as Gaveston had been appointed to his own. There could be a kind of retributive justice about it.

"I did not say my bed need be *empty*," she said, appreciating the swift look of alarm that crossed her aunt's austerely lovely face. And with dramatic effect she made that her parting shot, being neither entirely serious about Robert nor in any mood for listening to a warning about discretion in high places.

CHAPTER 6

FANNED to yet further discontent by a second grievance, which in happier circumstances she would have accepted for love's sake, Isabel began to complain to her kinsman Lancaster about the financial difficulties reported by the Comptroller of her Household. And in spite of Edward's charmingly worded orders that "his dearest consort should be honourably provided with all things necessary" the discomforted Earl had to confess that the Treasury was far too depleted to provide for her as befitted her birth and rank.

Even that part of her aunt's dowry which had been allotted to her by her parents was not forthcoming, and it was certainly not Marguerite who had had the spending of it.

"The King himself is in sore straits about money," admitted his treasurer, Sir Walter Reynolds, when summoned by Lancaster to a family consultation in the Queen-Dowager's apartments.

"Because of the way he and his friends have spent the revenues which should be mine on foolish things like gorgeous trappings for their horses and decked stages for their play-acting," said Isabel who, but for her hurt pride, could have taken as much delight in these frivolities as any of them.

"And in part because of the accumulated expenses of his father's wars," Reynolds reminded her with justice.

"Whatever the cause, your penury, my dear Isabel, shall be brought up and carefully considered when this long-overdue Parliament meets," her uncle of Lancaster promised her.

"And how do you suppose the voting will go, Thomas, for your motion to expel Piers Gaveston from the country?" asked Marguerite.

"Excellently, I hope. If only we can get a good backing from the people. Gaveston has been a popular figure with them, I admit, because of his lavish entertainments and his spectacular prowess in the lists. But our lovely niece and her cause are becoming ever more popular with them."

The May Queen, who had been trained to take a national view of affairs, tried hard to hide her dislike of a kinsman who wasted so much time on his own personal grievances. "What a pity, my dear Thomas, that Piers cannot be persuaded to leave without all this talk of 'causes'," she sighed. "It is like driving a wedge between King and Queen, and nothing could be worse for the country."

"What Aunt Marguerite really means is that I should suffer my marital wrongs in silence," retorted Isabel.

"People in high places would often be well advised to do so," said Marguerite, wishing that her lovely impetuous niece would sometimes learn to curb her tongue.

In spite of momentary annoyance, Isabel tried as usual to take her advice. In her heart she envied her aunt's serenity and had the sense to see that complaining to the barons only made things worse for Edward. And soon, God willing, she would have Edward to herself. In spite of everything she still hoped to forge some future happiness out of that. But, however patiently mute she kept, further enlightenment on the more intimate nature of her wrongs was to be provided to the public, tipping the balance against Gaveston.

During the feasting which went on for weeks after the Coronation she and Edward frequently ate in public in the vast hall at Westminster, with the doors open to all the gaping citizens and 'prentices who cared to ride out from London. Not only did these people get a view of their new young Queen but they also had a free view of the mummers and acrobats and minstrels who performed during dinner, and it became quite customary for the Guilds and prominent citizens to send congratulatory messages, which were read aloud during the meal. As each vied with the other in the grandeur of their orations and began to present them in more and more original guise this became one of the regular items of entertainment—particularly amusing to Isabel and her ladies because the authors invariably became hyperbolically poetic on the subject of her beauty. Pandering to Edward's taste for theatricals, the bearers of the orations were frequently disguised as gods or goddesses, satyrs or sprites, and came masked. Their entrance was cheered by the delighted crowd around the doors and the scrolls they brought were read aloud by the King's Master of the Revels.

Inventive novelty had reached such a pitch that little more than the usual admiring exclamations rippled from crowd to royal party when a masked woman on a black horse rode into the hall and urged the nervously excited creature up to the dais. Like those who had preceded her, she handed her scroll to the Master of the Revels, who stood waiting to receive her before the royal table. Nobles and ladies alike stared admiringly, and Edward and young Gilbert de Clare were busy laying wagers as to whom she might be. All present were far more interested in the graceful, daring lady than in the message she had brought. The Master of the Revels broke the seal and unrolled the scroll with a flourish. He cleared his throat and began to read the message aloud in his trained, far-reaching voice. Because he had declaimed so many of these orations during the past few days, and was momentarily far more concerned about the powerful black horse prancing restlessly near his feet, his mind scarcely took in the meaning of the words he read. Indeed, it was only when the cheering and talking and laughter died down to a tittering from the direction of the doors and then to a horrified silence on the dais that he took in something of their sense, and began to realize what was amiss. Instead of containing the usual fulsome flattery, the message was a forthright condemnation of the relationship between the King and Gaveston, and a strong appeal to the people to drive a canker out of their country. Mention of the Queen there was, but rather of her neglected state than of her beauty. The writer did not mince his scathing words, and in the first few sentences had made his point that unless the royal favourite were sent away, her Grace could not be expected to know happiness or to produce an heir. The flustered Master of the Revels got no further. Looking up he found himself surrounded by faces that expressed every kind of reaction—fury, horror, fear, grinning amusement and unmitigated delight. His frightened gaze passed to the centre of the table. What mattered most to him was the sight of his royal master's face, flushed with shame and anger. A few paces from him sat Gaveston. The sardonic grin on his handsome mouth told nothing of his feelings as his strong, fine fingers went on imperturbably paring a peach.

The unfortunate official, realising that his career as Master of any Revels must be over, ended it with a fitting gesture. Without reading another word he strode to the log fire blazing in the centre of the hall, screwed up the scroll with both hands and threw it into the midst of the blaze.

Before anyone had the wit to stop her the masked lady had wheeled her horse and clattered out of the hall. No man put out a hand to stop her. And the people clustered around the doors, cheered her with a whole-hearted vehemence which blanched the King's face from red to white.

After that the laughter-loving Londoners, who had hitherto derived some of their best jokes from the ways in which Gaveston managed to score off the barons, for once joined forces with his haughty enemies, and the result of the Parliamentary debate was a foregone conclusion. The King's beloved friend was to go.

The woman who had ridden into Westminster Hall was found and questioned. She had probably been chosen for her dangerous mission, people said, because no Plantagenet—least of all the second Edward—would torture information from a woman. Judging by the steadfastness with which she refused to give away the man who had employed her it was felt that she must be ardently in love with him, and because her fine horsemanship was traced to friendly instruction she had had from le Messager, suspicion quickly fell upon the Queen's Master-of-Horse.

The moment Isabel heard of this she sent for him to warn him, and because of the dangerous nature of the matter she dismissed her women from her room. "Is it true that it was you who took this crazy risk at dinner time?" she asked, remembering the extravagant vow which he had made to get Gaveston out of the country.

"It would be useless to deny it," he said, wishing her to know what risk he had taken for her sake.

"As Ghislaine du Bois crossed the courtyard just now she overheard the King giving the Captain of the Guard orders to arrest you in your lodgings before dawn."

"Then we have only to-night," said the hot-blooded young man, and had the hardihood to take her in his arms. He had been hungering for her for weeks. The ardour in his eyes promised exciting hours. Her great bed stood empty and, as the widowed Marguerite had said, nights in an empty bed can seem so long. Isabel had intended only to chide him lovingly and warn him. Instead, persuaded by his passion, she closed her eyes and allowed herself the intoxicating experience of being so eagerly desired. It was what she had expected of marriage. "Oh, Robert, Robert, why did you have to do this dangerous thing for me?" she whispered with what little breath his embracing left her.

"Because I love you to distraction," he said, his mouth urgent against hers.

"Distraction? Indeed, we must both be distracted!"

With a little cry of horror, she pushed him from her. It cost her the greatest effort at self-denial of which she was capable, but once free of his touch sanity began to return to her. "You will have to go. Now, before they take you," she said.

"What do I care?" he argued. "Even if they kill me I shall know that you live more happily. Isabel, I entreat you, let me stay this night. God knows I may not live to see another!"

Isabel shivered and, by a touch of inbred hauteur, reminded

57

him of her regality. "They will not kill you," she assured him. "They mean to put you in that terrible Tower."

"I may find means to escape."

"No one ever does," she said, touched to pity by a memory of its gloom.

The thought of it seemed to cool his crazy ardour. "Forgive me, Madam, if I have presumed."

Isabel smiled at him, shamed and tremulous. "Some of the blame was mine," she allowed with generous candour. "And I am sorry now that I struck you—that day when we over-heard——"

"I understood, even at the time. And to-night your lips have wiped out the smart of it. Remembering will warm me—even in the Tower!"

Isabel was all common sense now. She had not loved him, only wanted to share his all-consuming desire. She was so young, so inexperienced. It was frightening, she thought, how one's body could betray one into the most dangerous foolishness. "There is no need for heroics or the Tower if you go by the back-stairs now," she told him. "Why else do you suppose I sent for you?"

"Even now you can scarcely suppose the Guard will let me pass."

"Why not? The King is listening to those Italian minstrels and Gaveston is not vindictive." It began to exasperate her that, in his exalted mood, he should prefer to court danger in her bedroom than to go. She poured him some wine to speed him on his way.

"Did you know that the detestable Gascon is married?" he asked, almost conversationally.

"To Gilbert de Clare's young sister. I did not know until recently. He never brings her to court, poor child."

"Perhaps she suffers less that way."

"Not being humiliated openly as I am, you mean?"

He set down his empty glass and took her hands. "You must not talk so bitterly, beloved. You must tell yourself that many of us would risk their lives, as I do now, for the favours which their King seems to hold so lightly."

She knew that he was making a last bid for them, and drew away her hands. She allowed her glance to rest upon the vast, uncurtained bed, and laughed.

"Why do you laugh, Madam?" asked Robert, ready to take offence.

"It was nothing, really. Just something foolish I said to the Queen-Dowager a few days ago—about an empty bed. And the scandalized way in which she looked at me." She turned to him and added gravely, as though it were a matter of the utmost importance to her, "I love her very dearly, Robert."

"I thank God you have someone."

"And perhaps—partly thanks to you—I may yet have my husband."

That had been the thought which had steadied her through the clamour of her senses. She remembered now how she had run to the window and seen him for the first time down in the courtyard of Boulogne castle. So gay and attractive that his image, as she had seen him then, would be for ever graven on her heart. It was Edward Plantagenet her husband, whom she loved. The great lifelong romance which she had dreamed of was something to share with a king, too fine to shame by an hour's cheap tumbling with some impertinent Master-of-Horse. Pride came to her aid—pride, the cold deterrent. Though she had ached for the warmth of Robert le Messager's embraces, she sent him away.

CHAPTER 7

"They drove me to it, Piers. To think that I, their Sovereign, was forced to fix my seal to their horrible sentence upon you. Sentence of banishment, on pain of death and Excommunication if you should ever return to this country!"

"What else could you do, my dear Ned, seeing that your pugnacious barons had taken the precaution to come to Westminster fully armed? Not that I imagine my sanctimonious friends among the people would have raised a finger to protect me now—not since that charming little recommendation Robert le Messager sent us by the black horse lady."

"At least the meddling fool is caught and in the Tower for his pains," replied Edward.

Gaveston glanced affectionately at his worried friend. "You have no need to reproach yourself on my account. Their smug Parliamentary findings may prove equally bad for you. It was the shrewdest thing I ever heard of, trying to cover their insubordination by an announcement that their oaths of allegiance were made rather to the Crown than to the man who happens to be wearing it. That buffoon of Lancaster's idea, no doubt."

"And he my own cousin. As though they could juggle with the powers of an annointed king!"

With the Queen and a few of their more intimate friends the pair of them had retired immediately to Windsor in order to recover from their defeat, and to steal a few weeks together before Gaveston's irrevocable departure. Although they were in Isabel's apartments they sprawled before the fire discussing their own affairs with the utmost freedom.

"I will give you Carisbrooke Castle, Piers," offered Edward, desperately anxious to make amends.

"Where is that?"

"On the Isle of Wight. The Lady Isabella de Fortibus, whose family owned it, sold it to the Crown when she died. My father had always coveted it because the island makes such an effective screen between the French and Southampton."

"You have already made me Lord of the Manx. Why this obsession about remote and unproductive islands, Ned?" enquired Gaveston, more sore than he cared to admit at having been stripped of all his more productive English possessions.

"I thought I could slip across the sea sometimes. That at least I could hope to see you." Edward pushed aside an importunate hound and began pacing the room. "The thought of your being right down in Gascony again leaves me desolate. It takes days even to send a letter."

Gaveston, thoughtfully building himself a flimsy castle of playing-cards, laughed shortly. "I shall have difficulty in living *anywhere* now those fiends have seen fit to deprive me of the Cornish earldom you gave me!"

"But, Perot, that is the least of our difficulties." In his extravagant concern, Edward reverted to the affectionate nickname of boyhood and of their more intimate hours. "Surely you do not suppose that I would leave you to starve for my sake? Any more than I did that first time, when my father sent you home to Guienne."

"You were extravagantly generous, Ned. I sometimes think you must have sent me everything you owned except the princely diadem of Wales."

"The time seemed so long. I thought my father would never die."

"It was not much more than two months really," mused Gaveston, who had managed to amuse himself quite well. "No sooner had I set up my household in the splendid manor you granted me and entered for a tournament or two than the poor old King was dead and you were able to summon me home again. And during all that summer of thirteen hundred and seven your people were coming from London to Paris so that I was always able to keep in touch with you."

Isabel, sitting embroidering by the window, hated the way Edward spoke of his father and remembered that most of the court folk from London had, officially, been in France to arrange about her marriage—the marriage which her betrothed had appeared to be arranging with so much urgency. Could it be possible, she wondered, that even that had been only an excuse for sending them with messages to his exiled friend?

"But this time it will be longer," the Gascon was saying. "Ah, well, we must keep cheerful. That dissatisfied mountebank Lancaster may soon think of someone else to bait, and the wild boar of Warwick will probably die of apoplexy. Such a happy conclusion would be almost worth going abroad for!"

Isabel's hands had dropped from her embroidery to fondle a small, fluffy kitten in her lap. She had made a pet of her in the first place chiefly because Minette arched her back and spat so courageously at the hounds which were for ever around Edward's feet. But now she doted on the dignified little creature, as well as envying her ability to express so effectively some of the sentiments which a King's wife dared not voice.

She herself would have liked to spit out her annoyance over Edward's latest manœuvre. At first, when she had complained that he spent scarcely any time with her, he had taken little notice. But now, being forced to heed the reiterated complaints of his people, he complied with the letter though not with the spirit of her remonstrances. Whenever he was not out racing or hunting he spent much of his time lounging or dealing with necessary State business in her apartments—but invariably brought Piers Gaveston with him. Their manners towards her were charming and they were punctilious about inviting her to join in any music or games of chance which they enjoyed, so that no one could deny that it was her own fault if she sat proud and dull with her ladies at the far end of the room. Haughty daughter of France and Navarre as she was, her husband was King of England, and she could scarcely turn him out, even had he chosen to bring his grooms along.

And so Isabel endured this odd, three-cornered ménage. She knew that Bringnette and Ghislaine fumed on her account, and that because of her outraged withdrawal from them Edward and Gaveston had fallen more and more into the habit of discussing their own affairs regardless of her presence.

And yet at times, because they were all three young and gay by nature, she had felt herself drawn irresistibly into their conversation. Their comradeship was such that she could even enter into their feelings about this approaching parting. "Were you not discussing at supper last night the deplorable state of affairs in Ireland?" she asked of Edward, as his restless peregrinations brought him near her chair.

"Why, yes, my dear," he answered, dragging himself from his own preoccupations with surprise. "Each month more and more of the dissatisfied Irish are forcing their way inside the Pale."

"The Pale?"

"A kind of reserve we keep for English settlers in order to strengthen our rule there."

"You were saying that your Lord Lieutenant there is not nearly firm enough with them?"

"I may have said so. Certainly Aymer de Valence and old Hugh le Despenser, one of my father's ablest advisers, seemed to consider him inefficient." But Edward had more immediate problems of his own to think out. He was not particularly interested in Ireland at any time, and turned on his heel again. Until Isabel put down Minette and suggested calmly, "Then why do you not recall the man, and make Piers Lord Lieutenant of Ireland in his place?"

At least, she thought, it would get him out of the country and lessen for both of them the painful reproach of exile.

Edward stopped short in his tracks, clapping a dramatic hand to his forehead. "God, why did I not think of that before?" he exclaimed.

Piers Gaveston himself turned from the hearth, where he had been moodily kicking at a half-burned log. From where she sat Isabel could see his quickly veiled glance of admiration for a mind quicker than his own. It took him only a moment or two to assimilate the idea and find it good. His handsome face, from which he was usually so careful to exclude any real personal emotion, lit up with relief. "It needed your brilliant little French Queen to stir up the wits of both of us," he said, and strode across the room in a flurry of flowing scarlet scolloped sleeves to kiss her hand.

"What should we do without you, sweet?" applauded Edward, leaning over the back of her chair to kiss her. "I will send for old Hugh le Despenser and my Treasurer Walter Reynolds and set the plan in motion this very hour. Apart from anything else, it holds the pleasing possibility that, in the event of the Irish becoming still more troublesome, I can legitimately recall my Lord Lieutenant for consultation."

"And, by Heaven, how it will enrage my enemies in England!" chuckled Gaveston.

"I am glad that the prospect pleases you, Sir Piers," said Isabel stiffly, by the form of her address rubbing in the loss of his earldom. "I only hope that it will please your wife as well. Ireland, by all I hear, is an even poorer place to live in than this country. But perhaps you will find that a useful excuse to leave her behind!"

Gaveston stood before her, smilingly immune to her stings. He picked up Minette, who was pawing her way delicately towards him, and ruffled the fur about her neck until she purred with sensuous pleasure beneath his caressing hand. "The nimbleness of your Grace's suggestion has scarcely left me time to give the matter a thought. I should imagine that Margaret, being a Clare with possessions in Ireland, will probably prefer to come. But why the savage thrust?"

"Because we do not have the pleasure of seeing her at court. Indeed, I had been in England several weeks before I even knew that you were married. My ladies here were remarking only this morning that they do not even know what the Countess of Clare looks like. And she the King's niece!"

"Ah, I see. Between you, you have invented a pretty legend about my keeping my wife locked up in the grimmest dungeon at Wallingford." Edward laughed, and Isabel could have sworn that Gaveston winked at Ghislaine and that the silly girl blushed at the conspiratorial attention.

"A legend which can soon be disproved if we all go and visit her," suggested Edward, glad of the diversion. "Piers will in any case need to go home to make arrangements for his journey, and we can take young Gilbert along to bid his sister farewell."

"The hospitality of my house is always yours, Ned. And even though Margaret may be unaware of your tender solicitude on her account, Madam, I am sure she will be happy and honoured to have your Grace's company," said Gaveston, bowing with that faint suspicion of irony which always informed his more formal utterances—perhaps because he had small need to make them in private.

"Where is this Wallingford of which we have heard so much?" asked Bringnette, whose ageing bones were already beginning to rebel against the dampness of the climate.

"Only a morning's ride, Madam, and I will tell Dickon, my head groom, to find you the softest saddle," promised Edward.

"And I pray you, Isabel, let Mistress Ghislaine be of your company," said Gaveston, less formerly, "because she has just that bloom of unspoiled youth to match with Margaret's."

"By which he infers that I am not such a child as they thought me," concluded Isabel, remembering her farewell hour with Robert, and taking malicious pleasure in reminding them that she now had no Master-of-Horse to attend her.

"We will send for Hugh Despenser's son to come along in his place," said Edward. "I think you will like him."

And so they all set forth from Windsor Castle, leaving that lovely reach of the Thames and riding briskly through the greening Berkshire lanes, eating up the miles with spontaneous laughter and zestful enjoyment of a sunny morning until the stately walls of Gaveston's manor rose before them. "It is a fair enough place," allowed Bringnette, as the menfolk rode ahead through the gates, "but I should be sorry to be the royal favourite's wife and so neglected."

"For which reason I shall be glad to meet her," said Isabel. "Perhaps we can be of comfort to each other."

"If he *does* leave her behind perhaps your Grace could persuade the King to arrange for her to come and live with us at Westminster or Windsor," suggested Ghislaine of the tender heart.

Whereupon the three women rode into Wallingford full of noble sentiments and ready to relieve their own annoyances by pouring sympathy over Gaveston's royal young wife.

The entrance hall into which they were shown was as luxurious as all the rest of his possessions, and Isabel's fury rose at the sight of one of her mother's finest tapestries hanging on one of the walls.

"Fetch wine for our guests, Dragon, while I go to warn milady," the Master of Wallingford called to a wizened Gascon servant with a long scar down his cheek. But Isabel would have none of it. Tired as she was from trying to ride just as Robert le Messager had taught her, she preferred to meet a hostess unprepared. "Let us go to her now, so that she may drink with us," she said.

"Or so that you may catch her among the dungeon rats?" grinned Gaveston. "Your wishes are my command, Madam. But since the dungeon steps may be ill lighted, allow me at least to lead the way."

Hating to be made fun of, Isabel followed him, with Edward, Gilbert, the clever-looking young Despenser, and her two ladies at her heels. Edward motioned her to go first. As she had suspected, there were no steps at all to negotiate. Only the handsome service screens at the entrance to the Great Hall, lightly carved as lace, where they halted and through which they could all see what went on within. Although it was almost spring a cheerful fire crackled on the hearth and at the far end of the hall, in the clear light from a tall oriel window, a young girl was laboriously picking out a tune upon the strings of a gaily-ribboned lute. She had authentic Plantagenet red-gold hair like Gilbert's. So deep was her concentration and so quietly had Isabel contrived their approach that the girl remained unaware of them until her brother gave Gaveston a friendly push and he strode forward into the hall. At the sound of his footsteps Margaret swung round and saw him. For a moment she stood transfixed with glad surprise, then flung the lute down on the nearest chair and ran like the wind to meet him. As soon as she turned Isabel saw that she was not beautiful, but though her lashes were sandy and her cheeks freckled, her whole face was radiant with joy. "Piers! Piers!" she cried, flinging herself upon him with childish abandon. And, sustaining the shock of her onslaught in mid-hall, Gaveston lifted her shoulder high and kissed her.

"I have brought the new Queen to see you, sweeting. She is very lovely," he said.

"Oh, that will be wonderful! And Uncle Edward too, I hope. And Gilbert." Set down on her feet again, Margaret looked beyond him towards the screens, prepared to curtsy, but not seeing her peeping visitors, turned back to hug him once again. "But having you yourself to visit me is what I care about most of all," she confided vehemently.

"Not with very good news, I fear. I am going to Ireland, Margaret."

"For long?"

"To live there." Eavesdropping with the rest, Isabel noticed that there was none of the usual brittle joking in his voice when he talked to this child-wife of his. To her he explained things gravely and carefully. "The King is making me Lord Lieutenant."

"Oh, but that will be another splendid honour for you, will it not?"

"Honour?" Gaveston repeated the word doubtfully. There was a short silence while he stared over her head, seeming to have forgotten her in the self-reproaching of his thoughts. Perhaps, thought Isabel, she was used to being forgotten for, withdrawing her adoring, importunate little hands from the gold-flecked grandeur of his *cote-hardie*, she folded them sedately before her. "Although you will miss all your friends, we should find interesting work to do there," she said, with a dignity inherited from generations of ruling forebears.

Gaveston came out of his trance-like preoccupation. "So you really want to come with me?"

She drew back in momentary horror. "Oh, Piers, *please!*" she entreated. "You would not be so cruel as to think of going without me?"

He drew her to him again and kissed her with unmistakable gratitude. She was his wife, she must go or stay as he ordered; but in his moment of defeat it meant something to him that she could not bear to be left behind. "Of course not, my little love," he promised. "But you must come now and welcome our guests. We must not keep the Queen waiting any longer."

The surprise visit to Wallingford was a success, with their hostess playing her part to perfection. Gilbert teased her with brotherly candour about her unmelodious efforts with the lute, and Edward picked up the beribboned instrument and sang to them. As a family the Plantagenets were delightful, Isabel decided, and far less prone to formality than her own. But, knowing only too well how seldom the young Countess of Clare had her husband to herself, she hastened her party's departure In fact, Isabel was glad to get away. She found the amused glances which she had caught Edward exchanging with Gaveston very mortifying, and throughout the return journey she and Bringnette and Ghislaine were uncommonly silent, never once referring to the generous pity they had entertained for Gaveston's wife.

Isabel rode home very thoughtfully, without once noticing the features of the countryside. She had been surprised and shamed. Her young notions of good and bad were all confused. Life seemed to be more complicated than she had imagined. While all England snarled at Gaveston, while she herself had cause to hate him, while undoubtedly he encouraged her light-minded husband to be indolent and worse, he was, as her aunt had said, far from being all bad. "And if only Aunt Marguerite had been with us at Windsor yesterday," thought Isabel, "she would somehow have prevented me from making such a fool of myself!" But by the time she had reached Windsor she had decided that it was probably better to feel a fool and learn.

CHAPTER 8

EDWARD saw Gaveston off at Bristol and even lent him his own ship, the *Marguerite*. He arranged for an escort of other craft, and had his own tailor design fine new clothes for him. And to the further annoyance of the Barons, who had stripped Gaveston of his earldom and publicly burned the enfeoffment charter, their exiled enemy was wildly successful as Lord Lieutenant of Ireland. His fine presence and the trappings of his servants overawed the people he was to govern; without carping critics his energy and talents had full scope, and the very fact that he had been banished by the hated English ensured him a welcome. Judging by the accounts which began to filter through he was working hard to make the King of England's power felt. Instead of issuing useless orders to the chieftains of the more inaccessible and troublesome counties, he lost no time in collecting an army and personally leading it out against insurgents; he built new strongholds, and his personal bravery appealed so strongly to his Irish soldiers that they were proud to serve under him. Flauntingly he enjoyed the role of proxy prince, and the Irish, with their poetic patriotism and their starved love of pageantry, played up to him.

"Which all goes to show that without the entertainment of the King on his mind Piers can be both a spectacular and a capable ruler," said Marguerite.

"If only Edward would follow his example and attend to all the piles of State papers which mount up on his secretary's table!" sighed Isabel. "It would help him, at least for an hour or so, to forget a friend for whom I appear to be no substitute, and at the same time stop all this disloyal grumbling. Is there *always* such dissension in this country?"

"It was never so in the late King's time."

Isabel picked up her mirror, which was frequently near at hand these days. "The people always shout and throw up their caps for *me* whenever I go out of the Palace gates," she remarked complacently.

"They adore you. And I am thankful they do. It is part of what I was trying to explain to you in Boulogne. About the ordinary people's sense of justice protecting you. But it does not help to ease the tension."

"Perhaps not. Though with a husband who seems little moved by the fact that other men call me 'Isabel the Fair', even a drayman's admiration is pleasant."

Marguerite regarded her thoughtfully. That she should enjoy all this adulation was natural enough. But her aunt was well aware that the lovely little Queen had taken to riding out frequently of late, and smiling more devastatingly at the crowds, in order to encourage public applause. Marguerite suspected that Lancaster had suggested it but, while deploring the manœuvre, there was nothing much she could say about it. "Did you know that Edward has written to the Pope asking him to absolve Gaveston from his oath if he should return?" she asked, changing the subject.

"No!" Isabel laid down the mirror instantly. "Then he means to try to get him back?"

"For the sake of your happiness it is to be hoped that his Holiness will refuse. In spite of all Edward's apparent frivolity, he is, as you know, in some ways very devout, and would not imperil the eternal peace of his friend's soul, I think."

"Whether Piers is away or not seems to make very little difference to my happiness," confessed Isabel sadly.

68

Marguerite laid a loving hand on her shoulder. "Go on trying, my dear. Even if my step-son stills fails you, you yourself have courage and good intent enough for two," she said.

That evening Isabel talked with Sir Walter Reynolds and the King's secretary, and next morning she coaxed Edward to deal with some of the documents which had been awaiting his signature for weeks. She even sat in his work room, quiet as a mouse, hoping to keep him at the hated task. Isabel was growing up. She had already come to know that this weak, charming husband of hers could work as hard as any man at tasks which he enjoyed, but lacked the self-discipline to stick at those which bored him. Had he been emulating one of his craftsmen in carving some beautiful design in wood, or even learning to thatch a house, he would probably not have noticed when the sun came out. As it was he soon complained of cramp, stretched his long limbs and grew impatient to be out riding.

"There you are, Walter," he said, throwing down his pen. "That ought to satisfy them."

Isabel knew, too, that when her husband spoke of "them" in that hating voice he was alluding particularly to a half-dozen or so of his most powerful barons. "What is it that they are specially wanting you to do now?" she asked, as soon as treasurer and secretary had gathered up the papers and bowed themselves out. "Was not Piers' going enough?"

"Nothing would ever be enough for my uncle of Lancaster. He was probably born grumbling at the quality of his mother's milk. And he and Warwick stir up the others. Of course, they are always girding at me because we have lost Scotland. That is perennial. And also because we are lax—or less brutal—in Wales and Ireland and all the other places my famous father set his heel on." Edward got up and called to a page to have his horse saddled, and stood for a few minutes by the window looking out at the parklands of Windsor and wishing forlornly that his friend were with him on such a lovely morning.

"Well, Piers is putting that right in Ireland far more efficiently than any of them could, for all their war-obsessed minds and standing armies," he said, turning back to grin at her triumphantly.

For the first time Isabel tried hard to take an intelligent interest in the complicated affairs of a kingdom for which she really cared little. "But those are big national questions, Edward. I meant what are all those documents they keep sending you to sign, and the things which Parliament keeps trying to force you to do?"

"Mostly dull and niggling matters which are not worth wrinkling your pretty forehead over like that," he told her, perching on the arm of her chair and bending to kiss away her frown of concentration. "The fluctuating value of the coinage, for instance. Admittedly it is debased, but the shopkeepers and merchants agreed to accept it at its face value, and they should stick to their agreement. A nation has to pay for its wars somehow. And my father was foolish enough to expel all our Jewish and Lombardy money-lenders. Then there are the people who claim that they have been robbed or assaulted and cannot bring the offender to justice because some important person or other is shielding him with a writ of protection. And the outcry about my courts selling pardons to criminals——"

"Oh, but surely that is shameful! My father would not——"

"Yes, yes, I admit it is all wrong, and I intend to do something about it." Edward got up and wandered back to his work-table, picking up first one undealt-with petition and then another, and glancing at each with brief distaste. "There are so many matters that need investigating, including the everlasting whine against my bailiffs and servants. They are supposed to pay far too little for our fish or poultry, and to cheat small, struggling farmers out of their fields by means of clever legal quibbling, though in half the cases the trouble arises because the freed peasants who have acquired land cannot read their title deeds in the first place. Nothing my men do is ever right, although Warwick's men are far more abusive and acquisitive."

Having witnessed the overbearing ways of the "Black Dog of Warwick", as Gaveston so aptly called him, Isabel was quite willing to believe this.

"If only Parliament, instead of wasting so much time prying into my private affairs, would support me in setting up a flourishing staple for our cloth trade in Flanders!" sighed Edward. "There would be no need then for any of us to keep trying to raise money by dubious means, and more of the people might be able to send their sons to school, or to study for the priesthood, which I should be glad to see."

"Why cloth particularly?" asked Isabel, who had more personal experience of silk brocades and furs.

"Because this country teems with sheep. Our farmers shear them and our merchants export the wool. The Flemish weave it into cloth and make fortunes selling it all over Europe. And still the short-sighted Londoners get furious with me every time I encourage a few foreigners over here to show them how to make the cloth themselves and get much bigger profits. The people up in East Anglia are beginning to have more sense. They know that our wool is the best in the world and are setting up their own looms. But even when I tackled those numbskulls in Parliament about it only Aymer de Valence of Pembroke had the wit to see or the honesty to admit that that is why Norfolk and Suffolk are becoming the richest counties in England."

Watching with affection his enthusiasm for his pet industrial project, Isabel remembered how his step-mother had once remarked what a good manorial husbandman he might have made. "I see now what Marguerite meant about the wealth of this country being on the sheep's backs," she said, with a smile. She had intended begging Edward to release Robert le Messager from the Tower, but decided that with so many other worries on his hands this was not the moment. With the instinct of an alluring young woman, she realized that a request for something she had set her heart on was likely to be more propitiously received in bed. Approaching the subject of her admirer's release more circuitously, she asked her husband if she might accompany him on his ride, and, when he seemed genuinely pleased, improved the occasion by remarking how much she missed her Master-of-Horse. It seemed unlikely that it would occur to Edward's unobservant mind that it was not in that capacity she missed Robert most; but he made no comment and her complaint resulted as usual in the inclusion in the party of old Hugh Despenser's clever son, whom she did not very much like. He had, she understood, been brought up in the Prince of Wales's household together with Gaveston and young Gilbert of Gloucester but, although he appeared to be more stable, Isabel thought that he had shifty eyes and lacked the raffish charm of any of them. Disliking his company, and missing Robert's compliments, she began to share Edward's depression and even caught herself thinking that without Piers Gaveston court life could be decidedly dull.

As the weeks passed even the barons had to admit the brilliance of Gaveston's rule in Ireland, and the gloom lifted. When a favourable reply came from Rome, Edward went about singing and was seized by an unusual spurt of energy. He began to cut down his personal expenditure and to attend to the various grievances of Parliament with new vigour, hoping to be in a better position to bargain with them. Incensed with his neglect of the realm, which they had hoped would be lessened during the royal favourite's absence, barons and prelates sat for long hours in the Painted Chamber at Westminster solemnly preparing documents by which they intended to control their sovereign's private life and force him to rule the country conscientiously as his father had before him. They drew up ordinances which stipulated that he should not go to war or leave the country without the consent of Parliament, that he must curtail his own extravagance and the gifts he made to favourites out of his wife's dowry or the country's money, that all taxes should be properly audited and that all Gascon hangers-on at court must go. And much as he disliked some of these clauses, Edward intimated that he would sign and accept them in exchange for Gaveston's return. He would, thought his exasperated wife, have signed away his own life if it would have done Gaveston any good.

Because of his compliance, public opinion began to veer in his favour. Aymer de Valence and a few of the other more moderate peers were prepared to put the well-being of the country before their personal prejudices. Young Gloucester, who stood well with both sides, good-naturedly acted as mediator, so that in the end even Lancaster and Warwick were persuaded to give their reluctant consent.

And so Piers Gaveston came home, covered with heartily grudged honours. Not being sure of his welcome and having learned some modicum of wisdom during his lieutenancy in Dublin, he had the sense to come quietly across Wales, and had the pleasure of finding Edward in Chester to meet him. There was a new air of responsibility about the man which tended to lessen his enemies' animosity and even made some of them afraid to thwart him. And as soon as he and Margaret reached London and he found that the earldom of Cornwall had been restored to him, he improved public opinion still more by returning to the Crown all those revenues which Edward had given him in exchange.

"My ownership of your Isles of Man and Wight was short-lived!" he remarked cheerfully to Edward.

"May you never need them!" prayed his friend fervently.

"As things are, if nobody bothers me to sign those insufferable ordinances before the New Year, we shall be able to hunt together all autumn and then devise some stupendous revels for Christmas."

December brought the coldest winter within living memory. From Gravesend to London the Thames was frozen over so thickly that citizens, looking out from the windows of their houses on London Bridge, beheld the amazing spectacle of a bonfire blazing on the icy surface of their river. Edward took Isabel and her ladies, muffled in fur to the eyes, to watch people dancing round the warmth of it, while 'prentice lads played furious games of football among the frozen shipping.

On the surface life appeared to be full of goodwill and merriment, but underneath all the movement and shouting flowed a tide of anxiety and suffering. Neither by road nor barge could food be brought into the city, ravenous rats gnawed winter stores in warehouse and granary, wood piles could not be replenished, old people died and prices rose. Before the court left for what Gilbert of Gloucester called "a real country Christmas" at Langley, in Hertfordshire, that amiable young man persuaded Edward to abolish the tax which Parliament had levied in order to pay for a spring campaign against the marauding Scots— a move popular enough at the time with the hungry southerners, but less likely to prove popular among men of the north whose homes were burned and raped along the Scottish borders.

At Langley the festive season was kept with wild abandon. Even in France Isabel had seldom enjoyed Christmas and Twelfth Night revels more. Edward Plantagenet and Piers Gaveston together could have enlivened a charnel-house. And after all those weeks of worry, Edward was happy. He had the ability to be completely happy, like a child, in some isolated segment of time, without either regrets for the past or forebodings for the future. Isabel and his step-mother, Gilbert and Margaret of Clare were all there, and he loved to have his family about him. And above and beyond all, his friend had been given back to him. Gaveston soon forgot the self-restraint so essential to a busy ruler. Their high spirits soared and became contagious, spilling over in a largesse of pleasure to enrich the present hour for many whose minds were far from easy about the future. They were both so colourfully dressed and so good to look upon, so perpetually encircled by animated young people, that even to sit and watch them could be an aesthetic kind of pleasure. So,

73

at any rate, thought the May Queen, sitting comfortably by the fire, where her niece came briefly and breathlessly to rest beside her from a capering dance in which her light-footed loveliness had been much in demand.

"Do they never think beyond the moment?" said Marguerite, half laughingly, half anxiously, as they watched the two tall young men, in the middle of a laughing, shrieking group of men and girls, toss the King's protesting jester almost to the rafters, bouncing him with willing helpers from a hastily seized table-cloth.

"Edward is happy, and how absurdly young he looks!" said Isabel, conscious of a queer pre-knowledge that this particular fragment of time would remain static in her mind; and that even though she might grow to be quite old she would always choose to remember him as he looked now. "What made you say that just now?" she added, realizing suddenly that her aunt's concern was neither for Robert the Fool nor for the fine table-cloth she had embroidered. "What is there that you feel they should be thinking about beyond this lovely moment?"

Marguerite, who was no kill-joy, tried to shrug her anxiety aside. "Oh, just something I heard Guy Beauchamp of Warwick say, perhaps. Or because John of London, my scrivener, tells me that those solemn ordinances the barons have been working on so hard all these months are almost finished." But even at such a festive moment she found it difficult to speak lightly of something which might affect them all so much. She had not been feeling too well during this bitter weather, and even in the warm, holly-decked hall at Langley she could not rid herself of an awareness that the hatred of the barons was waiting, cruel as an icy blast, somewhere outside the thickness of the walls. When Isabel would have risen to rejoin her companions, Marguerite laid a detaining hand on her knee. "You do realize, do you not, Isabel, that once these ordinances are enforced they will deprive Edward of all but the outward trappings of kingship? That they will take away all his real power?"

Isabel looked round to where Gaveston, resplendent in scarlet and Capet jewels, was showing Ghislaine and some other girls the steps of a new masque he had invented. Because of her aunt's warning the spell was broken. "And he will have bartered it all for that greedy peacock. How I hate Piers Gaveston!" she said fiercely. "How I wish he would go away again!"

"Yet his love for Edward is genuine, in spite of all the spoils he gathers."

"Then why hasn't he the sense to see that the greatest kindness he could do the King is to go away so that the barons stop this terrifying muttering? Not just for a few months in Ireland or Guienne. Go away altogether, I mean."

But how would that profit her step-son in the end, wondered Marguerite, who had known him for so much longer. The removal of Piers' dominance would but leave Edward's weakness. Had he once bestirred himself to emulate his father's fine example while his friend was away in Ireland? "You see how it was last time," she wanted to say. But being Marguerite, she could not bring herself to put into words anything so hurtful and, in any case, chattering people were beginning to swirl around them again. "If you cut down the oak the ivy only finds another plant to lean upon," she said ambiguously.

But Isabel, too, had a Frenchwoman's quickness of perception. "Would it twine round a golden lily, do you suppose?" she asked, getting up from the unpretentious stool she had rested on.

"I pray that it will—when the time comes."

"*When* it comes—not *if* it comes!" The chattering group had drifted on their way again, and they were momentarily alone. Isabel leaned close to Marguerite, her eyes bright as a cat's in the firelight. "You sound very sure that Piers will go—for good." Much as she loved to dance, she was momentarily unconscious of the gay voices calling to her. Her mind was working upon a matter which concerned her and absorbed her, and by some swift association of ideas she hit upon the touchstone of her aunt's certainty. "What was it you heard the Black Dog of Warwick say?" she asked.

Marguerite held her hands to the blaze, turning them this way and that against the blaze, as though considering their beauty. But she was not a vain woman. They were a good horsewoman's hands, light at guiding and control; and she was wondering how much she could guide and control a sensitive, highly strung girl into happiness when the chance of a smoother course came. At the urgency in her niece's lowered voice she roused herself to explain. "He was standing on that dark staircase leading to the landing stage at Westminster, talking to young Arundel whose new lance did not, as you know, bring him any better luck against Piers in that last tournament. I was just coming up from my barge, but Ghislaine had gone back for something and neither of them heard me, I suppose. Arundel had been repeating some tactless joke Piers had made at his expense, and complaining about how he always refers to all of them by those ridiculous nicknames of his. And I heard Guy of Warwick say, 'Let him call me dog or whatsoever he will, but one day when I see my opportunity the dog may turn and bite him.' It sounded so—horribly convincing—because for once he said it quietly, without foaming at the mouth as he usually does when speaking of Piers."

CHAPTER 9

BACK in London the storm began to break. With their ordinances almost drawn up, the barons already felt capable of dictating to the King. To their mind it was a sovereign's duty to rule, and the more firmly he did so the better. All down the dynasty there had been good Plantagenet rulers and bad, but never one who had so neglected the whole royal business. But nevertheless Edward was their anointed King, to be spoken to with subservience, and so a scapegoat must be found for him. It was easy enough to point to the all-powerful favourite. Speaking half the truth and relieving their jealousy at the same time, counsellors accused him of having turned away the King's heart from his people, and of having committed every kind of fraud and oppression. With more complete truth and some small compassion, they declared that his attractive presence came between Edward and the Queen. And this time they refused to omit the clause which insisted upon Gaveston's banishment from the realm.

Edward tried to prove his own sweet reasonableness by sending a copy of the stern document to the Pope, and in order to gain time tried to get the clergy on his side. But Gaveston's greed was a by-word in England. Though he might throw spectacular largesse to a crowd or send generous support to his impoverished relatives in Gascony, abbeys and churches seldom benefited by any offering of his. The Gascon pretended to no devoutness.

Both clergy and barons had given him a chance, they said. Men like Pembroke and the elder Despenser had sincerely hoped that he would have learned his lesson by the time he came home from Ireland—that he would have lived less flamboyantly, and sharpened his wits on others less painfully. But such behaviour seemed to be in the structure of the man himself. Contrary to their belief, Piers Gaveston really did not seek to offend them nor did he work himself into such a prominent position for any politically ambitious purpose. As the Queen-Dowager could have told them—having watched him grow from orphaned adolescence—it was just that he had to have blood-horses and beautifully cut clothes, and was too arrogant and reckless to curb his tongue. And because his enemies, being but human, found it harder to forgive a few ill-timed words of ridicule about themselves than any carefully thought-out treachery against the State. Marguerite even knew that, being without deliberate animosity himself, Piers often found the intensity of their desire for vengeance incomprehensible; but that, unlike Edward, he did not invariably underestimate it. Of late he had had a pretty shrewd idea of the lengths to which his enemies would go.

"It looks as if I shall need one of your island fortresses after all," he said, for once scarcely covering his irritation with a show of indolent amusement.

"My contentious uncle of Lancaster tells me that they intend to read their precious document in public from the steps of St. Paul's," Edward told him.

"The ten commandments according to Saint Thomas, complete with fanfare and heraldry!"

As usual, they were talking unreservedly in the Queen's solar, from time to time including her in their conversation in the casual manner which annoyed her most.

"My subjects up in the north have been complaining about this Robert Bruce raiding their villages, and Parliament wants me to lead an army up there against him," said Edward. "And to crown everything, Isabel, your father chooses this depressing moment to insist upon my going over to France to pay homage for Guienne."

Isabel knew only too well that her frequent complaints to her family were building up a barrier between herself and her husband, but she always hoped that her father's backing would help the barons to get rid of Gaveston. She merely shrugged, but Gaveston caught at the news with relief. "What could serve us better?" he asked. "If we go up and fight the Bruce you have an excellent excuse not to go to France, Ned. And we shall avoid being in London either when all this baronial storm of self-righteousness breaks."

"Piers probably thinks that if only he can be as brilliant in Scotland as he was in Ireland, Uncle Thomas and the rest will have to forgive him," said Isabel, wondering why the man did not hit her for all the jibes she made at him, instead of just lounging there with a grin on his face as though he rather liked her.

"That is a good thought," agreed Edward, ignoring the half-weary, half-contemptuous tone in which it was made, and seeming, for once, quite pleased to go to war. "Let us set out as soon as Gilbert and our Constable Segrave and the rest can get sufficient forces together."

Isabel noticed that even his own familiar friend looked at him with puzzled amazement, as though marvelling how one who had gone campaigning with that arch-strategist Longshanks could have imbibed so little military sense. "There will be no grazing for our horses up there until early summer," he pointed out. "March is all very well for the hardy Scots who can make do with a fire under a hedge and a griddle and sack of oats under their saddles, but surely you remember, *mon cher*, how they used to burn their own villages sooner than let our men have a crockful of food?"

"I suppose you are right. And with Gilbert having talked me into remitting the war tax, we shall be hard put to it to take sufficient stores with us."

And so the expedition was put off until June when Isabel, surprised to find that Edward wanted her, went along, too. She could probably have coaxed him to leave her in comfort with Marguerite and her two boys, but, much as she hated sharing him, she hated still more the thought of being left behind.

"It is no fit traipsing for a gently nurtured woman," grumbled Bringnette, reluctantly superintending their packing.

"Queen Marguerite always went," pointed out her rapidly maturing nursling.

"*Her* husband knew how to look after her," muttered the old lady, unappeased.

And as if that were not enough, Lady Badlesmere, the most spiteful of the English ladies, whose menfolk had fought with

Longshanks, said patronizingly, "I do not think you need worry over much about her Grace's comfort. The second Edward is not likely to go far over the border."

Isabel could have struck her. "My husband may not choose to spend his life encamped round besieged castles, but he is a Plantagenet," she said witheringly. For was not the name, all over Europe and the Holy Land, synonymous with courage? Although one member of the family might happen to have more civilized interests it did not prove that he would not fight brilliantly when occasion arose. Even Gaveston, whom everybody knew to be a fine fighter, often talked in that bored, cynical way about war so that anyone hearing him might be excused for believing him to be lily-handed. It was, as Marguerite had been at such pains to explain, because they had both had too much military science dinned into them as boys.

Tired of the conversation, and intent upon snubbing Lady Badlesmere, Isabel drew Ghislaine into another room to help pack the jewels and headdresses she would take. "Little did your mother, the Queen of France and Navarre, think that all these lovely wedding things would be crushed on to army baggage carts!" complained the girl. "But you really *do* want to go, do you not, Madam?"

"Where one's heart is——" answered Isabel lightly. "And by the sheep's eyes you cast at the Gascon I imagine you want to come, too?"

Ghislaine blushed and busied herself with folding a gauze veil or two. "One cannot help enjoying things more when he is there—partly for the pleasure of looking at him, I suppose," she began, quite seriously for her. "Even with so much cause to hate him, your Grace must have noticed that he has a beautiful voice. And when he smiles, persuading one to pretend to be a mermaid in a masque or to do something else outrageous that he has set his mind on—— Oh, please try not to think me foolish, Madam, if I say that sometimes it seems almost as if he casts a spell. As if one can neither refuse nor dislike him any more."

Isabel removed a favourite filigree circlet she was trying on, and stared down at it abstractedly. "I do not think you at all foolish about some things, Ghislaine, and you are very dear to me," she said, with equal seriousness. "Although it appears that most people are quite immune from this—spell, I think you called it?"

"Oh, Madam!" Ghislaine seized her hand and kissed it, all the more grateful because the other women had laughed at her for a superstitious little nit-wit when she had minded so much about the breaking of the mirror on the Queen's wedding day. As if to increase such unexpected recognition of her small store of wisdom, she added sedately, "Of course, exciting as the Earl of Cornwall is, I always pray our Blessed Lady never to let me really fall in love with such a man. When it comes to a matter of *marrying*, I should prefer a steadfast person like Robert le Messager. Someone devoted whom one could trust."

Isabel noticed that her blue eyes were soft as pansies, and that her busy fingers were perking up the petals of a velvet fleur-de-lys with quite unnecessary vigour. "Wise child!" she laughed, kissing the warm childish cheek. "I will do my best to see that you get him one day."

"Oh, but, Madam, everybody knows that he is desperately in love with *you*!" blurted out the astonished girl. "And, anyhow, Heaven help us, the poor man is in the Tower."

"For my sake. So one day I may summon up enough courage to ask the King to release him. Violent fires are apt to burn themselves out quickly, people say. And who knows but what a few months in that gloomy place may have cooled our good Robert's present ardour?"

"Then you do not want him?"

"I am a married woman who wants no man but her husband."

Ghislaine's cheeks began to dimple deliciously. "Yet there is another we all want for you."

"Another, Ghislaine?"

"Small and helpless, with red-gold hair like the Gloucesters. I light a candle to kind Saint Joseph every day. Oh, Madam, we should be so *happy* if you had a son!"

"My fond Ghislaine! You are as sentimental as you are superstitious!" chided Isabel, ashamed that she herself did not pray for this final blessing as monotonously as most women. But who can blame me, she thought. And even if my marriage were unmarred, perhaps, to me, children would be but another gift to add to the wild prodigality of my wifely love?

"Robert le Messager told the men who took him that he would escape from the Tower," said Ghislaine, returning bright-eyed to their former discussion, and supposing the boast to be new to her mistress.

"Only a lion among men could do that," said Isabel, remembering the grim thickness of the walls. Laying aside her finery, she moved to the window and stood staring out with a sad, secret smile. She was caught in the snare of her wasted capacity for passion. She was thinking of the ineffectiveness of Edward and trying to imagine what it must feel like to be loved by the type of man who could, single-handed, break out from the Tower.

But the short campaign against Scotland brought forth no lions, unless it were Robert the Bruce, battling for the freedom of his country. Apart from a brief march into the Highlands, accomplished with considerable loss and danger, Longshanks's son seldom left the border town of Berwick. The place became an army headquarters to which men like Gloucester, de Warenne and Nicholas de Segrave returned between sorties. And Isabel, living there in comparative comfort, wondered sometimes whether her husband were merely prolonging his stay there in order to avoid the barons who had refused to accompany him. Piers Gaveston held the key town of Roxburgh, with its great sprawling castle, all the time hoping for the kind of victory which even the Black Dog of Warwick could not ignore. But his urgent desire to engage the Bruce's army seemed fated to frustration, and the whole campaign, lacking a fiery leader, resolved itself into the capture of a series of strongholds which the canny Scots had already dismantled. After a maddening winter spent mostly in trying to trap the most mobile army imaginable in the southern Highlands, Gaveston travelled secretly and painfully to Berwick to report. Or to set eyes on his friend again. And even Isabel, being bored to tears, was not ill-pleased to see him. The exasperating winter had taken toll of him. For once he was sick and subdued and could not stay for long in the saddle, but as soon as he had rested and been treated by the King's physician, Bromtoft, even Edward's blandishments could not keep him. He returned to Roxburgh full of a premonition that only a spectacular victory could save him; but the barons, learning of his sickness, were only too glad to relieve him of his command. The Earl of Angus and Sir Henry Percy of Northumberland were sent to take over the armies, while the King of France offered to negotiate a truce. And by the following summer King, Queen and court were back in London, where Gaveston faced a foe far more implacable than the Scots.

The ordinances which twelve chosen barons had been preparing were read in public. This time the King would be forced to sign, and his favourite would have to go. In all London there was scarcely one dissentient voice. Even Gloucester and the Despensers advised their sovereign to give in, if only to save his friend's life.

"Must he go to Guienne again?" sighed Edward.

"No. We said exile. Is not Guienne part of your Grace's kingdom?" said Lancaster, daring to rage more loudly now that the man who had so often discomforted him in the tiltyard was at last lying low. "Besides, peers and populace alike consider that the foreigner has feathered his nest there too well with English gold."

"Foreigner!" his royal nephew shouted back at him, in the nearest approach to a Plantagenet rage which Isabel was ever to behold. "Was not my sworn brother Piers brought up in England since boyhood? And has he not fought for her as valiantly as his father did before him? You lack common logic, milords. Guienne, it seems, is 'foreign' when it is a question of a subject's birth, but 'part of my kingdom' when it comes to a question of his exile."

But finding himself hopelessly opposed, he wrote to John, Duke of Brabant, his sister Margaret's husband, asking him to receive his friend. He asked for, and received, letters of safe conduct for him. And Piers Gaveston was seen no more about London. Edward spoke a good deal about the papers and about a ship lying off Dover. But there were some who said the papers were never used, and seamen who claimed the ship never sailed, and rumours began to spread that someone answering to the tall Gascon's description had been seen wandering about in Devon and Cornwall. The King did not deny it. At the barons' bidding, he obligingly ordered investigations to be made. "Make a careful search in all the castles of the said counties," he wrote, in his own rather niggling little writing, to Hugh Courteny of Devon. "For we have commanded all our county sheriffs, and the constables and wardens of the said castles, to assist you whenever they shall be required to do so in our name."

Graciously, with his own hand, he gave the order to Aymer de Valence of Pembroke. "I, too, should be comforted to know the whereabouts of my life-long friend," he said to the Archbishop of Canterbury. Sadly but charmingly, he stood on the steps of Westminster Hall, speaking to individual members of Parliament as they went out. He had brought his Queen in order to show on what good terms they were, and because the sight of her always pleased them. He was the bereaved and reasonable monarch, and everyone was grateful that the threat of civil war had been averted. The departing barons bowed low. Even Warwick bowed as low as his girth and his armour would allow, believing that he had licked some sense into Longshanks's feckless cub at last.

But Isabel noticed the lightness of her husband's lithe stride when they were gone. Returning to their private apartments she watched his eyes, and saw nothing of that desolate lost-boy look which had depressed her days all the while Gaveston was away in Ireland. "Are you *really* very anxious?" she ventured to ask, laying a hand on his.

Edward kissed it and shrugged sadly, so that the stiff gold cape about his shoulders touched the soft brown of his hair. "The May Queen tells me she says a daily prayer for him to St. Christopher," he said evasively. "To her Piers must be almost one of the family and she was always kind to him. Her sympathetic heart pictures him hungry among the ruins of Tintagel or half-frozen on some Welsh mountain."

"I will have those new musicians play to her this evening. The ones my Uncle brought me from Paris last week. And you should come too, Edward. They will cheer you."

After supper, when her visiting uncle and Marguerite with her two boys were gathered in the hall, and the French musicians were tuning up, Isabel sent Goodwin Hawtayne, her steward, to tell the King that they were ready.

"Edward loves music when he is depressed," Marguerite was saying to her brother, while the boys, glad to be released from their tutors, seated themselves on stools at her feet.

But Goodwin Hawtayne returned alone, and seeing that he looked worried Isabel drew him aside. "Is the King not coming?"

The man spread deprecating palms. "Madam, I regret, I do not know."

"But you left a message with one of the gentlemen of the bedchamber to remind him, surely?"

"The door was closed. There was no one about. Except that someone within was singing softly to a lute."

"The King himself, of course. Then why did you not——"

"No, Madam, it was not the King. At that moment I heard

his Grace's voice down in the courtyard. Looking at his sorrel mare that went lame, I think. And——"

"Yes, Goodwin?"

"That wizened-faced Gascon with the burn scar was standing on the stairs with drawn sword outside the King's room."

Isabel's fingers flew to her mouth. "Dragon!" she whispered, her lips scarcely sounding the word. "Did you say that I had sent you?"

Apparently the man had said nothing. Shame-faced, he stood looking down at the points of his shoes. "He was glaring at me. He squints. He has the Evil Eye. And he is said to be the best swordsman in all England and France," he muttered.

"And you were unarmed," agreed Isabel, knowing how terrifying Gaveston's man could look. "I understand that there was nothing you could do, stumbling on him unexpectedly like that. There is nothing you can do now, Goodwin," she added, pressing sharply warning fingers on his wrist, "except keep your mouth shut."

At that moment the King arrived, all charming apology for having kept the company waiting, and it was as the steward had supposed. "It was that mare your brother Charles gave me, Capet," he explained to his wife's visiting uncle. "I fancy the damp of our climate must have got into her shoulder joints. My head groom is good, but I wanted to run a hand over her myself on my way here. Forgive me, dear Isabel. These new French musicians of yours should be a treat for all of us."

Edward took a tray of sweetmeats from a servant and passed it to his elder half-brother Thomas and stooped to ruffle the head of young Edmund Plantagenet, who worshipped him whether he gave them sweetmeats or not. At a sign from the Queen most of the candles were snuffed out. He seated himself in the high-backed chair set ready for him beside her, the musicians struck up and he was soon absorbed by their fine performance.

Althought Isabel would have wished it otherwise, it was in such family moments that she came nearest to finding complete happiness. Herself unobserved, she could enjoy looking at her husband's flawless profile and at the contented relaxation of his athlete's body, and forget that she did not come first with him. Poignantly aware that her own beauty was matched well with his, she could believe for a little while that they were the perfectly wedded couple of her dreams. At such times she had only to stretch out her hand and he would hold it affectionately on his knee, and she could almost beguile herself into imagining that he held it with secret passion as a lover.

But this evening, under cover of a lively passage, Isabel leaned instead towards her aunt. Her fingers pressed meaningly on Marguerite's, claiming covert attention, while all the while her eyes kept careful watch on the King's face, making sure that he was still wrapped in enjoyment of the music. "I do not think you need pray for Piers in the Welsh mountains," she whispered, tilting her low chair a little further back into the shadows. "Goodwin tells me that when Edward was down in the court-yard there was soft lute-playing behind the closed door of his bedroom. And Dragon with drawn sword on the stairs."

Marguerite gripped her hand and, after a moment's amaze-ment, whispered back. "You think—Piers is here all the time? While sheriffs search the country. That Edward is hiding him?"

"Have you not noticed that he does not look *bereft* as he did before?"

"Yes, now you say so. He must be mad!"

"He cannot hope to trick them for long, can he, Marguerite?"

"They will kill Piers if they find out."

Isabel's only fear was for her husband—fear mixed with fury for his folly. "And what will they do—to Edward?"

"It will mean civil war. With almost everybody on one side."

"But you do not believe that even for Piers Edward would stand up to them—alone?" gasped Isabel, remembering her secret shame over his indolence at Berwick.

The King was quite unaware of their whispered conversation, and the gaze of each of them was upon his face—fearfully, consideringly, measuringly. "I do not know. I think he might," said his stepmother. "To those whom he loves Edward can be amazingly loyal."

CHAPTER 10

FOR Isabel, so young and capable of pleasure, the extraordinary shocks and disappointments of early married life were a bewilder-ing disillusionment. Only her vitality and power of retaliation saved her from being physically stunned by them. The misfortunes which Edward courted seemed incredible. Little had she dreamed, when coming in so much splendour to be Queen, that in a few short years she would find herself a fugitive from her husband's capital, and sharing his ignominious retreat before his subjects' wrath, in company with the favourite who was the cause of it!

They had fled northward and every step of the way since Gaveston had joined them had been resented by her.

The great hall of Tynemouth castle was stark and draughty, with no feminine touch to render it suitable for the reception of a Queen. The flight from Newcastle had been too hurried for Edward to bring any of their furnishings, so that no cushions softened the window-seats and no tapestries warmed the walls. An insufficient supply of torches threw shadows on the flagstones and a keen wind howled up-river from the sea. In spite of gusts of smoke which kept bellying out from the vast chimney and soiling her green brocade gown, Isabel crouched over the fire to keep warm. Except for Bringnette and Ghislaine, in their hastily prepared apartments somewhere up in one of the towers, she was the only woman in the grim Northumbrian fortress. Judging by the Captain of the Guard's report, the garrison was as inadequate as the lighting, and in spite of an assumed air of composure, the proud little daughter of France was really frightened.

Edward had gone out on to the battlements to hold yet another consultation with the Captain, but she was not alone. Piers Gaveston was lounging by a table at which he and the King had been playing chess before Edward, rising hurriedly on hearing of the approach of a messenger from Newcastle, had sent half the carved pieces rolling to the floor with a sweep of his sleeve. Since his departure Gaveston had been idly making an intricate military formation with such pawns as remained on the board, his long scarlet-clad legs stuck out before him. He had invited Isabel to join him in a fresh game, but she had ignored him. And now the thoughts of each of them were far away, his on the uncertainties of his future, hers on the cruel buffets of the immediate past.

Small wonder that she did not want to talk to him. But for him she and Edward and poor rheumaticky old Bringnette would be comfortably at home at Westminster enjoying the pleasant new apartments he had planned for her, with the Thames and not the Tyne flowing beneath their windows. But for Piers Gaveston she and Edward might be happy together in mind, instead of being driven apart by the casual nature of his kindness and by her burning jealousy and resentment. But for Piers Gaveston this country of her adoption would not be riven by force, with the barons in arms and their sovereign in flight before them. The whole situation was so incredible that she dared not dwell on it. That way lay a madness of rage and frustration. Better to hold to the one spot of comfort so strangely thrown up by the very desperateness of the circumstances.

As Marguerite had foretold, Edward had stood firm for his friend, and in so doing had shown a Plantagenet's courage at last. Obstinate, senseless courage, but still something in which Isabel could find pride as well as humiliation. "If only it had been for *me* he had so rashly defied our whole world, how I could have worshipped him for it!" she thought.

Practically alone, sometimes threatening, sometimes cajoling, he had refused to sign the ordinances unless Parliament allowed Gaveston to remain. As a last hope he had taken up arms and appealed to the Londoners to support him, but even the Mayor and Sheriffs had sided against him in this particular issue. And the barons, determined to impose their decisions, had parcelled out the authority of the country between them. Gilbert of Gloucester, still trying to mediate, had been made responsible for the orderliness of Kent and Surrey, Lancaster for the rest of the south, and the Earl of Hereford for the eastern counties. When Edward had prepared to march northwards Henry Percy of Northumberland had been warned to guard the Scottish border, and a final insult flung at the King by a suggestion that he might try to betray them by making common cause with Robert Bruce. Pembroke and de Warenne were sent in pursuit of Gaveston, with orders to bring him to trial. And Edward, refusing to abandon him, had met him in York, bringing Isabel with him and hastily strengthening the defences of the city.

She could have refused to accompany them. She need only have appealed to the Londoners and they would have protected her. She was their idol, the beautiful helpless young wife whose husband's affections had been unfairly tampered with. Her kinsman Lancaster would have been only too glad to make capital out of her complaints, and to use her very barrenness as a further argument against his nephew's unpopular friendship. By raising an outcry she could have stayed in comfort with Marguerite. But, looking back, Isabel was honest enough to admit that she had not really wanted to. · She had clung to Edward because, in spite of everything, she loved him. She had even shown him sympathy in those last days of extremity when the Londoners had refused help and Gaveston was really wandering about in hiding with a price on his head. And she had had her brief reward. Edward had clung to her as a woman, no longer treating her as a child. Because Isabel could ignore danger and discomfort for the sake of satisfying her desires, they had been happy in a queer transient way until Gaveston joined them again in York.

So deeply immersed was she in reviewing the immediate past that she scarcely noticed how low the fire had burned, until Gaveston saw that she was shivering. "You are cold," he said, rising and throwing on some more logs without interrupting their unsought solitude to call a servant.

"Edward is a long time out there," she said, speaking to herself rather than to him.

"It may be that Lancaster's army is already advancing from Newcastle."

"And you stay idling here, knowing what it has already cost Edward to stand by you!"

"He has stood by me to the last ditch," agreed Gaveston, without complacency. "And this may well be it."

"You mean that they will besiege us here?"

"It is only a matter of time. If it comes to that I promise you that I will go before they harm him."

They were talking in the level tones of people accustomed to each other's company. He picked up Edward's cloak and put it round her shoulders, and while she jerked it more closely about her he seated himself in Edward's vacated chair on her side of the chess table. They had been in this unwilling kind of partnership for so long that even their personal safety had become a shared concern, and neither of them had much doubt about his ultimate danger once he separated from the slender protection of the King's company.

"Isabel, if the worst should happen to me—will you show kindness to my Margaret?" he asked. "See her sometimes— let that kind girl Ghislaine console her——" He looked across at her with a wide, wry smile. "In spite of that rat-ridden dungeon, she is absurdly fond of me, you know."

"She worships you." Isabel could feel a new mothering tenderness softening her, born, she supposed, of the strange languidness in her body. "You know that I will, Piers," she promised simply. Forgetting her resentment against him, she leaned across a corner of the table, chin cupped in palm, allowing herself to realize how attractive he must be to girls like Margaret and Ghislaine. "You must have been casually kind to your Margaret as Edward is kind to me—only she is too childish to realize the humiliation of it. Have you never really loved any woman, Piers?" she asked, with a genuine interest which wiped out more antagonistic issues.

Gaveston seemed to be turning back the pages of his mind. "Yes, once," he said.

"You mean—a long time ago?" asked Isabel, wondering if Edward knew of it.

"A very long time ago."

"And for some reason you could not marry her?"

He laughed with sudden, short amusement. "There was a very good reason why I could not."

Finding some part of him which she had never known, Isabel momentarily forgot even the last vestige of her hatred. "I am sorry," she said. "What was her name?"

"Claremunda."

"And was she as beautiful as the name?"

His fingers were setting out the chess men for fresh conflict, but his thoughts were far away. "I suppose that for me she had the beauty of all women, because no other has ever taken her place. She was brilliant and gay, and if I close my eyes when passing the roses in your garden, I can draw back into my being the scent of the lovely clothes she wore. Sometimes she would read me poems or dance with me. I was barely seven and she was the shining centre of my world."

Only the sound of a charred piece of log falling with a soft little plop on to the hearth followed the warm melody of his voice. With her vivid imagination, Isabel had followed him into a happier, younger world. "She was your mother?" she said softly, hoping that one day some unborn son of hers would think of her like that.

"Yes." Gaveston's fingers were stilled on the table, his eyes stared into the red heart of the fire. "They burned her as a witch in Guienne."

"Perot!" For the first and only time the pet name passed her lips, her hand leaped forth impetuously to one of his.

"My father was not there to save her. He had offered himself as one of Edward the First's hostages to the French."

"And you——"

"Dragon told our servants to keep me away, but I struck at them with my ridiculous little dagger and ran after him into the market-place. He would have dragged her from the faggots if the French soldiers had not pulled him back. He will always bear the scars of it."

"And you—as a child of seven—saw it happen?"

"And was terrified by the stench of her dear, scorching flesh." Gaveston's words came slowly, as though dragged up from an old deep well of suffering. "When the person who is the centre of one's world is burned to death it is not something which happens, and then is finished. It is something which is always there, embodied in the element itself—something which one sees in every proud beacon fire, on every homely hearth. The consuming flames lick on through the years, devouring one's heart."

The two of them sat in silence. They might have been alone in all that great castle. "Why did they do this to her?" asked Isabel at last, knowing all words of pity to be inadequate.

Gaveston roused himself to speak with everyday briskness. "Unfortunately my mother, Claremunda of Marcia, was as clever as she was beautiful. Besides nursing me almost miraculously through some violent childish fever, she lent her healing skill to our village sick and tried to beguile the King of France into setting my father free."

"And so the people of Guienne must needs accuse her of witchcraft!"

"They believed she used some spell. But the miracle that cured me was probably no more than a mother's devoted love. And are there not people in every generation who are born with that fatal thing called charm?"

Isabel relaxed and leaned back, aware that during the last revealing minutes she had come beneath it. "Does Edward know this?"

"Only Edward. Not even your adorable aunt. No one else in this country except Dragon."

"That is just as well," said Isabel, feeling oddly flattered. "Why?"

"Because your enemies would soon twist yet another accusation against you out of it. Do you not see how they would love to tell the credulous that your mother was known to be a witch, and therefore it must have been through devilish machinations that you gained so much domination over the King? Can you not hear Lancaster bringing it up against you in Parliament as a final argument for your death?"

"Ah, well," shrugged Gaveston, "they cannot know unless you tell them."

"Then why are you such a fool as to trust me, Piers?"

"You speak as though you, of all of them, were my worst enemy," said Gaveston, with that one slowness he had—a slowness to comprehend the ill-will of others.

"Have I not good reason to be?"

He rose and leaned his arms upon the high carved back of his chair, looking down at her. "But do you not realize, Isabel, that but for our mutual love for Edward you and I might have been very good friends?"

The same thought had occurred to her more than once of late, though never more strongly than at that moment; but she only shrugged, hating to admit it. "Knowing all we both know, how could you blame me for using *anything* against you?" she asked coldly.

"I, more than any man, would find it impossible to blame you, but all the same I do not believe that you will," he said, adding with half-tender, half-jesting lightness, "It is odd, is it not, how life twists us into what we are and decides the kind of things we do? A tragic agony of childhood, bewildering loneliness, sudden poverty—these can produce a rudderless braggart who bolsters up his secret insecurity by making himself of importance by any means, however vile, and grasping greedily at every present pleasure, and so brings disaster to a far more important friend whose sweet affection refilled his empty life. And because of these two worthless fools an eager, generous girl, exquisitely moulded for high destiny, grows bitter with good cause, harbouring, for all I know, the seeds of eventual cruelty. It is like the widening ripples on a lake. Whatever you may become or do, dear Isabel, will to any thinking mind be justified."

"Yet not to Marguerite's," thought Isabel, grateful for the

tolerant working of his own. Though life might grip and twist and wound, yet women like the May Queen would maintain that one must strive to hold inviolate the original standards of one's soul. But then nothing half so cruel or violent had ever happened to Marguerite. . . . Isabel rose and stretched her white arms above her head in a gesture of weary exasperation. "How much longer must we stay in this bare and horrible place?" she demanded, exchanging her subtler grievances for the material.

"Not long, I imagine, once Lancaster gets wind of where we are," said Gaveston, stooping to gather up again the cloak that slid from her shoulders.

"Could we withstand a siege any better here than at Newcastle?"

"Rather worse," he answered sombrely. "I could, of course, take what few men we have and go out and fight."

"And Edward?"

He looked at her without shame or subterfuge. "I do not think he will choose that way. And after all, he is the King. He has already risked so much for me. I could not persuade him to any course which would endanger his life."

"Then you think we shall have to—run away—again?"

He kissed her hand formally, understanding both her humiliation and her resentment. "Your grace takes this very bravely."

They both turned sharply at the sound of footsteps descending the tower stairs. Edward appeared in the doorway, his face pale and his hair ruffled by the wind on the battlements. He dismissed his handful of attendants and came hurrying across the hall. "That rumour the shire reeve had yesterday is true," he told them breathlessly. "Newcastle must have fallen to Lancaster's men a day or two after we left."

"We got away only just in time," murmured Isabel, but Edward and Gaveston went on talking quickly without noticing her.

"But now they are on their way here. A fully equipped army against a garrison already depleted by the Scots and riddled with sickness."

"How far off does this messenger say they are?" asked Gaveston.

"Close behind him. A dozen miles, perhaps. He must have ridden like the wind. His poor sweating beast almost dropped under him."

"They would attack from the land gate."

"What does it matter where they attack from?" asked Edward. "Constable and Captain both say we cannot possibly hold out for more than a couple of days."

"It is only I whom they want. I could give myself up," suggested Gaveston.

"No. I forbid it, Piers. There is still Scarborough. One of my strongest castles. The Percys have lived there so you may be sure it is kept in good fettle, and I will make you Constable, *mon cher*. It is only about seventy miles."

"It wouldn't matter if it were only twenty, with all our best horses left behind at Newcastle! I suppose it was unavoidable hurrying away down the river like that, but what would I give for my fleet roan now!"

Edward was too distraught to bemoan even the loss of his most valuable horses. His hands were shaking with nervousness and his eyes glittering with the excitement of his urgent plan. "We can take ship again. Go round by the coast," he said. "I looked down from the battlements just now and there is a small boat tied up against the steps of the river postern. And it was almost high tide. The Captain of the Guard pointed out a coaster with a trustworthy master who would take us round to Scarborough. I swore him and my squire Beaumont to secrecy. I have told Beaumont to see to it."

"Now? To-night?"

"To-morrow may be too late. Lancaster and the rest of them may be here before dawn. They will surround us as far as they can and have the river watched."

Immersed in their own concerns, neither of them heard the Queen cry out.

"But there is no need for *you* to come, Ned," protested Gaveston. "You can stay here and make your peace with them. Tell them I slipped away without your knowing to France."

Edward went close to him and clapped a hand on each of his shoulders. "It is no good, Perot," he said. "I will not leave you until I see you safely established in Scarborough. With your sound military sense you would stand some sort of chance there."

They stood looking levelly, anxiously into each other's eyes, each concerned for the other's safety. But it was Gaveston who stood in the greater jeopardy, and Edward's more single-hearted, dependent love which won the argument. "I will tell

Dragon to bring our swords and the barest necessities," said Gaveston, and went from the hall without more ado.

Isabel felt shut out and unprotected. "How soon do we start?" she asked, rising shakily from her chair.

By the way that the King swung round at the sound of her voice she knew that he had completely forgotten her. He stood frowning for a minute or two, as though confronted with a fresh problem. "It is a stormy night and you will be safer here," he pointed out. "Beaumont will look after you. I will leave orders that the gates are to be opened without an arrow being exchanged. After all, Lancaster is your devoted kinsman."

Isabel scarcely heard his words. The bare sense of them struck her too cruelly. Her hand still gripped the carved arm of her vacated chair for support. "Before God, Edward, you do not mean to leave me behind?" she cried, her voice croaking with fear.

"You will be better here with your women. I tell you, the storm is rising."

She ran to him and clutched at his arm. "But, Edward, how can we know for certain that the approaching army is Lancaster's? It could be de Warenne's or Warwick's, and we have all heard of the way the Black Dog's men have with women."

"Even he would not dare to harm you."

"I have Ghislaine to think of."

In his own anxiety, Edward shook aside her pleading hand with unaccustomed roughness. "The fellow said it was Lancaster's men. And what speed could Piers and I make with three women and their gear?"

Isabel faced him angrily. "You mean it is your friend's safety against your wife's," she accused.

"There would be far more question of your safety out in an open boat with this storm rising," Edward flung back at her sullenly. "Are any of the barons likely to harm you? Have they not turned my whole country against me by making a crusade of your wrongs? Are you not the apple of Lancaster's eye?"

"But I tell you we cannot be sure who is on the march against us. And you admit this place is obsolete and ill-manned. If my father knew that you——"

"I have taken enough orders from your father. And now I order you to stay."

He was the King, angry and aloof. No longer her gentle, compliant husband. Desolation gripped her. She went down on her knees to him on the cold stone, seizing his resisting hand and holding it against her cheek. Her tears flowed over it. "I entreat you, Edward, do not leave me. You cannot leave me now! I am three months gone with child."

His hand no longer pulled away from her. She felt him stiffen with surprise. "Isabel!" he exclaimed, torn between pity, surprise and incredulity.

"Doctor Bromtoft—Bringnette—any of my people—will tell you."

"Then why was I *not* told?"

"I forbade them. Because I was afraid you would make me stay with Marguerite in London."

"God knows I should have done!"

"And missed what happiness we had?" she asked softly, pressing her lips against his hand. She knew him to be sensitive, and seldom wantonly unkind. In all save the quality of his love she had always managed to get her own way. "I will have Bringnette and Ghislaine get my things ready quickly. Going to Scotland, coming here, have I ever been a whimpering nuisance on your journeys?"

"You have more resource and courage than I," he admitted.

"Then do not leave me here alone." Seeing that he seemed to be thinking something out she made her last appeal, more proudly. "All your life—you would despise yourself. All down the years it would be held as shame against you that you left your wife and unborn child in an endangered castle to save your precious friend."

"Isabel, you swear that this is true—about our child?"

"On all the vows I made on that most lovely day I married you."

He was unhesitant and kind again, as though he had suddenly made up his mind. "Then go now and have them pack your things. You have a good half hour. Come down and wait here until we come for you. You would get wet outside."

Isabel kissed his hand and obeyed. She wasted no words but went swiftly up the tower stair. Her limbs still shook, her face was white and smudged with undried tears; but her husband had not deserted her. Sickness and storm, battle and siege might lie ahead, but she would not be left behind in this grim place where she knew no one and where men spoke a dour Northumbrian tongue. She slammed the door of her candlelit room and found her two women preparing her bed. In quick, staccato words she told them what had happened, what they must do, and why.

"You mean the King would have left you here?" exclaimed Bringnette.

"With his child in your womb?" cried Ghislaine.

"He did not know. And he is not leaving me now," said Isabel, waving the matter aside impatiently. She was always at her best in an emergency. "Bring my travelling cloak. And do you, Bringnette, borrow my warmest furs because of your aching joints. We shall be going out to the estuary in an open boat. My jewel case, Ghislaine. You have ample time to pack my rose damask and the gold tissue which the King loves, so see you fold them carefully."

"You are shaking, Madam. There is some warm spiced wine by the bedside," ventured the girl, hurrying to her task.

"We must not keep his Grace waiting," remonstrated Isabel, with a nervous glance at the hour-glass.

"You will drink it before we stir out of this room," decreed Bringnette, with all the old authority of the nursery. And by force of habit and because of the cold feeling in her stomach Isabel obeyed.

Cup in hand, she moved to the window to drink the warming stuff while her poor harried women made up a most unregal-looking bundle. In spite of the beating rain she pushed open the slatted casement and leaned out. The Tyne flowed wide and full against the castle walls, lit fitfully by a cloud-racked moon. Ships' lanterns swayed out in the estuary, and beyond the bar white horses glimmered on an angry sea. She hoped that she and the other two women would not be hideously sick. Why, why had she become Queen of England if it meant living like a hunted vagabond?

The bobbing light of a lantern drew her attention to a man moving on the steps below. It must be Dragon, making ready their boat. "Heaven save us, how small it looks to take six of us!" she thought. She saw Dragon deposit a bundle of some sort in the stern sheets and could just discern two other figures emerging from the postern door. To Isabel, peering down the sheer surface of the wall, they looked foreshortened but familiar. "Hurry!

Hurry!" she cried over her shoulder. "The King and milord Gaveston are already down by the river, although not half the time his Grace gave us has gone by."

But the two foreshortened figures stepped without hesitation into the swaying boat. A rope splashed into the water and Dragon, already kneeling in the bows, pushed off. Swiftly and silently the King and Gaveston set oars in the row-locks and rowed out across the river towards the nearest lighted ship.

"Bringnette! Ghislaine!" cried Isabel, half-crazed with horror. Edward had meant to do this. He had tricked her. The cup fell from her outstretched hand, tinkling against the outer wall and falling with a faint splash into the water. It must have caught Edward's attention. Sitting amidships, he looked up, his face a moving disc of whiteness as he rowed. She knew that he must have seen her outlined against the lighted room, heard her cry out to him to wait. But he made no sign, only rowed steadily on with long, powerful strokes, setting the pace for Gaveston in the bows. Piers Gaveston, his beloved friend, who must be put safely in the stronghold of Scarborough at all costs.

Her two women, their arms laden with treasured possessions and with garments trailing from their hands, peered over her shoulders, too shocked to say a word. It was left to her to comment on their desolate situation.

Anger surged through her, crushing out misery and fear. Her slight pregnant body shook and, like a she-wolf's, her lips were drawn back viciously from the strong whiteness of her teeth. "I will kill him for this!" she vowed, her gaze fixed on the pale receding blur of her husband's face.

CHAPTER 11

DURING the desolate weeks which she spent in Tynemouth castle Isabel assumed a new, pathetic young dignity beneath which to cloak her hurt pride. For once reticence curbed her natural impetuosity. She no longer discussed events unguardedly with Bringnette and Ghislaine. She was very conscious of the indigant sympathy with which even the roughest castle servant sprang to serve her, and because their pity hurt she walked among them proudly, never letting them forget not only that she was their Queen but also that she came from the royal house of a more civilized country where women were not abandoned, with neither comfort nor entertainment, in bare fortresses.

The thought of bearing a child in such circumstances appalled her. Glad as she was that she might at last produce an heir, she was too full of resentment to share Ghislaine's store of excited loving to be lavished on the baby for its own sake. While realising that she had much excuse, Isabel tried to salve her conscience for this lack of maternal feeling by showing concern for the sick and poor in the town, and by taking charge of a small Scots boy whom she had seen singing for scraps at the castle gates. His parents had been killed in some border foray, and besides having him clothed and fed she was only too thankful to pass some of the time which hung so heavily by allowing him to sing his sad, incomprehensible Gaelic songs in hall.

"Thomeline has not only a sweet voice but a good ear," she decided one evening after supper when she had been teaching him the gayer air of a French song. "We must take him back to Windsor, Bringnette, and have the master of my musicians train him to sing the canticles in chapel."

"If ever we get there!" sighed Bringnette.

"The King has left Scarborough and is in York again raising another army for milord Gaveston's defence. As soon as he has time he will come for us," said Isabel. She spoke with more pride than confidence, and began picking out the tune again on her lute for Thomeline.

The Constable of the castle, who had been talking apart with his captain by the half-cleared supper-table, came forward and bowed to her. "Madam, forgive me, but it is meet you should know there is no longer need of an army for Scarborough."

Isabel's hands were stilled on the strings. "You have news, Sowerby?"

"The Earl of Cornwall has surrendered. It seems that he had little chance to do otherwise. The place was not sufficiently victualled, nor so strongly garrisoned as he and the King had supposed. And once the King had left the town the Earl of Lancaster sent milords Pembroke, de Warenne and Percy to besiege it, and most of the northerners flocked to join them."

"Instead of joining their lawful King?"

Sowerby accepted the hauteur of her tone with respectfully bent head; but he was a Yorkshireman, sturdy and blunt. "Like the rest of us, they had heard how the two of them abandoned your Grace," he said.

"To obey the Earl of Lancaster instead of their King is treason," Isabel insisted, but her heart sang with a glad sense of power because they had risen to protect her.

"What will they do with Piers Gaveston, Sir Constable?" asked Ghislaine anxiously.

"They will certainly bring him to trial for all the dissension he has caused, Mademoiselle du Bois. But he surrendered only on the condition that his life should be spared and that he should be taken to speak with the King first. And the King himself sent an urgent message to milord Pembroke promising to agree to any terms they may make if only he will see that no harm comes to his friend."

"And you think they will do this?" asked Isabel, wondering how much the barons thought Edward's promises were worth and how they could not see that he was only playing for time.

"It seems so, Madam. Milord Pembroke has managed to persuade the more violent among them, and has pledged his estates to the King and his word to Gaveston that he will bring him safely home to Wallingford. They are marching southward now, and the King, they say, is on his way southward too, so that a meeting may be arranged at Windsor."

"And the Queen's grace is left here while the Gascon goes home, outwitting his betters once again!" raged Bringnette, unable to control her indignation any longer.

The Captain of the Guard, who had not as yet spoken, did his best to reassure her. "I do not think he will outwit anyone this time, Madam," he said dourly. "The messenger who rode in this morning and reported all this told us that people in the streets and villages were shouting execrations after him, and that the stern border lord, Percy, had insisted upon his being brought south in chains."

The thought of Gaveston's fine, strong body in chains came as a shock to Isabel. "All this is only second-hand hearsay," she complained, twanging an angry discord from the lute and dismissing them. "I would to God we could be told definitely what is going on by someone in authority."

To be left like some chatelaine of no particular importance in such a backwater of a place while events were going on which concerned her husband and his kingdom so closely was more than Isabel's proud spirit could bear. So great was her longing to be back at Westminster or Windsor that she would have set forth herself with her meagre handful of followers had not the Constable warned her of the dangers which were likely to befall a party of women travelling during such disturbed times, and reminded her that he himself would be held responsible to both England and France for keeping her safely in his castle. And, futile as the days of her loneliness seemed, her wish for contact with someone of importance from the outside world was fulfilled sooner than she had expected.

One morning just before midday a well-equipped body of horsemen appeared at the gates, and before the excitement of their arrival had died down Aymer de Valence of Pembroke himself was waiting upon her; but a very different de Valence from the dignified, composed statesman whom she had last seen at her husband's court. He looked more lined and sallow than ever, and appeared to be extraordinarily agitated.

"You are more than welcome, milord," said Isabel, greeting him with unfeigned pleasure. "We had heard that you were conducting the Earl of Cornwall to Wallingford but, as usual, rumour appears to be a lying jade."

The tall, thin earl bent over her hand so low that she guessed he had come to beg a favour. "He *was* in my charge, but was stolen from me," he said, with none of his usual euphemism.

"Stolen from you?" repeated Isabel.

"I was fool enough to leave him for a day or two at Deddington, a small village near Oxford. Your Grace may recall that my manor of Bramthorp is near there, and with all these disturbances it was months since I had seen my wife. Besides which, the Gascon was badly chafed because some of those hot-heads had insisted upon his riding in chains. God knows I have no cause to show mercy to a man who has gone about calling me a play-acting buffoon, but he was the King's friend, and I am not, I hope, completely inhuman. So I left him in the house of the village priest, adequately guarded, while I went home to spend a night with my wife. I told him to rest——"

"Why are you telling me all this?" said Isabel, puzzled by the note of apology in his usually suave voice.

"Because I am hoping that your Grace will persuade the King that what I am saying is the truth."

"Does your lordship suppose I can persuade the King of anything, shut away in this God-forsaken place?" asked Isabel bitterly.

But Aymer de Valence was far too concerned about his own awkward situation to consider hers. "There are some evil-minded persons who are putting it about that I, who had given my solemn word to escort Gaveston safely, pre-arranged all this with Warwick."

"With Warwick? What had Guy Beauchamp of Warwick to do with it?"

"Some spying busybody must have told him of my movements. As soon as he heard where Gaveston was he hurried from Warwick with over a hundred men, overcame my guard, and took him. In the early hours of a Sunday morning it was. The priest had gone to celebrate Mass in another village. Guy surrounded the sleepy little rectory and shouted to the Gascon to come out just as he was, bare-foot from his bed. He clamped the chains on him again and took him off to some foul dungeon in Warwick Castle."

Isabel rose from her chair, half choked by the quick beating of her heart. She was aware of the silk banner Ghislaine had been embroidering slipping with a slithering hiss to the floor, and of Bringnette's sharp grunt of satisfaction. She was aware, too, most vividly, of the way Piers Gaveston had looked only a few weeks ago, when he had last talked with her in this hall. She was back under the spell of those few moments when she had come inadvertently upon the real man, glimpsing the tender beauty of his initial human relationship and realising what life had made of him. She knew that she should be rejoicing because her enemy had been trapped and taken, and was badly shaken at finding herself instinctively on the captive's side; but not for worlds would she have admitted it, after all her months of bitter complaining. "Warwick would show him no mercy," she said with apparent indifference. "He swore that one day Piers should feel the bite of the Black Dog he had baited."

"He has already bitten, most savagely," said Pembroke. "He held a trial of sorts, with few of the rest of us present. They brought up all the Gascon's crimes, real and imaginary, and some unimportant squireen said, 'We have followed our prey for a long time, and should not now let him go. It behoves us to consider the annoyance and expense he has been to the State, and to decide that it is better for this one man to die than that civil war should spread because of him.' So they condemned him to death as a traitor—as a traitor *against the King*, mark you!" Pembroke's strained voice broke into an angrily contemptuous laugh.

"And what then?" prompted Isabel, out of the shocked ensuing stillness.

"Warwick had him taken out onto a lonely hill beyond the city wall. Blacklowe, I think it is called. Although Gaveston stood there chained and helpless, it seems that even those who had shouted after him and mocked him by blowing on their hunting horns seemed afraid to touch him—either because he was the King's friend or because he exercised some peculiar power over them. Until a Welshman who knew nothing of the business came along and for a few pence stabbed him, and brutally severed his head with a borrowed sword."

Ghislaine stifled a scream and Isabel, standing with her back to the rest of them by an open window, felt the babe jerk in her womb. The warm June sunshine flooded all about her as it must have warmed the world on Blacklowe Hill that earlier noontide, and mocked the young man who stood there, loving life. But it was not for her to be pitiful. Had she not always said she hated him? Had she not had cause? More intimate cause than all the harsh barons put together. "What did they do with his body?" she asked evenly, without turning.

All emotion had been drained out of the Earl's voice too. "Left it lying on the ground among the blackberry briars and bracken," he said expressionlessly. "Until two cobblers found it and carried it up to the castle on some kind of farm ladder. But Warwick would have none of it. 'Take it back and let it lie where you found it, outside the borders of my land,' he ordered." Aymer de Valence sighed heavily as one who has completed a difficult mission, and laid down his hat and gloves. "I am just come from Oxford, Madam, and the Jacobin friars, who told me all this, have given Gaveston decent burial there. But Thomas of Lancaster, who rode into Oxford with me, insisted upon seeing the corpse first, to make sure that this terrible thing had really been done. Relieved as he was, I cannot think that he would have been a party to it. 'Take him,' he told the friars, 'and may he be received of God.'"

Ghislaine crossed herself, wide-eyed with horror, and Isabel stretched out a hand blindly towards Bringnette. She suddenly felt ill, as though she must faint or vomit. "Our Constable will see that a meal is prepared and that such poor hospitality as he can offer is yours, milord Pembroke," she said unsteadily. "But if you will forgive me I will retire. This will be a terrible blow for my husband, and I—must go to him—somehow——"

Bringnette's arm was about her, supporting her. "If only we could go to Windsor, my sweet poppet! It is not fit that you stay here," she soothed, helping her to a chair again before ever she reached the door. "But dare we, with the country in such a state, and without his Grace's permission to leave this horrible place?"

Ghislaine ran for peacock's feathers burned in the kitchen fire and held them beneath her mistress's nostrils, and gradually the faintness passed. "When the King hears of this he will be too heartbroken to so much as notice whether I come or stay," murmured Isabel.

"I would that I could have that same assurance about myself!" said Pembroke. "Warwick he will never forgive, and if his supporters try to lessen his fault by persuading his Grace that I purposely betrayed Gaveston to him, I am ruined. I pledged my estates that I would bring Gaveston to Wallingford. That is why I hurried to Oxford, to entreat the University to vouch for my honest intent in the matter, since the execution happened over the border in their county. But they refused to be drawn into it. And so I came to you, who have always been gracious to me and whose beauty no husband could withstand."

Isabel sat silent for a minute or two, weighing what advantage she could cull from his distress. "If you will take me and my ladies to Windsor with you I will do what I can," she bargained.

Pembroke looked up. His shrewd eyes met hers, and smiled. "I dare not stay after to-morrow lest Warwick's men get the King's ear first," he temporized.

"We shall be ready by sunrise. We will pack our possessions now," promised Isabel, rising with renewed vigour. And because she had always liked the man she smiled at him in passing. "Though you must not expect me to have much influence with the King."

With her movement the draperies she wore fell away from her gown and for the first time his eyes rested observantly upon her swelling body. Because he was a born opportunist, a brightness snapped into them. "Not now, at this misfortunate moment, perhaps, but in a few months' time you will have every influence," he prophesied, bending a knee to kiss her hand with all his old courtly grace. "And think, Madam, what we can do! Without Gaveston, who has been this country's bane for years, we could begin afresh. Gilbert of Gloucester, de Warenne, the Despensers and I. We could advise your husband more wisely, stop all this seething discontent and make England the law-abiding, respected land it was in the late King's time. With Thomas of Lancaster and other moderate men on our side, and with your help, Madam, and the popularity your Grace has with the people, so much would be possible."

His words seemed to open up a vista of happier times. He was cleverer than the rest of them, and more gentle. More like the cultured nobles she had been accustomed to in France. He had the sense to see that her interests and his own might well run together, and so long as they did so he would be an astute ally. He and the Despensers would keep the mighty Warwick's power in check, and Warwick she never wanted to see again. Nor did she ever want to see again the hall of Tynemouth Castle. She went up the winding stairs with Bringnette and Ghislaine to prepare for the morrow's journey. It was better to busy one's hands so that one's heart had not time to picture Piers Gaveston parting with life in the noonday sunshine.

CHAPTER 12

ISABEL lay snug and triumphant in her great state bed at Windsor. The warmth from an iron brazier made her feel deliciously drowsy, and the memory of austerity and neglected loneliness at Tynemouth had taught her to appreciate almost as a novelty the comfort and good service which now surrounded her. Some of her relatives had come all the way from France to attend her lying-in, and respectful congratulations had been showered upon her. As one whose long-dreaded ordeal is over, she lay at ease against her pillows, empty-minded, enjoying her room—enjoying the rich colours of her tapestries, the exquisitely embroidered lilies on her bed cover, the cessation from tearing pain. All the bishops and court officials whose duty it was to be present during the birth of a prince were gone at last, and the bed hangings had been drawn back at her request so that she could watch the charming group by the brazier. She could see old Bringnette's back, stiff with pride because she held the heir of England on her knees, young Ghislaine in an attitude of kneeling adoration holding a ewer of warm water, and beside them the wooden cradle on its sturdy rockers, with fierce Plantagenet leopards carved round its hood.

From beneath half-closed lids Isabel could also see the Queen-Dowager smiling down at the infant, and looking, in her nun-like wimple and plain girdled gown, more like a pensive Madonna than ever. Although she felt too tired to make any effort to call her, she was glad when Marguerite came to her bedside. "My dearest Isabel," she said, bending to kiss her. "I have been so concerned lest all you went through during the early part of your pregnancy might have harmed you. But already the colour is coming back into your cheeks."

Isabel smiled, and clung to her hand. "I am stronger than I look. But, oh, I am glad it is all over!"

"And, God be praised, you have a boy. All across the country, as the news spreads, they will be lighting bonfires and rejoicing," said Marguerite, for whose sons—offspring of a second marriage—there could have been no such wild rejoicings.

"My women were so anxious to clutch him away and array him in all those clothes they have been embroidering that I have scarcely seen him."

"They will be bringing him back to you as soon as he is washed and oiled and grand enough to please them. He is strong as a little lion, *ma chère*. Bigger than either of my boys were. And you such a fragile little thing!"

"He takes after the Plantagenets, no doubt." As everyday thoughts began to flow back into Isabel's torpid mind, she turned her dark head petulantly on the pillow. "Where *is* Edward? Has no one told him I have done my duty at last and provided him with an heir? Does he not care?"

"Your steward rode out at once and caught up with him before hounds were away, and the King was so delighted with the news that he gave him a pension for life."

"Another of his sudden, disproportionate extravagances! Did he *have* to go hunting this morning?" Isabel sighed and closed her eyes so that Marguerite supposed she had fallen asleep, and moved away. But behind defensively closed eyelids the new young mother's thoughts were resentfully busy about her husband. She recalled how he had looked when the Earl of Pembroke had first brought her home from Tynemouth. She had expected Edward to be heart-broken over Piers Gaveston's death, but his white and stricken face had appalled her. It was as if all the gay youth in him had been quenched. He would shut himself up and weep for hours, or pace about his room planning vengeance on the barons, or go out walking for miles, forbidding even Gilbert to follow him. His complete detachment from any other call which life might make upon him made his physicians fear for his sanity. And in spite of all her wrongs, Isabel's heart had bled for him. Instead of reproaching him for deserting her, she had tried to soothe him, but—as she had foreseen—he scarcely seemed to notice whether she had come home or not. Forgetting how she had stood at her window and sworn to kill him, she had forced herself against her nature to be gentle and patient, but all to no purpose.

"Why feign sorrow?" he would ask. "Everyone knows you hated him."

"Not altogether—not at the end," she had once tried to explain.

But in his frenzied grief he had not heard her, or saw her new-born sympathy only as hypocrisy. "You bayed with the rest of the jealous, bloodthirsty pack, helping to hound him to his horrible death."

"I?" she had protested. "How could I have done anything, mewed up like a winged bird in that bare fortress?"

"You could have sent out messages to Lancaster. One of the accusations they brought against my beloved friend was that he was the son of a witch."

"That! Oh, no!"

"That he used his mother's sorcery to enslave my affections."

"Her charm, perhaps. The charm which he inherited. Fatal, he called it. He spoke about it once, the last time I was with him. That evening when you both——"

"Then you admit you knew. And you hated him. Only you could have told them," Edward had reiterated.

"I swear I did not."

"You expect me to believe that you had this weapon in your hand and did not use it?"

"*He* believed I would not."

Lying in her sumptuous bed, Isabel recalled how Edward had still stared at her, sullen and unconvinced. "They held Dragon prisoner at Scarborough, but *he* would not have spoken even had they tortured him."

"Other people besides us three must have known about Piers' mother, and in any case there were other, far more important reasons why he had to die," she had pointed out. But she had never known whether she had really convinced her husband, nor whether he forgave her past animosity towards Gaveston. During all those unhappy weeks after her homecoming Edward had been wrapped away from her in the wildness of his grief and anger. He expressed appreciation when she sent for his friend's distraught young widow, but only as the time for Isabel's delivery drew near had his thoughts begun to reach out to her again. With his own hands he had wrought the handsome iron candle sconces for her room, he had seen to it that his cleverest physicians attended her and given orders that everything possible should be done for her comfort. "He gave me everything but his companionship," she thought. "And now, while I have been needing him most, he had gone out hunting."

Although she knew that it was the way of most anxious royal husbands, two hot tears of self-pity slid beneath her long lashes and coursed slowly down her cheeks. Marguerite must have noticed and mistaken the cause of her weeping. She whispered to Bringnette, who brought the baby in all his princely finery to the bedside. But Isabel glanced at him only briefly, then turned her face away. The unhappy conditions of her marriage had soured even the triumph of motherhood. How ugly he is, she thought, with his crumpled red face and crop of straight auburn hair! All new babies must be disappointingly ugly, she supposed, and as though, having been so recently a part of her, he could instantly divine her thought, her son endeared himself to her still less by setting up a protesting howl.

"I should have kept to my resolution and denied Edward my bed," thought Isabel, shocked out of natural emotions because she had been so callously abandoned at Tynemouth. But months ago when she had been so resolved Marguerite had laughed at her and said she was no nun, and as usual the May Queen's words had proved right. Momentarily, in her exhaustion, Isabel hated even Marguerite. Why did all these women want to disturb her? Why could they not leave her to her enjoyment of her comfortable room and to the blessed relief of having her body to herself again? Passing appreciative hands over her flattened belly beneath the bedclothes, she fell to thinking of all the things she would do and enjoy when she was beautiful again.

But suddenly she was aware of a stir at the door. Eager voices shattered the quietness of the room, and the King came striding towards her bed. Isabel opened her eyes. Resentments were momentarily forgotten, and because there was something of the old light eagerness in his step life was suddenly exciting again. Edward was still in his plain leather hunting tunic, which showed up the splendour of his limbs and made him look so young. The men who came crowding after him were all peering curiously over each other's shoulders, the women who attended her were curtsying like a windswept field of multi-coloured flowers. It pleased Isabel that, in spite of the lusty insistence of his son's yells, her husband came to her first. He lifted her hand from the coverlet, kissed it gratefully and enquired kindly how she felt. Then Bringnette proudly held out to him her beribboned wailing bundle.

Isabel watched him take his firstborn, not awkwardly as most new-made fathers do, but with such efficient gentleness that the wailing stopped instantly. After the ministrations of a bunch of over-anxious women, his strong arms must have provided a satisfying sense of security. He put out an exploring forefinger, and a tiny red hand ceased waving aimlessly and clutched it tightly. The new-born, wrinkled ugliness of his son meant nothing to him, only the helplessness. From her vantage point against the pillows Isabel saw the smile of dawning delight, the tenderness on his face. Edward Plantagenet had found something weaker, more dependent, than himself. A small being who, for years, would be dependent upon *his* knowledge, *his* strength, *his* love. Someone infinitely dear, and so guileless and royally important that no one would resent or try to bar his love. Someone, thought Isabel, who had succeeded in driving that bereft look from his eyes—who had succeeded where she herself had failed.

"What is our son to be called?" she asked, with awakening interest in him.

Trumpets had already sounded shrilly from the battlements, and church bells were ringing out down in the town. "How shall the heralds announce the birth of England's heir?" the returning bishops and barons wanted to know. Her uncle of Evreux was saying how much pleasure it would give his countrymen if the child might be called Philip after the King of France, and her uncle Thomas of Lancaster, now back at court, was smiling at her and backing the suggestion. But Edward, with the child still in his arms, glared across the room at him with unforgiving aversion. "So foreign a name would not be pleasing to my people," he said, with a new crisp decisiveness reminiscent of his father. "He shall be a third Edward, thoroughly English. And by God's grace he will grow to be the kind of man who will revive all those glorious exploits of my late father which you are all so constantly lamenting." For once his allusion to them was not wholly cynical. He spoke with a dignified humility, as though wishing for his son much which he knew to be impossible for himself. Carefully, reluctantly, he handed his new-born heir back to Bringnette and turned back to Isabel. "What can I give you, my wife, in return for this inestimable gift you have made me?" he asked.

For once Isabel the Fair found herself unprepared to profit by a propitious situation. There was so much that she wanted. Happiness, a great love affair, first place in her husband's heart— all intangible things which could not be handed over as a gift, nor even put into words. But all of them things which she now dared to hope might be coming nearer to her grasp. Because she had wanted them so passionately and for so long, no lesser material gift would come into her mind, but her eyes happening to rest on Ghislaine's sweet face, so alight with happiness for her, she said involuntarily, "I should be well pleased if your Grace will pardon my Master-of-Horse, and release him from the Tower."

Edward looked surprised, and frowned. "I had not supposed that you entertained for him such high regard."

"Say rather, pity," pleaded Isabel. "To be young and eager, and shut behind stone walls——"

Without passion, jealousy finds poor breeding ground; and the rash young man's offence against him and Gaveston lay in the regretted past, over-shadowed by the murderous deeds of more powerful men. "It shall be as you wish," Edward promised, almost negligently. "But I meant something you want for yourself, dear Isabel." He came and sat on the bed with his back to the rest of the room, contriving a few moments of privacy. "You must often have been alone and unhappy during the months when you were carrying my son," he added, as though for the first time his mind were free to realize the fact.

Because his eyes and voice were kind there did not seem to be much that she *could* want. She felt, as she so often had of late, that Edward possessed two separate personalities—the man obsessed by another who had tricked her at Tyneside, and the attractive bridegroom whom she had fallen in love with at Boulogne. And now the bridegroom had come back to her. Her lovely eyes filled with tears. In a sudden overwhelming realization of all she had been through, she had a great longing for her own country. It was years since she had seen her parents and her beloved brother Charles. "Some day will you take me home to France?" she begged. And because she was emotionally spent and still weak from her travail, she began sobbing against the King's shoulder.

"To go abroad could be good for both of us, and it is high time I visited my subjects in Guienne," she heard him saying above the luxuriant disorder of her hair. "We will go, my poor sweet, as soon as you are strong again. But first we must prepare for our son's christening. Here, in the chapel of St. Edward. If your people carry you in a litter do you think you can be ready for that in four days' time?"

It was cheering to have fresh things to think about. Delighted, Isabel assured him how resilient she was, and they began making their plans, just as he and Gaveston had planned so many ceremonies in the past. "We must ask your uncle of Evreux to stand as one of the godfathers, of course. And my sister's husband, John of Bretagne. And I should like to honour Hugh Despenser."

In their new hour of accord Isabel forebore to show how much she disliked the Despensers. "And Aymer de Valence," she urged. "He has been kind to me, and I do assure you he is loyal to your cause."

Edward got up from her bed abruptly. "If he had not left Piers in that accursed Oxfordshire village——"

"So that he might rest, because the chains had chafed him so badly. Do not forget, *mon cher*, that De Valence of Pembroke was the only one who showed him humanity. He would have brought him safe to Wallingford." Seeing that her husband's eyes were still smouldering with anger, and knowing how much Pembroke's support meant to her now that her kinsman of

Lancaster was out of favour, Isabel ventured on a yet more urgent appeal. "You always say he is far cleverer than the rest of them. With him and Gilbert and your Despensers we could form a strong party against those who would for ever be coercing you. And do you suppose he will ever forgive Warwick for fooling him?"

"Warwick's enemies will always be my friends," swore Edward with sudden violence. "We will have Pembroke, then."

Isabel sank back exhausted. He beckoned to her women to come to her, and went to look again at his sleeping son. "On the day of his christening I will make him Earl of Chester," he said, with restored good humour.

And so, after the solemn pomp of the christening and all the excitement of public rejoicings, the King and Queen of England sailed for Guienne, leaving a chastened and apprehensive baronage in England.

All who had hounded Gaveston to his death knew that the King would never really forgive them. His subjects were rid of the expensive favourite and at last an heir to the throne had been born. And Isabel had brought new popularity to the royal cause. Throughout her journey to the coast people ran from field and shop and homestead to gaze at the radiant beauty of their young Queen, and to cheer her wholeheartedly.

Motherhood and happiness became her, and weeks of sunshine in Guienne warmed the petal fairness of her skin. Afterwards, in holiday mood, she and Edward sang snatches of *chansons* to the cheerful strains of his fiddlers as they rode leisurely northwards towards Paris, where a wealth of lavish hospitality awaited them. There was the joy of meeting her family again, the long intimate talks, the exchange of gossip with girlhood friends. Philip le Bel tactfully made no reference to his former exasperation with his English son-in-law, but entertained his English guests with feasts and pageants and morality plays far more splendidly mounted than those which Edward and Piers had thought so fine at home. And all the humiliations which Isabel had been forced to bear because of the inordinate affection between these two young men seemed to be soothed away by the sense of superiority she was able to feel in the magnificence of her father's court, and all her resentments were softened by the suave compliments which Frenchmen paid her. So that, moving about the luxurious rooms of the Louvre or riding through the formally kept forests outside the city walls, she could almost persuade herself that the jealousies and violent factions of her married life had never been, and that these two halcyon months were but a continuation of her honeymoon.

The same idea must have been in the mind of her youngest and favourite brother, Charles, as he drew her away from the rest of the royal party to stroll with her quietly in the palace garden on the evening before her departure. "One would say a marriage made in Heaven!" he remarked, with an ironic glance in the direction of Edward's departing back as he walked conversationally with his host in the opposite direction. "Were all those frantic complaints which so disturbed our father really necessary, *ma soeur*?"

Isabel walked beside him with downcast eyes. "They were unbearably true—at the time. And I was the world's most helpless innocent! I suppose you all knew—here—what sort of a marriage I was being sent to?"

"We had heard rumours—my brothers and I." Charles glanced down at her with a quizzing sympathy. "But now the worst of your troubles are over, it seems?"

"Please God!"

"Since the Gascon favourite got himself killed?"

"Say rather since an heir was born."

"A felicity which, quite understandably, it took you years to achieve, *ma pauvre*. Every conceivable excuse that Adonis of yours wrote in reply to our father's protests. Such abject letters! He must have guessed that French influence was stirring up his own subjects."

But Isabel was scarcely listening. She stopped by a laden quince tree, picking absently at its foliage, with the last of the evening sunlight all about her. For weeks she had wanted to talk seriously with this clever, worldly wise brother of hers. It was difficult to discuss one's own husband. Yet there were so many things which puzzled her. At home there was only Marguerite, and Marguerite was tolerantly fond of him. Perhaps, without fondness, a man might see more clearly, more objectively ... Edward came into sight again, gorgeous in purple and gold, at the end of a transverse path. The glances of both of them were upon him. Absently, her small bejewelled fingers tore a quince leaf to pieces and scattered it in a small green shower on the grass. "Charles."

"*Ma chère?*"

"How can a man of such splendid physique be so——"

"Weak?"

"I suppose so."

Hearing the depth of her sigh, and knowing the proud fire of her nature, Charles Capet realized what even this confidential admission must have cost her. He kicked thoughtfully at a stone with his long tipped scarlet shoe, trying to answer her with honesty. "It is not an over-rare type. A man with all the outward graces who is incapable."

"Oh, no! Neither incapable nor indolent, as people pretend!" Isabel swung round on him in eager defence. "You know how musical he is. He knows more about dogs and horses than his own grooms. I verily believe he could build and thatch a house as well as any of our craftsmen. He—he made me the loveliest wrought-iron candle sconces for my lying-in——" Isabel began to realize how childish her words must sound, and her voice tailed off in face of her brother's sardonic grin.

"My dear child, how would even so fine a list of accomplishments help me or either of my elder brothers to rule France? Do you not see why Edward takes pains to perfect himself in these manual tasks? It is often so with people who are—insufficient—for the demands of their own administrative calling. It soothes their sense of failure—to do *something* well."

"You talk as if he were a fool!" she cried out angrily.

Charles shrugged tolerantly. "When a king infuriates his most powerful subjects and then allows them to chase him about in his own country, that could be the kindest view to take. And few of our royal houses are immune from cases of degeneracy. We have to inter-marry too much. Oh, my dear, do not stand there looking so aghast. I am not seriously suggesting that your handsome English husband is insane. Merely that he has unfortunate tendencies. Why, even though, with your interests at heart, I have good cause to dislike him, at times I find it extraordinarily difficult to do so. He can be such merry company. You must not take it all so sadly. Spend his money, and turn that fog-bound island of his into a scene of glittering revelry with your light-hearted zest for life. And next time he starts fondling some attractive young man you must retaliate and take a lover."

"Next time?" Isabel stared at his blond, laughing face in horror. "No, Charles, I could never go through that again!

And you do not understand. Piers Gaveston was someone whom he *loved*. Someone real whom he will grieve for all his life. Whom no one could replace—except perhaps our son."

To a sophisticated young cynic like Charles her words were almost meaningless. "You may be right," he granted lightly. "But unless you want civil war you had better persuade him to come to terms with the man's murderers, who after all had vast provocation. You must remember that to the fortunately normal nothing is more hateful than abnormality, and if life in that barbarous country should become more uncomfortably complicated than you can bear, you must appeal to the Dauphin or to me."

"To brother Louis or you?"

King Philip of France was still to be seen walking slowly back to the palace, solicitously assisted by his stalwart son-in-law. "Have you not noticed how feeble our father becomes?"

Isabel's glance followed her father pityingly. She shivered involuntarily as the warmth from the setting sun slid down behind the garden wall, reminding her that the last day of her happy visit to France was nearly over. To-morrow she and Edward would be on their way to the coast. Given a fair wind, they would soon be back in England. They would stop perhaps in the dim grandeur of Canterbury to kneel at the shrine of the murdered Archbishop whom the English thought so much of, then trot briskly between the Kentish hedgerows past Marguerite's lovely castle of Leeds, dreaming in the middle of its lily-covered lake. And soon, soon, they would be back at Westminster. The roses would still be in bloom in the garden which Edward had made for her; on gentle summer evenings merchants' families from London would row past the palace in their skiffs, sending snatches of songs and laughter across the rippling water; and in the cradle with the carved Plantagenet leopards her baby would no doubt have grown prodigiously. And always, when she rode through the streets, there would be homely, cherishing love for her lighting up the faces of the people. As long as she kept that love, England could not be a bad place to go home to.

"Everything will go well, Charles—you will see," she assured him, reaching up to kiss his smoothly shaven cheek. "But always in the back of my mind I will remember what you have said."

CHAPTER 13

Through the golden October forenoon all London seemed to be flocking to Westminster Hall. People poured out through Ludgate, making their way westward along the muddy Strand and through Charing village. A stiff autumnal breeze from the river caught at their caps and coifs, and russet leaves swirling from rich merchants' gardens came to rest on their billowing cloaks like beneficent showers of gold.

The beneficence of hope warmed their hearts. Better days, they all felt, must lie ahead. There was an heir to the throne at last, and King and Parliament were coming to terms. With peace at home, trade with the Continent would improve. All up and down the country young men would be free to settle down to their sheep-rearing or their shop-keeping without being called away at any moment to fight in some quarrel which did not concern them. Men of goodwill like the popular Earl of Gloucester, and men of good sense like Pembroke were beginning to make themselves felt. The May Queen, God bless her, had always had the people's interests at heart, and now their beautiful young Queen Isabel, hitherto so shamefully ousted from her rightful place, seemed to have come into her own in the King's affection. Since her return from France she had appeared with him on all State occasions, and only a week or two ago she had been seen wandering hand-in-hand with him at a Michaelmas fair when he had taken his two young half-brothers to watch a performing bear.

As the people crowded into Westminster Hall there were many who declared that the Queen's influence was now almost as strong as the Gascon favourite's had been. That ever since their return she had been trying to persuade the King to issue this general pardon to his rebellious barons, and that it was she whom the country had to thank for the prospect of a less brutally disturbed era. She was there inside the hall now, lovelier than ever in the new maturity of her motherhood, and the hearts of all the women went out to her, well aware of all the slights and trials she must have been through.

The ceremony in Westminster Hall was Isabel's personal

triumph. Her family jewels had been returned to her. The barons had stripped them from the hated favourite, but even the priceless brooch of Charlemagne, rising and falling with each excited breath, shone no more brightly than her eyes. She sat erect beside her husband on the dais and watched the impressive scene. She heard a herald's voice proclaim, "This pardon and remission is granted by the King through the prayers of his dearest companion, Isabel, Queen of England," and the words which Edward had so generously insisted upon rang through the lovely building so that all should know and appreciate the peacemaker's part which she had played. She looked up for a moment to exchange a glad smile of understanding with her aunt, knowing that this day was an even happier one than either her wedding or her coronation days had been. From beneath decorously lowered lashes she glanced sideways to admire her husband, grave and handsome beneath his golden canopy of state; then watched the long line of barons filing past, each mounting the shallow steps to the throne and kneeling before him in submission. This time it was not they but the King who called the tune; and he had made it a condition of his pardon that they should kneel humbly in the sight of their peers and of as many of the common people as could crowd within the doors. "And now he will forgive them for what was largely his own fault," thought Isabel, with a cynicism caught from her brother Charles.

Graciously, Edward forgave each of them for taking up arms against him—even Lancaster and Warwick, who had been responsible for Gaveston's death. Because his uncle Thomas of Lancaster was a Plantagenet, he was quick to raise him with out-stretched hands before ever his knees had time to touch the stone floor, but the smile on the King's lips was a mockery when Guy of Warwick, looking, without his armour, no more important than any other sick and ageing man, went down on creaking knee joints. All who had witnessed Edward's love for Gaveston must have recognized those particular moments of remission as a blasphemous fraud. And the memory of them marred Isabel's triumph and became linked in her with a yet more disturbing moment. For when the ceremony was at last over and she passed out from the hall with the rest of the royal party, she was surprised to see Dragon, who had been held prisoner in Scarborough castle, standing in the shadow of the great doorway. "Why, Dragon!" she exclaimed involuntarily. But although she passed so close that her stiffly jewelled dress brushed against him, he neither saw nor heard her. Being short of stature, he had raised himself on the plinth of a pillar so that he could see over the heads of the crowd, and the cold hate in his eyes made the mockery of Edward's smile seem almost kind. Turning her head to follow the direction of his gaze, Isabel found—as she had expected to—that it was concentrated upon Guy of Warwick, the man who had taken his defenceless master at Deddington and hustled him to ignominious death.

A cold shudder passed through her body, so that she was glad to step outside into the sunshine and to be received into the warmth of the people's welcome. She paused with Edward on the threshold, smiling down at them, fully conscious of what an ideal royal pair they must look, and wondering how much Edward realized that the wildest of the cheering was for her. Although it usually was so he never showed resentment. "Is it just that he is sweet-tempered? Or that he does not care?" she wondered. "Or can it be possible that he is so out of touch with his subjects that he is not even aware of their reactions?" Yet surely that awareness, that common touch, must be a primary asset of a successful sovereign. As a princess of France the idea had never occurred to her. But here in England one came in closer contact with the sturdy-willed people. Gradually she had come to learn that she herself had this common touch, this ability to move them. And now for a bewildering moment a sense of power gripped her, a surprised assurance that she, a woman, might rule successfully where Edward failed. A fleeting suspicion came to her that all those solemn oaths of submission given by the barons might, in a crisis, weigh less than the warm, united love of the people. It was a heady, revolutionary thought; but times were changing. It had been part of the first Edward's policy, so her kinsman of Lancaster had explained to her, that the voice of the Commons should be heard and so help to curb the power of barons who might thwart him, and already the masters of trade were beginning to hold the purse strings of Parliament.

"Let us get some fresh air after all that solemnity," Edward was saying, rousing her from such grave speculation and drawing her towards her peaceful riverside garden.

"It has been such a mild October that there are still a few roses in bloom," said Isabel, and then, as their retinue fell respectfully behind, she seized the opportunity of asking him if he had seen Dragon.

Edward stopped short by her sundial. "No," he said, tracing the sharp shadow of the metal gnomon with his forefinger. "But it is fitting that he of all men should have been there—if only to see them all kneel."

"You had him fetched, unharmed, from Scarborough?"

"I made it my first concern."

"And you will take him into your service?"

"Naturally. If he wishes it. I sent Nicholas Huggate, my chief clerk, to tell him so."

"If he wishes it?" Edward's humility with regard to anything relating to Gaveston never failed to amaze her. "Surely, a King's service would satisfy him?"

"Who can see into the thoughts born of so strange and violent a loyalty?" Edward turned to examine her rose bushes with knowledgeable interest. "This sweetbriar has grown so tall that it will need drastic pruning. I must tell Job. And, see, there is one of your favourite damask roses still in bud."

"How sweet it smells!"

He leaned across the low box hedge that bordered the flower-bed and broke it off, and as he tucked it into her jewelled belt she touched his down-bent head caressingly. But her thoughts were still on Dragon, and the disturbing fierceness of his eyes. She did not want him about the palace. "Whenever I meet Dragon I shall always see him rushing into the flames to save the lovely Claremunda," she murmured.

Edward stared unseeingly over the sunlit garden, the sharp thorns of a rose bush crushed unnoticed between his bleeding fingers. "Dragon would do the same for any of the family," he said.

"Then you think he may go back to Gascony?" asked Isabel with relief.

"He will find it very difficult to serve any other master. Even me."

Isabel's quick mind hit upon an idea. "There is your niece Margaret. The poor child is with me now, but when she goes back to Wallingford she will need some trustworthy man about the place."

"That is perhaps the solution," agreed Edward, as they strolled back towards the palace. "At any rate until I find her another husband."

"But not so soon!" protested Isabel.

"Before we go to Scotland."

"Her heart is still raw with grief."

"All the more reason why I cannot go campaigning and leave her unprotected. An alliance with a Plantagenet should prove a tempting bait to ensure the loyalty of one of my ambitious lords. And other young widows remarry almost immediately."

In spite of his frequent easy kindnesses Edward spoke with that dispassionate detachment which showed him to be so out of touch with other people's hearts. Isabel sighed, and changed the subject. "Then you really intend to march on Scotland?"

"Not before spring because there would be no fodder for our horses." There was one of those painful silences while each of them realized that he had unwittingly been quoting Gaveston's words. "But nothing less will satisfy Pembroke and the rest. This firebrand Bruce is marching on Stirling, they tell me. He may well be at Berwick and over our border next."

Never at any time had Edward's heart been in any war, but now Isabel realized how dreary the prospect of this fresh campaign must look to him without Gaveston. "Do you want me to come with you?" she asked, smothering a twinge of involuntary contempt with conscious pity.

He turned to her at once with eager uncertainty. "You know how you hated Tyneside——"

Again his lack of understanding rose like a barrier between them. It had not been the castle, but his betrayal, which had been unbearable. With all her fastidious love of luxury Isabel knew that remoteness and grim walls might but have added fervour to her ecstasy had she been cut off there with a husband who was her lover. "I could have been wildly happy even at Tyneside——" she began passionately.

But he pulled her close and kissed her to silence. A flame of loveliness always made her more vivid when she was angry. And, like most men of weak character, he accepted the easy palliative of self-deception and avoided discussion of anything that was unjustifiable in his past. "I only meant that I once promised not to drag you from battlefield to battlefield as my poor mother and step-mother were dragged. But perhaps, dearest Isabel, if you were to bring your household northward to some comfortable stronghold I shall be able to visit you sometimes . . ."

He was conciliatory, tender, pleading. "You know that I

will," she whispered back. For a moment or two she gave herself, pliant and receptive, to the pleasure of his embrace, wishing the discreetly following courtiers at the bottom of the Thames. His arms were strong, his clothes smelled deliciously of some not too feminine fragrance. But why, why could he not *order* her to come? Take her because she was his? "If the oak is cut down the ivy will find some other plant to lean upon," Marguerite had said before Gaveston was killed. And her encouraging prophecy had proved true enough. "But already I begin to weary of being leaned upon," thought Isabel. "It is high-spirited jades like me who need a master. Someone who can dominate me, afford to smile while I spit out my fury, then bend my will to his and take me on equal terms of desire, holding me his by natural right against the world. And until God gives me such a man must I go hungry?"

She freed herself and left the garden, walking almost unseeingly with down-bent head to her apartments. In spite of her husband's newly found need of her, a sudden craving for a very different kind of man had assailed her of late. Horrified at the strength of her errant desire, she had often gone straight to her private oratory and flung herself down on her knees to pray for seemly gratitude and wifely chastity. But now she only called sharply to her women to prepare her bath with the new lavender essence sent from Paris, and to lay out an even more becoming gown for the King's midday banquet to which all his humbled and forgiven lords had been invited. And while she waited their ministrations she sank down in her high-backed chair, less wearied by the day's long ceremony than by the buffets of her own emotional temperament. And being torn between triumph and dissatisfaction, she was not over-pleased to find Margaret and her more sophisticated elder sister Eleanor whispering confidentially with Ghislaine in the privacy of the window embrasure. She had kept her promise to Gaveston and shown every kindness to his heart-broken little widow—indeed both she and Edward would have done so in any case. But all three girls should, she felt, have been full of the impressive success of their Queen's efforts for the internal peace of their turbulent country rather than immersed in their own small affairs.

The girls rose and curtsied at her entrance and Ghislaine immediately brought one of the bright window cushions for her head. Touched by her solicitude and noting how childish

Margaret looked in sad black with a widow's barb swathed beneath her chin, Isabel felt her momentary irritation dissolve in pity. "What is that glittering thing you were showing Ghislaine?" she asked.

Margaret knelt on the stool at her feet and held out a jewelled cross hanging from a fine gold chain. "It belonged to milord's mother. He always wore it beneath his grand clothes," she said. "Dragon brought it. He says that my dear lord gave it to him before they—took him at Scarborough. Piers charged him to give it to me with a message."

"Was it a very private message?" asked Isabel gently.

"No, Madam. But a very—foolish one. He said not to grieve for him because he was not worth it."

Looking at the desolate, tear-swollen face before her, Isabel wondered involuntarily how it must feel to love a man so undemandingly and be so plain. It was all very well for Edward to remark dispassionately that other young widows remarried, but few of them, she supposed, could have been married to men of Piers Gaveston's misfortunate charm. She let Claremunda's cross and chain run through her own richly jewelled fingers. She judged the cross to be a thing of fine taste and foreign craftsmanship, but of small intrinsic value. Of far less value, for instance, than the fine French rings which now sparkled again on her own fingers, or the Charlemagne brooch which Gaveston had flaunted outside his doublet. Yet it was the cross which he had always worn intimately against his heart. "So you have seen Dragon?" she said.

"He came to the garden door yesterday at dusk and asked for my sister," volunteered Eleanor of Clare, who was Hugh le Despenser's wife.

"Without having leave of either the King or of me?"

"He had to assure himself that I was well cared for," pointed out young Margaret sturdily. "Piers would have wished it."

"And, as we all know, milord Gaveston's wishes must always override those of anyone else. Even after he is dead." Remembering how vulnerable the girl was, Isabel took a hold upon her bitter tongue. "And it gave you and this servant of his great pleasure to see each other?" she asked, more gently.

"Oh, Madam, of course!"

With odd reluctance, Edward's much-wronged wife handed back Gaveston's last gift. "Would you like to have Dragon stay and serve you?"

"I have told him that there is nothing which would comfort me more."

"So you took it upon yourself to suggest it?"

"I think Dragon would be willing, but——"

Irritating as it was to have one's kindly suggestions forestalled, it was still more irritating to be told that a disfigured Gascon man-at-arms should presume to receive such royal generosity with reservations. "But what?" snapped Isabel.

"It seems there is something which he must do first. Something, perhaps, which more closely concerns his—late master."

"And what could more closely concern him than your welfare, child?"

"Truly, I do not know, Madam. He did not tell me. As your Grace knows, he is not a man to talk, and even I—am a little afraid of him." Margaret rose and stood politely with clasped hands before her. "All I know is that he was leaving London immediately and going on a journey. Somewhere in a north-westerly direction I should think because he promised to take some money to the good monks of Oxford who received my dear lord's murdered body, so that they may say daily masses for his soul."

"He will have need of them!" muttered pert Eleanor from behind Ghislaine's back in the window embrasure.

Isabel, who abhorred her, dismissed them all. She had enough problems of her own. When a page came to announce that her bath was ready she rose to beautify herself for her husband and for the further enslavement of men who might be useful to him. And later, at dinner, when she repeated to him what his niece had said about Dragon, Edward showed no surprise. "The man was always a law unto himself," he remarked indulgently. "Piers always said that he forestalled his orders, and that by the time he came to give them everything necessary had usually been quite efficiently done. He has probably bethought him of some last thing to do for Piers now. But there was no need for poor Margot to send money to Oxford. I have already done so."

No matter upon what mission Dragon was gone, Isabel was only glad that they were rid of him since the sight of him must always recall his master. London was full of gaiety that winter and she entered into it with all her natural zest. There was ease from internal tension coupled with that uprising of general good will which brings out the best in a nation preparing for war.

Edward, who liked to have his family round him, persuaded his younger sister Mary to leave her convent at Amersham and stay for a while at court. He spent happy hours playing with his small son, and generously bestowed on Bringnette the revenues of rich lands in Ponthieu in gratitude for the loving care which she expended on the child. "It will ensure comfort in your old age, dear Countess," he said laughingly, "if the Queen and I should ever come to penury." He granted a commission in his newly-formed army to Thomas of Norfolk, the May Queen's elder son, who talked of nothing but driving back the Scots; and even young Edmund of Kent, the King's favourite half-brother, was given his first suit of armour. And all day long out at the butts or in the lists beside the river the eager shouts of young men and boys rang out as they practised the art of war.

And so it came about that just before Christmas when the two Queens had invited Edward and a few of his courtiers to admire a magnificent pearl-embroidered cope which they had been making for the Pope, Marguerite's two sons burst into the room, still hot and dishevelled from the tiltyard. "The Black Dog of Warwick is dead! The Black Dog of Warwick is dead!" chanted young Edmund, prancing excitedly around the room as though still mounted on his pony, and making an imaginary thrust at stern old Lady Badlesmere's embroidery frame.

"Death is no subject for rough jubilation," reproved his mother, putting out a hand to stay him.

"The Black Dog was poisoned!" persisted the boy.

"Edmund is so gullible," explained his elder brother Thomas, struggling to remove his helmet. "It is only what people are *saying*."

"They always do if anyone dies these days," said Marguerite.

"And why should he have been? He certainly looked a very sick man when he was in Westminster Hall last October," added Isabel hastily.

"But everybody hates him, don't they?" said Edmund, too excited from his morning's prowess to heed maternal restraint. His shrill young voice was guilelessly audible, and he looked straight at the King. He had no fear of Edward, from whom he had never received a cross word. Anyone who was Edward's enemy was his. And how often had he heard Piers Gaveston being exquisitely funny about Warwick, and his step-brother laughing? Edmund Plantagenet was still childish for his age, and with the uncanny acumen of childhood he sensed how Edward now hated the Earl, and all he wanted was to see him look pleased.

If Edward's face showed satisfaction, it expressed no surprise. "What makes people suspect foul play, Thomas?" he asked sharply.

Having freed himself at last from his tilting helmet and seeing that the King was present, Thomas of Norfolk was already looking sheepish and embarrassed. It was one thing to burst in upon the news-starved ladies with the latest wild scandal, and another to give tongue to it incautiously before the King. A possible implication of what he had just heard began to be apparent to him. "Milord of Lancaster's man who brought the news saw that scar-faced servant of—that scar-faced Gascon servant—in the streets of Warwick," he mumbled reluctantly.

Isabel remembered the cold hatred in Dragon's eyes and the smile on Edward's lips that day when Guy Beauchamp had been officially forgiven. Her hand flew to her breast to still her quickening heartbeats and she was grateful when Aymer de Valence moved in front of her, shielding her from the rest of the company, as he selected an unused pearl from her needlework box and held it aloft to examine it by the light from the window. "And why should our good friend Dragon not be in Warwick?" he was enquiring negligently.

Isabel was glad of their alliance, and Edward gathered time to assume an air of indifference. "He was probably on his way to the Welsh border," he said.

"He had an errand for his master's widow in Oxford," put in Isabel helpfully, hoping that her sense of direction was right.

"Then undoubtedly that is the route he would have taken," concluded Pembroke cheerfully, returning the pearl.

"Then your Grace saw this man Dragon before he left?" asked Hugh Despenser, more to emphasize his new familiarity with the King than with any thought of discrediting him.

"I did not," denied Edward.

His uncle of Lancaster looked at him long and searchingly. "Then may one enquire, my dear Edward, by what sixth sense you know that the man was making for the Welsh border?"

"Certainly, my dear uncle," replied Edward blandly. "I had offered him a place in my own household, and so I believe did my niece, so it was only civil of him to send me word that he had decided to take service with Roger Mortimer instead."

"Roger Mortimer!" exclaimed more than one voice. "When he might have been in the royal household!"

"Not surprising, is it, seeing that Mortimer was trained to arms in the late Earl of Cornwall's household? My friend thought highly of his military prowess and as we all know Mortimer has since made himself felt in enforcing order." As if to dismiss the subject Edward took a corner of the gorgeous cope from Ghislaine with appreciative fingers and signed to her to help him stretch it out again. "It really is an exquisite piece of work, my love," he told his wife, "and it is to be hoped that his Holiness's special blessing will rest upon you."

Marguerite sent her sons in chastened mood to clean themselves up before dining and no one in the room alluded again that morning to the Earl of Warwick's death. Only when Edward came to her that night did Isabel dare to question him. "Poor Margaret will be disappointed if Dragon does not come back to her," she said, loitering by the window in her miniver bed wrap.

"He may find the mountain air of Wales healthier," said Edward, unfastening the belt clasp of his own.

"Then you think he did this thing?"

Edward shrugged irritably. "I should expect him to. But, as you yourself observed, Guy of Warwick was old and sick." He snuffed the two tall candles at the foot of the bed and stood waiting. "Will you not come to bed?"

But Isabel still stood with her back to the window, both hands resting on the cold stone sill behind her. Her face was in shadow but the moonlight sketched a silvery outline to her unbound hair. "Some of the barons are suggesting that you sent him," she had the temerity to tell him.

"I was sure they would!" agreed Edward, with a short mirthless laugh. Then, realizing that she was still waiting, he leant forward trying to read the expression in her shadowed eyes. "You are not seriously asking me if I am a murderer, are you? Trying to add Warwick's death on to the other crimes your eyes used to accuse me of? Good God, Isabel, are you wanting to make sure that I have not blood on my hands before you come to bed with me?" She did not move or answer and he caught at her slight, resisting shoulders. "Don't be a little fool, Isabel!" he said, half pleading and half exasperated. "Has any of the violence you have seen since you came into my kingdom been of *my* doing? It would be absurd to pretend to you that I do not feel glad and revenged that that vile dog is dead, but whatever way he died I swear to you I had no hand in it. Do I *look* like a murderer?"

The moonlight was full on his face. On his kind eyes, his finely cut features and the feminine weakness of his mouth. "No," agreed Isabel with complete conviction. "Forgive me, oh, forgive me, but I had to know." Standing heart high, she laid her head upon his breast and he held her close, telling her that he admired her courage. That he would sooner have her outspoken doubts than the secret, venomous, trumped-up sandalmongering of others. "Who is this Roger Mortimer?" she asked idly after a while.

He lifted her chin and kissed her. "One of my fiercest border lords. He and his uncle, Mortimer of Chirk, own half Wales. If Dragon has done this thing he would certainly be safer with them than here from the vengeance of men who wear the Warwick badge of bear and staff. The Mortimers know how to hold what is their own. Or for that matter," he added laughingly, "what they take."

He drew the miniver from the slender whiteness of her body and carried her to her bed. The moonlight lay in bands across the rich tapestry of the coverlet, illuminating the bold fierce leopards *couchant* of his race. With eyes half closed it was easy enough to pretend that he was bold and fierce, too.

"Roger Mortimer," murmured Isabel, even while lying in her husband's arms. "I like the name; I like the sound of him."

CHAPTER 14

SHE saw him for the first time across a heath alive with armed men. She heard a trumpet sound and from the raised ground where she sat her palfrey she saw him ride up at the head of some Welsh soldiers who were to join the expedition against Scotland. She noted how the ranks of archers and pikemen and men-at-arms seemed to make way respectfully before him and how the more important knights pressed forward to meet him. The newcomer was less tall than Edward, who reviewed his troops beside her, and less resplendant than Gaveston, who was in his grave. He was not even particularly handsome. But there was an air of purposeful strength about him which pleased her.

"Who is that bareheaded man with the green and yellow stripes on his surcoat who is stopping to speak to Aymer de Valence?" she asked of her uncle Thomas of Lancaster.

"Roger Mortimer, the old lord of Chirk's nephew," he told her. And at that moment Mortimer, having come much closer to the King's mound, looked up at her across the sea of excited faces. Their glances held for a moment or two, each full of curiosity. "Even in Wales, he has probably heard about my beauty," thought Isabel, glad that she had worn her rolled-back headdress laced with rubies. And obviously he approved of what he saw, because his stern face broke into a slow smile. Involuntarily, she smiled back at him, and it was as if they two were somehow alone and detached in interest from the campaign.

The morning sun shone on the bright head of Gilbert of Gloucester as he slid from his horse to greet the newcomer. "Why, Roger, how are my lands in Wales looking?" he cried, drawing off a gauntlet to wring him by the hand.

"Have you seen our new trebuchets for hurling barrels of flaming pitch over castle battlements, Sir?" enquired young Thomas of Norfolk, eager for an expert's opinion.

"Give me old-fashioned bows, which can be used on any terrain," grinned the hardy Welshman, unimpressed.

"Under your command I can well imagine they would be equally efficacious," laughed Edward, greeting him with easy charm. "It is a rare pleasure to have you with us, Mortimer. If I remember rightly you kept the border peace while your uncle came to our Coronation. Come and let me present you to our Queen."

The border lord bent over her hand with due formality. When he looked up she noticed that his eyes were grey, curiously flecked with brown, and was aware that they had already introduced themselves to each other with that first spontaneous smile.

Sharp words of command, jangle of harness and the sudden shrill neighing of horses filled the air, and the movement of multi-coloured banners wove a constantly shifting tapestry of brightness around them. Scraps of opinion from tried warriors and bits of the boasting of excited young men like Thomas of Norfolk assailed their ears.

"Victory should be assured."

"There never was so fine an army."

"Robert Bruce will count himself lucky if he can raise a quarter of the men."

"Or train them, in the wild hills of Scotland!"

Isabel gazed bright-eyed at the splendid spectacle before her. Steel gleamed as far as eye could see and it was impossible not to be stirred by all the clamour and preparation. But she could not quite put out of mind the last inglorious campaign.

"Is it true what they say, milord Pembroke? Or are they over-confident?" she asked, when the King had moved forward to welcome a contingent from Guienne.

"Undoubtedly we should win, Madam. But one must remember that a small army well disciplined and well led can be very dangerous," answered Aymer de Valence cautiously. "So much depends on the strategy of the leaders."

"Meaning that this Bruce could be cleverer than any of you?" Isabel turned to the newly-arrived defender of the western marches. "What say you, Sir Roger?"

Mortimer, sitting his tall bay beside her, assessed them with an experienced eye. "It is true that England has never raised a *larger* army," he answered non-committally.

"Then I suppose it would be the more shame if they were to lose."

Presumably he agreed with Pembroke about the importance of leadership. "Given such an army, I should count defeat inexcusable. But then I am more accustomed to cut-throat border skirmishes with only a handful of men."

More fanfares were being sounded and the troops were beginning to march. Last farewells were being said. Isabel waved to Gilbert of Gloucester and to Thomas of Norfolk and to Robert de Messager. Surely they at least must come back covered with glory. They were too enthusiastic and too young to die. She bade a more formal farewell to Pembroke, to Lord Clifford, to Sir Henry de Bohun of Hereford and other seasoned warriors, and allowed a dignified old knight, Sir Giles de Argentine, to kiss her hand. Because he had gone Crusading with Longshanks he was allowed pride of place at Edward's side. "Look well to the safety of milord the King!" she charged him almost gaily, and he promised on his knightly honour that he would. Isabel suffered no agonizing anxiety at parting from her husband. Remembering the long, dull days spent in Berwick, she realized with a swiftly crushed twinge of shame that he was not likely to push himself unnecessarily into the forefront of a battle. As soon as Stirling was taken he would send for her to come north, she supposed, and take advantage of some lull in the campaign to join her in some reasonably safe and pleasant stronghold. "In the meantime stay at Westminster and keep our son with you," he said, leaning from his splendid horse to embrace her as well as armour permitted. "The air and produce should be better for him there than in the Tower."

His last thought was for their child, who was still small and helpless. And Isabel, watching Marguerite bid farewell to her elder son, was glad that it would be many years before her own babe would be old enough to ride away into the unknown like that. With the other women, both Queens waved to their men as long as they could see them, and then sat silent in their saddles watching the rest of the army depart. When the trampled heath was almost empty of men and the sun was glinting on long, snakelike lines of spears in the distance, Isabel turned with a feeling of flat depression and found Roger Mortimer still beside her. "So both of us are left behind," she said with a wry little smile.

"I should like to have gone, but the King has left his borders in my care. Those fine fellows cannot afford to have any trouble brew up behind them," he told her.

She looked at him appraisingly—at his broad shoulders, his firm, clean-shaven mouth and at the reddish hairs on the back of his bare, right hand. "I shall be at Westminster and you far away on the Welsh border when we hear news of them from Scotland," she said.

"May it be good news!"

"Even so it may be years before we meet again."

She did not know what drove the impulsive words to her lips, and was furious with herself when he smiled at her naïve betrayal of how much he interested her. His lips parted over square white teeth in a way which she found too likeable for her peace of mind. "A pity," he said, looking down audaciously into her eyes, "when like calls to like."

"In any case they will be lean years," she said hurriedly, trying to hide the shock of pleasure his words had given her. "Did you notice the poorness of all our crops as you rode through our home shires towards London?"

"With deep concern, Madam. I am obliged to be something of a farmer, having my own wide estates to watch over."

"And what little our peasants have garnered the army must have taken," she added.

He stretched out that strong hirsute hand and laid it on the pommel of her saddle so that their mounts edged very close and his mailed leg pressed sharply for a moment against her thigh. "I will see that you do not starve," he said.

His promise banished her desolate feeling of being left behind. She suddenly felt cared for, excitingly. Being Isabel, she did not jerk her horse aside. "In what way do you think we are alike, milord?" she asked, with lowered eyes.

He withdrew his hand to strike at a gadfly which was tormenting his bay's sleek neck. "Strength of will, intelligence, spirit—the making of a partnership," he answered consideringly. "I do not care for mouselike women."

Astounded at his impertinence yet oddly satisfied with his response, Isabel offered him in duty bound the hospitality of the Palace. But having attended Parliament and brought his feudal quota of men for the King's service he must return immediately, he said. So she motioned to her retinue to follow her back to Westminster; and to the long weeks of waiting.

They were lean and tedious weeks indeed. Few market carts came in from the country over London Bridge. Even in the Palace the shortage of food was felt, but the army must be fed first and Isabel encouraged her household to make a jest of the simpler meals they ate. Thomeline, the orphan whom she had brought from Tyneside, was becoming a fine musician and delighted to sing for her. Robert Withstaff, the King's jester, had been left behind to amuse her. The roses in her garden had never looked more beautiful and her barge was always waiting to take her up and down the winding Thames. Drawn together by anxiety for their menfolk, Isabel and her ladies devised which sport they could to while away the long summer days.

May wore into June and still no news came. All they knew was that their men had long since passed over the border and must be somewhere north of the border town of Berwick. They supposed that they must by now have relieved the strong key town of Stirling, which the Scots were said to have been besieging. Probably they had left strong reinforcements with Sir Philip Mowbray, who had been holding it for the King, and were already marching southwards. Through the hot days and nights London waited breathlessly for the glad tidings that the Scots were routed. They had seen a splendid army marching through their streets and were impatient to be hanging out their banners and lighting bonfires to welcome them home again. Going a little hungry and being skinned short of money would seem well worth while then. Their feckless king was no fool after all. He would come riding back one sunny morning with King Bruce of Scotland in chains behind him. And then what rejoicings there would be!

Or perhaps, one fine day, he would send a messenger on ahead with the good news. But it was pouring with rain and scarcely light when the news really came—which was just as well, because few people saw the man who brought it. His horse was flecked with sweat and he looked gaunt as a ghost. The sleepy guard at Moorgate pulled back the great bolts and let him through without question when he showed the Clare badge on his stained surcoat and asked for the Queen.

He rode through the sleeping city to Westminster, and Isabel rose from her bed to receive him. Rain and sweat glistened on his lined face. Beneath the grime of travel she recognized him as a favourite squire of Gilbert's. She had seen him riding out with the young men whom she had waved to that day on the heath, but he looked much older now. "Have you a message for me from the King?" she asked sharply, drawing her wrap about her.

The man shook his head, his lungs still working too hard for speech. "I served—the Earl of Gloucester," he panted.

"I know you did, Richard Overbury. I will have his sister wakened and brought so that she, too, may hear your good news."

But he stayed her order with a gesture of entreaty. "I pray your Grace—not yet!"

For the first time Isabel began to suspect that his news might not be wholly good. "And how fares your Earl?" she asked, motioning to a servant to take his sodden cloak and bring him wine.

"He was killed. Leading a charge of cavalry."

Isabel closed her eyes and pictured young Gilbert, ruddy and vital, urging his horse into the thick of the fight, calling back encouragement to all those splendid knights who thundered after him. "Not Gilbert!" she murmured. "What cruel, improbable mischance that it had to be he!"

"It was no improbable mischance, madam. He was only one of thousands. It was wholesale slaughter."

The Queen's women groaned and she herself sank down onto the chest at the foot of her bed, staring at Overbury incredulously. It seemed that he could neither drink nor rest until he had said what he had ridden through a nightmare of days and nights to say. "The Scots defeated us—utterly."

For a moment or two the amazed silence in the room was broken only by the steady beat of rain on the deserted courtyard outside. The eastern sky was growing light, making the hastily lit torches look garish. "And what of milord the King?" asked Isabel in a small frightened voice.

"He is safe, Madam."

The young man gulped thirstily at his wine, and Isabel had the impression that he was glad to hide his face behind the uplifted tankard. "What do you mean by safe?" she persisted.

"He—left the field. With Sir Giles de Argentine. They were making for Stirling when I last saw them. The castle was still in our hands then. I know no more, madam," he went on with almost surly reluctance. "But other messengers—half the army —will be scurrying back here soon. Some of them should be able to tell your Grace."

"Then they, too—fled?"

"The Scots had prepared the ground," he muttered.

"What ground?" snapped Isabel.

"The flat marshy ground beside the burn that we must ford. Every furlong of it. They'd dug holes and then covered them with brushwood, and strewn murderous spiked iron balls among the young green heather. The screaming of our horses was horrible. Either they broke their legs or their bellies were impaled. Milord of Gloucester almost managed to get across. He was fighting brilliantly until his horse stumbled on the edge of one of those pits and rolled on him. I could not reach him but I could see the murderous down-thrust of a score of enemy lances. They say his golden head was battered to bits." Richard Overbury was weeping unashamedly. "A few of us lived to flounder back," he went on. "But a man fully armed without his horse is ludicrously helpless."

Isabel rose, stunned but outwardly composed. "Fetch milords of Lancaster and Arundel who sent their men but so churlishly refused to go in person," she ordered. "Tell all members of the Council who are left in London to come without delay. Ghislaine, you must break this sad news to poor widowed Margaret Plantagenet, who has now lost a brother. And go, one of you, and bring me my miniver cloak. Leaving my bed so hastily has made me cold."

But it was more than hasty rising which had chilled her. It was fear. The same stark sudden fear which drew lamentations from her women and made their pale hands shake uselessly. Fear of the Black Douglas with hordes of barbaric kilted Scotsmen pouring down over the border to slaughter, burn and rape. But she would not admit it. She sat regally in her state chair all through that dismal summer morning listening to the defeat of England's pride. Other messengers from the broken army came and went before her, sodden and befouled with mud and blood, and each filled in some further details of that devastating rout. And all the time the rain beat down steadily outside the windows. The steady, merciless rain.

"It was at a place called Bannockburn," they told her. "A brook runs through it below the mound of Stirling castle, and now the brook runs blood."

"We were trying to relieve the castle. Sir Philip Mowbray and his poor devils there had had no food for days," said Thomas of Norfolk. He had come in quietly and was standing behind the Queen's chair. Hearing his voice, she put up a hand to touch him, immeasurably thankful for Marguerite's sake that he was back. "Lord Clifford took eight hundred of our cavalry—all picked men—and tried to push through from the eastern side. He made a furious charge and at one time things looked black for the defending Scots, but the next thing we saw was English horses galloping off in all directions, mostly with empty saddles."

A rugged old Warwick pikeman with a store of battle experience took up the tale. "They'd all the advantage of knowing their ground," he explained. "And they never left anything to chance. They do say 'twas the Marshal of the Scots army hisself who rode out to a hilltop to see what kind o' an army was comin'; and a right skeerin' sight we must ha' made, twenty thousand or more o' us spreading out all over the countryside."

"*We* went out scouting too, and but for an inch or two the

whole battle might have gone the other way!" broke in a Herefordshire squire to whom his master, Sir Humphrey de Bohun, would always be the hero of the day. "We went so close we could see the Scots king riding along his lines giving last-minute instructions. Just mounted on one of those wiry little ponies they use in their mountains. He'd no lance, nor even a sword. Sir Humphrey spurred forward and thrust straight at King Robert's bare throat. You should have heard the groan that went up from the Scottish lines! But at the last moment the Bruce jerked his pony aside so that the English lance missed by an inch. And before my master could pull up King Robert swung round at him with his axe. Such a hefty blow that it cleft helmet and skull together." The young squire put a hand before his face and turned away. "Only a matter of inches," he kept repeating, "and the day might have been ours."

"And where was milord the King?" asked Isabel, trying to piece together each man's particular aspect of the battle into one comprehensible whole.

"His tent was pitched on a little hillock behind our main divisions," said his half-brother, Norfolk. "He rose at dawn and joined us. Everything was very quiet, only the birds singing sleepily. We looked across to the enemy's lines and saw men going down on their knees. 'The rebels have seen the size of our army and are praying for forgiveness!' he cried out, hoping that all bloodshed could be averted. Then we realized that an Abbot of some sort was walking among them, and Aymer de Valence said in that dry way of his, 'Yes, they are praying for forgiveness, but from God, not us'."

"The King gave the order for action then an' we let fly," broke in a brawny Sussex bowman. "The air was full of arrows and the Scots falling like ninepins. But the Bruce sent the pick of his cavalry chargin' right through the thick of it. 'Twas a turbel risk to take, but once the lucky ones as was left alive come to close quarters we was done. We'd no weapons save our bows, an' their gurt horses trampled most o' my comrades. The Earl of Pembroke saw our plight an' was quick to send a fine bunch of cavalry to help us. They come thunderin' across the flat ground by the burn, an' the young Earl o' Gloucester—God rest his soul!—was leadin' 'em. An' then I dunno how 'twas but the whole pack of 'em seemed to be sinkin' down in the earth like the Devil was pullin' at 'em."

"You see, Madam, it is as I said," interrupted Richard Overbury, glad of corroboration.

"With our bowmen gone and half our knights bogged down by pits and caltrops what *could* we do?" asked a shamed and shaken old knight.

They seemed almost to have forgotten their silent, white-faced Queen. Absorbed in their subject, they began reliving that dreadful day among themselves.

"But the thing that really finished us was when the King's party looked up and saw a second army of Scots coming over the brow of the hill behind the first. Though some do say it was only the baggage men who'd heard the day was won and were coming after the loot——"

The Queen cared little *why* the English had taken this unexpected defeat. All that mattered was that they had. She made an impatient gesture to her steward to send them all away to fight their battle over again elsewhere. She sent everyone away. Even Bringnette and Ghislaine. But she gestured to Thomas of Norfolk to stay. "Tell me what happened to Edward and tell me the truth," she ordered, as soon as they were alone. And rising from her chair she moved to the window embrasure, her silken skirts swishing over the scented straw as she went.

"He left the field," the unhappy youth repeated.

"You mean he fled?"

He made no answer until she turned, and then he spread his hands deprecatingly and bowed his head. He would not look at her. "One of the first."

"Alone?"

"Sir Giles de Argentine went with him."

"Yet you tell me that his Grace is safe. And I heard the others say just now that Sir Giles died, fighting furiously." Somehow she must drag the truth from him. He might be Edward's half-brother and hate to tell her, but she was Edward's wife. If she had to live with him, she must know. "Answer me!" she ordered, and her eyes were two probing points of brightness.

"Sir Giles told me to escort the King to Stirling castle. But he himself went back."

"Why?"

"As soon as we were safely out of the press he begged Edward to excuse him. He said it was not his custom to run away."

"He said that to the King?"

"Yes, Madam. He said that in his family the men stayed and fought. Then he set spurs to his horse and galloped back to the battlefield. As we rode towards Stirling I could still hear him a long way off shouting his war cry 'de Argentine! de Argentine!' Then suddenly I didn't hear it any more—nor the thud of his horse's flying hoofs. I suppose that was when he was killed."

Isabel's skirts swished after her like angry snakes as she mounted the few stone steps to the window. She stood with her back to the room, covering her face with both hands. Ever since the time of Cœur de Lion the courage of the Plantagenets had been legendary. She had been proud to marry a Plantagenet. But in that bitter moment Edward, as a man, ceased to exist. And in the grip of her shame she thought involuntarily of Roger Mortimer, the fierce border lord, and set him up as a symbol of the only kind of man she wanted.

She had almost forgotten her waiting relative who was telling her how he and the King had ridden on to Dunbar, not daring to stop even for food because the Douglas was so hot on their heels. "A mercy Edward is so splendid a horseman," he was saying.

Isabel supposed that he was too obtuse to see that the fact added shame to shame. "And at Dunbar?" she asked wearily.

"Patrick, Earl of the Northern Marches, found us a fishing boat. Some other stragglers, mostly older men, had joined us by then. So I begged a fresh horse and rode down through Berwick." Once again Thomas offered doubtful comfort. "It was a calm summer night when they embarked so the King should make some English port quite safely."

"Quite safely!" echoed Isabel, making a savage little gesture of dismissal. After he had gone she stood for a long time by the window staring out into the gathering twilight. The rain still fell with desolate monotony down into the courtyard. All her life she would hate the depressing sound of steady rain.

CHAPTER 15

The army straggled home, as Gloucester's squire had foretold. And Edward's little ship came safely to port in England. There were no bonfires on the hills nor was there any cheering in the

London streets. "Twenty thousand they were against six thousand," men kept muttering in a bewilderment of unbelief; and by the time the survivors of the twenty thousand had been paid there seemed to be no money left in the exchequer. And less and less food in the country, so that people went about dazed by anxiety and hunger. "Food is only for the rich," the fathers of young families said, but even at the King's table there were few luxuries. Acting on Pembroke's advice, he tried to keep his poorer subjects from starvation by fixing the prices of staple foods, but even with the money in their hands shopkeepers waited in vain for farmers' carts to bring the daily provisions into London. Slaughter yards stood empty and shrill-voiced 'prentice lads had few wares to call. Herds found so little fodder that there was scarcely enough milk for country children. Even the oak trees, no matter how violently shaken by anxious swineherds, seemed to let fall no acorns for the pigs. And now, with the new year, the Scots were over the border pillaging the precious crops in the North. There seemed nothing for it but to gather together another army and march northwards to oppose them.

"But how raise another army without money?" sighed Edward.

"Why are we so poor?" asked Isabel, who had never wanted for anything in her life until she came to England.

"Because of my father's unending wars," he had told her, with some truth.

"Or because of your extravagance? And Gaveston's?"

Seeing the sharp look on her face, and the sudden whiteness of Edward's, Aymer de Valence had, as usual, hastened to intervene in the cause of conjugal peace. "If only your father had not expelled the Jews, Sir!"

Isabel had looked up at him quickly—seeing his dark little beard and his clever, sallow face, and remembering how Piers Gaveston had always baited him by calling him "the Jew", she wondered for a moment if he had any cause for racial feeling. "Did he persecute them?" she asked, her interest suddenly side-tracked, as he had intended.

He had smiled then as if reading her thoughts. "No. Edward Longshanks was always just. When he ordered them to leave the country he gave them reasonable time, and forbade his officers to ill-use them. But all the same it was one of the few serious mistakes that great king ever made."

"Why?" Isabel remembered asking. And the answer had been succinct. "Because there is now no one to borrow from. Centuries ago, when the Jews were persecuted out of their pastures, their flair for finance grew. Now we have no moneylenders, and no way of raising money save the false economy of a debased coinage."

That had been months ago. And now, after a Christmas spent at Westminster, Edward had gone north again and Isabel was glad enough to be left at Eltham, quietly out of it all. There had been no question of her going with him, because she had been again with child, and now she had just borne him a second son. He had been delighted with the news and had quite characteristically made her messenger a present of a hundred pounds without any thought for their financial difficulties. "Will he never learn?" she had thought and, although still abed, had set about making arrangements for a quiet christening, sending only for her uncle of Lancaster and the Bishop of Norwich as godparents, and calling the child by the thoroughly English name of John, which she knew would please both her husband and the people.

The birth had been easy, but now that all the fuss and effort were over, post-natal lassitude lulled her to a contentment foreign to her restless nature, so that she was glad to sit idly with Marguerite in the warm September sunshine. It was really very pleasant in the Kentish palace garden with its parterre of small, square flower-beds intersected by stone-flagged paths. From where she sat in the shade of a mulberry tree she could see four-year-old Ned playing with the wooden hobby-horse which his father had lovingly carved for him and which the boy called *Cher Ami*. Somewhere in the background Thomeline was singing softly to his lute. Thomas of Lancaster had come to enquire after her health, laden with gifts for herself and for his new godson. In his lordly way he had also been distributing money to all who had cared for her during her confinement and now most of her women had withdrawn to the herb garden, babbling with delight.

"What a satisfactory Queen you make, my dear Isabel, producing sons," he was saying. "You will be more popular in this country than ever."

"I doubt if John will be as strong as Ned," said Marguerite anxiously. And her glance strayed admiringly to the sturdy boy urging his brightly-painted *Cher Ami* across the grass.

"All the same it might be a popular move to show him to the

people, after so quiet a christening. A procession through London, perhaps, with our dear Isabel holding him in her arms."

Thomas of Lancaster was always thinking of moves to enhance his own and his niece's popularity. They did Edward no good, she knew. All the same, a little shiver of anticipatory pleasure ran through her at the thought of being seen in London again. It seemed a long time since she had heard the gasps of admiration and the wild cheering of the people, and this time, with the King away, all the tumultuous welcome would be for herself and her two children. Ned, perhaps, being led on a white pony. "We need to have the charettes done up, and all the cushions re-covered," she said. "Flame-coloured silk, I thought, and I would wear my silver lamé. You, my dear Marguerite, look your loveliest in that myrtle green——"

But even as they fell to discussing it Hawtayne, her steward, came through the archway into the walled garden bringing a letter.

"It is from the King, Madam," he said. And they all fell silent while she broke the royal seal and unrolled it. "He is near York, and wants me to join him," she told them in a flat expressionless voice. A year ago, before Bannockburn, she would have been glad. Now she let the stiff parchment roll back across her lap and looked up at her two French relatives appealingly. "It is so pleasant here in late summer. Must I go up north?"

Marguerite smiled at her sadly. She knew that the beauty of the season had less to do with Isabel's reluctance than the new value one puts on solitude when out of love. "If the King wishes it," she said.

"When does he want you to come?" asked Lancaster, from the stone bench where he sat resplendent in a high-collared, belted houppelande, a becoming fashion for older men which he had introduced from France.

"He says as soon as I am stronger." Isabel got up, stretching her arms above her head as she went to join him on the garden seat. She even lifted Ned experimentally, when he left his play and ran to her. "See, I am quite strong already, dear uncle. Why do men always think of me as frail?"

"I should not disabuse them of the idea, if I were you," advised her aunt. "There is nothing makes a man feel so beneficent as giving in to a helpless-looking woman who barely reaches his heart."

Both of them laughed, and Isabel helped herself from a dish of marchpane squares which Ghislaine had brought for the Duke's refreshment, and popped one into her first-born's ever-ready mouth. It was an hour for gossiping in a warm garden, for smiling indulgently at the antics of a child, for making exciting plans for a procession or a pageant; but now Edward's letter had spoiled it. And Lancaster sat there, suddenly resentful, inveigling against the dragging, ineffectual war which so spoiled their lives. "Why not come to reasonable terms with the Scots instead of wasting our lives and substance?" he grumbled. "For all their pillaging, the Bruce is a civilized man."

Isabel felt provoked by the innate pomposity behind his pleasant façade. "I notice that you did not risk *your* life, milord," she could not refrain from saying. "Was it because you feel some sympathy with the Scots that you refused to go?"

He did not answer directly. "I am no longer young. I sent as many retainers as my allegiance to the crown demands," he reminded her self-righteously.

"You sound as though you sent them unwilling. But surely you wish to protect your people and possessions in Lancashire?" said Marguerite.

"So far the King of Scotland has not touched them."

"But even so, with Cumberland and Northumberland already being raided, surely you consider that England should put up some resistance?"

"Resistance? With no virile leaders, and such as there are still half disaffected from the Crown? And your good husband, Isabel, marching to the sound of fiddles, they tell me. Such resistance as we show to-day is a mere farce! A joke in the streets of Stirling, where mere 'prentices swear to bring back the stolen stone he was crowned on!" The Earl arose, a fine figure of a man growing to paunchiness, with the arms of Hereford, Lincoln, Lancaster and Derby blazoned on his houppelande and anger snapping from his eyes. "Do you know what King Robert of Scotland says? 'I fear the bones of the first Edward of England dead more than I fear his living son!' And he swears by all the saints that it was more difficult to get a foot of land from the old king, than it will be to take a whole kingdom from this present popinjay."

The hot blood rushed to Isabel's face. She sprung up and faced him. "How do you know that he said that? Whom did he say it to?" she demanded.

But her uncle looked shiftily away, preparing to depart. He realized that he had over-stepped even the intimacy of their mutual foreign relationship. "Robert Bruce will assuredly take

Berwick unless Edward has the sense to come to terms," he repeated evasively.

Marguerite rose too, cold with anger that he should say so cruel a thing before the Queen. She knew him to be jealous of Edward, lustful of power for himself and scheming enough to link himself with his niece's popularity to that end; but never before had she so clearly seen the evil genius he must have proved to their marriage, with his efforts to push them into separate opposing parties. "Your Grace seems very well acquainted with the King of Scotland's mind," she said, with a formality that wiped out all their former friendly ease.

He saw the eyes of both women rest upon him with suspicion, and immediately bethought him of some council table at which he should, at that precise moment, be presiding. And as he went hurriedly out into the bailey to join his retainers the young Prince went bounding through the archway after him, trying to reach up to his brightly jewelled dagger. He preferred men, and was never one to hang about his mother.

"How could he repeat such words in your presence!" exclaimed Marguerite, staring after him.

"But they were true," said Isabel. She strove to speak as though she did not care, but felt physically sick with shame. The bright marigolds and modest pansies were all a haze before her eyes, so that she wondered if, after all, she could be as strong again as she had thought herself. She sank down again on the bench, bowing her head on her arm against the back of it. "I sometimes wish I were a widow like you and Gaveston's Margaret," she said.

"A wicked thing to say," chided the May Queen. "You do not know what it is like to lose the man you love."

Isabel lifted her head and stared unseeingly before her. "Even that could be less bitter than to realize that the man you loved has never really existed." While the older woman assimilated the full meaning of her cry, Isabel just sat there staring into her future. She had forgotten that she was a queen, and even her resentment because she must share the uncomfortable consequences of Edward's ineffectual rule. She was only a beautiful young woman, capable of passion, with the bright image of her love-life lying in fragments like a broken mirror about her. "Oh, Marguerite, must I go back to him?" she cried. "And bear yet another Plantagenet babe?" Without turning she reached up a hand and the May Queen came and held it. Her own was warm and comforting, as it had so often been when Edward had clutched it as a boy, battered by paternal wrath. "He is a good and loving father," was all she could think of to say.

"But every time he makes love to me I shall see him running away from that battle at Bannockburn."

Her aunt, who loved them both, sat down beside her where Lancaster had sat. "You were so romantically in love with him at Boulogne—on your honeymoon. Have you no pleasanter pictures of him to remember? None culled from the years when you cried for him as children cry for the inaccessible moon?"

Isabel thought back, relaxed and smiled. "Strange that you should ask me that, *ma chère*. There is one picture that will always stay in my mind. I see him—not often, but at the oddest times—as he was that crazy Christmas at Langley. Before he and Piers went to Scotland. I have only to shut my eyes sometimes to see them carefree and laughing, tossing poor Robert the jester up to the ceiling in one of your best tablecloths. Do you remember? I can see the blazing logs on the hearth, the wreaths of holly hung against the tapestries, the torchlight on their lithe bodies and lovely clothes. And Edward's happy face. Do you know, Marguerite, Edward never looks like that now."

"But he needs you and seeks your advice. It is as I said, about the ivy clinging to the fleur-de-lys."

Isabel shook her head. "Although I am his wife and the mother of his children, I believe that he has never really loved anybody as he loved Piers Gaveston. I cared so much then. I was sick with jealousy. And now it is only my pride that minds. Now I see the poor—popinjay, did my uncle say?—as he really is." She laughed, unsteadily; and, rising, began pacing back and forth between the small, square flower-beds. "Alack-a-day, how handsome he was! And how I loved him!"

"He is handsome still," said Marguerite.

"And beginning to grow a beard!" agreed Isabel lightly. "He says it will make him look older and will help to overawe the barons."

"And even that suits him."

"It would! His beauty is incorruptible. Neither dissipation nor his country's ruin can lessen it." Isabel swayed dancingly between the flowers, arms hugging her breasts, her very insouciance a barbed mockery born of suffering.

"Oh, Isabel, try to see him more tolerantly. All men are not military heroes. My youngling Edmund is rather like him, but neither you nor I love him the less for it."

"He is only a boy."

"Yet I must admit it sometimes worries me that he is growing up weak of character. Too kind to crush an adder. Too easily pursuaded by the last person he was with—too gullible, as his brother says."

Isabel pursued her way back and forth between the flower beds. "Weak and impressionable perhaps, but not a proven coward," she said, pursing her lips aggressively in the direction of a tall hollyhock that nodded knowingly against the garden wall.

"Neither is Edward," argued his step-mother. "Look how he stood by Gaveston. He might well have lost his crown through it. It is just that he has no stomach for war." There was no answer, so she added hesitantly, "There are different kinds of courage, Isabel, and they are not all spectacular. Like bearing suffering patiently——"

Isabel looked up quickly and instantly stopped her irritating perambulation. For the second time of late she noticed that her aunt's face was white and drawn, and recalled how she had stumbled hurriedly from chapel during Vespers, with both hands pressed to her abdomen and Lady Vaux helping her. "Perhaps she is often suffering, though she never speaks of it," thought Isabel anxiously. "I must ask Lady Vaux." Aloud, to cover her sudden panic, she remarked with careless disloyalty, "My brother Charles says that if Edward is incapable of ruling he deserves to lose his crown."

Mentioning Charles turned her thoughts from England's difficulties to the changes that had taken place in France, and to the last conversation they had had together in the gardens of the Louvre. As he had foreseen, Philip the Bel had not lived long, and then Louis, her eldest brother, had died, childless, after a brief reign. So that only her second brother now stood between Charles and the throne. "If only I could talk to Charles!" she thought, as she always did during the disappointments of her life. But at least she had Marguerite. Marguerite whose good counsel she always disputed, and then tried—usually quite successfully—to follow. "What should I do without you in this difficult country?" she exclaimed impulsively, and linking arms walked back with the May Queen to her apartments and called her women and saw to it that she rested. She was unusually gentle with her, regretting her former out-pourings which must have given her pain. "I will tell my people to prepare for the journey north before the autumn cold comes and the roads get bad. And I will try to take only the best of my marital memories with me," she promised smilingly.

It was no small task to remove a whole royal household. The sun shone through a golden mist and the trees were turning to russet on the mid-October morning when she started, and to one of Isabel's mercurial temperament the beauty of the day lent cheerfulness to begin life afresh. All was excitement and the courtyard packed with her gay cavalcade. Her steward was shouting last-minute instructions and her household servants were spruce with new fleur-de-lys badges on their cloaks. Her women were already seated in their charettes, a special one for the children and their nurses followed her own, and grouped in the background were the baggage wagons with her tapestries and bed linen and clothes presses, and a string of sumpter horses laden with the possessions of the rest of the company. Before the palace doors stood her own eight-wheeled charette with the arms of England, and France painted richly round the woodwork of its sides, and the seats furnished with the cushions of new scarlet silk as she had wished. It would be pleasant riding through the country, and the people in the towns and villages would all turn out to welcome her. And the Dowager Queen and the Earl of Lancaster had both come to see her off.

"If the King wants you to stay long in Yorkshire you must use my castle at Brotherton," offered Marguerite, kissing her good-bye.

"You will not be needing it?"

"No. I am going to my manor of Marlborough in Sevenacre forest for the winter. To set my affairs in order with my head steward."

"Brotherton, Marlborough, and Leeds in the middle of its Kentish lake—what lovely castles you have!" called down Isabel laughingly, as Robert le Messager helped her climb up into the charette.

"They will all be yours one day," smiled Marguerite.

"Not for many a day, let's hope!" called back Isabel, spreading out her stiff damask skirts and putting a white hand out through the drawn-back curtains of the vehicle for Lancaster to kiss. "Take care of her while I am gone, will you not, milord? She grows much too thin."

"I will send her venison from my own forests every day," he promised gallantly.

"And she will give all the best pickings of it away to the poor!"
Marguerite was bidding the children farewell and marvelling that they should be taken so young. At the time of her own more spartan journeyings towards the seat of war her husband had always left his heir at home. But not so the second Edward. He would sooner a thousand times be playing with young Ned than killing Scotsmen. She supposed that Thomas of Lancaster must be remembering and marking the difference, too. She came close to the open side of the charette and spoke more privately. "I hope Edward will let you stay at Brotherton. For me it is full of happy memories because my first child was born there, and men say it is impregnable. You and the children should be safe there."

"Safe?" echoed Isabel, surprised. "But of course I shall be safe anywhere in Yorkshire. Edward will only come to visit me from time to time. The trouble is further north."

"Isabel is right," corroborated Lancaster. "There is no fighting going on within a hundred miles."

Marguerite glanced uneasily at Ned, jumping about the nursery cart and clamouring to hold the reins. "All the same, I shall be happier to know that she and the children are at Brotherton with a double curtain wall and my own loyal people about her," she persisted.

"All will be well with us," Isabel reassured her, forgetting how loath she had been to go. "My only regret, dear uncle, is that we did not have that procession for the Londoners which you suggested," said Isabel, sorry that on that occasion she had parted from him in anger.

He had kissed her on both cheeks in the French fashion. He had brought some delicious mulberries from his London garden to refresh her, and even remembered a basket of cinnamon sticks to keep Ned quiet on the journey. He had been everything that a kind and important relative should be. But now he seemed preoccupied, as if mulling over some new idea in his mind. And almost as glad for her to go, she thought, as he had previously been anxious to keep her.

"A strange, tortuous sort of man, though he be my own kinsman," whispered the wise May Queen warningly, but Isabel was already waving a flowered scarf and the high wooden wheels of the charette had begun to turn. Only Robert the Fool heard her, and he was full of his own ideas for new jests and junketings against the glad day when he would be reunited with his master.

CHAPTER 16

As THOUGH to reward her for her docile acceptance, Isabel did not have to stay long in Yorkshire. The Scots, it seemed, swooped down in sudden raids but avoided another decisive battle, so that Edward soon tired of the long-drawn-out border warfare and brought her back to Westminster. He wanted to be home for Christmas and Twelfth Night, and Isabel was only too thankful to find herself in the midst of preparations for revelry instead of preparations for battle. Being by nature as luxury-loving as he, she tried to shut her mind to the fact that, with his usual thoughtlessness, he was giving lavish rewards to all those stay-at-home members of his household who provided him with amusement and soft living while up in the bleak north half his army remained unpaid.

"It is not every day a Plantagenet gets married. We must make a show for my niece's wedding," he said, when the Archbishop of Canterbury had the temerity to try to restrain him.

"It is all arranged then that Margaret de Clare is to marry Hugh de Audley?" said Isabel.

"And half of poor Gilbert's inheritance she will bring him."

This time Isabel made no protest on the girl's behalf. She stood with Edward on the steps of the Abbey and helped to fling marriage money over the heads of bride and groom as they plighted their troth before the crowds before passing in to the more solemn part of their nuptials before the high altar. "After all, Gaveston has been in his grave a long time now, and she does not seem to mind this new marriage as much as I thought she would," said Isabel, when sitting with her women after the ceremony was over.

"She seems to accept it," agreed Bringnette. "She is always quiet and withdrawn now—even with Ghislaine."

"It is because of what her sly-faced sister told her," said Ghislaine, stabbing her needle with quite unnecessary violence into an unoffending heraldic beast on her embroidery frame.

"Eleanor of Clare?" said the Queen, laying aside her own work before it was well begun. "What did she tell her?"

"About her husband." Feeling the warning pressure of Bringnette's slipper upon her own, Ghislaine stopped short. She bent lower over the frame hoping the padded wing of her headdress would hide the hot blood sweeping up into her cheeks; but the Queen bade her go on and the girl had courage. "About Piers Gaveston and—the King," she said.

Isabel rose, cold with fury. The bright-hued silks cascaded from her lap, and the eyes of both women followed her apprehensively as she went with sweeping skirts towards the hearth. "I never could abide that sleek, precocious little cat!" she exclaimed. She stood tensely, staring down upon the leaping flames while an awkward silence hung in the room. "Ghislaine," she called presently, making an imperious little beckoning click with her fingers.

"Madam?" Ghislaine, all frightened repentance, was instantly at her side.

"You think—that Margaret of Clare never realized?" she asked so softly that no one else could hear.

"I am sure of it. She always had a kind of naïvety about her which armoured her against gossip, and she worshipped him."

"That is why it was so wicked of Eleanor. To destroy the thing her sister loved. To destroy it forever. Even his murderers had not done that. It would have been better and more merciful had Margaret gone to her new marriage bed with loathing, keeping a shining image in her heart." Ghislaine saw that the Queen's eyes were closed, her forehead bowed against the cold stone of the chimneypiece. "I know! I know whereof I speak!" she kept murmuring inexplicably. But when at last she turned the pupils of the eyes were bright pinpoints of anger, and her lovely mouth was hard. "Send the others away, Ghislaine—all but Bringnette. And have one of the pages see if the Lady Eleanor of Clare is anywhere about the palace. Bring her to me, and I will make her rue the day she broke the brightness of another woman's dream."

"Yes, Madam," said Ghislaine, wishing she had never spoken so unguardedly. She had supposed that the Queen would be hurt by her words—so hurt and humiliated that she might even send her away. And surely, she deserved it. Old Bringnette, with her sharp warning frown, must have thought so. For had she not blurted out the thing which was never spoken of by those who loved the Queen? The thing which everybody but fond, foolish Margaret had always known. Yet the Queen had not upbraided her, and somehow Ghislaine sensed that although her mistress's humiliation remained, she was no longer tearingly hurt by past memories.

And when Eleanor of Clare was found she came readily, with no sign of fear or reluctance; but rather, one would have said, with some strange secret elation. But once in the Queen's presence she was far too sly to show it. With clasped hands and downcast eyes she listened humbly to the flaying words of her uncle's French wife. She never once excused herself or answered back. She kept her enjoyment until the last, savouring the anticipation of it as one might push some tit-bit of food to the side of one's plate. She was a Plantagenet, like Margaret, and she could afford to wait. Only at the end of her royal aunt's tirade did she open her cruel little mouth to speak.

"Did you know that the King has promised my husband the whole of Glamorganshire and several strong castles including Ludlow!" she asked, looking up at last.

The triumph was hers. Clearly Queen Isabel did not know. And nothing could have displeased her more. Neither dared she harangue the wealthy Lady Despenser further.

Eleanor Despenser allowed herself time to look round at the amazed faces of the two women who had been allowed to overhear her dressing-down, and to savour her patiently awaited moment. Then she added insolently, "*And* he has promised to give him Gilbert's earldom."

With the Queen's covertly watching women she saw Isabel's face whiten with anger. With hate or love, according to their allegiance, they all noticed the trembling of her hands. All three of them were forced to admire her proud effort at self-control. "Then I wish you and your husband joy of it, and of each other," she managed to say, realizing how her just rebuke had been made a mockery of. "It grows dark, no doubt, along the stairs and passages. Ghislaine will go with you to your apartments."

"I would like to whip the smirk from her meek, sallow face!" broke forth Bringnette, before the door was well closed behind them. "No two sisters were ever more unlike than she and this day's sweet bride."

"Had you heard rumour of—this second marriage—before, Bringnette?"

"No, or I would have warned your Grace." The old lady went down on stiff joints to gather up the scattered silks, grumbling to herself the while. "Eleanor Plantagenet and that upstart Despenser! A pretty pair they make."

"A *dangerous* pair." Isabel began to walk thoughtfully about the room, trying to estimate how grave the danger might be to her hardly won influence over Edward. The danger of two clever people so ill-disposed towards herself, so close to the King's ear, now being united in their mutual ambitions. "Before he left me for this last campaign—a few months ago even—Edward would not have done this without telling me," she thought. "*Mon Dieu*, how high the Despensers grow!"

The servants were bringing in lights and soon Robert le Messager came, bowing before her and asking if she would be pleased to join the hunt over Nutting Hill on the morrow. While scarcely heeding his suggestion she was glad of his presence, welcoming him unceremoniously as one who could ever be counted on as an ally. "Robert," she said, pursuing her thought, "what was the extent of the late Gilbert of Clare's possessions?"

"Immense, Madam. Except for milord Pembroke's lands the Clares and the Mortimers between them owned most of Wales and the border marches."

"The county of Gloucester, of course——"

"And Hertfordshire and all their lands in Ireland."

"Send for that map your late King had made and show me." Almost from habit she glanced up at him sideways with an effective trick of feminine allure. "You forget I am a Frenchwoman. I still find your little patchwork counties confusing."

When the map was brought and unrolled across a table they pored over it together, but their touching shoulders and the closeness of their bent heads no longer stirred the old delicious excitement in her blood. Her whole mind was absorbed by the names and contours on the parchment which he held outspread before her. "Ludlow," she read, picking out the strong Shropshire castle. "Surely that should be Mortimer land?"

"I have heard my father say that it came to them through marriage with the Genvilles, and that the Mortimers grew strong and kept the border well throughout the last two reigns. I suppose that bit by bit they have taken over the supremacy. There have been two minorities in the Clare family, and neither the late Earl Gilbert, nor Piers Gaveston when he married the Lady Margaret, bore milord Mortimer any ill-will. They were all very good friends."

"And now the King is intending to give Ludlow to the Despenser." Isabel straightened herself and faced the man who had so adoringly championed her but whose body no longer stirred her. "Robert, do you know that he is also to get Gilbert of Gloucester's title and half the inheritance?"

The young man busied himself rolling up the map again. "I had heard a rumour of it," he admitted harshly.

"And you bear him no more liking than I do?"

"Madam, you know that I do not. Nor any man whose very breathing bodes you ill."

"Bodes me ill? What do you mean, Robert?" she asked, with fear in her voice.

He shrugged, but would not meet her eyes. "He grows too strong, even without his royal marriage."

"But Roger Mortimer is stronger," she said quickly.

"He certainly knows how to hold his own."

Isabel smiled, a warm joy about her heart. "I have been told that before."

"All men know it to be true, Madam. But hitherto he has held land *for* the King. I do not see how even he can hold what the King desires to take from him."

"Not unless he is warned."

Their eyes met then in mutual understanding and Isabel, the Queen, moved closer so that had he wished she would have stood within the circle of his arms. Her slender fingers played familiarly with a button at his breast. But a movement which once had sprung from her own ill-suppressed desire was now a calculated wile to arouse his, and so strengthen her plea. "There is a small thing you could do for me—you, who always said that you would die for me."

"Your Grace has but to tell me."

"You could send Mortimer fair warning by some trusty messenger."

He made no attempt to hold her but a slow confederative grin curved his pleasant mouth. "And so assure Hugh Despenser of a harsh welcome when he rides west with his insufferable bride to grab her lands in Wales?" he said with relish. Although he was no longer crazily in love with her, although he was the kind of man whose fine boast that he would escape from the Tower had come to naught, he was still her man, eager to protect her from all enemies and even from the follies of the King. "Thank you, dear Robert," she said, turning from him with a dazzling smile.

No harm, she thought, in letting him know the ill she wished for Hugh Despenser. Of the good fortune she wished for Roger Mortimer he had no inkling. Perhaps, if he had, he would not do this thing for her. Perhaps Ghislaine's charms had not so far cured his jealousy. But there was one wish she could not bring herself to hide. The strong, attractive border lord must know that it was she, Isabel the Queen, who had thought to warn him. He must be reminded of her beauty, of their intimate smile across a crowded hall and his impertinent words about a partnership. And here was the opportunity. Did he, she wondered, still remember her? Sallying forth with his men from some grim border castle, or riding home from hunting at eventide, did he sometimes catch himself thinking of her, as she so often thought of him?

"Send whatever trusty messenger you like," she said. "But tell him to say to milord Mortimer that he comes from the Queen. You have already suffered imprisonment for me, dear Robert, and I would not have you risk more. And if the King or Hugh Despenser should come to hear of it at least no one will dare to send me, the King of France's sister, to the Tower!"

After le Messager had gone Isabel sat thinking of the man whom they were warning, and—with her usual lack of self-deception— realizing how hard she had hitherto tried to deny herself that pleasure. Upon reflection she feared that her impulsive interference might prove to be ill-judged. Was it perhaps foolish to try to foster remembrance in a man whose life and duty lay so far away? Yet could any woman's foolishness equal the King's in provoking such a man to wrath? She began to realize, too, how little she knew of Mortimer save his public reputation which appealed to her. And that her loyalty should lie solely with her husband at whose wishes she had struck an underhand blow.

With his usual love of family gatherings, Edward had insisted upon the May Queen joining them for Christmas. But the journey had fatigued her and they had both noticed how often she excused herself from all the merry-making and rested quietly in her room. And Isabel, frightened at what she had done, made occasion to visit her there alone and to take her into her confidence.

"Of course, Hugh Despenser inheriting all that land in Wales is bound to make trouble. But the Mortimers would have heard soon enough—as soon as the settlement is made public," said Marguerite, frankly horrified. "Surely it was undignified—and disloyal—for you, the Queen, to warn Mortimer secretly?"

"I should not have done so," Isabel defended herself, "had Edward not been underhand with me."

"Probably he did not tell you because he knows how much you dislike Hugh Despenser."

"Who does not?"

"Could it not be partly jealousy, *ma mie*? He complained to me once that you hated *all* his friends."

Isabel moved away to her aunt's prie-dieu and began turning over the illuminated pages of her Book of Hours. "Oddly enough, in the end, I did not hate Gaveston," she admitted, in a half-shamed voice.

"I am glad. God knows he needed your forgiveness!" The May Queen leaned back in her chair, a little weary of her relatives' affairs. "But with any kind of person whom Edward loves it is the same. He goes to such extremes. He is beginning to behave like that now about Hugh Despenser. Advancing him in every possible way, marrying him into the blood royal, lavishing gifts upon him as he did upon Piers Gaveston."

Isabel, standing idly by the window, turned sharply. Her eyes probed her aunt's pale face. "As he did upon Gaveston." The words repeated themselves like a sudden warning in her brain. "Not that! Dear God, not that!" she prayed in momentary panic. But of course it could not be. The idea was absurd. What vestige had quiet, clever, sallow Hugh of Piers's radiant charm?

"Of course, the Despensers, father and son, have both been useful to him." Marguerite pulled herself together and went on a shade too quickly, putting the whole matter on a basis of services rendered, as if reading her unfortunate niece's thoughts. "Their policy is sound and sane if only the country as a whole would accept it, and Edward has the sense to see it. If they ever succeed in getting our laws made and enforced by a Parliament in which land-owners and commons are fairly represented, it would stop all this wrangling between the powerful barons and provide a basis for some sort of law and order. Gaveston may have fought for the King, but Hugh Despenser serves him as statesman."

"I prefer men who fight," said Isabel shortly. "And if Hugh Despenser lays claim to a foot of Mortimer land he will *have* to fight. Roger Mortimer knows how to hold his own."

The toss of her head and the pride in her voice betrayed her. The May Queen sighed and sat in silence for a while. "You know that the man is married?" she asked at length, in a carefully expressionless voice.

She saw Isabel's back go suddenly rigid, her fingers stop turning the pages. "No. No, I didn't," she answered almost lightly, after the briefest pause. "But what difference should that make to me?"

"None at all. I just wondered if you knew."

"Who is she—Mortimer's wife?"

"A woman of French descent like ourselves. Joan de Genville. A granddaughter of Hugh the Twelfth of Linsignon."

Isabel closed the great leather-bound Book of Hours very carefully. She seemed to be a long time fastening the metal clasp. "Marguerite," she said, still bending over it.

"*Ma chère?*"

"Is she very beautiful?"

"I have no idea. I have never seen her. They live so far away from court." She smiled suddenly, and held out an inviting hand. "Perhaps, dear Isabel, it is as well."

Isabel came and took her hand, smiling back at her without offence. "Yes. Particularly as I have played the dutiful wife so well that I believe myself to be with child again."

"My dear! What a success you have made of your married life—in spite of everything!" Because of her weakness there were tears of gratitude in Marguerite's eyes.

Forgetful of all queenly dignity, Isabel pulled up a stool beside her. "It is to be hoped there will be enough food for him!" she said laughingly. "Hawtayne, my steward, says the sheriffs were making the people line up for loaves in Pie Lane yesterday. One loaf to a family."

"You seem very sure you will produce yet another son!"

They were laughing and happy again, more like sisters than aunt and niece. "*A vrai dire, je voudrai une fille cette fois,*" said Isabel. "A small daughter to name for you. You know, Marguerite, when I look back over the years since I came to England I can see that I should have been a much more hateful person had you not been here."

"You have had much to put up with, *ma chère.*"

"You admit it now?"

"Now that I am going away." The May Queen slid her loose rings up and down the thin fingers in her lap as she looked back through the strange disturbed years of her widowhood. "If I have sometimes seemed hard it is because I have believed that your inherent generosity of heart would ultimately triumph over the hurts life offered you. But who are any of us to play the mentor who have not come young and eager to our marriages—to find a Gaveston?"

When Marguerite returned to Wiltshire Edward himself picked out the steadiest horses in his stable to bear her litter and young Ned proved his love for her by offering his precious wooden horse *Cher Ami*, which she tactfully refused on the grounds that he looked so ferocious that everyone would mistake him for a seasoned war-horse. All the family went out into the courtyard to bid her good-bye. "Are you sure you are strong enough to make the journey, *ma belle-mère?*" asked Edward with compunction.

"Do not be anxious for me," she reassured him. "Edmund will ride with me as far as Windsor."

How she loves that younger son of hers, though he is weak like his half-brother, the King, thought Isabel. "Will you not change your mind and stay with us?" she urged.

"I have things to see to at Marlborough Castle, my loves."

"What sort of things?" piped Ned.

"Affairs of my estate to set in order."

Impulsively Isabel reached through the gay curtains of the litter and clung to her, her cheeks wet with tears. "Marlborough—Brotherton—Leeds. How often have you stayed away from us in one or other of them. But never before have I minded your going so much."

King and Prince stood hand in hand, waving. "Feed yourself up on good Wiltshire fare, dear woman, and come back to us soon," called Edward teasingly, as grooms and horses began to move. "You know that nothing ever goes right for any of us without you."

CHAPTER 17

SOON AFTER the May Queen's departure news came that the Bruce had taken the strong border town of Berwick, and even Edward of Caernarvon could no longer go on frittering his time away with the northern gateway of his kingdom in the hands of the enemy. Once more Thomas of Lancaster refused to lead the expedition on the grounds that his nephew had made little attempt to comply with the ordinances. "Particularly the clause in which he promised to get rid of bad advisers," he had said, thrusting at the man who had been brought into the circle of the royal family and usurped the place in the King's counsels which he, a Plantagenet, should have had. And so Edward had been forced to bestir himself and, mustering what men he could, march north again.

"And while I am kept busy with these marauding Scots your brother seizes the opportunity to be awkward about Guienne," he had complained to Isabel, handing her a letter from the King of France.

Since the King of France was now her brother Charles, Isabel read it with avidity, hoping for home news. But the letter was brief and business-like. "He merely mentions that it is high time you crossed the Channel again to do homage for it."

"Did I not do so at the time of our marriage?"

"But that was to my father. You have never done homage for it to Charles." Isabel sighed, sick for a sight of home. "It would be lovely to be in Paris with all this insular bickering left behind."

"My dear Isabel, devoted as you are to Charles, surely you can see that I cannot be in two places at once."

It was only too true. But Isabel's nimble mind saw other possibilities in the problem. "You could perhaps send someone in your place to put your cause to Charles. To placate him, and yet insist that he leaves the question of Guienne until you are free to come. Someone both tactful and strong."

Edward was sitting beside her, stroking Minette's soft fur as the cat lay curled on her lap. When in her beguiling presence he still heeded her advice. "It is a thought," he said. "But whom among all these jealous curs can I trust, save Pembroke and those who come north with me?"

Isabel leaned against him and took his hand between her own. "Were it not that I bear your child within me I would go myself," she said regretfully.

"And who could be a more persuasive messenger?" he said, bending to kiss the tip of her short little nose. She could not tell if he took the idea seriously or not, but at that moment it rooted itself in her own mind as an advantageous suggestion to be stored against some future crisis. "Then what about that border lord whom you left to keep the peace on the western marches when you went to Stirling?"

"Roger Mortimer of Wigmore? Why, yes, if he has at last subdued his unruly vassals in Ireland."

"Surely his uncle—the elder Mortimer of Chirk—could see to that?"

"I will speak of it to Hugh Despenser."

Isabel pouted and shrugged away from his encircling arm. "Can you not even arrange something with my brother without that man's approval? Can you not send Mortimer because *I* suggest it?"

Because he would be leaving her within a few hours and because she was pregnant he assured her she was cleverer than all his councillors put together, and then and there dispatched Nicholas Huggate, his chief clerk, to Wigmore.

"I will tell Roger to bring Sir Griffin's boy with him when he comes," he said, alluding to a Welsh knight who had been killed at Bannockburn. "The boy is spirited and not much older than Ned, and should be good company for him while I am away. You remember how he fretted last time."

"Milord Mortimer can deliver the child into my care," agreed Isabel, with a pleased secret smile.

But after Edward had gone the days of her confinement dragged slowly. There were no knights left to tilt at tournaments, and no one seemed to have the heart to devise plays or pageants any more. She seldom went into London because the bells of all the city churches seemed to be for ever tolling for the dead instead of pealing joyously to welcome her. Crowds no longer lined the streets with cheerful shouting. The people's faces were pinched with anxiety and hunger, their thoughts turned inward upon their own misery and upon the means of finding the next meal for their families. Ships were moored idly by deserted wharves. The wool trade with Flanders was at a standstill because so many sheep had died for lack of pasture, and in the empty warehouses men and boys were catching rats for food. "It will be our helpless babies next," whispered parents of the better sort, keeping careful watch on them because of the horrible rumours they had heard.

"Just when your Grace needs cheer and good food most," lamented Bringnette.

But Isabel the Queen did not go short for long. When Roger

Mortimer rode through London on his way to take ship from Dover to Bordeaux a convoy of carefully covered wagons was driven into the palace yard. Hungry as the citizens of London were, and suspecting that the wagons were piled high with food, they dared not touch or pilfer since the fierce, dark little Welshmen in charge of them wore the great border lord's badge. The wagons were their master's gift to the Queen. Roger Mortimer's wordless answer to her friendly warning. "I will see that you do not starve," he had promised, half in jest, that overweening day when Edward had reviewed his troops before the Scottish victory at Bannockburn. That had been long before the famine in England became so serious, but he had kept his word. And Isabel felt warmly happy and cared for as she watched her servants unload the welcome sacks of flour, the tubs of salted meat, the haunches of mountain venison, the cheeses and the bowls of honey. She bade her steward count it all and divide it out among her household and, since she could not share it with the May Queen, she gave some of it to the good Grey Friars at Newgate, whose church Marguerite had built, so that they might distribute it among the most desperately poor and sick.

But although Mortimer lodged a night in London she would not see him, being already clumsy in her pregnancy and knowing herself to be pallid with poor living. "I would have him remember me always as beautiful," she decided reluctantly, "lest he compare me unfavourably with that French wife of his." Like a girl in love, she would have liked to talk about him to one of her ladies, but because she was the Queen and married she was too proud to do so. Even with Marguerite she was reticent, although she knew that her aunt had guessed at the strange attraction the man had for her. All the day of his departure she sat reading love poems by a window which overlooked the courtyard, telling other people that the light was better there, and telling herself she was a fool. But although the wagons rumbled away she saw nothing of him. Only when the sun was high in the heavens did she learn that he had ridden out of the palace before dawn—furious, she hoped, because she would not see him.

The boy Griffin had been brought to her, and she sought to dispel her disappointment by watching him and her own two boys at play. Ned was delighted with him because he was strong and bigger than himself, and had picked up thrilling information about training war-horses and discharging iron arrows by means of some modern explosive. But she only found herself still further reminded of Roger Mortimer because the sturdy war orphan seemed to have developed an immense hero-worship for him during their journey from Wales, and was for ever showing Ned and small John of Eltham how milord Mortimer vaulted into his saddle, how milord Mortimer bellowed an order so that it could be heard across the river Severn, or how milord Mortimer rounded up deer in some stupid Englishman's park whenever his men were hungry.

"After my baby is born I will go north to join Edward and forget all about the wretched, over-bearing man," she told herself virtuously, and called Ned away from his amateur soldiering to gather the very best bunch of rosemary he could find in the herb garden to sweeten a cushion she was embroidering for Marguerite. "We will send it to her with our special love for St. Valentine's Day," she told him, remembering how the boy's grandfather, grim warrior as he was, had always sent his second wife a love token on that day; and how Marguerite, although widowed so young, always insisted "When Edward died, all men died for me."

But soon after the cushion was dispatched with so much love news came that the May Queen was desperately ill. The wasting sickness kept her helpless in her bed and the physicians gave little hope. Messages were immediately sent to Thomas and Edmund Plantagenet, but they were away on the Scottish border. Isabel would have given anything to go to her, but her own hour was at hand. And by the time her daughter was born, news had come from Marlborough castle that the beloved May Queen was dead.

She had died on St. Valentine's Day with her head on the sweet-scented cushion, and Isabel and small Ned could only be thankful that she had received their message of love.

Isabel held her new girl-child to her heart, for some strange reason finding more comfort in her than she had found in either of her sons. Perhaps it was because she herself had become more mature.

"Where is the dear lady to be buried?" asked Bringnette.

"In her own Grey Friars church, and clad in a habit of the Franciscan order as she always wished. Her elder son is having her body brought to London, and the King has ordered yards and yards of that lovely striped lucca silk to cover her coffin on the journey. The very best the Italian merchants can produce."

"Why yards and yards, Madam?" asked Ghislaine, taking the baby to the wet nurse to be fed.

"It seems it is a custom in this country for each church where the bier rests for a night to keep the pall, so if it is a long journey several palls are needed," Isabel told her listlessly.

"He loved her as though she really *were* his mother," sighed Bringnette.

"Say rather as an elder sister. Poor sweet, she was only thirty-six—not so many years older than I. And how I shall live without her——" Isabel broke down then and Bringnette hastened to comfort her. "There, there, my hinny. *Le bon Dieu* has given you the babe instead. Perhaps that is why, in His mercy, He sent you a daughter."

"Then we will call her Marguerite," decided Isabel.

But to her grief she was not permitted to do so. Sincerely as he mourned his stepmother, Edward insisted that his first daughter should be called Eleanor after his niece, and to the new Lady Despenser must go the honour of standing sponsor for her at the font. "It is to please Hugh Despenser, but if Edward were here I could still persuade him," Isabel raged privately to Bringnette. As it was she dared not disobey the King's instructions, and had to endure his niece's ill-concealed triumph at the christening.

As soon as she was strong enough she was not sorry to travel north again, hoping to counteract the younger Despenser's influence. This time she went with her young family to Brotherton, which Marguerite had loved so well and which, by the arrangement made at their joint betrothal, had now become part of her own dowry. The walls were marvellously strong and the garrison loyal, as Marguerite had told her. Yet while she was there the incredible thing happened. The Black Douglas swooped southwards secretly with ten thousand men hoping to take her and the young heir of England as hostages. It was one of his daring plans which might have succeeded by its very unexpectedness. "Be good, or the Black Douglas will get you!" was a common enough threat made by all mothers to disobedient children, but it was only those north of Yorkshire who experienced any real terror when they said it. To be afraid of such a thing had never occurred to Isabel, yet when she heard of the attempt she realized with horror that had the much-feared man got hold of Ned the Scots could have dictated any terms they liked to his devoted father.

It seemed almost incredible when Robert le Messager came

thudding over the drawbridge to tell the Constable of Brotherton that Douglas's men had spent the previous night encamped in a wood only a few miles from their walls. A Scotsman sent to spy out the approaches to the castle had been captured by a mightily surprised hunting party, it seemed, and dragged before the Archbishop of York. At first he had pretended he did not understand the English tongue but finally, to save himself from torture, the man told the truth and was called an ingenious liar for his pains, until he directed them to the wood to see for themselves. The Douglas, finding himself discovered, had made off as silently as he had come, but not before every man who could be spared in York had been rushed to Brotherton to bring the Queen and her household away. So urgent had their concern been for her and for her children that half her possessions had been left behind, and after a night's rest in the Archbishop's palace she had been taken for greater safety to Nottingham, that massive stronghold in the very centre of England which she hated then and was sure she always would hate. "There is something sinister—something ill-omened—about this place," she had said, shivering and drawing her cloak about her as le Messager showed her round the battlements.

"Nothing half so sinister as might have happened at Brotherton," he answered laughingly, to rally her.

Isabel leaned against a merlon of the wall to look over the sunlit countryside. She was trying to rid herself of the foolish antipathy she felt towards the place and to regain her usual gaiety. "Well, it did not happen and your Ghislaine is safe," she teased. "And now instead of being off at the wars you will see her daily again, being set in charge of us by milord Archbishop's express commands."

"It was of your Grace's safety we have all been thinking," he replied stiffly. But she saw the colour mount beneath his sun-tan and wickedly enjoyed the embarrassment of a man whose sworn affections had shifted.

"And the country's," she added, more seriously. "With the King's heir an hostage I imagine the campaign would have come to an end."

"Had the Douglas taken your Grace and the Prince away into the Highlands I doubt if we could ever have found you."

"You are right, Robert, and do not think I am ungrateful— although I dare swear the Scots king would have treated us honourably. Milord Archbishop's parting words to me were, 'You should make a pilgrimage to the sainted Becket's tomb at Canterbury, my child, to thank God for such a timely deliverance.'"

They stood there in the morning sunlight, with the wind ruffling her becoming coif and his curly hair. For the moment they were two young people in serious mood rather than Queen and household officer, and their minds were quick to mutual understanding as they had always been. Presently le Messager glanced at her and said, "You know what men are saying?" and when she looked back at him questioningly and shook her head he added gravely, "I should be an ill friend were I not to tell you, even though you may hate me for it."

They were away from court formality, high above the city with the swallows circling about them. They found it easy to speak with complete naturalness, and she knew his reckless passion for the truth. "I could never hate you, Robert, even though you have transferred your heart to Ghislaine. What are they saying?"

"That the Earl of Lancaster had a hand in it."

She swung round on him then with a flash of anger. "My own uncle! Oh, come, Robert—you are as gullible as young Edmund of Kent. My uncle Thomas has always made so much of me, so championed me. Why should he wish to be unfriendly towards me now?"

"Probably he does not. But he could wish still more to be friendly with the Scots."

"Why?" Amazed as she was, Isabel knew that he would not willingly misinform her out of any personal enmity.

Le Messager shrugged. "To oppose the advice of Hugh Despenser whom he loathes, perhaps. Or to create a powerful party of his own. After all, he is a grandson of the third Henry and *should* be a power in the country."

"It is true that he has twice refused to fight them," murmured Isabel, thinking that her master-of-horse might not be so gullible after all. And she recalled how Lancaster had been present when Marguerite had urged her to go to Brotherton, and how he had veered round from wanting to make a display of her to the Londoners and seemed quite glad for her to go. "And it does seem strange that the Scots have spared his land when Northumberland and Cumberland have both been ravaged," she added thoughtfully.

"That is what the Despensers are taking care to point out to the King."

"And Edward will believe anything of him since he let Gaveston fall into Warwick's vengeful hands."

Her master-of-horse waited until a passing sentry had disappeared out of earshot round the bend of the next embrasure of the wall. "They are telling the King that Lancaster was paid to betray the times and routes of your Grace's movements to the Scots. They even name the figure." As she stared at him in shocked silence he named it himself. "Forty thousand pounds." At the sound of more approaching footsteps he gathered up her cloak and lowered his voice. "I suppose that having the laugh over England after all these years would have been cheap at the price."

Isabel was too stunned to speak. She turned and allowed him to escort her down the dark winding stairs to her apartments. She began to wonder whether she had so much to be thankful for after all. Life might have been pleasanter in the hands of the chivalrous Bruce than among her own relatives and her husband's countrymen. "If I go on a pilgrimage to Canterbury it will be mostly for other reasons," she thought. "To pray for the soul of by beloved Marguerite, and to beg for strength to stop hankering after that capable, over-bearing Welshman."

CHAPTER 18

ISABEL hated every hour of her sojourn at Nottingham. The very efficiency of that key fortress of the Midlands oppressed her. "*Why* should I feel it to be so full of foreboding?" she asked petulantly, staring down into the cleanly kept bailey.

"It is probably only the result of the shock your Grace sustained at Brotherton, and all the scurry and anxiety afterwards," suggested Bringnette, who had herself been badly upset by it. "Such experiences are apt to make one fanciful."

And when the King at last came to join them he, too, was all concern for her. He blamed himself for having sent for her for his own pleasure. "To think that that fool of an Archbishop refused to believe your danger even when he was told," he kept saying, "and that you might all have been taken as hostages!" But Isabel noticed that his gaze was generally on Ned when he spoke of it, and that he scarcely let the boy out of his sight. "All the same I would have you make a pilgrimage to Canterbury on my account as well as your own. And I will have the children cared for here until I am able to return to Westminster."

"Then I pray you keep Robert le Messager to be in charge of them. Going through the peaceful south I shall not need him."

"I will. But, do not tire yourself, my sweet."

"I can stay and rest awhile at Leeds castle now it is my own," she said. "Hitherto I have only seen the lovely place in passing on our way home from France."

"Then send Lady Badlesmere word to have it in readiness to receive you. Her husband is away, I hear. Somewhere with Thomas of Lancaster."

Half the years of Isabel's marriage seemed to have been spent moving from castle to castle, first because of the barons' jealous quarrels over Gaveston and more recently on account of these everlasting Scottish wars. The colourful days of plays and pageants and tournaments, the summer jaunts by river in her barge, and the winter evenings spent with music and dancing in the great hall at Westminster or Windsor all seemed to belong to some former, brighter existence. But at the moment she was so out of tune with gaiety that she scarcely regretted them. The loss of Marguerite had cast a lasting shadow over her life and she was not sorry to be going quietly to Canterbury to spend contemplative hours in the solemn hush of the vast old cathedral. She bade Edward good-bye and set forth from Nottingham in the rich sadness of a mild October. And she went with sincere intent to sort out the muddled values of her mind, to seek strength to control the swift surges of her lusts and animosities and to live more gently, as Marguerite would have wished.

Because she was going humbly as a pilgrim and because she was heartily sick of the sight of men-at-arms she rode beneath russet beech trees and along nut-laden lanes with only a small company of women and servants, having sent John de Jargemoc, her almoner, on ahead to warn Lady Badlesmere of her coming.

"The sharp-nosed old dragon will be putting the whole household through their paces," Isabel overheard Ghislaine say laughingly to another of the younger women.

"Arriving as the new owner of any place calls for so much tact," she herself confided to Bringnette, being the type of mistress who took pains to make herself liked.

"To be sure, Madam, we could have wished for a sweeter hostess," agreed Bringnette, who had frequently had to endure Lady Badlesmere's ill-tempered jealousy.

"If only we could have arrived to find the May Queen waiting to welcome us!" sighed Isabel. But, like the rest of them, she was pleasantly tired after the ride, and Leeds castle was looking its loveliest. The grey towers were silhouetted against a pale lemon sunset, with long evening shadows lying across the surrounding meadows, and the bright reflection of the sky still gilding the brooding stillness of the lake where a few belated waterlilies were cupped on the flat green tables of their leaves.

"It is like a fairy castle out of some old Provençal legend!" exclaimed Ghislaine ecstatically. "So peaceful, so inviting."

The Queen and her ladies reined in their tired horses and waited in a bright-hued bunch at the far end of the long causeway which led across the lake to the main gateway. They were quite content to survey the pleasing scene and to enjoy the prospect of a good supper. But although they could see the westering sunlight glinting on the helmets of men-at-arms moving about the battlements, as yet no one had thought to haul down the Badlesmere standard floating aggressively from the keep, and the great oak doors deep in their stone archway still remained shut.

"They are too busy getting out the best bed linen and basting the boar to notice us," suggested a young ward of Edward's.

"And perhaps old Baddy herself is stuck half in and half out of that tight puce velvet we always had to help her fasten," giggled a very young tiring woman irreverently.

Isabel, full of fellow-feeling, pretended not to hear the impertinence and ordered her herald to sound a fanfare. But when the great doors were opened at last and the drawbridge lowered it was neither chatelaine nor seneschal who stood there to receive them— only fat old John de Jargemoc, his hands fidgeting nervously with the cord of his habit and his face unusually red against the silvery hair encircling his tonsure. He stood uncertain between a couple of joking men-at-arms, then began to waddle quickly out across the causeway while, to the mystification of the waiting party at the other end, the gates closed again behind him. Aware of the expectant hush and of all the curious eyes upon him, he went down on his knees in the dust beside the Queen's horse. "Madam," he gasped, sorely out of breath, "'shamed am I to bring so impudent an answer——"

"From Lady Badlesmere? Is she sick?"

"Far from it, your Grace. She shouted at me from an upper window. 'While my lord is away I open the castle to none without his orders,' she bawled. 'Go tell the Queen that if it be a night's lodging she is wanting she had best seek it elsewhere.'"

In the still evening air his incredible message was audible to all, and horrified amazement held them still as statues. Never had they imagined that any person would dare speak so to a King or Queen. Isabel's face flushed as if some varlet had struck her, then paled to anger. "Ride forward to my gates and demand that they be opened in the King's name," she ordered briefly. "What we have hitherto asked with courtesy we now demand." And setting her horse in motion she fearlessly led the way. Her retinue crowded after her. In their fervour some of the men-servants even took it upon themselves to scramble before her that they might batter at the door, and young Thomeline, who was never far from his mistress's side, dodged between them to hold her bridle lest her horse should shy or stumble on the rough stones. But when the company were half-way across they were startled by a sharp whirring sound through the air and, before the Queen could recall them, half a dozen of her men were pierced by a slick rain of arrows from the battlements. Being completely unarmed, they dropped dead where they fell, blocking the narrow causeway, and the arrow which came nearest to her pierced her Scottish songster's heart. It must have been a brave man or an exceptionally confident marksman who had dared to aim at a target so near the Queen. Her horse reared, almost throwing her, and as the pawing hoofs came back to earth again Isabel found herself staring down at the dead face of Thomeline, whom she had come to love. He was lying spreadeagled on his back, his smashed lute beside him, and almost before her women's screams had ceased she saw his slender body slither over the slippery stones at the edge of the causeway and disappear with a splash into the deep water beneath the green carpet of lily pads.

So cruel and sudden had been the onslaught that Isabel sat stunned in her saddle until Goodwin Hawtayne, her steward, touched her urgently on the arm. They were a peaceful party of women on pilgrimage, not a beleaguering army, and there was nothing for it but to withdraw before more lives were lost. But grief and indignation raged in Isabel's heart. Never had she witnessed such unnecessary callousness. Never in all her pampered life had she been treated with such brusque impertinence. Where she slept that night she neither knew at the time nor remembered afterwards. In secret she wept for Thomeline and her other faithful servants, in public she appeared like an angry Medusa because of the insult offered to herself. Canterbury and all good spiritual intentions were forgotten. In the white fury of her wrath she sent immediately to tell her uncle what had occurred. Since the first day of her arrival in England he had never failed to champion her, drawing public attention to her wrongs and associating himself with her consequent popularity. She never doubted for a moment that he would rush to avenge her now. But to her amazement Lancaster took no notice of her plea. Lord Badlesmere was with him, it was said, and they were to form a party strong enough to force the King to rule according to the ordinances and to send the Despensers permanently out of the country. And so Isabel rode back to Westminster and poured out the story of Lady Badlesmere's outrage to the King. She was sure that he would sympathize with her very charmingly but had little hope that he would drag himself from his own private amusements to do anything about it. Peace was too rare a pleasure, the shameful treaty with Scotland too newly ratified. But to her fierce joy his indignation matched her own.

"It is all part of a plot. Bartholomew Badlesmere openly supports his wife's conduct," he told her after he had demanded an explanation. Through the drawn-back curtains at the end of her bed she could see him standing by her table prodding at a scent pot with one of her jewelled pins like a petulant child. "I would like to pull their castle down about their ears!"

"Except that it is mine, and that I love the place. But you *will* punish the old virago and her impudent seneschal?"

"If I had the men I would. But Badlesmere boasts openly that Leeds is well victualled and evidently they both count on your uncle coming to their aid. And my soldiers are sick of war, my sweet, and glad to get home, as I am!"

He came and sat on the bed and would have taken her into his arms, but she held him off, her mind too set upon revenge for love-making. "I do not think Uncle Thomas would go as far as that," she said. "But he deserves putting in his place. Surely you

can raise enough men to take a small castle like Leeds. And in so
just a cause. Appeal to the Londoners, Edward. You know how
they love me. And you remember how Marguerite always used
to say that the people's sense of fair play is our best protection."

She sat up in the great bed, vitally alive, with that familiar,
heady sense of her own power rising within her. Here was a
chance to put to the test that exciting conviction she had experienced when coming out from Westminster Hall after the barons
had been pardoned at her request—the conviction that the people
of England would bestir themselves for her when they would not
move for Edward. Her eyes were bright, her cheeks flushed, and
her husband was staring at her admiringly. This was her moment,
with the Despensers' away, to prove her power over him. And
over them. "If I ride out and appeal to them I believe the Londoners will rise as one man," she said.

"And I myself will lead them," he promised, catching her
enthusiasm.

"And think, *mon cher*, in what a much better position you will be
afterwards with that army behind you—to turn to your own uses."

She let him take her then, surrendering with glad abandon.
She did not want to bear him another child. Since Bannockburn
she had sworn unavailingly that she would not. But her ardent
senses were too easily stormed, and her vanity appeased. She had
always seen herself as the partner of a great lover, a beautiful
woman championed by a powerful husband. Ever since adolescence it had been her unfulfilled dream. And now Edward was
stirred violently to military action, prepared seemingly to act
with the same strange, single-minded courage which he had
shown when Piers Gaveston's life was in danger. But this time
it would be for her. It was the vindication which her jealousy
had always craved.

The next morning he issued a proclamation explaining the way
in which his beloved consort had been insulted and obstructed
in the use of her own property, and mustering all men between
the ages of sixteen and sixty to join him in an expedition against
Leeds castle in Kent. And to his surprise and to Isabel's deep,
secret joy an army larger than their wildest expectations assembled, only too eager to fight on her behalf. The city of London,
where her beauty and her previous wrongs were so well known,
justified her boast and rose to a man. The King led them in
person. And although Lady Badlesmere and Walter Colepepper,

her seneschal, held out stubbornly in the hope that the Earl of Lancaster and Lord Badlesmere would relieve them, the days passed and no relief came. Clearly Lancaster, although he had not come to avenge his niece, had no intention of further affronting her. And before the last of the October leaves had fallen the castle had surrendered, and the bodies of Walter Colepepper and eleven of his men were dangling hideously on gibbets before the gate. Two of them for each of the Queen's servants who had been so wantonly shot there.

It was a vengeance to satisfy the pride of any woman. But thrilled as she was that Edward's rare ruthlessness should have been roused on her account, Isabel did not particularly want to picture them swaying and swirling there in the first winterly winds. They had but done bravely as they were bid. "It will not hurt their mistress as the fate of my poor men hurt me. The woman has no feelings," she said, thinking of poor gentle Thomeline. "Are you not going to punish the virago herself?"

"She will have plenty of time in the Tower of London to repent her rudeness to you," Edward told her.

"But why do you let her off more lightly than her men? It was she who gave the treacherous orders."

Edward had turned to look at her, surprising the hardness in her small, heart-shaped face. "My dear Isabel, you do not expect me to put women to death, do you?" he had asked, half-disgusted and half-amused. "We Plantagenets are accused of all kinds of faults, God knows, but scarcely that."

She knew that she had wanted to retaliate by making the old lady suffer, had hoped to be able to picture her overfed body dangling with the rest, and was appalled at her own wickedness. Momentarily she suspected she must have had the instincts of a murderess. But Edward was no murderer, though she had suspected him of it that night after Guy of Warwick died. The punishment he had meted out at Leeds was stern, but would be accounted in most men's eyes as just, and he himself would be thought the more of in consequence. Indeed, his stock had gone up throughout the land.

Isabel had supposed that after doing all he had set out to do he would return to her, but unaccustomed success and the size of his willing army seemed to have gone to his head. "While I have them I will use them to break up this growing opposition of Lancaster's," he wrote, and knowing that she herself had half suggested it and rejoicing in his sudden spurt of mastery she did nothing to dissuade him. Kind as Thomas of Lancaster had been to her in the past, and much as her annoyance with him had been mitigated by the fact that he had not come to the relief of Leeds castle, she wanted Edward to crush his power and reign more absolutely. It would do pompous Lancaster no harm to be shown who was master. And, as though sensing the coming conflict, men were still streaming in to join the royal cause. She was proud to know that for once the second Edward was leading them in person.

But there were two things which she had not counted on.

The first thing Edward did after his success at Leeds was to recall the Despensers to his side, and although Hugh urged him to use his unexpected force to crush Lancaster and the rest of the resurgent barons once and for all, so that for once his council upheld her own, she knew that her hour of exclusive feminine influence was over.

With the King and all his fine standards marching north-westward towards Lancashire there was nothing to do but to wait quietly for news at Westminster. And one evening after her two younger children had been brought to say goodnight and they and their nurses were gone, Aymer de Valence, Earl of Pembroke, was announced. She always enjoyed his suave and entertaining company. Guessing at her loneliness, he stayed and talked awhile, praising his godson Ned's achievements on his new pony and at the quintain, assuring her that the wool trade was gradually improving and the famine abating, speaking in his interesting way of this and that. "And now to add to this gratifying surge of loyalty on your behalf," he added, "there comes good news from France."

"Is Roger Mortimer back so soon?" she asked quickly.

"In the King's absence I met him as he passed through London yesterday."

"And he succeeded in his mission?"

Pembroke smiled, with expressively spread hands. "I imagine he is the kind of man who usually does."

"Did he get on well with my brother?"

"Very well, apparently, since King Charles has promised to withhold his hand from Guienne for a few more months, until such time as the King is free to come and do homage for it."

Isabel bent over a childish posy which small toddling Eleanor had deposited adoringly in her lap. She busied herself smoothing out each wilted petal so that the revealing torchlight no longer illuminated her face. "In the King's absence milord Mortimer did not come to see *me*," she remarked.

"He bade me make his excuses to your Grace. On arriving in London he heard of the Lady Eleanor's marriage to Hugh Despenser."

The Queen straightened herself up abruptly. "And about the lavish grants of land, I suppose?"

"He is already on his way to Wales," said Pembroke significantly, bending to pick up the posy which the suddenness of her movement jerked unheeded to the floor.

"And what now, milord?" she asked, scarcely above a whisper.

Aymer de Valence, Earl of Pembroke, the most farseeing of them all, sighed heavily. "Yet more trouble in this quarrel-racked country, *ma pauvre chère reine*," he said. "And what will be the end of it God knows, with Roger Mortimer taking part."

Long after he had bowed himself out Isabel sat there staring before her, her small strong hands gripping the mythical beasts carved on the arms of her chair. She thought of the powerful army Edward now commanded, of his sudden spurt of energy and of the part she herself had played in provoking it. She had thought with complacency of troublesome Uncle Thomas being taught a lesson. She had not said a word to deter her husband from using it to put down the power of the barons with whom she had for so many years been on good terms and whose pardon she had once obtained. But never once had it occurred to her that that very army might be used against Roger Mortimer. Never until now had she visualized the possibility of the King and his loyal border lord being on different sides. But now that Pembroke's words had shocked her into seeing that Edward's final folly must make them bitterly opposed, she knew beyond doubt whose side she was on. For much as she had enjoyed the triumph of being championed so fiercely by the King, she knew now—as she had known ever since Bannockburn—that her first wild physical love for him was dead.

"If only I had never set out on that ill-fated pilgrimage!" she thought. "That Badlesmere hag's discourtesy may well cost far more than my servants' lives and my own indignity. God knows I was in the right, but as usual I had to pursue my vengeful fury to the uttermost. And there was no Marguerite to tell me I was behaving like a fool!"

CHAPTER *19*

AFTER all, Isabel saw Roger Mortimer before he left for Wales
—hurriedly, soon after dawn, with the horses of his retinue
champing impatiently outside in the street. Almost peremptorily
he had sent Ghislaine to waken her. "I owe your Grace thanks
for warning me about Eleanor of Clare's marriage contract," he
said without preamble when she came to him. The torches had
not been lit and he was standing in the shadows so that she could
not well see his face, but he spoke in the half-angry way of a man
who hates being beholden to anybody.

Her composure was ruffled as only he could ruffle it. "And
that is why you are hurrying home to the Welsh border? Aymer
de Valence says that you and my uncle have succeeded in persuading a strong party to use force if necessary to banish the
Despensers," she said, feeling how history was repeating itself and
hurrying over the inept words like any nervous serving wench.

"What else did the King expect me to do, with Gilbert's inheritance divided at my very doorstep between two men who
hate me!"

His anger against her husband was like a tangible thing in the
shadowed room and he made no effort to hide it, seeming to take
her partnership for granted. She made no protest, but came and
seated herself nearer to him on the deep window seat. "De
Audley, the other Clare girl's new husband, I should have thought
is negligible," she said, as if considering a tactical position which
personally concerned her. "And in any case you did not seem to
mind when Piers Gaveston had Margaret's lands."

"Gaveston did not hanker after political power. He wanted
the glitter of possessions so that he might enjoy life. You of all
people should know that this Hugh Despenser is the most ambitious man in England. And it is *my* lands, *my* castles, by which
he thinks to climb." Mortimer came nearer to her, resting one
foot on the window step, beating fist into palm to emphasize his
words, and yet retaining a quality of stillness which emphasized
his strength. Although he achieved more than most men his
economy of movement matched his economy of words. "A Mortimer's command was heeded throughout Wales. We practically

ruled the country, and in return kept the King of England's borders. I could have made a mort of trouble when Robert Bruce and the Black Douglas kept him busy in Scotland. Yet we kept faith with England. But now——"

"Pembroke has no cause to like this redistribution of land either."

Mortimer laughed harshly. "Pembroke will come in with me and Hereford and Berkeley, whose castle guards the Severn Valley. But do you suppose I shall allow it to happen?"

"Men say you know how to hold what is yours."

"And if the King provokes me to it I shall know how to take what is his." He did not move or touch her, but his eyes looked into hers so boldly that she knew it was not only Edward's kingdom of which he spoke.

She rose and faced him, striving after dignity. "You forget, milord, that King Edward is my husband."

"Is he?" At sight of his contemptuous grin she felt herself cringing before the blow of what she divined he would say next. "Or is he merely the lover of H igh Despenser?"

"How dare you?" she cried.

She reached up and struck him savagely across the mouth, but he only shrugged, shaking aside her anger as a dog might shake drops of water from its coat. "Ask Pembroke. Ask that clever master-of-horse who is so enamoured of you. Ask anybody."

"Why ask them—or you——? It is I, who have lived with Edward amicably these many years and borne his children, who should know."

"He has been away from you a great deal of late," he reminded her, with a rough kind of pity.

"And so that is what men are saying—again?"

But this time she minded more that they should say it, sniggering behind their hands in palaces and taverns, than that it should be so. Roger Mortimer did not answer but watched her admiringly as she stood there tearing the King's Christmas necklace from her throat and blazing with anger because she could not shout aloud that she no longer loved the King, nor cared with whom he might consort.

"How anger becomes you, Isabel!" he said after a while. "When I devastate Glamorganshire I shall be striking for you, too. And taking vast pleasure in the fact."

He spoke as though he were her equal. As no man without royal blood had ever dared to do before. And the shock of it almost made her forget her anger. "Why tell me what you intend to do?" she asked, without hauteur.

"Have I not always said we should be partners?"

"But why trust me? How do you know that I will not warn the King—as I warned you a while ago?"

She was staring up at him, already regretting the savage red weal deepening on his weather-beaten cheek. When he took a step towards her she knew what he would do, and made no effort to stop him. He pulled her against his body so that she could feel the strong beating of his heart and, bending, crushed her mouth beneath his own. It was a long kiss of possession and surrender, and when he released her both of them were aware that it was not she who moved first. "*That* is why," he said.

She sank limply to a near-by stool. She did not know whether she loved or hated him, and at the moment it did not seem to matter. All that mattered was that he could move her as no other man ever had, and satisfy the full capacity of her senses, and that in that close and silent embrace some power of proud resistance had gone out of her. For the first time in her life she had met a man who could master her. "A woman like you was not made for that half kind of marriage," he was saying, roused to a kind of tenderness, but more controlled than she.

In this first demonstration of what they meant to each other even what he had said about Hugh Despenser seemed of small account. She knew that he was on the point of leaving her, and only things which concerned themselves, however small, had any place in her mind. "I, too, am in your debt, Roger, and—unlike you, proud Welshman—I rejoice in it," she said, smilingly pushing back a lock of hair which had escaped from her elaborate headdress. "I have not thanked you for these welcome food waggons." Even then, with their mutual defences down, she could not bring herself to tell him that all that time ago it had been his solicitude rather than the food upon which she had fed. "You *must* have cared to send them?"

He laughed and shrugged, dangerously attractive in his careless virility. "I had seen Englishwomen in Ludlow, who had managed to reach relatives over our border. All scrawny and haggard, they were, with withered breasts. I did not want your beauty to be blemished like that."

Isabel sighed with pleasure. "You remembered me then. Am I so beautiful?"

"You have a mirror, vain woman."

"It could lie. A woman can have perfect features and lack some lure which plainer women use. Her only true mirror is in men's eyes."

"Then look in mine." He pulled her up from her stool and drew her close again, but was clever enough to leave her unkissed, so that she could only assuage her hunger by learning every line which life had fashioned on his face—the heavy reddish brows, the battle scar on his left cheek, the wide and sensuous mouth. "But you will not be here to keep me convinced. You are going away," she complained. "Is Joan, your wife, very beautiful too?"

"Beautiful, but cold."

"Yet I have been told you have a son." Above her own pre-occupation she heard approaching footsteps and the voices of her women, and turned from him reluctantly. "Is it for them you hurry away from me to Wigmore before it is well light?"

A horse whinnied impatiently down in the palace yard. There was a clattering of restive hoofs in the direction of St. Margaret's Lane, and a raising of men's voices. When her women came into the room to dress her for the day, the great border lord was gathering up his gloves and swinging a fine green cloak about his shoulders. "You will soon hear why I go, Madam," he said, bending formally to kiss the Queen's hand.

And soon all England heard. While the King was proclaiming Thomas of Lancaster a traitor and preparing to do battle with him in Yorkshire, Roger Mortimer called his fellow border lords together and devastated Eleanor of Clare's property to the last acre so that when her ambitious new husband came gloatingly to take possession there was nothing but wasted pastures and burned villages to inherit. Mortimer took Newport, the capital. And four days later Cardiff, the main stronghold of all Glamorgan-shire, and then Caerphilly. The English, hearing of it, were appalled. But because of their sense of fair play and the dislike they had for the King's new favourite they were not wholly sorry.

In spite of all older loyalties, Isabel's heart sang with secret pride. Here was a man who would vindicate his own rights and dispel her enemies. But Wales was so far away and she had to wait hungrily for further news. Mortimer might have joined up with Lancaster. Fearing the King's retribution, she half hoped that he had. But the next she heard was that Edward had defeated and captured Lancaster at some place called Borough-bridge. The fact that for once he was marching at the head of his army had put heart into them, and the rumour that Lancaster had been in league with the Scots put an end to all the Earl's former popularity.

"It must be in Yorkshire because they have taken the earl to Pontefract Castle," said Isabel, consulting her husband's precious map. "I never dreamed that Edward would so decisively defeat the poor man."

"Badlesmere was with him, but he escaped," Goodwin Hawtayne told her.

"And he the cause of all the trouble," sighed Bringnette.

And a day or so later Ghislaine came into her mistress's presence with a crumpled letter in her hand and tears in her eyes. "Oh, Madam, Robert has sent me this—from Yorkshire."

"And what does he say, beyond that he loves you? Anything of real import?" Isabel spoke unkindly, being herself extremely anxious, and hurt, because she, the Queen, had had no word from Edward.

Honey-haired Ghislaine knelt on the cushion beside her, her first love letter, too precious for other eyes, crumpled against her breast. "Oh, yes, Madam. That is why I came to tell your Grace. He says that milord of Lancaster was brought from Borough-bridge to Pontefract with about a hundred of his followers. He was made to ride on a shambling white pony many hands too small for him—to make him look ridiculous—so that the people jeered. And that when he was brought to trial he kept saying 'May my God have mercy on me, for my King will have none!'"

"Brought to trial? My uncle, a Plantagenet—as much grandson of your third Henry as the King himself! To trial for *what*?"

"Treason, Madam," explained Hawtayne, seeing that the frightened, weeping girl could not speak. "It is now proven that he entered into negotiations with the Scots, hoping to gain power against the King's party and the Despensers. That he accepted forty thousand pounds to betray your Grace and milord the Prince as hostages on condition that neither of you was hurt."

Isabel rose, one jewelled hand at her throat. "But the penalty for treason is—death. Oh, Bringnette, Ghislaine—when the King rode from Leeds to intimidate those barons with a show of such splendid force I never thought it would end like this. I thought that my uncle would see reason. I pictured them both coming back together. I thought we should all be friends again. But I see now——"

She saw now that it was as it had been when Gaveston was in danger. That although the King's first eager spate of indignation and energy had been inspired by her, it was now for Hugh Despenser. His strange mind would be piteously set against all who would remove the favourite from him. "Get up, Ghislaine," she ordered. "Tell them to send one of my clerks to me with pen and paper, that I may write to the King. I must intercede for my poor uncle as I did before."

"And so successfully, Madam," murmured Ghislaine, remembering how she and the two Clare girls had been gossiping in a corner and had not shown sufficient admiration when their Queen had come back from her triumph in Westminster Hall.

But willingly as Ghislaine would have hurried on her errand Hawtayne stopped her with a gesture before she reached the door. He, too, had heard news, it appeared. "Did Sir Robert not tell you?" he asked, his plain flat face as white as it had been on the evening when he had found Dragon outside the King's bedroom.

"Tell me what, Goodwin?" said the girl, wide-eyed.

The Queen's steward made a helpless gesture with his ungainly arms and stood wretchedly before his mistress. "It is too late to write, your Grace," he said.

"Too late?" The words framed themselves almost soundlessly on the Queen's lips. "You have had some later news?"

"I was trying to bring myself to tell your Grace. It seems the King called together a few of the lords who led his army and formed them into a jury, and he himself presided over the trial in the great hall at Pontefract Castle." Hawtayne's eyes sought Bringnette's, beseeching advice. It was already rumoured about the Palace that the Queen was pregnant again since her husband's last visit and the poor man was afraid to go on lest he should shock her. But Isabel made an impatient gesture and he had no choice. "They brought in a verdict of Guilty. After all, Madam, he had taken up arms against the King and he had received that money from the Bruce. So—he was condemned to death."

Isabel rose unsteadily and Bringnette put an arm about her. "You hear what Goodwin says?" she cried. "That Edward did this—condemned my own uncle to death. Uncle Thomas was foolish and pompous and discontented, I know. But he had to put up with those upstart Despensers. And he was kind to me when I first came—when I was so shocked and unhappy." For a moment or two Isabel hid her face against Bringnette's thin breast and allowed the older woman to comfort her. Then she pulled herself together and turned with a spark of hope. "But they will bring him to London. To the Tower, no doubt. And I will be able to plead for him in person then." She looked around at the circle of devoted friends. "Why do you say nothing, Goodwin? Why do you look at me like that?"

Goodwin Hawtayne went down on his knees before her. "Because they beheaded him a few hours later—at Pontefract."

Isabel thought that the room grew dark and her women's anxious faces began to swim before her. But anger saved her from swooning. She sank weeping in her chair. "It was done purposely. The King did it purposely. So that I could not write to my brother, in France, or intercede here," she moaned, forgetful of all who could hear her. She believed that Edward was all too well aware that, had she been given but an hour's chance to do so, she would have beguiled him into sparing a man who, with all his faults, had been a part of his family life. And suddenly it occurred to her that the hated Despenser must have feared this, too, and persuaded Edward to such inhuman haste.

She wept for her uncle because he had been a link with her relatives in France and had so often formed a conversational trio with Marguerite. She ordered mourning for her ladies and for herself, although it did not suit her. But her feeling for Thomas Plantagenet was more a surface grief augmented by her indignation with Edward, and in no way comparable to her deep and lasting longing for the companionship of her aunt Marguerite. And the whole unhappy affair was swept violently from her mind when she heard that both the Mortimers, uncle and nephew, were in the Tower.

Taking advantage of the haste with which he had rid himself of Lancaster, Edward had led his victorious army further westward to punish his erstwhile border lords and allies for the humiliating blow which they had struck against Hugh Despenser. He had summoned them to his presence, but they had defied him and refused to come. But, with that strange intermittent courage and energy which had informed him when Gaveston, his former friend, had been in danger, he had forced even the Mortimers to surrender.

"These two men, Gaveston and Despenser, must be all he

really cares about," thought Isabel, tossing sleepless in her bed with all her sympathies projected towards the grim stronghold of the Tower.

CHAPTER 20

MANY times towards the end of that winter the Queen called upon her watermen to row her down-river from Westminster to Wapping stairs, and invariably as they drew level with the Tower of London she would order them to rest awhile upon their oars. Her bargemaster was amazed that she should want to make such a journey, wrapped in furs and big with child, and her women dreaded the days when the whim took her, less because of the bleak grey weather than because it meant shooting the turbulent rapids between the starlings of London Bridge. And although they knew that all skilled watermen could do it they never failed to scream as the strong tide drove them beneath the shadow of one of the narrow arches, remembering how a lady of some former Queen had once been rocked overboard in panic and drowned.

Isabel always spoke to them sharply telling them to be quiet, because their frightened jabbering disturbed her thoughts. She herself seemed scarcely to notice the dangerous moments, her gaze being fixed upon the bank to starboard for so long as the Conqueror's stronghold was in sight. It was as if she would learn every feature of its river frontage. The keep rising white and massive in the centre, the low wide watergate with slimy steps and ominous bars through which traitors were taken to their doom and through which Thames water fed the moat, and the various odd-shaped towers built strategically along the encircling walls.

"Which gloomy tower shuts in Roger Mortimer, who is used to riding all day in wind and sunshine on the Welsh mountains?" she wondered, but was far too shrewd to ask outright or show concern for him. Only when the time of her delivery drew near did she pretend to grow fanciful and frequently voiced a desire to spend her confinement in the Tower.

"But you have always said how much you hate the place. That night we had to spend there before the Coronation you complained that it was damp," Edward reminded her.

"I was but newly come from the sunshine of France, and your kingdom was at peace then. Now, with all these unending disagreements with the barons, I fear violence."

"But what cause have *you* to fear?" he had asked impatiently. "The people adore you. And surely you would find the time pass more pleasantly at Windsor or Eltham than cooped against the evil-smelling gutters of the City?"

With her gift for play-acting Isabel had managed to combine a fond look with a convincing shudder. "With you away, *mon mari*, I should feel safer in the Tower."

Other royal children had been born there, and Hugh Despenser, who seemed to have a voice in even the most domestic matters these days, was quick to second her wish. As she had foreseen, he would be only too glad to have her out of his way. And so Edward, who was usually so careful about anything concerning his children but who now seemed to care little either way, had given the necessary orders before leaving for York. Isabel's goods and chattels had been removed to the royal apartments in the Tower and in due course, to the delight of the Londoners, her second daughter had been born there. "'Joan of the Tower' people will call her, just as they call your Grace's second son 'John of Eltham,'" prophesied Ghislaine, hoping soon to marry Robert le Messager and have children of her own. "And she is the prettiest baby of them all, with her fair skin and hair reverting to true Plantagenet auburn."

At nine years old Prince Edward already had his own tutor, and Isabel had left the other children in the care of their nurses. And, reminding her steward that there would not be overmuch room, she had been careful to bring only a few of her women and such as she trusted most. The birth of her child had been only an excuse for living within the Tower precincts, and she wanted no clacking tongues or prying eyes.

And now the spring's ordeal of childbirth was over and the privy garden in the Tower was bright with summer flowers, and she walked there in the afternoon sunshine, wondering how she could make contact with Roger Mortimer and what she could do to save him from the executioner's axe. The garden was small, being confined on one side by the long, low range of royal apartments and on the other by the south-eastern section of the outer wall, guarded by the Cradle and Well towers jutting out into the moat. At either end of the apartments rose the bulk of the Salt tower and the Lantern tower, all of which she had so carefully noted from her barge. Walking in her garden, she had no view of the busy wharf outside the wall nor of the swiftly-flowing Thames such as she had from her windows above, nor could she hear any sounds of life save the mournful cry of gulls, rough seamen's voices and the harsh squeak of pulleys. She knew that people marvelled how she, who so loved gaiety, could choose to stay there.

"But with so much unrest in the country, and the poor lady not long over her fourth lying-in——"

"And she always lookin' like some lovely fragile flower——"

Only that morning she had overheard men talking thus about her as they came ashore with the armful of rushes which was the Constable's due from every Norfolk wherry bringing thatching reeds and floor rushes to London. And when the Constable's wife had voiced much the same kind of sympathy for her fragility, Isabel, remembering the May Queen's advice, had made no effort to disabuse her of the notion. When her own women offered a supporting arm or the kindly solace of their company she told them that her head ached with the heat and that she preferred to wander about the place alone. And when Edward sent a message congratulating her upon the birth of another princess for the European marriage market, and suggesting that she might now return to Westminster, she had sent back word that she did not yet feel strong enough to make the move. Seizing upon a complaint which need show no symptoms, she had described nights of sleeplessness and the good physician Bramtoft had prescribed a potion made from crushed poppy seeds. "It is a cure which our Crusaders brought back from the Holy Land," he told her. "And vastly potent, since the Saracens use this opiate for deadening the pain of their wounded when they have to sever a gangrened limb. I do assure you, Madam, that having taken a few drops of this soporific draught your Grace will enjoy a sound and happy sleep as soon as head touches pillow." Isabel had thanked him languidly and each night when the potion was brought she had managed, with Bringnette's connivance, to hide the phial beneath her pillow or slip it into a corner of her jewel casket.

And now her various ruses had given her time to act. Edward was away in York and the windows of his apartments, stretching at right angles to her own from Lantern tower to outer wall, looked down like empty eyes upon the privy garden. And Roger

Mortimer, she knew, was somewhere within the Tower facing the thought of death. Her first move had been to invite Sir Stephen Segrave, the Constable, to sup with her and draw from him confirmation that Roger and his uncle were imprisoned in some lower part of the Lantern tower, but Sir Stephen was a man of stern and conscientious disposition and not even her subtlest wiles had succeeded in drawing from him more details of their lodgings or their well-being. But he had brought his lieutenant with him and the pleasant young man had proved far more susceptible. Utterly thrilled at being noticed by the Queen, he had mentioned that while the younger Mortimer kept his body fit by such athletic exercises as his cramped lodgings permitted, old Mortimer of Chirk seemed to be failing rapidly through poor food and the past winter's severe cold. "His nephew is much concerned for him and tries to press all the best morsels of their meat upon him," he added, encouraged by the Queen's interest. "But in their rigorous quarters there is little he can do for him, and I doubt if the old man is long for this world."

Detaining him on some pretext, Isabel had beguiled him with her sweetest smile. "In the cause of humanity could you not find means to let the poor old man have something from my own too abundant table?"

Thinking her the most charitable of ladies and flattered at being talked to privately after his superior had left, young Gerard Alspaye had promised recklessly. "There is a most efficient servant with them, a scar-faced Gascon, and the Lantern tower lies near the royal kitchen. I make no doubt he could gain entry there and if, in the performance of my duties, I should pass him on the stairs bearing an extra dish or two I could admire the view from the nearest arrow slit, if it would please your Grace."

And so food had been sent, ostensibly out of pity for an old man who was dying, but always with a surfeit for a younger man who was trying to keep up his strength. And now she walked in the sparse shade of the plane trees wondering how she could send a message with the food. Roger Mortimer must know that she was in residence. Perhaps he could even see her from his window. She stood for a long time looking towards the lower windows of the Lantern tower, but when she turned in her pensive promenade and saw the Bishop of Hereford being brought towards her, she guessed that Mortimer had already devised some contact between them.

Adam Orleton was a portly churchman whose interests, like the Earl of Hereford's, had always been linked with the Welsh marches. His very name was taken from a manor given him by the Mortimers. "For whom does the chapel bell keep tolling?" she asked hurriedly after she had greeted him, and her women had withdrawn.

"It is for the Lord of Chirk. At his age he could not be expected to support the rigorous conditions here. He went to his Maker an hour ago. He asked for me, and his nephew persuaded the Constable to let me come. And what more natural, Madam, that being in the Tower I should ask leave to wait upon your Grace?"

"Or what more fortunate?"

Isabel looked searchingly at his bland, pink face. "Your Grace may trust me and speak openly," he said, after a backward glance to assure himself that none of her people was within earshot. "I have reason to believe that it was as much for his own ends as for his uncle's spiritual needs that Roger Mortimer sent for me. He tells me that these past weeks they have received gifts from your Grace's table, and asked me to express his thanks."

"A small thing, milord. And I would do more," said Isabel, leading him to a garden seat. "Do you suppose that the King really means to put him to death?"

"The Bishop of Durham and I have pleaded for him, and at one time his Grace seemed only too willing to reduce his sentence to imprisonment. I think the King is mindful of all Mortimer's years of loyal service. I think, too, that he would not willingly destroy a man whom Piers Gaveston liked. But I fear Despenser drives him to it."

"Hugh Despenser drives us all to disloyalties we would not otherwise dream of." Even now her conscience held her back from what she would do. She must have justification, know for certain. She laid an entreating hand on the Bishop's sleeve. "Do *you*, milord, believe what they say of Hugh Despenser—and my husband?"

He did not answer her directly, but sighed and looked down at his strong, silver-buckled shoes. "Madam, our Blessed Lady knows that you have been called upon to bear much."

"Then, as a churchman, you do not condemn me if I strive to help Roger Mortimer?"

Christian conscience and political ambition struggled in the man. "So long as you do not go beyond helping him, my child."

"Then how can I see him?"

The eagerness in her voice would have betrayed to the merest moron that it was more than help she wished to give, but Adam Orleton's desire for Mortimer's release matched her own, and the pause was almost negligible before he answered. "It would seem that since the older Mortimer's death Segrave has relented. Roger is to be allowed to walk on the Well tower battlements for an hour a day before noon. There is, as your Grace knows, a small door to the Well tower from your garden. And young Alspaye, who will be on duty tomorrow, has promised to send the sentry on some errand."

Forgetful of all that she had suffered in the past, all Isabel's being became suddenly vibrant with joyous expectation for the future. "Did Roger Mortimer ask you to tell me this? Does he hope that I will contrive to be there? Alone?" she asked, her voice low and deep with excitement.

But the portly bishop would burden his conscience in the matter no further. "I am merely acquainting your Grace of the fact, since of your kindness you have shown concern for the Mortimers' welfare," he said sanctimoniously, well aware that to one of her temperament he had already said enough.

By the next day the Queen had taken a strong dislike to the pattern of a wall tapestry her women had been embroidering and, although the sun shone temptingly, kept them indoors at their frames unpicking it. Only old Bringnette was allowed to sit sunning herself on a bench with an advantageous view of the garden while the Queen of England, in a chambermaid's borrowed cloak, ran lithely as a girl to a lover's tryst up the Bell tower stairs.

And Roger Mortimer, sure of her coming, was waiting for her at the top, with the sun on his face and the wind in his hair.

"Was there ever such a courageous woman?" he whispered approvingly. He would have taken her into his arms. But, although that merlon of the battlements was deserted, she was all nerves, her senses too much engaged in listening to imaginary footsteps. "I am grieved for your loss," she whispered.

His face saddened. "My uncle was a fine old man. Never in his life had he been caged like this before. If only our inhuman gaolers had allowed him to get out into the sunshine some times——"

"And yourself?"

He stood before her in the pride of manhood, flexing his muscles. "See—do I look ill?"

She was as helplessly impressed as a peahen before its mate. "The young lieutenant——"

"Alspaye?"

"Yes. He says you do all manner of exercises."

"And now I am allowed to walk on the battlements, as you see. And my meals this week have been almost feasts. I imagine Segrave's conscience was jolted when my uncle died. He becomes quite affable. But it was really the food from your kitchen which kept me fit."

"A mere *quid pro quo* for your waggons during the famine. I will go north and entreat the King for your life. I will do any-thing——"

"And do you suppose he will remember my lifetime of useful service, with Despenser at his elbow? Save your steps, Madam, and stay to help me here. I would not have you humiliate your-self begging favours for me when I can escape."

For the first time Isabel's gaze passed from him to the solidity of stone with which they were surrounded. "Escape? From here? From the Tower of London?"

"And why not?"

"Robert le Messager boasted that he would, but only my pleas released him."

"Le Messager!" he repeated with careless contempt.

"But what man ever has since prisoners were first incarcerated here?"

"None that I know of. But no Mortimer has ever tried." The very naturalness of his arrogance fascinated her, so that when he spoke more gently and took her hands in his she allowed them to remain there. "Remember, my sweet, there must always be a first time for every achievement."

"You are crazy, Roger."

"Not if you will help me."

"But what can I do?"

"Consent to be my partner in all things, as nature intended. Come and sit here and I will tell you." He drew her down on to a low stone platform on which the sentries sometimes stood. Although he sat close beside her he no longer held her. They might have been two men talking desperately together. "Thanks to your ingenuity Dragon has often been in your kitchen of late. Those snapping dark eyes of his miss nothing. He tells me your great kitchen chimney goes up at this end of the royal apartments against this tower. That the two buildings join, in fact. He drew a plan with his dagger on the circular wall of our room, and together we have gradually prised away some stones in our side of it, so that a man could crawl through into the chimney."

Isabel was aghast at the daring of their scheme. "But the Constable—or the guards—if they should come in and see what you have done?"

"In the day-time we put everything back, and push my bed in front of it. Since we came Dragon has waited on us so that no prying servant knows. We find there are rough projecting slabs in your kitchen chimney by which an agile man may climb—put there for the sweeping of it, I suppose. Once up it and out into the open air with a rope wound about my body, I could let myself down on to the roof of the King's apartments and crawl along it to the outer wall which, as you know, is strengthened just there by the Cradle tower jutting out into the moat. With all the tackle kept in that tower for raising cargo left for the Constable it should be child's play to let myself down into the moat, swim across and pull myself up onto the wharf."

"But there are guarded gates at either end. You would never pass them either to St. Katherine's steps or into Thames Street. And I have wormed this piece of information out of Gerard Alspaye—that by the Constable's orders all rowing boats moored at the wharf must have their bungs taken out at night."

Mortimer nodded, agreeing but unperturbed. "Then I must slip quietly into the Thames and swim across to the Surrey shore. It would need to be a dark night, of course."

"Swim the Thames? At its great width below bridge?" Isabel shuddered and clutched at his arm, remembering the swift tide swirling beneath the dark arches, and picturing his drowned body being dashed against the green-slimed starlings.

But he only smiled at her reassuringly. "I should remember to take off my boots," he teased. "And was it not in hope of some such possibility that I kept my muscles in trim? But Dragon and I never arrived at a workable plan till now—and, in any case, I could not have left my uncle in his helplessness."

"And what next did you plan?" she asked, carried along by his enthusiasm in spite of all her doubts. "If you reach—*when* you reach the Surrey shore?"

"Milord Bishop of Hereford might happen to leave a couple of horses over there in some ill-locked tavern stable—to be used for some worthy episcopal errand, of course. If he knew which night."

He turned to her, grinning, with one eyebrow quizzically raised, and Isabel was quick to take up her cue. "He is staying with the Bishop of Durham, I understand. When I know the night I could ride along the Strand to take the air, and stop to admire the roses in his host's garden," she suggested with a smile. "So simple a thing to do. Was that all the help you wanted?"

Mortimer raised her hand to his lips, and then forgot to let it go. For a Welsh border lord his gallantry was sometimes surprisingly Parisian, but that, she supposed with annoyance, came of his having acquired a rich French wife. "Your Grace probably knows if anyone lodges above me who might hear us move the heavy stones or see me from the upper windows of the Lantern tower?" he said.

"No one," she assured him. "It is the King's bedchamber. He has gone north. And as you just said, the chosen night must be dark."

"But do not forget the lantern itself. Shining from the top of the tower on a pitch-black night it must be of great guiding comfort to mariners sailing up the Thames, but at some point along the palace roof I shall have to cross its beam. But that is a hazard I must take—— And then there is the matter of the Constable himself. And his officers who go the rounds. I could make them drunk, I suppose, first. But how can I, mewed up in one locked room, get to them?"

"Make them come to you. Give a feast and invite them all."

"A marvellous thought. But for what occasion? If I should make a feast so soon after my bereavement they would suspect me of some such purpose. It must happen naturally—and soon— before the King and that rat Despenser return to London."

Isabel rose and stood leaning thoughtfully upon the coping of the wall. "Next week, so they tell me, the foundation will be celebrated of the chapel which the first Edward had built down there in the bailey and dedicated to St. Peter ad Vincula."

"Scarcely good cause enough, since they know I hate everything within this place. Now if only it were St. David's day—— Still, the desperate must seize on straws. Upon what date does this commemoration day fall?"

"The first of August."

"The first of August! Witch that you are!"

At the exultation in his voice she turned and found him, in spite of all his danger, looking as excited as a boy. "Why?" she asked, laughing. "Why do you sound so glad?"

"Because it is my birthday. With all this pother I had forgotten. That and my accession to the Lordship of Chirk should make a worthy occasion. And by my reckoning there will be no moon. *And*, I fear," he added ruefully, "precious little wine. Certainly not enough to make a dozen men drunk."

"A ship put in this morning from Bordeaux. Perhaps for such an occasion Sir Stephen might provide you with a bottle or two from his perquisites."

"And have his well-disciplined servants serve it," Mortimer reminded her. "Besides, drink takes men so differently. Some are more dangerous drunk than sober. And the Constable himself would probably remain abstemious."

They stood looking at each other, nonplussed, in silence, until suddenly Isabel found herself inspired. "My sleeping potion!" she exclaimed, on a delicious burst of excited laughter. "The one my physician gave me when I tried to stay here. A drop or two apiece should settle them all."

He held her, laughing in unison, while she explained. "Dragon can put some in the wine. According to old Bramtoft the officers should be in a very stupor of sleep in a few minutes. But you must see to it that they all begin their drinking with a birthday health to you lest one should succumb before another and suspect your trickery."

"That is well thought of. But how am I to get the stuff?"

"The lady of Bringningcourt will invent some errand to the kitchen at such time as Dragon will be there. The other ladies you may trust, milord, but she is the only one who is completely in my confidence."

Roger Mortimer stood looking out across the river to the open south bank streets, the sunlit marshes and the homely villages beyond. "And so in a week's time I may really be gone," he said, drawing in a deep breath. "Merciful God, how good it will be to bestride a horse again!"

And Isabel the Queen stood small and still beside him. "And ride back to Wigmore—leaving me here," she said, thinking of that other Frenchwoman who was beautiful but cold.

He swung round at once and caught her to his heart. This time she knew his ardour to be untinged by any thought of expedience, since dalliance could but endanger him. "We were made for each other. No woman ever so rose to all a man's demands. We are still alone. Give me yourself before I go, and so let us make it the complete partnership."

Her eyes were closed, her eager senses clamouring to obey. But some lingering potency of her lovely, cheated marriage vows still held her chaste. She must give herself time, set an almost impossible condition upon her surrender. "Wait awhile, my love," she whispered, freeing a hand to restrain his hot, demanding lips. "Escape from here first, prove yourself so much more a man than any of them, and one day you shall have me. I swear it."

He had not expected her to make terms and stared down at her, angry in his frustration. "You can bargain, at such a moment, about love as fierce as ours? So that you may enjoy the thrill to your vanity, I must buy your body's softness with *my* body's danger."

"Is not a Queen's surrender worth it?"

His eyes were still angry, but he let her go. "You are a proud woman, but worth waiting for," he told her, deliberately ignoring the royal blood in her veins. "I would not have a mouse-like prude."

They talked indifferently of this and that, filling in what might have been such precious time. Ships with billowing sails passed busily along the river below, gulls screamed overhead, but their thoughts were all of themselves. "Why did you speak of *two* horses waiting over there?" asked Isabel, still listless from the tearing battle with her senses.

"Had we stolen a boat Dragon would have come, but unfortunately he cannot swim," Mortimer answered almost woodenly. "At one time I had thought of Gerard Alspaye, but am not sure how far I can bribe him."

"I, too, have tried with him."

"So I gathered."

"I think he would go far——"

"No doubt he would, for you. But do not try too hard. Your lips are mine. There will be no need to bemuse the lad out of his few senses after I am gone."

A door banged loudly at the bottom of the turret. Feet began to tramp heavily up the stairs. An approaching sentry was whistling a popular tune from one of the King's plays. Isabel moved quickly into the shadow of the great well wheel around which the bucket ropes were coiled. "Where will you make for?" she whispered, all eagerness again.

"Paris," Mortimer whispered back, his jealous antagonism forgotten. "If the Despenser's reign proves unbearable, move Heaven and earth to join me there. Somehow I will contrive to let you know."

Their precious stolen hour was finished. It had been invaluable because it had set the seal upon Mortimer's plans for escape, but they both felt that emotionally it had been wasted or had slipped away too fast.

"All through the first night of the month I shall be watching and praying for you," she whispered, looking upon him with the thought that it might be for the last time.

He gathered up her forgotten cloak from the stone platform and, putting it about her shoulders, bent to kiss her white throat possessively. "And before we grow old some other night will come when you will be keeping your sworn promise to me," he told her.

Pulling the dark material of the cloak across her face, she slipped into the shadows behind the wheel as the sentry's rubicund face appeared level with the flagstones of the well chamber floor. The moment he appeared Mortimer was shouting to him from the doorway and pointing excitedly to some strange foreign ship. The man stumbled hurriedly up the few remaining steps, all agog with curiosity. "Where be she, Sir?" he called out, and ran clumsily across the well room to join the prisoner on the battlements. And in that contrived moment the Queen slipped unobserved down the way he had come and joined Bringnette, who appeared to be nodding placidly on a garden seat.

CHAPTER 21

ALL THAT first day of August the Queen had been restless and difficult to serve. First she had wanted to do one thing and then another, until her women were worn out. "It is this oppressive heat, or maybe she is sickening for something," they whispered among themselves.

"And small wonder, shut in like this so near the stench from the City ditch, with the smell of stale fish in Thames Street and the butchers allowed to do their slaughtering anywhere they like instead of having a proper abattoir outside the gates," grumbled poor Ghislaine, who had twice been reduced to tears. "I cannot think why her Grace stays here!"

"If only poor Thomeline were still here to soothe her with his music!" sighed Bringnette, who knew only too well why the Queen stayed.

By the time the long day was ended and Curfew rang from the Bell tower, all members of the royal household were thankful to seek their beds. And so no one saw the Queen herself slip down the garden stairs with a dark, hooded cloak drawn about her. A light still burned in her bedroom, but only old Bringnette was there, nodding in her chair. Isabel paced the garden until dawn, watching and praying and listening to the least sound. "If he is caught now while attempting this mad escape, there will be no doubt about his death," she thought. But Roger Mortimer's calculations had been right. Mercifully, the night was dark as pitch and, even by the faint downward glow of the beacon which was kept burning on top of the Lantern tower, she could discern no one moving on roof or chimney.

Saying that she could not eat roasted meat on such a day, she had ordered a supper of cold venison pasty and peaches so that the cooks should go off duty early and the roaring kitchen fire be damped down. She had tired out her household so that all were abed. A few days earlier she had visited the Bishop of Hereford. In fact, as a useful partner, she had done everything she could think of to help Mortimer. But she was still racked with fears. "If he should be suffocated in that foul black chimney. . . . If he should slip from the sloping roof of the King's apartments. . . . If he should be more weakened than he thinks by long confinement so that he cannot battle with the tide—if he should be drawn down, down into the deep dark waters of the Thames . . ." All through the breathless summer night she lived in the life of the man she loved, as women do. The scent of stocks from the flower beds was so overpoweringly sweet that it almost made her swoon, and every step of the sentry on the battlements and the least rustle of leaf or cheep of bird came to her strained ears like a thunderclap. Earlier on there had been a light streaming out from a deep-set lower window in the

Lantern tower and a converging of bobbing lanterns. She had heard a coming and going of footsteps and then, from the lighted window, the sound of men's voices and bursts of convivial laughter. But all had been silent for a long time now and the light had gradually guttered out. And no one, so far as she could tell, had come out again from the Lantern tower. It seemed almost as if Mortimer's plan must have succeeded. "Either he has really escaped, or he lies dead," thought Isabel, shivering beneath the warm texture of her cloak in spite of the midsummer heat. "And somehow I must wait until it is morning to know."

A chill little breeze was blowing up river with the tide. A faint streak of yellowish light above London Bridge heralded the dawn. There was nothing else to stay for. She turned, and saw gratefully that the welcoming warmth of candlelight still shone from her own window. Her feet and legs ached with standing, so that she almost stumbled along the path towards it. For the first time she considered the danger of suspicion if she herself had been seen, and was startled by a hoarse angry croak and a whirring sound swooping towards her out of the thicker shadows by the wall. She stifled a scream as something black flapped within a few inches of her face. Then forced herself to walk on, realizing that she had only disturbed one of the ravens which were said to have nested in the Tower since the Norman Conqueror's time.

Bringnette, still sitting in her chair, had hours ago nodded herself into the facile sleep of old age; and Isabel, having no heart to waken her, had lain sleepless on the curtained bed. And when morning was fully come the whole Tower seemed to be abnormally astir. She sat up against her pillows and listened with fast-beating heart. She could hear men running, sharp orders being given, and horses being brought round and clattering out under the archway of the Byward tower, and the curfew bell giving tongue in broad daylight. And as soon as she was dressed the Constable himself came to her. He looked sallow and unshaven and horribly afraid. "Madam, my most important prisoner, Sir Roger Mortimer, has escaped," he blurted out, all unwittingly giving her the news she seemed to have been waiting a lifetime for. He said a great deal after that, about some wine that had been tampered with, about Mortimer's servant being held for questioning, about the necessity of questioning even her own household. Only as a matter of form, he was assuring her, since in so grave a matter no stone must be left unturned. But Isabel scarcely listened to the rest, her relief being like a lightness flooding all her being. She knew that the man was terrified, not knowing how to face the King—or worse still, she supposed—the quiet fury of the Despensers. She guessed that Dragon was down in some foul dungeon being tortured, although she felt sure that because Gaveston had loved the man the King would set him free. But nothing mattered at the moment save that Roger Mortimer had done this impossible thing. And that because he had done it she belonged to him.

She herself was the one person within the fortress whom the distracted Constable never dreamed of questioning. So, complaining of all the turmoil, she bade Bringnette bolt her door and, exhausted by hours of tension, threw herself fully clothed on her bed and slept for hours.

But on waking she found the first flush of relief was gone and fresh fears beset her. "Bringnette," she called, when a servant had lit the candles and withdrawn. "Anything might still happen to milord Mortimer. You heard all those men-at-arms clattering over the drawbridge in pursuit. He had so short a start."

The old Countess hurried to the bedside with a soothing drink. "A man who could escape from the Tower could do anything. It would be child's play to him to get back to his old haunts."

"But he is going to France."

"All the better," declared the indomitable old woman, "because all those goggle-eyed men-at-arms will be frantically searching for him in Wales. Now drink this, hinny, and call Ghislaine and the others to dress you in your coolest silk. If you dine gaily in hall it will look as if you could not care less what happens to Sir Stephen's escaped prisoner."

The old Countess had been right, and a few days afterwards Isabel blamed herself for not having had enough faith. Hers was a man indeed. News came to her through one of those London merchants who so much admired her. Taloise, her tailor, fitting her for a ruby red gown, said that he had bought the lovely Utrecht velvet from a merchant called Ralph Botton whose ship had just returned from the Continent. And folded in the velvet was a letter from Roger Mortimer.

Like all his communications, it was brief and unemotional. Instead of the two episcopal horses which he had hoped to find in some stable, seven of his own men were waiting for him on the Surrey side. Men whom the Bishop of Hereford had thought to summon and who would fight for him to the death. Making the most of their few hours start, they had all managed to reach the Hampshire coast. At the little port of Lymington they had hired a rowing boat, letting it be understood, in case of pursuit, that they had business on the Isle of Wight. But instead of putting in at Yarmouth haven opposite they had rowed round to the extreme westerly point of the island and there, in a little bay under the lee of the dangerous Needles rocks, Mortimer and two of his men had climbed aboard Ralph Botton's trading ship, leaving their companions to return the rowing boat next day. The wind was fair for France. Botton had set him ashore on the Normandy coast, and he hoped soon to arrive safely in Paris.

"Would I were with him!" thought Isabel. It was her first letter from him and her instinct was to cherish it in the bodice of her gown as Ghislaine had carried Robert le Messager's, but —caring so much for Mortimer's safety—she resolutely tore it into shreds.

There was nothing more to stay for in the Tower. Hoping she might never see the inside of it again, she returned to Westminster. And there, as in London, all the talk was still of Mortimer's escape. That any man, taken in through Traitors' Gate, should get out again save by the King's favour seemed incredible. And the King, still up in Lancashire, had immediately set a huge price on his head, and urged by Hugh Despenser, had roused the whole country to search for him. Sir Stephen Segrave was arrested for neglect of duty, and Lord Badlesmere had been caught and executed for his part in the Earl of Lancaster's rebellion.

"Half the King's army is out searching for Mortimer," Despenser told Isabel, with gloating satisfaction, when they were all back at Westminster and he had followed Edward unbidden into her apartments.

"And where are they searching?" enquired Isabel, ostensibly giving most of her attention to some materials she had ordered for her costume in a Michaelmas mask.

"Where else but in Wales?" answered Edward with that hint of impatience which now so often marred his manner to her when his new friend was about.

"Where else indeed?" agreed Isabel politely, slanting her lovely head this way and that the better to admire the result of her selection.

But it was Hugh Despenser, as usual, who had the last word. With all the assurance imaginable he, too, came and admired her draperies for the part of Saint Catherine. "One must commend your Grace's skill in blending colours," he said condescendingly, just as if she and Piers Gaveston had not devised some of the most striking masques in London in the old days when people had peace in which to enjoy them. "A splendid piece of blue velvet, with just the right touch of silver tissue to lend it sheen." His long, tapering fingers tested the material as sensitively as any woman's, though his thin lips were pursed disapprovingly. "But one trembles to think what your Grace must have paid for it. A pity it is for the entertainment of but a single night!"

It was not the first time he and his sharp-faced father had made remarks like that, drawing her husband's attention to some extravagance or other, and Isabel could have killed him for it.

"It would probably have paid for one of those new siege bombards of which we stand in so much need, Hugh," remarked Edward.

Isabel noted the look which passed between them and opened her mouth on a stinging retort about the cost of their everlasting disputes with her late uncle's party, but Despenser silenced her with a pleasant and seemingly innocuous remark. "You had the velvet from Ralph Botton, did you not? I see he has a ship just in. One of our most enterprising merchants, I always think."

She was afraid to say another word. What had he heard of Ralph Botton's enterprises? Had one of the crew talked? What did he know of her own part in Roger Mortimer's escape. Had his sharp-eyed cat of a wife wormed some significant detail from one of her women? Had gossip got busy about the Queen's long sojourn in the Tower? "Probably I shall never know. He is the first of these stolid Englishmen who has been too clever for me," she thought. And from now on she must pit her wits against his. It was a battle *à outrance* for the King's favour, and Hugh Despenser's star was in the ascendant.

Their struggle began on the level of finance. Leeds castle had been captured by the King and therefore must belong to him,

Despenser argued. And other domains which had been included in her dowry or which she had inherited from the May Queen were gradually taken from her, to be handed over to the favourite. It was the Piers Gaveston situation all over again.

In return, and because she never had been able to accept injustice tamely, Isabel made a belated outcry about the execution of her Uncle of Lancaster, never losing an opportunity of holding up the bungling, discontented traitor to the people as a martyr for their liberties and for better government. And such was her popularity that she soon had them making pilgrimages to his tomb at Pontefract. What good it may have done them she did not care, nor did she greatly miss Thomas Plantagenet's amiable championship of her wrongs. She herself had grown more worldly wise than he. But during the difficulties and humiliations she was now forced to endure she would have given anything for the quiet converse and far-seeing advice of Aymer de Valence. But his power was as eclipsed by the Despensers as her own, and he had been away in Pembroke holding his Welsh possessions secure from their greed until the King had sent him to propitiate Charles in France for his own still delayed visit of homage.

Hating the constant presence of the Despensers at court, Isabel retired to Havering-atte-Bower in Essex, where she seldom saw her children. The two young princes were often with their father, and the only friend who still visited her in her retirement was Edmund of Kent, who, for his mother's sake, showed her what kindness he could. But to Isabel the value of his visits lay rather in the fact that his attachment to the King rendered him a prey to jealousy, and sometimes when alone with her he would let fall complaints about their common enemy.

"Despenser is always urging Edward to dismiss those attendants whom you brought from France and who are so specially dear to you," he reported regretfully, having entertained from childhood a great affection for Bringnette. "I am sure that Edward would never have harboured so unkind a thought, but the King's Shadow, as we call him at court, argues that they keep your thoughts too much in France."

That her thoughts were often in France Isabel could not deny, but none save Bringnette knew why. Each day she thought of Roger Mortimer in Paris and hoped that he had met Pembroke and had an audience of her brother and given him an account of how impossible things were for her in England. And what was there, save her children, to keep her unhappy thoughts in England? "If the King sends my fellow countrywomen away, I shall go with them," she told Edmund, impressing his gentle mind with admiration of her daring spirit.

But a Queen could not just give orders for her possessions to be packed, charter a ship and return to her native land. Not even with a world of provocation. Such things could be brought about only by diplomacy, she supposed. But more provocation was yet to come.

She knew from chance words of Edmund's that the Despensers, with devilish cunning, were always harping on her popularity, and she guessed that Edward, in his easy purblind way, was for the first time being made to see it as a menace to his power, and beginning to mind. He did not want her to go travelling about the country from castle to castle, charming the hearts out of his subjects as she went. And his new favourite was always casting envious eyes upon more and yet more land. So in order to clip her wings and to load yet more gifts on Hugh Despenser he offered her a totally inadequate pension in place of her royal demesnes.

"A pension! While I am still Queen of England!" cried Isabel, and, while still in the white heat of her fury, called for quill and paper and poured out the whole of her grievances to her brother in France. "The griping miser would keep me like a servant in his palace," she complained, forgetting how often she had railed against Edward's thoughtless extravagance. And she complained that she went in fear of her life, through the hatred of the Despensers. Much of what she said was unreasonable, but she was far too angry to care. And Charles *le Bel* shared her high temper. He made a far more satisfactory answer than her Uncle of Lancaster had done when appealed to for aid. He struck immediately. He raided Guienne and let Edward know that he intended to keep it until such time as he bestirred himself to come and do homage for it.

Proud and vindicated, Isabel walked on air when the news came. She might be robbed. She—one of the most beautiful women in Europe—might no longer be wanted by her husband, but the powerful arm of France could still stretch out to protect her. She dressed in her richest scarlet and gold brocade, wore the great Charlemagne jewel and dined in great state to celebrate her victory. And that night for the first time in months Edward came to her. She had been enjoying a selection of French *chansons* performed by her minstrels and had not yet undressed and, when her women warned her, she made no effort to do so. "I will never have him in my bed again," she said, without troubling to lower her voice.

He found her standing between the two tall candles by her reading-desk, turning the pages of some book. She looked up in assumed surprise and gave him a cool greeting. Her dark eyes challenged him, and either the candlelight or the grandeur of her garments seemed to make her look taller and to lend her an air of mature authority.

"I will see that you do not write to France again," he said without preamble, slamming her door behind him.

Isabel showed no sign of fear. Only her delicately drawn brows lifted a little. "Surely it would be inhuman—and difficult —to prevent me from writing to my own brother."

"Your family has been the bane of my life," he cried, kicking like an angry boy at a stool that stood in his path. "You know that he now insists upon my doing homage like some insignificant retainer for Guienne?"

Isabel shrugged and closed the book. "He has waited a long time," she reminded him. "And your Grace has always the option of fighting for it as your father would have done."

She had struck at his most vulnerable point and his light eyes shone with surprise and anger. "You grow too high. Answering back like any cheap market jade!"

"True, mine is only a woman's point of view," she admitted, with assumed humility. "And it is common knowledge, is it not, that your Grace has little use for women?"

"Vindictive shrew!" he cried, seizing her by the wrist with cruel strength.

"Ah, that is better," she jibed. "I like a man of spirit."

She thought that he would have struck her. Some frustrated part of her hoped that he would. Instead his fingers slackened. "Did I not come and take Leeds castle for you?" he asked, harking back to what must have been his highest hour with her.

"And then took it back again for yourself. And put my uncle to death—quickly, purposely, before I could interfere."

"You interfere too much."

"I seem to have heard those words before, a constant cry against me on your chief adviser's lips."

He took a turn about the room and let her stand there sucking at her smarting wrist. It was a new thing, totally outside of his experience, to be answered back like that. When he came back to her he looked more like the gentle, smiling Edward she was accustomed to. "Can we not be friends?" he pleaded.

"Friends? Ah, yes, I could wish it so." She wished it sincerely, but knew that because of her infidelity even that was something which she could no longer have of him.

But he took her words as half-surrender. He reached for her and was angered because her small hands held him off. "Take off that gown and gee-gaws. You are my wife," he ordered.

"I should do us both a greater wrong than you know." She still resisted, but felt herself helpless beneath his strength, and the thought came to her that he knew that he had always before had his way with her. He knew how easy it had always been to make her respond to his desire, remembered that more often than not the desire had been her own and that on the rare occasions when she had resisted him he had always had his way with her in the end. But this time she fought him like a tiger. There was no half-hearted reluctance, no dalliance with surrender. She was embattled against him by far stronger desires. Not for worlds would she conceive by him this night and so jeopardize her future plans. And suddenly in a flash of intuition a thought came to her. "That devil Despenser sent you," she accused breathlessly. "He encouraged you to come—or you had some coarse wager together that I would let you take me—so that I should bear you another child, and be out of his ambitious way for months. All you have ever wanted of me is children. All your anxiety about the Black Douglas at Brotherton was for your heir, not me!"

He let her go so suddenly that she fell back against the pillows. "That is a lie, and you know it," he said with more restraint. "For years we were happy together——"

"The years when I was some sort of comfort to you for Gaveston."

"Happier, God knows, than I am now," he added, ignoring her brutal thrust.

She sat up and looked at him, trying to see *his* point of view for the first time. "That is possibly true," she admitted. "You used to laugh then—you were lovable and spontaneously gay—

almost like you were when I first knew you. Else I suppose I should not have wanted you so desperately for myself."

He sat on the edge of her bed, looking at her sadly as if from a long way off. "Do not wholly condemn me, Isabel. My life has not been easy, either. You speak of urges which you do not understand."

"Perhaps. But I speak of things which I have been obliged to bear."

"I am sorry, *ma chère*." He got up with a deep sigh and he moved away from her with an air of regretful finality, as if all were finished between them. For a few moments he stood idly twisting the crimson tassels of her bed curtains. "You are clever, and full of perspicacity. Hugh Despenser did make the diabolical suggestion that I should come." He saw the spasm of rage which shook her, and hurried on with an endearing penitence which was the best part of him and might at any other time have moved her. "But I do assure you that it was not wholly his urging nor any politic desire to placate your brother which made me come to you to-night. I came here because sometimes—when the Church has been at me—I try to fight this taint which I seem to have been born with. And I hoped that you would forget and forgive."

She slid down from the great bed and stood facing him with blazing eyes. "I was fool enough to forget and forgive—once. But not a second time. What do men like you expect of their wives?" She saw that he was genuinely shaken by her savagery and liked him better in that pathetic moment, but was honest enough to see that a plea for reconciliation could but wipe out the comfortable justification for her own infidelity. "It is not I, or my body, that you really want," she went on a little impatiently, as though explaining something to a backward child. "Do you not see that it is some remembered state of life—a return to childhood security—which weak people crave—oblivion from your own self-contempt, that you are seeking? And because you remember those unreproachful domestic years of ours you hope to find it with me. But I am Isabel the Fair. I"—she groped for words and Roger Mortimer's came to her—"I was not made for a half marriage like that."

CHAPTER 22

ISABEL was to find that she could not deny the King her bed
with impunity. When he recalled her to Westminster she had
gone willingly, hoping that he had relented towards her and that
the conditions of her life would be improved. But it was only
to find that most of her trusted servants had been dismissed and
that Despenser's wife was appointed to her household—ostensibly
to take the place of a favourite French countess but in reality
to govern her actions and to spy on her. Considering the woman's
nature and the antipathy which existed between them, this was
the cruellest blow that Edward could have dealt her. But he
seemed to be more and more under the domination of Despenser.
And now he must have allowed himself to be persuaded to find
an appointment elsewhere for her faithful Robert le Messager,
who had hitherto managed to guard her from some of Lady
Despenser's malevolent annoyances. And this appointment
would mean losing Ghislaine, too, because she herself had already
given permission for them to marry.

When bidding the prospective bridegroom good-bye she walked
with him to the top of the water steps where his waiting barge
was moored, bobbing on a full, slapping tide. And because
he had been with her all her married life and she would miss him
so sorely, she stood talking with him in the morning sunlight
about his new appointment, the house she was giving him as a
wedding gift and the arrangements for his forthcoming marriage.
"Be kind to my Ghislaine," she said, laying a hand on his arm.
"There have been many times, God forgive me, when I have
been impatient with her myself, but my household will be dreary
indeed without her."

And all the time she was with him she was conscious of a tall,
lean friar in a brown habit who was watching her from the shadow
of the watergate archway. She had noticed him before when she
had been talking to Robert, and his presence made her uneasy,
so that she laughed a little more loudly and gestured more
vivaciously than she normally would have done. She wondered
if Messager, who had always been so watchful on her behalf,
had noticed the man. But what man who was going to marry

Ghislaine du Bois in a few days' time would not be blind and indifferent to anything else?

When Isabel returned to her women the sour-looking friar had moved away, but almost immediately Eleanor Despenser joined the group so that she would not ask about him. Nor, indeed, was she inclined to talk about anything in that woman's presence, but spent a dull and silent morning. In consequence she was all the more pleased to see Edmund of Kent coming across the garden from the King's apartments after noon. Pitying her new unenviable state, he often contrived to spend a short while with her after dining with the King, and even Eleanor—although in some sort his niece—had not the effrontery to join him and the Queen uninvited as they walked together by the river. "I am sorry you must have that spiteful piece forever at your elbow," he muttered, in spite of his loyalty to his half-brother.

"It is insufferable!" broke out Isabel. "I would not have minded if it had been her sister Margaret, who knows what unhappiness is——"

"It is done to please the Despensers, and so that you shall not write to the King of France."

"Nor spend a penny on pleasure, nor visit my friends, nor ride through the streets and stir the people's hearts to pity so that they clamour for me——"

Soft-hearted Edmund drew her gently to a bench. "I have a feeling that it would not have been so were my dear mother still alive," he said. "But try not to take these slights as coming from the King himself. It is hard for all of us, seeing him so—obsessed."

"And too weak to resist." Lulled by the rare company of a kind relation, Isabel sat for a few moments pleasantly relaxed, as she so seldom was these days. "Edmund," she said, her thoughts straying back to Robert's departure.

"Yes?"

"Do you know anything about a sinister-looking friar who hangs about the Palace—watching me?"

"A tall, lean man with deeply hooded eyes?"

She turned eagerly. "Then you do know him?"

"I am afraid it must be the man they call Friar Thomas."

"Afraid?"

"Because I suppose he *could* well be spying on you."

"But to what end? Do they suppose I have a backstairs lover hidden in the buttery or behind the curtains of my bed?"

But either Edmund would not divulge what he had heard in the King's apartments, or he could not bring himself to hurt her. He began to hedge vaguely. His facile sympathies always had betrayed him, first to one loved person and then to another, so that it was difficult to be sure which side he was really on. "In spite of your loveliness you have led such an exemplary married life that they can scarcely suspect you of that," he said, with a nervous laugh. "But it would be as well, my dear Isabel, to be careful in all things."

He should have known his spirited French sister-in-law better than to suppose that such vague warnings would satisfy her. As soon as he was gone she sent for Despenser's wife, who had no such inhibitions. Lady Despenser came in her own good time, when the Queen's women were preparing her for bed. It seemed that she preferred to have an audience. She stood there smug and unsmiling, her hair strained back from her high shiny forehead and her hands folded secretively in the sleeves of her gown.

"Who is this friar—this hired creature in your husband's pay?" demanded the Queen, in a high rage. "Why do you set him to spy on me?"

"If your Grace is referring to the learned Father Thomas he is awaiting his final instructions before setting off on an important mission to Rome."

"One would imagine that a mission of any importance would call for someone of slightly more standing," remarked Isabel sarcastically.

"One might indeed, Madam," agreed Eleanor, with that hateful meekness which the Queen was beginning to fear. The woman could afford to be meek, knowing very well that Isabel's curiosity in the matter would force her to question further, and knowing too that all the cards lay in her own and her husband's hands.

Isabel, sitting with unbound hair, began drawing off her rings and laying them in the velvet-lined casket held by a pert chit who had taken Ghislaine's place. "What is the nature of this mission?" she asked, as casually as she could.

"To persuade his Holiness the Pope to agree to a divorce."

The Queen's head shot up, jerking a long tress of wavy golden hair from her tiring woman's hands. "A divorce," she repeated, well aware that such a thing could usually be obtained only by royal or important persons. "Between what two parties?"

Eleanor paused for a moment to moisten her thin lips and to enjoy her exquisite moment. "I understood, Madam, that it was between the King's grace and yourself. Have you not heard?"

Isabel sprang to her feet, her half-braided hair falling about her. In a mirror held by two of her new young women she saw her face whiten and the pupils of her eyes brighten to fierce bright pin points. One of the kneeling girls, being clumsy and untrained, lost her balance; and the other, from sheer fright, began to giggle hysterically. Between them the mirror fell with a clatter to the floor and broke. For a moment or two Isabel stared down at it in horror, almost shocked from everyday sanity. It was the second time such an ill-omened thing had happened. "My marriage!" she thought, momentarily forgetting the frightening present because she was reliving so vividly her wedding morning in Boulogne. But now, alas, there was no Ghislaine to bemoan the ill-omened accident and gather up the pieces. No wise Marguerite. No Aymer de Valence of Pembroke. No one at all to care. Nor, come to that, did she care so greatly herself, she thought, coming back to present reality. A divorce would leave her free. She waved away everyone but Edward's ambitious niece, and faced up to her as a royal daughter of France should. "It was your husband's idea, not the King's. You can spare your breath if you think to deny it. On what grounds does the meddling parvenu think to obtain it?" she asked, with a cold pride which abashed her tormentor.

Eleanor's audacious eyes were lowered, not for effect, but because she no longer dared to meet the outraged Queen's. "Since you refuse the King your bed," she mumbled, "why should he keep you as his wife?"

"So he went straight to your immaculate husband and told him? Then all three of you, doubtless, discussed it?" Isabel peered at her as though she were some species of vermin beyond her understanding. "Answer me!" she almost shouted, when the woman remained abjectly silent.

"How else could we have known?"

"How else indeed? And now, I suppose, the very scullions know. But do not hug to yourself the delusion that it would hurt me to cease to be the King's wife."

"No, Madam—save that your Grace would also cease to be Queen of England."

The retort came swift as a rapier thrust, and was true. Isabel knew in that moment how intensely she would care, even apart from the humiliation. "But your foolish scheming is doomed to failure," she said. "His Holiness shall be made to understand that the reason for my refusal to cohabit with my husband is no shame of mine."

Eleanor raised her eyes then. "I do not think so," she said, with quiet confidence.

"No, perhaps not, my gaoler," allowed Isabel, "since that is what you are here for. To forbid me pen and paper. To remove any friend of mine who might be trusted to convey my side of the case. But his Holiness is neither deaf nor blind. The hand that wears St. Peter's ring rests on the pulse of Europe. Does it not occur to you that he may already be aware of my husband's habits—and of the accommodating ways of those who climb to power?"

"It is only your word." The voice of Hugh Despenser's wife was sharp with fear.

"It is common knowledge. But in case that should not be enough to justify me you hope to pin upon me the scandal of some lover. Even Robert le Messager, who is to marry one of my ladies next week."

"There was a time when he looked higher. I was only a child then but often about the Palace. And children have sharp ears."

"Yours could never have been dull. But there again it is only *your* word." Sickened of the subject, Isabel relaxed and sighed. "I am glad to talk straightly to you this once, Eleanor Despenser. And since your tortuous mind is interested in such things I will tell you that there was a time when I could have taken Robert, my susceptible master-of-horse, but—because of the love I bore my husband—I would not. That should be proof enough that I kept *my* side of the marriage. But I suppose that for your own ends any man would do—to discredit me."

All polite pretences were down indeed. "And I doubt not we shall catch you yet," said Eleanor venomously. "Although you are my aunt by marriage you are still young enough. And hot-blooded, they say. And men still call you Isabel the Fair."

Instead of crying out in indignation, Isabel laughed aloud.

"No, you will not catch me," she said, confident in the knowledge that her lover was safely in France and she immune from the demands of any other man.

Surprised and shaken by such spontaneous laughter, Eleanor sought for some final weapon with which to quench it. "I must ask Hugh to try to persuade the King to send away that proud and secretive old woman who now shares your room, and whose dismissal his Grace still stands out so obdurately against."

The weapon was cleverly chosen. The thought of being left without Bringnette in the midst of so much scheming hate almost broke the Queen's confidence. "She cared for me when I was small. She has lived with me nearly all her life. She is old and was early widowed by war," she said, with a gesture of entreaty. "And I love her."

"And no doubt, since the King gave her those estates in Ponthieu, it is she who smuggles your disloyal letters to France."

There was a sweep of silk skirts across the floor, stirring the scent of some pungent herbs from the rushes, and the Queen was shaking her by the arm. "If you try to take Bringnette from me I will kill you," she said. And Eleanor Despenser had the good sense to believe her, and to let the matter drop.

Baiting the Queen was her niece's private privilege, but Hugh Despenser and the King had more urgent matters to occupy their minds. The voice of the people was beginning to make itself felt. They were sick and tired of years of bloodshed in their betters' quarrels, of inefficiency and misrule. Bad kings they had had before—some of them men of far worse character than Edward. Hard-working Plantagenet despots they had endured and obeyed. Courageous, pride-giving Plantagenets like the Cœur de Lion and Longshanks, who had bled England for their foreign wars, they had made heroes of. One way and another they had stomached them all. But at least they expected their kings to understand the business of State and to be strong enough to rule. Edward's incompetency became their despair, his defeat by the Scots their personal shame. The more deeply thinking clergy and land-owners began to talk about degeneracy, as Charles of France had done. The throw-back of an over-martial father. A born weakling who could scarcely be held responsible. It was a good thing he had sons, they said, and that the elder of the two grew daily more like his grandfather, bidding fair to become a man of decisive personality to whom towns and individuals could take their problems, confident that they would not be shelved or muddled into something worse. But such good fortune lay in the laps of the future generation, rather than to be enjoyed in their own lifetime. And in the meantime that much-hated man, Hugh Despenser, held the country in thrall and, although undoubtedly he was clever, his ambition and the way he sought to over-shadow his royal master sickened them.

The Londoners, with their usual sprightliness, joked about the discomforts of a state of affairs they could not mend. They even encouraged a good-looking crazy fellow who traipsed about from tavern to tavern leading a dog and a cat by a chain and declaring that he was the real firstborn of Longshanks, and Edward a changeling. Nobody seriously believed in him, of course, but his antics suited their humour. After all, they bore some sly resemblance to the frivolity of taking performing animals and fiddlers to war. And the very fact that men laughed and listened tolerantly to his pretensions showed how low respect for their real King had fallen.

That spring the country suffered a grievous loss. Aymer de Valence, Earl of Pembroke, died of a fever in Paris. Like Gilbert of Gloucester, he had stood for moderation, and with his death the people lost all hope of a final reconciliation between the King's party and the barons and some sort of struggle back to better times. King Robert of Scotland had made his own victorious terms, and now King Charles of France was preparing to take possession of that rich wine-growing duchy of Guienne for which their fathers had fought. And all because their own king would not bestir himself and leave his hunting and his hated favourite to go and do homage for it.

Soon the muttering in England and the news from Guienne grew so serious that Despenser could no longer disregard it. It was he who had always advocated that the people should be heard equally with the barons and churchmen in Parliament. He had hoped that, for the safety of the crown, *vox populi* would sometimes keep in check the demands of the peers. But now their voices were beginning to be heard dangerously in the village squares and streets. Trade would come to a standstill again, there would be more famine, they shouted, and with proper government all of it could have been prevented.

And as if in answer to their complaint an idea came to fruition in the Queen's mind. An idea which she felt to be worthy of her deeply lamented mentor, Pembroke. She had suggested it once before to Edward, but it had been unfeasible then because she had been awaiting the birth of one of their children, and they had both treated the idea almost as an idle jest. "Why should your Grace not send *me* to Paris to negotiate with Charles?" she suggested. "Perhaps he will listen to me, his sister, and stop this senseless ravaging of Guienne." It had not been easy to make Edward listen to her, but there was so much good sense in her argument that in the end she got her way.

It had meant begging for an interview with the smooth-tongued Despenser, because at that time the King would no longer see her. It had meant being civil to him even though he had purposely kept her waiting, as she had guessed he would. But she was prepared to do anything to get away. She had promised Roger Mortimer that she would join him if it were humanly possible. "And if he could climb a kitchen chimney and swim the Thames, a little lickspittling will not hurt me," she told herself.

She had the satisfaction of knowing that Despenser must have gone straight to the King and discussed her proposal. She supposed that Edward saw in it a way of getting out of difficulties of his own making without altering his pleasant habit of life; and that Despenser—who desired above everything the King's undivided attention—must feel that since Edward had failed to put her out of the way by getting her with child again, the next best thing would be for her to go abroad. Isabel believed and hoped that he had found it more difficult than he had anticipated to stir up her husband's enmity against her.

However that may have been, an expedient reconciliation was patched up between the three of them. Dispatches were sent to Paris, the Cinque Ports were ordered to place a fleet at her disposal, an escort provided—an escort so lavish that it would give Charles the impression that her complaints about parsimony must be all lies. As if to make up for past neglect, Edward busied himself personally with preparations for her comfort on the journey. While pretending to listen carefully to Hugh Despenser's diplomatic instructions, Isabel looked past him to her husband's diligently bent head as he wrote meticulous orders for one of his sea captains, and the thought went winging almost impersonally through her mind, "How little does he suspect that he is sending me to my lover! And if he knew, how much would his heart care?"

Ned and John were to ride with her as far as Eltham, and she had the younger children sent to her to say good-bye. Which was almost the undoing of her plans. Small, chubby Eleanor clung and kissed and plagued her with innocent questions about how long she would be gone, and tiny Joan of the Tower gurgled happily in her arms. Isabel paced the palace garden holding one by the hand and the other against her breast. "I will come back, my pretty sweetings," she vowed softly. "I will come back and bring you fine dresses from Paris, and one day I will make you both queens. Though perhaps," she thought, looking down at their sweet, trusting faces, "it may prove small kindness to send either of you across the sea to marry a handsome king."

As she rode over London bridge on a May morning and southwards through busy Kentish villages the people ran into the streets and waved from upper windows, throwing their caps in the air and shouting for her as though she were the saviour of their country as well as their Queen. And the following day, after a storm of rain, countrymen hooked down branches from the trees and dragged their precious winter fuel to fill in the muddy potholes before her horse's hoofs, while their women risked being crushed by the crowds or bruised by the pikes of her guard just to kiss the hem of her riding cloak. At least there was one royal personage, they felt, who knew how desperately their country needed peace and who was willing to do something about it.

Gervase Alard, Lord Warden of the Cinque Ports, rode out from Winchelsea to meet her. Beyond the harbour bar blue sky met blue sea, and the wind was favourable for her voyage. Standing at a window in Alard's best room looking out at a fleet of graceful ships flying the leopards and lilies from their mainmasts, and watching her horses and goods being stowed on board, Isabel could scarcely believe her good fortune. Only a few weeks ago she had been humiliated and watched, and now she was free, with a new pattern of life before her. It had all been too easily come by. How could Edward have failed to guess at the cause of her eagerness, how could she at last have hood-winked the wily Despenser? Suppose even now his sly wife should be whispering to him about some unsuspected lover overseas? Suppose at the last minute the King should change his mind and refuse to let her go? In sudden panic she found herself listening for the hurrying hoofbeats of some messenger sent to detain her, and watching the small scudding clouds lest the wind should veer. The memory of all she had endured drove her to urgent restlessness. To be made to turn back now, with love and happiness almost within her grasp, would be unendurable. She turned to the kindly and susceptible Lord Warden, entreating him with every wile she knew. "Make them hurry so that we may sail to-night, good sir. As we came through Tonbridge a soothsayer foretold that the weather would break before dawn. And I am impatient to be away by then to serve the interests of milord the King, and of your countrymen who have ever been kind to me."

So the Queen's fleet set out to sea that evening. The stars were shining when she stepped on board. Brightly twinkling stars portending some brighter destiny, she hoped. Though who could see into the future? For the moment it was enough that a widening wake of water put all fear of recall behind her. That every billowing of the great sails carried her nearer to the man she had always wanted—a man strong enough to control their joint destinies, in whose arms she would find a sure and satisfying haven. A man who by his self-confidence and by his own physical exploits had achieved a spectacular escape where other men had always failed.

Stepping ashore at Boulogne was to Isabel a homecoming. The Governor and the aged Abbé were waiting on the quay and the town was bright with banners. France was welcoming her own. Riding through the flower-strewn streets and entering the castle, Isabel found her thoughts returning vividly to her wedding day. Almost as though she were some other being she looked back at that shy, romantic princess who had come there to be married, and who had been so easily pleased with the outward beauty of her English husband. A foolish child, her head stuffed with romantic dreams, and good, no doubt. Anxious to comport herself in public so as to please her parents, and immensely impressed by the vows and solemn beauty of her marriage service. Isabel looked back at her nostalgically from the distance of time and of her present maturity. "I am a woman now with few illusions, but still, please God, some years of beauty," she thought. "And this time, instead of taking brittle dreams to my bridegroom to break, I am going with fierce joy to a lover."

CHAPTER 23

RIDING into Paris on a May morning seemed to Isabel like coming back into the heart of the world. "It is so much larger than London!" she exclaimed proudly, not having seen it since her eldest child was a babe.

"Seven times as large, they say," answered the Abbé of Notre Dame, who had been sent to meet her. "And a seat of learning with a growing university as well."

"Such as the Clares and the Pembrokes are so anxious to benefit at Cambridge," recalled Isabel.

She had passed through the busy towns and fertile fields of northern France, where shopkeepers and peasants worked unhindered by constant alarms of warfare, and had contrasted their peaceful prosperity with the ever-shifting violence of life in England. Now that she was on the Continent, the ports and towns of her husband's island kingdom seemed to her memory like toys. For the last few miles of their journey her party had followed the course of the Seine through a well-tilled valley between richly wooded hills, until the splendid city lay before them. And soon the river divided to cradle in its arms the island on which past kings of France had built their palace, the fantastically towered and turreted Louvre sprawling within its high strong walls. An arched, stone bridge joined it to either bank, and over the Grand Pont rode Isabel with her French and English escort. To her, that day, Paris had seemed an enchanted city because it held her lover and because within the palace, Charles, her brother, was waiting to receive her.

"There never was such a homecoming," she thought. All the people seemed to be shouting a welcome in the streets, and all the church bells rang for her. And at the end there was the kindness of Charles's smile. "You will rest and eat first, and talk politics afterwards," he insisted.

"And meet those few of our relatives who are left," said Isabel, looking round the familiar rooms where there were so few familiar faces. Parents and both her elder brothers were dead, but Charles, for all his cynicism, had ever been the dearest of them all and the one most likely to listen to her. So she pushed aside the shadow of sadness and supped with him merrily. There was music and laughter, and a great state and profusion which, with each trumpet-heralded course, proclaimed the unquestioned wealth and power of the King of France. "Short work would *he* make of any insubordinate barons who rose in arms to quarrel with him," she thought. "And short work will he make of Edward's French possessions if I do not intervene."

After supper he gave her her opportunity, having a chair of state set for her near his throne, and motioning to his courtiers to withdraw. She complained bitterly of the Despensers' influence, but loyally pleaded her husband's difficulties and the war-impoverished state of his kingdom.

"It seems to be much as your lord of Pembroke put it to me," said Charles thoughtfully, "though you paint the picture darker. A pleasant and intelligent man, that Pembroke, with many useful years before him by which we might both have profited. I was grieved by his untimely death."

"And I, with still more cause. Since I first went to England he has been my friend and counsellor. Almost the only one of those clamouring English barons who looked beyond the aggrandizement of his own power. A tolerant man, a steadying hand to me in a bewildering world, God rest his soul!"

"He, too, has always pleaded Edward's difficulties. And I was patient, as you know, during the Scottish wars."

"Most patient," agreed Isabel, guessing that with his usual shrewdness he had been waiting to see which way victory would go.

"But now that my unwarlike brother-in-law has come to terms with Robert Bruce I see nothing that should detain him from doing me homage for Guienne."

"There are fresh and bitter disputes with the barons, chiefly stirred up by the Despensers who, with Edward's favour, grasp their lands."

"So I hear from this Roger Mortimer who escaped from your Tower of London. An incredible feat, that, by all accounts. A man whom Edward would have been wiser not to offend, I should imagine."

Isabel looked up, warm with pride. "For years the Mortimers have kept the north-westerly marches and been like uncrowned kings of Wales."

"Certainly the man has initiative and strength. I will send

for him to attend our official council meeting on this matter to-morrow. And in the meantime, my dear Isabel, you may rest assured that if you can persuade that husband of yours to bestir himself to cross *la Manche* and swear fealty to me I will stay my hand in Guienne. So take some rest, my sweet sister, after your long journey." When she would have knelt to him he rose and kissed her on both cheeks, holding her face affectionately for a moment or two between his hands. "You are all that I have left, *ma chère*."

Isabel's eyes suffused with tears. "Until you have a family of your own," she said sympathetically.

"That I hope to do," he said. "But unfortunately our brothers' wives were both barren and unfaithful. So that we two, Isabel, are at the moment the only remaining Capets."

Ridden by her own urgent concerns, Isabel failed to notice the gravity of his words or to realize their full implication. Hers was the eagerness of a girl in love, coupled with a woman's zest. "Did your Grace mean that Roger Mortimer—is actually housed here within the Louvre?" she asked hurriedly as Charles beckoned to his Chamberlain to escort her to her apartments.

"I could scarcely do less than offer hospitality to any man who had brought me news of you, *ma chère soeur*," smiled Charles negligently.

Isabel curtsied low and gratefully. While her procession formed she allowed the more important of his admiring courtiers to kiss her hand. And all the way along the torch-lit corridors and up the staircase to the ladies' bower, with Chamberlain and ushers and torchbearers going before and her women and pages following after, she was thinking, "Roger is here, somewhere within these walls, and to-morrow I shall see him." And had she not promised herself to him if he escaped?

In her bedroom her women performed their nightly ritual of taking off her glittering garments, bathing her with rose-water, unpinning the jewelled rolls of her headdress and unbraiding her hair. It had been a long day and some of them yawned secretly behind their hands. Bringnette, she supposed, must be already in bed, having asked leave to retire because the motion of the sea had brought on one of her bad headaches. But there was no sleep in Isabel. She moved restlessly about, touching first one familiar thing and then another, delighted that Charles should have thought of giving her the room she had occupied as a girl, though now there were grander tapestries on the rounded stone walls and rich Eastern rugs brought from the crusades, and the finest wax candles such as were to be seen before the high altar in Notre Dame. Everything was fit for a queen. But the tall arched window was the same, and the carved chest where she had once kept her girlhood treasures, and the bed with its blue-and-gold hangings, and beside it the small door leading to the *garde-robe* turret with the winding stair by which she used to run down singing to her mother's privy garden. She stood for a while, forgetful of her tired women, looking out across the Seine and over the sleeping moonlit city, then turned to finger the thickly embossed *fleurs-de-lys* on the crimson hangings of her bed. The hangings were snugly drawn save for a space by the window, the linen sheets invitingly folded back, the small stool set for her to climb on to the thick, feather mattress. And there, to her surprise, stood Bringnette half hidden in the shadows between the bed and the garden door. "Why, Bringnette, I did not see you come in with the others, I had thought you were long since asleep!" she exclaimed, with a little start. "I so much wanted you to have a good night."

"And may Heaven send your Grace a happy one." There was something in the old lady's face which made Isabel look at her again. A guarded, troubled look. And when she sank down as well as her old bones would let her to kiss her mistress's hand she slipped into it something hard and cold.

Warned by such stealth of manner, Isabel kept her hand hidden in the folds of her rose-pink bedgown until the others had all curtsied and were gone. She watched Bringnette move slowly after them across the room. Only when they were alone did she open her hand and look upon the small iron key that lay there, and then questioningly at Bringnette.

"The little garden door," the Countess said laconically. "In case your Grace should wish to take the air."

Shrugging resignedly as one who would have nothing further to do with the matter, she made to follow the other women; but Isabel, lithe as a young girl, sprang after her. "You mean, you exasperating old woman, that Roger Mortimer is down there?"

But Bringnette, brought up in rigid traditions, sniffed disapprovingly. "I am too old to have any part in such affairs. It is for your Grace to decide whether to use the key or not," she muttered mulishly. Then added, with a twinkle in her sharp eyes, "At least he had the sense to cajole instead of trying to bribe me."

She seemed thankful to go, and Isabel bolted the main door again behind her. She stood barefoot in the moonlight, the key in her hand and her heart hammering in her breast. "It is years since I first saw him, when he looked at me with those brazen eyes of his and told me we were meant to be partners in all things—and now the moment has come." By the tumult in her blood she knew that there would be small need for decision. Her marriage, her life in England, her prayers and spiritual struggles and lapses were all forgotten. Only the urgent joy of the moment remained. She pushed her white feet into fur-lined slippers and ran down the turret stair, her heart singing—though no longer with girlish innocence—and unlocked the little door. The walled garden was streaked with silver moonlight and sable shadows, and he was standing in the deepest shadow of all beneath the old mulberry tree where she had first sat dreaming about some future lover. How foolish she had been these last hours! All Paris knew of her arrival, and so must he. And all day, throughout the glitter and the ceremony, she might have known that he would be waiting there—he who invariably succeeded in all that he contrived. He moved towards her and smiled, and with a low cry she ran to him, letting him hold her in the long wordless embrace for which both their bodies had so long hungered.

Half laughing, hand in hand, she led him up the turret stair, and her night was happy indeed, as Bringnette had hoped. "Charmed hours stolen out of the ugliness of time," she murmured, resting against his shoulder in the blue-and-gold bed when the hours of night were done.

"We will make them a lasting reality," he said, having little use for fantasy. "Our destinies are now joined, my sweet."

"And, even less than ordinary lovers, we have no idea where our joined destinies may lead us."

"Or others," he added, almost grimly. "But for good or ill we go on together."

And hearing him say it she was content.

Through the open window she watched the city flush to the pale warmth of dawn. It was one of those things which she was to learn, getting to know him intimately, that no Mortimer could bear to be closed in. He was mountain born, accustomed to campaigning cat-sleeps beneath the stars. His curtains must be drawn back, all windows open to the earthy sounds and smells of the outside world. And she, luxurious child of palaces, would shiver and suffer, she supposed; but always, because the foible was part of him, she would do so with an indulgent smile. And she would be warm in his arms.

"But now you must be going," she warned, dragging herself back to the reality of the coming day. She let him take her again, and then, fulfilled and listless, began to laugh weakly. "How amusing it will be to meet again this morning over a council table, discreetly clothed, among a group of stuffy statesmen, discussing the fate of Guienne! And Charles with no inkling that I lay naked in your arms last night."

"I am afraid he is not the sort of man to remain without an inkling for long," said Mortimer, rising reluctantly from her bed and beginning to pull on shirt and hose.

"You think that he will mind?"

"It is the men who were wildest in their youth who are most apt to be scrupulous about their wives and sisters."

Isabel sat up against her pillows to argue with him. "But he advised me to it, only the last time I was here. 'If Edward should take another favourite——' he said. And I, poor fool that I was, cried out indignantly that he never would."

"Must we speak of Edward, who has so despitefully used us both?" Testily, Mortimer shook out his crumpled cloak, then turned and spoke to her more gently. "*You* have no cause to let your conscience ride you, Isabel. Certainly not the good cause that I have, with a chaste and self-righteous wife in Wales. But there is always the political aspect, I grant you. Charles will not want to seem in the eyes of the world to be harbouring scandal, nor in the eyes of the Pope, lest it turn sympathy towards England in this Guienne quarrel. And certainly it will not suit our future plans if he should withdraw his support and hospitality."

"*Our* plans? *Our* future plans?" questioned Isabel, all surprised attention. He did not answer, seeming to be occupied by the unaccommodating buckle of his swordbelt. "Am I then so soon become but part of a plan?" she demanded.

He came then to the foot of the bed, looking across at her, with a hand grasping a drawn curtain on either side of him. "If our lives are to be linked we shall both need plans," he told her reasonably. "And for the moment, in this business of Guienne, I suggest that you get the boy here."

Isabel stared at him in amazement. She was still warm and love drowsy, he as businesslike as if he were giving directions to one of his captains. She found such sudden change of mood disconcerting, but suspected that it was another of his peculiarities that she must learn to live with. "The boy? Ned, do you mean?" she repeated hazily. Then, all broken up by what she took to be his kindness, "Oh, Roger, I minded so much leaving the children. It was the only thing I *did* mind. Leaving them for— for this, I mean. It would be wonderful to have Ned, but I doubt if his father would ever——"

"Then bring up the idea in council this morning. Suggest that the King of England might be persuaded to send his son over to do homage in his stead," he told her.

She had always wanted a man who was decisive and masterful. She was immediately out of bed and clinging to him admiringly. "It is true what you say about our partnership. Together we could bring almost anything to pass!" she exulted, with a happy laugh. "Why did I not think of this before leaving England? It should delight the English and stop all this bickering."

"And leave you with all the cards in your own hands, my most ingenuous sweet," he said, with his boisterous laugh. He bent to embrace her, saw the key of the garden door lying on her table, slipped it into the leather pouch hanging from his belt, and went swaggering down the stairs.

Isabel was given an honourable place at her brother's council table. The assembled notables of France listened with flattering attention to her description of affairs in England. Starry eyed when she should have been languishing with sleeplessness, she brought up the matter of her elder son, and all present considered her a veritable Minerva of wisdom. "It is a possible way out and could be arranged. Of what age is he?" said Charles. And when Isabel told him that he was thirteen and well grown and *bien serieux*, he seemed pleased with the idea.

"It is by no means the first time that a King's son has sworn fealty in his father's place," urged Mortimer from further down the table.

"And apart from this question of homage I would willingly make acquaintance with this young nephew of mine," said Charles, drumming his fine fingers thoughtfully on a pile of state papers before him. "If his father allows him to come he will become Duke of Guienne."

And that evening after supper when he and Isabel were watching a masque he leaned across to her and spoke of it again under cover of the applause and laughter. "That son of yours, if I should like him, might well become more important than he imagines. Unless I live to beget sons."

Startled, she turned and looked at him. Tired as he sometimes looked, she had not known that there was any real anxiety for his health. They were both too deeply absorbed in this new train of thought to hear anything of the talk and music. "But there is our uncle's son——"

"Pah! Son of a second son, and a Valois!"

"Yet surely France would never consider—continuing the Capet line through a woman?"

"Probably not. Not here, with our Salic law. A pity," said Charles wearily, "for at least it might make an end of this everlasting feud between our two countries."

Isabel sat looking at him—at his clever mouth and heavily-lined eyes, and at the parchment tightness of the skin across the fine bones of his face. "If he should die to-morrow," she thought, shocked into silence, "by English law, I should be Queen of France."

CHAPTER 24

As soon as the other members of the Council had drifted away Roger Mortimer sauntered into the room where Isabel was resting in the sunshine by an open window. He came and leaned over the back of her chair—a shade too intimately, some of her women thought. "You think that King Edward will let him come?" he asked, his lips almost against her ear.

"I think that he will grasp at any alternative to coming himself, and that the Despensers will so advise him," she answered, pretending to watch the antics of a performing bear down in the courtyard lest anyone should suspect how wildly his proximity made her heart beat. "All the more so as Charles now knows how they have treated me. Though, to be sure, it will mean a wrench parting from the boy."

"I scarcely meant for that reason, but rather because of his own prestige." Mortimer bent to retrieve the well-worn *Chansons d'Amour* which, in her agitation, she had let fall, and lowered his voice as some ladies of the French Court passed by in a chattering bevy. "You realize, do you not, Madam, that if your son swears fealty, it is he who will bear the title?"

Isabel laughed because his estimate of her husband's nature was so wide of the mark. "Edward is not one to covet titles," she said, almost unaware that she was defending him. "He loves Ned and will delight in any honour shown him. He is proud of the boy—particularly of those very qualities in him which he himself does not possess." As the words passed her lips it seemed as though she saw for the first time her husband's vulnerability. The painful stabs of inferiority which the weak son of a warlike father must inevitably feel. The desire to shine at *something*, however unsuitable, before a public which expected great things of him. And his youthfully bewildered need for strange, private solaces. She thought she saw how he was unconsciously seeking fulfilment in his son, as well as hoping that the lad's strength and ability would protect him from similar difficulties. And the suddenness of this new clarity of understanding shook her to a sense of wrongdoing. "Is it because I am now so removed from Edward that I can at last see him objectively, without resentment?" she thought. "Or, being at last physically satisfied, do I grow more capable of compassion?"

But having chosen her course for the future, she knew that she could not afford to dabble in compassion for the past. Yet when time proved that she had judged Edward's reactions aright, she was glad for some more obscure reason than because they served her lover's scheming and her own convenience.

At the close of that strange, exciting summer King Edward sent the Prince in charge of the most kind and trustworthy prelate he could find—Walter Stapleton, Bishop of Exeter. Fashionable young courtiers like John of Bretagne and John Cromwell rode in his retinue, and Isabel herself journeyed to Boulogne to meet him. Edward had seen to it that his son came splendidly as the representative of England, and the only two provisos which he had made were that the duchy of Guienne should revert to himself in the unlikely event of his elder son dying before him, and that no overtures for a foreign marriage should be made without his consent.

All Paris was *en fête* again, and the Prince's coming did much to heal old sores. As he rode through the streets all who saw him were impressed by his height and horsemanship and by a manly bearing which belied his thirteen years. Charles himself was evidently moved by the grave but fearless courtesy of a lad who had been accustomed to enjoy his own father's company without repression. And at the solemn ceremony of feudal homage when he knelt to place boyish hands between those of his *suzerain*, and took his oath of allegiance in a voice alternating touchingly between the treble of childhood and the gruff beginning notes of manhood, his mother felt tears of pride stinging hotly against her eyeballs. However bitter the differences which had marred and finally broken up her marriage with Edward Plantagenet, they two had between them produced an heir to be proud of.

For the first time she saw her elder son as an individual, disassociated from the familiar associates and habits of home. As a Frenchwoman she did her best to guide him, although sadly aware that he gave her little of his confidence. And in spite of his extreme youth and the difficulties presented by being in a strange land, the new Duke of Guienne acquitted himself well. If he seemed a little heavy in the company of the gay and witty gallants of the Louvre, or slow in paying compliments to the daughters of proud families who pressed their charms upon his attention, or if he had associated so easily with his father's masons and fletchers and falconers that his French was marred by a strong Anglo-Saxon accent, it but made him all the more an unmistakable Englishman. And Guienne had gone with England ever since Richard Cœur de Lion's mother had brought it as her heritage.

Being still young in experience in spite of his splendid growth, Ned enjoyed with zest the entertainments provided for him, and took a healthy pride in his new estate. To the disappointment of the younger ladies of the court his interest lay in jousts and feats of arms rather than in dancing, masques and music. He liked to listen to King Charles and his ministers discussing such matters as might one day help him to take an active part in the ruling of his much neglected duchy. Roger Mortimer he scarcely noticed save as an important Welshman who had displeased his father. If he marvelled at his mother's graciousness towards him, he was too unsophisticated to wonder why the man spent so much time in her apartments, and his lack of interest piqued the proud border lord from the first.

"I will tell him how you climbed my kitchen chimney in the Tower, which is sure to intrigue a boy. And do you, milord, enter for the Michaelmas tournament and unhorse all comers," advised Isabel, amused by his obvious annoyance and anxious to feed her own pride upon his prowess. To her, Mortimer was the epitome of virility and courage, and she wished her son to see him in the same light.

Mortimer boldly wore her favour in the lists and, with the ease born of many a border fray and of his early training under Piers Gaveston—though with none of Gaveston's careless amusement—he bore all before him; and it was a high moment for Isabel, as Queen of Beauty, when he knelt to her to receive his guerdon in the sight of all the chivalry of France. And after that, nothing would do for the avidly watching young Duke but that he must take lessons from the champion to improve his own promising but immature thrusts, so that all present supposed that he had conceived a great admiration for the spectacular victor, and even Isabel was deceived into thinking so. But she could read her husband's mind more accurately than her son's. His was a singularly stubborn nature, given to pursuing the few ends he cared about with patience and singleness of purpose. And at this period of his life it was proficiency in arms Ned wanted, no matter from what source he acquired it.

Ned had no idea that the man who instructed him was his mother's lover, but disliked him instinctively, whereas King Charles, who had quite liked the Welshman, shared none of his nephew's innocent blindness.

"You have a diligent pupil there, Mortimer," he called as he sauntered through the tiltyard with his sister and stopped to watch them practising at the barrier. "And you, *ma soeur*, have a most spectacular lover," he added, lowering his voice and turning to Isabel, who was watching, bright-eyed, beside him.

She started and looked up at him in dismay, but was relieved to see no forbidding anger, only an eyebrow quirked in teasing amusement. "Your espionage must be better than I imagined —or my ladies less discreet," she murmured ruefully, with a little shamefaced laugh.

"It is the Sieur Mortimer who takes no pains to be discreet." Charles Capet's eyes were turned again towards the two ill-assorted figures in the almost deserted lists, and Isabel had the impression that his enthusiasm for his uninvited guest had waned.

"I did but take your advice, Charles," she reminded him. "'Take a lover,' you said, here in this very garden behind us, 'if Edward should give you further occasion.'"

Charles turned his back on the lists and, leaning against one of the gaily-decked stands, looked down at her with his inscrutable smile. "And the occasion arose, as anyone but an optimistic wife supposed it would?"

"Unfortunately."

"Little liar!" he countered. "The second blooming of beauty on your face shows that by that time you found it mighty fortunate. Oh, do not spit out at me, little hell-cat! I admit that were I a woman in your place married to that type of man I should probably have murdered him long ago. So for so long as you are my guest, *amuse-toi-bien*, *ma chère*. But do not take your affair too seriously. The man is not worth it."

"Not worth it!" retorted Isabel. "When he is the man most capable of keeping order in all that turbulent island kingdom, and has but yesterday out-fought the flower of your chivalry here?"

It had always seemed to her that Charles, even in childhood, had enjoyed the unfair advantage of keeping his temper. He shrugged and spread his hands in tolerant admission of her facts. "But what ultimate happiness will he give a woman?"

"He is the world's most ardent lover!"

"He would need to be to satisfy Isabel Capet!" grinned the head of her house. "I am only warning you that he will always put his own plans first. Even now, it seems, he is too arrogant to take pains to guard your good name. Our countrymen, who are not backward at such things, begin to smile covertly when he approaches you, and I would not have the rumour reach Edward."

"I know your thoughts are for me, and will try to persuade him to act more discreetly," Isabel promised docilely. "But I cannot help asking myself what further harm could such rumours do me? You know how Edward depends upon first this person and then that—so ardently and so briefly? And for that reason, Hugh Despenser fears I may yet regain some ascendancy, so he is already trying his utmost to persuade Edward to divorce me."

All the anger she had hoped for snapped now in Charles's dark eyes. "The impudent dog! What are our domestic concerns to do with such as he? By Saint Denis, Isabel, I will defend you from such insults!" She reached for his hand and kissed it passionately, but although he was quick to control his wrath his manner was still grave. "With my new marriage upon which the succession depends I want no scandal in the family, nor any further arguments to offend the Pope."

In the lists Mortimer and Ned had dismounted, and squires were hurrying to collect their gear. Charles began to walk back with her through the palace garden, with a brisk autumn wind swirling russet leaves about them. And as he walked he relented, remembering that she was all he had. "Do not think me too stern, dear Isabel," he said. "*Le bon Dieu* knows I have ever taken my pleasures where I found them. And I suppose that a woman as beautiful as you must want *amours*."

Hearing hurrying steps behind them and knowing that they would no longer be alone, Isabel clutched urgently at his arm. "No, no, you are wrong, Charles. Even as a girl I did not want *amours*. What I wanted—*always*, Heaven bear me witness—was a marriage like that of *la chère reine* Eleanor, for whom my father-in-law erected crosses. A passionate, life-long married love——" Neither Charles nor she understood her sudden urgency, nor the compulsion she felt to proclaim this truth aloud just once before a witness. Her son came bounding after them, sweating from exertion and babbling of some marvellous counter-thrust, and her pathetic words were swept away with the dying leaves by the autumnal wind. Dead of their own initial improbability, she felt. For what chance had she ever had, poor hopeful fool, of constant married love?

Charles laid a kindly arm across his excited nephew's shoulder, though neither of them took in what the boy said. "Is that to be your epitaph—'She wanted married love'?" he teased, regarding her keenly across Ned's tousled and unheeding head.

"I scarcely expect so kindly a one," admitted Isabel, with a bleak answering smile, knowing well that such worldly quips seldom mirror the unseen struggles of the soul.

When she reached her apartments she found a messenger from England who knelt before her with a letter from King Edward. A letter begging her, now that the necessary negotiations and homage were done, to come home.

It was easy to make excuses. There was the matter of her own heritage of Ponthieu. Ned had done homage for this, too, and was styled Count of Ponthieu, but the terms had been ambiguous. It was only reasonable to point out, with all wifely duty, that since her estates were so curtailed in England, she would need the revenues from that province during her lifetime, and that for convenience' sake the matter should be settled before she left France. And then again, Ned was profiting so much from the tournaments. Charles, who had taken a most fortunate liking to the boy, was arranging a series of jousts for young competitors in which the lad was wildly anxious to do well. Edward, she knew, would be the last to curtail his pleasure. And she herself would like to stay through the winter for her new sister-in-law's coronation. She sealed her letter in the knowledge that Hugh Despenser, her bitterest enemy, would surely read it and see through each excuse. Because he did not want her back, he might, in his soft suave way, add his persuasions to her own. But the most she could hope for was delay. The future was like a dark wavering curtain, and so that she need not try to peer behind it she gave herself gaily, passionately to every moment of the satisfying present.

And then began a series of letters reaching out to her, dragging at her, to bring her back. Edward charged her to cease from all pretences and delays and to come at once. She wrote then, openly refusing, and giving the Despensers' enmity as her reason. Entreaty changed to indignation as he perceived how he had been tricked. His letters grew formal with his sense of injury. But he wrote Charles a reasonable and brotherly letter, asking him to compel her to return and discrediting her complaint that she went in peril of her life from Hugh Despenser, refuting the suggestion by referring to those hypocritically friendly letters and overtures which she had undoubtedly exchanged with the man in order to get to France. The letter was so excellently composed that Isabel suspected that Despenser had had a hand in it, but when Edward finally appealed to his son it was unmistakenly a personal *cri de coeur*. "Fair Son," he wrote, "at your departure from Dover you said that it should be your pleasure to obey our commandments, as far as you could, all your days. It causes us great uneasiness of heart that you now say you cannot return because of your mother. Neither for her, nor for any other, ought you to displease us. We do not doubt but that your uncle the King will grant you safe conduct. So by the faith, love and allegiance which you owe us, do not delay to come to us."

After that only constant surveillance kept Ned from trying to persuade some of the younger men in his suite, such as John de

Bretagne and John Cromwell, to help him to return to England, and it was clear that he must have sent messages to his father by the Bishop of Exeter who had hurriedly and rather mysteriously returned thither.

When Mortimer tried to exercise authority over the young Duke, and to restrain his freedom, the boy naturally resented it. "He grows sulky," he complained, being accustomed to dealing firmly with grown men and having small tact with youngsters. And Isabel—in order to keep the peace between them—tried to talk reasonably with her son and to persuade him that right was on her side. She spoke of the misrule and unhappy state of England, blaming it with more personal enmity than justice on the Despensers. She reminded him how money and freedom had been denied her, and how her faithful French attendants had been sent away. Of her more personal wrongs she tried to speak guardedly, but she was living in a state of strain and was at all times a woman whose emotions must flare up urgently. Ned had no choice but to listen to her, and she felt that many of her arguments were beginning to colour his hitherto uncritical viewpoint, but she knew how much he hated it when she said anything which seemed to disparage his father. And as the months passed Edward wrote to the boy again pointing out bluntly that she had shamed both himself and Ned by appearing at the French coronation in the company of that "traitor and mortal enemy" Roger Mortimer. Isabel would have intercepted the letter if she could, because King Edward made her relationship with Roger Mortimer quite clear to his son, and from that time Ned, inarticulate with the raw hurt of being young and shamed and helpless, closed up his heart against her, and never spoke to Mortimer unless he was obliged to do so. Only the arrival of his uncle, Edmund of Kent, provided him with congenial company at that time. For in that gentle younger son of Marguerite Capet he found someone as bewildered as himself. A man who, while hating the Despensers, and having natural sympathy with his French relations, still loved England's unsatisfactory King.

To Isabel's grief, her brother Charles's attitude gradually changed towards her. Although he still allowed her hospitality, she knew that he avoided her and that his court would soon follow suit. She knew, too, that the remedy lay in her own hands, but she could not bring herself to break with Mortimer. Her body was utterly his, and the conviction that they were born to share some vaguely shaped destiny grew strongly in her mind. All Europe knew how she had deserted her husband to take a lover, and tattled of her shame. And she was honest enough to realize the uncomfortable position which she had created for Charles. There was a sincerity about Edward's letter which must have moved him in spite of all his cynicism and, whatever his private feelings, she knew that he would feel bound to support a fellow monarch against the treachery and insolent adultery of a subject. Edward's unjust and foolish provocation in rewarding years of loyal service by taking Mortimer's lands and giving them to a new favourite would not interest him, nor Europe either. Only the people of England seemed to take into account the marital difficulties which she had been forced to endure. Isabel ate the bread of humbleness at his court until the Pope himself intervened. His Holiness must have been prodded, she supposed, by Hugh Despenser. He censured Charles for harbouring the Queen of England against her husband's wishes and threatened to excommunicate him unless he turned her out of France immediately.

It was a sad day for Isabel when she knew that she must leave her native land. Charles ordered her and all her entourage to go, and threatened to confiscate the estates of any of his subjects who offered them assistance. But Isabel half suspected that it was with his knowledge that a mutual cousin, Robert of Artois, came at dead of night to warn her that orders had been given for her arrest, together with that of her son, the Earl of Kent and Lord Mortimer, and that they would be shipped back to England by force unless they were gone from Paris by the following morning.

All of them knew that to return would mean immediate execution for Mortimer. "I have had horses ready these three days for just such an emergency," he told her, as soon as the kindly cousin was gone.

Isabel was already giving orders to Hawtayne to waken her son and her brother-in-law. "But where shall we make for?" she asked, remembering how she had once asked the same question of her husband during another terrifying night, and been left behind alone at Tyneside. At least that would not happen to her now. Her lover would think and act for her. He was the kind of man she had always wanted.

"Across the northern border into Hainault," he said. "It will be the quickest and safest way out of France."

Her eyes met his consideringly. "The Count of Hainault is married to a cousin of mine," she recalled.

"Do you know them?"

"I scarcely remember them. But I remember Queen Marguerite saying that she liked them, and how sad it was that they had a family of small daughters and despaired of ever begetting a son."

The mention of Marguerite's name at such a moment was unfortunate. "If I had only learned to accept life as she would have me do, instead of fighting it!" she found herself thinking, as the full horror of the situation in which she had landed herself forced itself upon her. At the thought that she, Isabel of France, was escaping like a thief in the night to some strange country without state or welcome the blackness of the curtain shrouding her future seemed more impenetrable than ever. But there was no time for regrets, and she strove to stem her rising panic and to give coherent orders to her distracted women.

Mortimer had sent Dragon to fetch Sir John Maltravers, a friend who had fled to France after the execution of Lancaster, and it seemed that they two were the only men whom he intended to take. She could see him through the doorway of an outer room sketching a rough map of their proposed route for Maltravers and giving Dragon orders about the horses. By the time he returned to her she was already dressed for their journey. "Capable woman!" he said, smiling for the first time since the news came. "One day I must put you in command of a successful army."

"You had thought all this out before?" she said, pointing to the map which, together with all the ready money he had, he was cramming into the pouch hanging from his jewelled belt.

"We knew this had to come, you and I."

"Yet we never spoke of it. I was content, I suppose—for this short time stolen out of life—to be with you."

"Why speak of our partnership as if it were impermanent? It can go on, if you will have it so." He grasped her shoulders with his strong, square hands, and looked down searchingly into her face. "This route I traced for John Maltravers leads to the French border, but eventually it can lead to London."

"You always intended to go back?"

"Surely you know that?" He pushed her gently into a chair, poured wine for both of them, holding hers to her lips because her shaking hand would have spilled it. Then he perched on the table beside her and drank his own at a single draught. The light of a candle set in a tall sconce beside him threw into relief the strong lines of his clean-shaven face. "Isabel, it is time we talked of this with no shadow of pretence," he said, when the warm Bordeaux had steadied her. "What is in *your* mind for the future?"

"To go back to England with you—if you dare risk the return. Alone, I could never face that tormented life again. All the more, now that my conscience knows that my husband really has something against me. I can go only as an enemy."

"And when we get there?" he urged, not deeming it necessary to assure her that he would go, but leading her on that he might read her inmost mind.

"We shall find many friends."

"Friends, yes. But to the point of being supporters?"

"My cousin, Lancaster's son, could scarcely be anything else."

"Orleton, Bishop of Hereford, is busy on our behalf and writes me that more than half the barons would rise to our cause."

"And the people——" Isabel's lips curved into a reminiscent smile, and Mortimer grinned with satisfaction. "They worship you, their beautiful and injured Queen, do they not? Your uncle of Lancaster worked on them well."

"They love me for myself, without his scheming. And Marguerite used to say that if the people are on one's side——"

Their voices had sunk to whispers inaudible to her bustling women in the next room; their minds were so well attuned that half-sentences sufficed. "Roger, what *is* our cause?" she asked. "What do *you* plan to do when we get there?"

He twirled his empty tankard thoughtfully on the table before him. "Reclaim all that is mine. And yours. See you reinstated as an unhampered Queen. Help you to rule."

His daring outran her wildest thoughts. "And who," she asked, picking her words slowly, "would be King?"

"Your son."

"A puppet king, with the real power in our hands. Until England is in better shape again. Roger, you yourself would not want to be——"

"No, I swear it. The boy should be King, at least in name. Edward the Third."

"You had this in mind when you persuaded me to send for him?"

Mortimer did not deny it. He threw back his head and laughed. "Lord, what fools they were to let him come!" Then suddenly he was deadly serious, leaning forward so that the candlelight was glitteringly reflected in his strange, brown-flecked eyes. "Say that you are with me in this, Isabel."

She stood up and faced him across the table. She remembered the tempting tingling of power that had sometimes taken her unawares when Edward had been particularly foolish. "I believe that I, a woman, could rule England better than that tortured country has been ruled for years. I have often felt it. And with you beside me——"

"Then that is our cause. Does it satisfy you?"

She did not answer. Her momentary elation passed—elation for something which she felt to be full of fine possibilities. Mortimer leaned closer and his eyes compelled her. "I have told you my inmost thoughts, but time presses and you still withhold a part of yours. If we are in this fierce enterprise together there must be ruthless candour, without reserve or shame, between us. Deep down in your heart there is something more. Some goal that you have lived towards as I have lived towards this pageant of power. What is it, Isabel?"

She was surprised by his unusual perspicacity, and the steadiness of his gaze seemed to have some hypnotic power. Sometimes of late she had wondered if he really *had* some such power over her. The words were drawn out of her slowly, as though she were sleepwalking. She did not even know that she was going to say them. "To break Hugh Despenser for all that he has broken of mine." Shamelessly, she had put into words her most pressing immediate desire. Desire to revenge her broken marriage. Beyond that all was still dark and unmaterialized.

"That I can promise you," said Mortimer, as hurrying footsteps on the stairs proclaimed that all was in readiness for their departure.

Neither of them had mentioned Edward. For the present it was as if they had extinguished his unavoidable existence by pushing the thought of him from their minds.

CHAPTER 25

IT WAS pleasant and peaceful in the privy garden at Valenciennes and Isabel, tired by her long and anxious journey, was thankful to wander without ceremony in the late spring sunshine. Sweet-

scented gilly flowers blossomed around her, and she found it soothing to listen to the contented cooing from the tall stone dovecote,
or to sit lazily watching a procession of small white clouds floating
across the vast inverted bowl of sky above the flat fields of the
Netherlands.

Although grave hazards still remained to be faced in the future,
most of her immediate anxieties had proved groundless. No one
could have received greater kindness than she, ever since her
party had come over the French border into Hainault. It had been
like living in another world. No scandalous notoriety seemed to
have preceded her into this sleepy province of the holy Roman
Empire, and her cousin, Joanna of Valois, and the chivalrous
Count of Hainault had received her with open arms. Her fragile
beauty and obvious distress had won sympathy for her from their
subjects. "Banished from her own brother's court," people said.
"And unkindly treated by her husband before that!" Isabel
could not understand their guttural tongue, and it was her cousin
Joanna who translated the remarks overheard in every street
crowd that turned out to do the English Queen honour and to
marvel at the latest Paris fashion of her elaborate winged headdresses. And it was Joanna, kind credulous creature, who had
repeated in shocked tones to her husband William of Hainault
the whole tale of wrongs that Isabel poured out to her.

"She shall not want for money or freedom *here*," he had vowed
in a rumbling attempt at French, nodding and smiling encourag-
ingly at his wife's distressed relative and finding himself rather
pleased to be able to tell his friends that he had a Queen staying
in his comfortable castle.

And so in the kindness of their hearts they gave several of their
prodigious banquets, and between whiles received Ned into their
family circle of growing daughters and frequently left Isabel to
sit in their own private garden with her own people—with her
gentle, good-looking brother-in-law who was also related to them
through his mother, and with the devoted Welsh lord who had
brought her out from Paris with so much efficiency and who
seemed to be in charge of her affairs.

"How right Roger was to come here!" exclaimed Edmund of
Kent with a sigh of grateful relief, as soon as the three of them
were left alone.

Isabel smiled at them both impartially, but Mortimer was
standing a little apart with a foot on the coping of a small fish

pond, chin buried in palm, his mind clearly on something else, so she went on talking to her husband's half-brother, who looked at times so disconcertingly like him. "I shall not soon forget the surprise or the kindness of that knight who took us in at Ostrevant. Nor of the way his wife cared for us. It was a poor sort of place and they had a family of growing children to feed, but they gave us of their best. What was his name, Edmund?"

"Sir Eustace d'Ambreticourt."

"I pray you remember it so that I may one day do something to repay them."

"As meticulously as you insisted upon doling out coins to pay your creditor before we left Paris, even though Roger was fuming and the horses were champing at the door!" teased Edmund, breaking a manchet of bread which he had brought to feed the rising carp. "But it is true that we have much to thank the d'Ambreticourts for. It was they who thought to send news of your arrival immediately to Valenciennes."

"And then that eager young brother of William's came to fetch us here."

"The impressionable Sir John of Hainault," said Kent, smiling at the pleasant recollection.

"A very knight-errant out of the Arthurian legends, with his Saxon blue eyes and his wavy flaxen hair."

"And all ready to fall beneath the spell of a beautiful damsel in distress, and to tilt for her against the whole wicked world!"

They laughed at the thought of how completely the inexperienced young knight had been bewitched by her beauty. "Well, if there was no such dramatic need to do that, at least he brought us all here in comfort and with an adequate escort," said Isabel, holding out a hand for a piece of the bread. The fish were jumping greedily and she began feeding them too, and would have been content to sit there in pleasant idleness for the rest of the morning.

But Roger Mortimer seldom suffered people to sit idle for long. His own mind had been on his next move ahead. "In spite of the kindness which your Grace's relatives have shown us we cannot afford to outstay our welcome here as we did in France," he said. "And it seems to me that now, at the flood tide of Flemish sympathy, we may be able to raise some supporters."

Isabel was relieved to notice that before her brother-in-law he had the good sense to address her more formally than when they were alone. Reluctantly, she ceased throwing breadcrumbs into the sunlit pool. "You mean, milord, that you think we should be preparing to leave as soon as possible?"

"I do, Madam. All the more so because it will give us the invaluable advantage of taking our enemies by surprise. But the question my mind has been working on is where shall we land? Naturally, I would suggest Wales, where every man would be for me, were it not for the twin facts that it would necessitate a much longer sea voyage and that, in my opinion, we should strike first at London." He turned to Kent. "Have you any ideas about a landing place, milord?"

"Why not East Anglia where my brother of Norfolk's lands lie? Somewhere near his great stronghold of Framlingham?"

"What port would you suggest? I do not know that part of England."

"There is the river Orwell, where the Flemish weavers' ships put in, and our own wool merchants' wherries set sail. It is a sheltered place, and not too far from London."

"We could run up this river Orwell at night. And you think that your brother the Earl of Norfolk will join us?"

"He hates the Despensers as much as I do."

Mortimer drew a small folded note from between the buttons of his green and gold *cote-hardie*. "Madam, I had this from England but an hour ago. It is from Bishop Orleton of Hereford. He says that he and my mother and your late uncle of Lancaster's son, Lincoln, have been working diligently for us. And that such is the response among barons and merchants alike all up and down the country, that they say they can promise success if only we will let them know the time and place of our landing and bring with us at least a thousand men."

"A thousand men! When we came here with only Maltravers and Dragon and a handful of Edmund's squires and pages. No wonder you have been so ponderously silent!"

"Foreign mercenaries are our only hope. They are usually to be got in these Empire states, and some of these German mercenaries are remarkably well trained."

"But how could we persuade them to cross the sea on what would seem to them a wild cause, unsponsored by their Emperor or by the King of France?"

Even Mortimer was forced to admit uncertainty by an expressive shrug. "Only by paying them good wages, I suppose."

"With what?" asked Kent pertinently. It was he who stood apart now, as if marshalling second and more cautious thoughts with which to confound their hopes. "Who among us draws a penny from his estate, being banished? And of those supporters in England many are suspect. Since that unfortunate accident in the lists, poor Lincoln is half blind. And what, my dear sister, do you propose to tell Ned? Is he to accompany us to England in the certain knowledge that we shall be bearing arms against his father?"

"His father and Hugh Despenser are, as we all know to our cost, indivisible," retorted Mortimer. "And in any case the Duke is but a child."

Ned's voice came to them at that very moment, calling cheerfully after one of Hainault's daughters as they pursued some game on the other side of a tall box hedge, and Isabel could not but feel grateful that he *was* still a child. That his voice held again that note of boyish eagerness which had been silenced too long in sullen resentment. This Court of Valenciennes was a good place, free from cynicism and scheming, and a small maternal part of her wished that the boy could stay in it, undeceived and unexploited, to grow to decent manhood among those guileless-faced girls of Joanna's. She saw Edmund go to join them, as if some element of simplicity in him were drawn from treachery towards their happy laughter. Mortimer turned too and watched him disappear through an arch cut in the thickness of the yew. "He is only half-heartedly in this," he said regretfully.

"Because his heart is still half with Edward. As a young man he adored him and now he is torn between that caring and his desire to destroy the Despensers," answered Isabel, reading Edmund's troubled state from her own.

"The same desire for revenge which obsesses you."

He put a protective arm about her as if to wipe out the hardness of his words. "Perhaps he is even naïve enough to believe that when we have achieved it Edward will be left to us just as he used to be," she added, following her previous train of thought in spite of her lover's proximity. And he, with disconcerting suddenness, moved away and remarked that Kent had been quite right about the difficulty of dealing with Ned when he should find himself placed in unwilling opposition to his father. And asked, in his most practical tones, how much she intended to tell the boy. It was, she supposed, a proof of the perfection of their partnership, that they found themselves as close in matters of policy as in the union of their bodies.

"At least he should be glad to get back to his own horses and hawks and to the lively companionship of that lad of Griffin's," he said. "With all his martial aptitudes he must be most uncommonly bored playing foolish games with all those girls."

"On the contrary, he seems to be enjoying himself immensely," said Isabel a little sharply, as another peal of concerted laughter reached them. "Have you not noticed, Roger, how much happier and more tractable he has been since we came here? It may well be that——"

"That what, my dear?"

But the thought taking shape in Isabel's mind was as yet too unformed, and too daring, to be spoken of. She was merely a woman, unauthorized to promote national alliances, so far-reaching in their results. But one of the immediate results of such a move might help her lover, and win that approving smile of his and the high regard for which she lived. "Leave him to me," she said. "I will go and enter into their gaiety—do all I can to prepare a happy approach—before I talk to him—persuasively."

She would have left the garden for the tiltyard where the younger people played, but before she reached the archway, Mortimer's words halted her like a sharp command.

"There is another to whom it is of yet more importance that you should talk—persuasively," he said.

"Of whom do you speak?" She stopped short and turned to look at him. He was smiling at her from across the pond, and for once the practical leader and the ardent lover seemed to have become a little mixed.

"That latest victim of your charms. Young John of Hainault. I am told he has the ordering of more than five hundred men. He could be useful to us."

"You think he would come and fight for us?"

"For you." Mortimer came to her quickly with that almost cat-like tread which never failed to surprise her in so muscular a man. Without touching her body, he bent and kissed her on the lips. "You could drive a man into doing anything, my woman. I hate the very thought of it, but go on bewitching him, the young fool. Offer him—anything. If only he will come and bring those five hundred men. After all," he added, standing back with a half-shamefaced laugh, "I can always hide behind the arras and kill him at the last moment if he tries to take too much."

But Isabel neither laughed nor fumed that he should ask it of her. She stood, eyes wide agaze, seeing something which would always be beyond his vision. "No, no, my love," she said softly, taking his weather-roughened face between soft fingers. "You need not so torture yourself. That is not the way to come by them at all."

"What surer way is there with a man?"

"All men are not the same. Some serve their ideals rather than their passions. They would sooner reach out for some unattainable Fata Morgana than possess a sinful woman. Oh, not many!" she admitted, seeing his restive shrug. "But when their mothers have made them that way it shows in the aspiring selflessness of their eyes. And what Edmund said in jest just now of John the knight-errant is true. We shall carry him further with us by leading him on some selfless crusade than by tempting him to my bed."

"You may be right," said Mortimer, who was always willing to allow the value of her more intuitive knowledge in such matters. "For myself, I am more at home with the workings of a siege-mine or an ambuscade."

"But you must have seen some of this gentle idealism in Edmund, too. He has some quality inherited from the loveliness of his mother but lacks strength to transmute it into the dedicated strength of a great leader, as we hope Sir John of Hainault will."

"So long as you persuade him to espouse our cause, no matter by what means——"

Isabel went to him and slipped her arms coaxingly about his neck, noticing as she did so how much less tall he was than Edward. "And as for you, my dear Roger, to whom such visionary qualities are not granted, the least you can do is to refrain from disillusioning him. I pray you curb that arrogance which I adore and do not come too openly as my lover. A too-blatant display of our relationship may blur the appealing picture of a much-wronged wife. Besides alienating Ned when I would most wish to influence him."

He gripped her wrists as if to disengage them. "You mean," he flung at her furiously, "that once in England you would have me keep away from your bed?"

But she pressed herself against him with sudden passion. Her small forefinger smoothed the sullenness from his mouth. "No, dear fool! I mean only—come softly and come late. Come disguised as my confessor or the chandler's apprentice or what you will. Only *come.*" She clung to him, laughing, then with closed eyes lay still for a moment or two against his heart. "For truly I think that if you ever cease to do so life will end for me."

He held her then at arm's length so that they looked closely into each other's eyes. "I myself will die before that happens," he said slowly, as though he were looking into the future and making her some solemn vow.

"Then anything else I can endure. Leave me to deal with awkward sons and dragon-slaying knights," she said, hiding beneath a show of light-hearted gaiety how much his words had moved her.

She left him then and went to join Ned and his new-found friends. With Edmund, she would have sat on a grassy bank to watch them play with their shuttlecocks. But at sight of her the straight-limbed girls, redeemed from plainness only by the freshness of their youth, sank to the ground in over-awed curtsies. The laughter died on their wide, kind lips. She perceived that to them she was not just their new friend's mother, but Queen Isabel the Fair and the pattern of all fashion and beauty, with a knowledge of court etiquette far exceeding their own. In an effort to put them at ease she would have set them all to dancing, herself trying to teach them the whirling steps of a gay new Provençal dance called a Waltz. But her efforts were useless. They clung together shyly, their good Flemish faces all looked alike, she could not even remember their names. All except the tall, dark one whom Ned had chosen as his partner in the short-lived dance.

But at least she had the satisfaction of knowing that Ned had been pleased by her attention. He was obviously proud of her beauty and her grace which still, in her early thirties, could make a group of almost marriageable girls look and feel like a posse of raw milkmaids. He escorted her back to her apartments, more smiling and talkative than he had been for months, and she took advantage of his closer filial approach to say what she had come to say.

She paused by 'the gate of her cousin's herb garden. "Just before we left Paris I had another letter from your father."

She saw Ned's face light up. "He is well?" he asked, with all his old naturalness. "And we shall be returning soon, Madam?"

"Yes, we shall be returning to England soon. The King did not mention his health, perhaps because there were graver matters afoot. His Grace is negotiating for a betrothal between your sister Eleanor and the King of Aragon."

Ned made a cheerful grimace. "Poor child, if she has to learn all their stiff Court etiquette!" he said, with the casual uncomprehending pity of fourteen. "But it will be some years yet before she will be old enough to go."

His face was turned towards her in full sunlight so that Isabel could read his least reaction, and she sprang the rest of her news upon him with purposeful suddenness. "His Grace is also arranging for *you* to marry the King of Aragon's daughter."

The youthful Duke of Guienne stood stricken. All happiness was quenched from his face. He put a hand to the neck of his *cote-harde* as if to loosen it so that he might breathe. "No! Oh, no!" he cried, in a hoarse incredulous whisper.

"But why should you mind so much?" she asked reasonably. "You must have known that a marriage would soon be arranged for you with *some* eligible princess."

"But I—I cannot spend the rest of my life with some Spanish girl who gabbles in a foreign language," he broke out.

"Marriage is certainly for a long time," she agreed, full of pity for him. "But we all have to accept this—political bartering —which takes no account of personal happiness. Particularly a King's elder son."

He did not answer, but she saw the desperation in his eyes. She wanted to console him by saying, "Some of us are driven to take our pleasures elsewhere," but she was his mother. She did not want it to be like that for him. She went and laid a hand on his arm. "Is it only the matter of the language, Ned? Or would you not have minded so much—*before we came here*?"

She knew that she had crystallized into words a fact which he himself had scarcely realized, and that in his deliberate way he was digesting it. "Come, come, Ned. Which one of them is it?" she teased, with a rallying smile. "The dark one whom you were dancing with?"

He shot her a quick glance as though resenting her frightening feminine divination. "That was Philippa," he said, in what he hoped were non-committal tones. "She can talk quite intelligently about herbal remedies for a wound or training a hawk— for a girl. And she cried when she heard I might be leaving—

236

soon." He would probably mature into one of those huge strong men who are rendered ludicrously helpless by a woman's tears, thought Isabel, repressing a smile. And suddenly he was appealing to her and, as he did so, looking almost a grown man already. "Can you not do something, *ma mère*—can you not persuade the King—you who can persuade any man to anything——" he was saying, incoherent as usual where his emotions were concerned. And saying it in that gruff, breaking voice of his which had a way of catching at her heart.

"We will see, my son," she promised soothingly. "Milord Mortimer and I will see what we can do." It would be good to win Ned's gratitude as well as to be making him an unwitting partner in their plans.

That evening at supper she took more careful stock of the girl with the blue-black hair and the kind, honest eyes who might one day be her daughter-in-law.

"Heaven knows what he sees in her," she said a few hours later, lying warm in Roger Mortimer's arms. "Of course, it may be only the *type* of woman he wants. The untemperamental, help-meet type which Flanders breeds. He once swore to me—rather unflatteringly, *n'est ce pas?*—that nothing would induce him to marry a Frenchwoman. This Philippa is not the eldest, and any one of them might do. But Ned has one of those tenacious memories and a kind of slow determination——"

"A most damnable obstinacy at times," agreed Mortimer feelingly.

"I told him that you, too, would try to help him in this. In the hope that it would make him like you better."

"That will be pleasant," said Mortimer with irony. "But I do not see how even between us we can betroth a lad without his father's consent. Particularly in face of these almost completed negotiations with Aragon which you speak of."

"Edward will not be in power for long after you land, and for a Valois my cousin Joanna tattles most indiscreetly. She is always bemoaning the fact that she cannot bear sons. 'William and I will find it hard to make good marriages for all four daughters,' is a favourite theme. Pressed upon me with intent, perhaps. So I do assure you there will be no difficulty in arranging an alliance before we leave."

"Before we leave?" Mortimer sat up to run frenzied fingers through the dishevelled crispness of his hair. "But who, in the midst of trying to raise money for an invasion, wants to be encumbered with the fripperies of a royal bride?"

Isabel laughed and drew him back against her pillows. "The bride is far too young to take," she said. "But considering the prosperity of these Flemish towns, William might be persuaded to pay her dowry *now*. Which would pay our troops."

Mortimer let out a long breath of amazement. Even up to that moment he had not realized the driving skill of his partner. Admiringly, he had to admit that it surpassed his own. "But Ned," he objected, with unaccustomed caution. "One day, I suppose, he must come to some sort of power. And one day he and his bride must know. They could say that we *stole* her dowry."

Isabel lay back against his shoulder with a sigh of content. "Without the troops—and the risks we take—he could not marry her at all," she pointed out, with incontrovertible logic.

CHAPTER 26

"There are some women who live gently all their lives, Ghislaine, but to me, whom men call 'Isabel the Fair', every conceivable adventure must happen." Laughingly, yet with tears of gratitude still glistening in her eyes, the Queen of England stopped dramatically in her restless pacing of a tavern room in Harwich. The light from hastily brought candles shone on the travel-stained grandeur of her rich brocades, on cheeks white with weariness and on eyes blazing with the heady excitement of success.

Ghislaine, who had come with her husband to be among the first to greet her, marvelled how anyone so utterly exhausted could still manage to look so spectacularly beautiful. "Or does she only bewitch us all into thinking so?" she wondered. "Let me take off that poor torn dress and unbind your Grace's hair," she urged, prodding doubtfully at the unpromising hardness of the bed.

Touched by her solicitude, the Queen stopped her pacing and went with swift steps to kiss her. "Oh, Ghislaine, it is good to have you back! Now that I have had to part with Bringnette there are so few people I can really speak my mind to. But her poor rheumatics were so bad that she begged me to leave her to rest awhile in that property the King provided for her old age at Ponthieu." Even present relief and success could not protect Isabel from a stab of sadness at the thought, and the loneliness went all the deeper because she knew in her heart that it had been disapproval of her adultery with Mortimer rather than rheumatics which had prompted Bringnette's request.

"I can make your Grace a soothing posset as she used to do. She taught me her special brew. 'Against the day when I am dead and the Queen might need one,' she said."

So here, in this humble impersonal place, her old nurse seemed to be still caring for her. Isabel threw open the casement, low under the thatched eaves, and the clang of church bells seemed to fill the little room, while out in the darkness the low Essex coastline was fringed with blazing bonfires. "How can I even *want* to sleep to-night?" she exclaimed, then turned to speak more soberly. "You know, Ghislaine, I never really *believed* that we should land—much less be so received. At first, when we planned this in Hainault, we had nothing. Except," she added with a laugh, "a very doubtful reputation!"

When she laughed like that Ghislaine recognized some subtle difference in her—a new and brittle hardness—which made her want to look away. "But Robert says you landed with twice the number of men we dared hope," she said.

Although it was only September Robert le Messager had insisted upon a fire being lit lest the guest room should be damp, and Isabel was glad to sit in the only chair before it. "The Bishop of Hereford wrote that we must bring at least a thousand men," she said, with the same secret, mocking laughter in voice and eyes. "And for some reason that charming Sir John of Hainault became inflamed by the sight of beauty in distress and begged Count William to allow him to espouse our cause and bring a sizeable army of Flemings. He himself is in charge of them, of course. And milord Mortimer is down there on the harbour now giving instructions to at least a thousand Englishmen who have joined us. So that already we have nearer three thousand. And, believe it or not, my dear Ghislaine, their wages will be promptly paid!"

It was this frequent unbending from royal hauteur to almost

youthful gaiety which endeared her to the closest of her attendants. "But *how*, Madam? You would need to pawn your crown to pay all those men," laughed Ghislaine, less timid than she used to be before she became a cherished wife and new-made mother.

"Oh—somehow," answered the Queen evasively. "I always believe in paying for service. Although—as I should well know— there is a service of the heart such as yours and Bringnette's which no mere coins can repay."

Their slow, mutual smile was settlement enough. "Since your Grace cannot sleep, will you not sit quietly and tell me of your journey?" suggested Ghislaine, to cover their moment of emotion.

"Life seemed to be all sunshine and kindness in Hainault," recalled Isabel, leaning her head back gratefully against a cushion. "My cousin and her huge kind bear of a husband prepared everything for the comfort of our journey. We slept at a place called Mons and sailed from Dort. Milords of Kent and Mortimer were anxious to disembark unobserved, at night, on some lonely beach; but, God pity us, it was so very dark and lonely on your beach that there seemed to be no habitation at all. They rigged up a kind of tent for me from the Syrian carpets which Sir John had put in the cabin. One of our smaller ships had run aground and been staved in on some rocks, and the sailors dragged some of her timbers across the shingle and lit a fire to warm me. But they dared not make too big a blaze for fear of attracting enemy attention. It was a blustery night and although I wore milord Mortimer's cloak I sat and shivered till dawn. By then I could stand the suspense no longer—the suspense of not knowing what lay ahead of us—so I gave the order to march, and as soon as it was light we saw this little town."

"And the workers out in the fields came running with news of your arrival, and Thomas of Brotherton, Earl of Norfolk, rode out through the city gates with all his armed men to meet you."

"And greeted me with the assurance that we were on his land and that already a small army of barons and knights and retainers were here to greet us. And even some of the Bishops, with Adam Orleton of Hereford. I do not think I have ever heard more welcome words. Though it seems so foolish now, looking round at all the friendly faces, to think how afraid I have been of failure." She sat for a while in brooding silence before remembering the lateness of the hour. "But I must not keep you from your bed any longer, Ghislaine, or I shall have black looks from Robert in the morning."

Ghislaine made her obeisance. "And you, Madam?" she asked, anxiously noting the return of tired lines which excitement had hidden.

"I must be alone awhile—to realise it all."

The Queen's voice sounded as if she were already alone, and almost before the door was closed she was pacing the room again. Trying to realize the magnitude of the thing she had done, and to assess the encouragement of success that had so far attended it. Realizing that she had put herself in the position of a traitor, and praying for strength to carry her plans through. Picking up her white ermine cloak which had been carefully brought ashore, she flung it about her shoulders and began rehearsing for the morrow when she would ride inland, through familiar towns and countryside, testing the heart of England. But her sure intuition made her throw the priceless thing aside. "*This* is what will gain the chivalrous indignation of the men, and the woman-to-woman sympathy of their wives. This once queenly gown all mired by exiled roads and torn with sitting on inhospitable beaches," she decided, spreading the spoiled skirts which Ghislaine would have discarded and controlling her dancing steps to a semblance of frail sadness. "This is how they shall see me—with neither heralds nor pursuivants nor crown. I will ride among them and smile and stretch my hands for their unwashed mouths to kiss." Enchantingly, she began to mime her rôle. "And they will shout for me as they used to do, only more wildly. And this time Edward will not ride beside me, a figurehead acknowledging an ill-deserved part of what was never his. This time it will be all mine, the shouting and the cheering. And this time it will carry me on—to Westminster? To God knows what."

And as she moved back and forth in the small tavern room, swaying and smiling graciously from side to side, remembrance of their cheering and her briefly-tasted sense of power rose in her, exquisite and heady as good wine. It was a part of her—a temptation and a weapon—a fierce secret enjoyment which even her lover could not share. And as the days of her journeying passed, with their scenes of wild enthusiasm, it became a craving and a necessity, a rich dangerous food from which she drew strength so that Mortimer and all her followers marvelled at her decisive courage and her determination to push forward.

Her cousin Lincoln had joined her. His men with the badge of the red antelope were everywhere. And as they all marched, four thousand strong or more, people flocked to them from every place they passed through. And everywhere her troops were fed, because it was a known fact that Queen Isabel paid people for their pains. Frenchwoman though she was, the English saw in her a saviour from a state of disorder of which they were sick to their very souls.

As they approached London they halted, coming upon a parchment signed with the royal seal, attached to the door of a town hall. Robert le Messager ran up the steps and read it aloud to her while her officers gathered round. It was a proclamation offering a thousand pounds for the head of the arch-traitor, Roger Mortimer, and all who had taken up arms against their King. And, coupled with the silent angry looks of the crowd in that part of the country, was enough to give them pause. Mortimer himself laughed carelessly, reaching across him to pull the notice down and tear it across and trample it beneath his muddy boots. But Edmund of Kent blanched, and Sir John of Hainault, uncertain of relative values and conditions in a strange country, came courteously to the Queen and asked if it was her pleasure to push on or to turn aside.

"The King makes special exception of your Grace, of the Prince and of myself," pointed out Edmund of Kent, retrieving a piece of the fluttering parchment and touched almost to the point of wishing himself back at his brother's side.

Isabel was touched too, but she looked at Roger Mortimer laughing carelessly on the steps of the little town hall with his strong body in danger from the poignard of any King's man, and steeled herself against such weakness. "My friends' lives are as dear to me as my own. I would neither profit by such exception, nor change our plans," she said, leaning from her saddle to touch her faithful Flemish knight on the shoulder.

"Then we ride on?"

"We ride on, but we will first give his Grace the King an answer to his proffered reward of a thousand pounds for the head of milord Mortimer. An answer which I fear he will not like," she said. And seeing that they all awaited her pleasure, she raised hand and voice to call an order to le Messager. "My good Robert, have one of the clerks of this town write a yet bigger parchment offering double that sum for the head of Hugh Despenser."

The great shout that went up almost drowned her words. She knew that it was the most dangerous thing she could have done—the biggest offence to Edward, who had shown himself desirous of treating her generously. But judging by the way in which her decision uplifted the hearts of her followers it was also the most popular. And she saw the look of admiring gratitude in Roger Mortimer's eyes as he swung round in sudden surprise.

"Would it not be wise, dear sister, to write a kind of manifesto to the people explaining that our coming in arms is in no way intended against the King, but rather to deliver the kingdom from the oppression of those who mislead him?" Kent was urging pacifically, after a few soothing words to the young Prince who had been urgently plucking at his sleeve.

Isabel's eyes sought Mortimer's, knowing well that both of them intended to go further. But he nodded assent. "It would be expedient," he agreed.

"Such a document can scarcely be prepared in the saddle. I should need time for thought," she objected, not too anxious to commit herself.

"If your Grace pleases we could turn aside and pass the night at Wallingford," he suggested, having been familiar with the place when in the household of Piers Gaveston. "Then proclamation of the reward and manifesto of our motives can be published together in London in advance of our arrival."

"Where would your Grace wish them to be affixed?" asked le Messenger eagerly.

There were cries of "St. Paul's" and "the Guildhall" and a daring suggestion that since the King and the Despensers had, upon hearing of their landing, taken up residence in the Tower, the Queen's riposte should be affixed, at dead of night, upon their own gates. And one huge bowman shouted amid roars of laughter, "Put the Queen's proclamation about Hugh Despenser on London Bridge to bide there till it be joined by his swollen head!"

But while they shouted and argued Isabel was thinking back into the past, and deciding upon a place which she felt would tend to touch the chivalry in men's hearts and be most suitable to the cause of a distressed and disappointed Queen. "Do you remember, Robert, riding with me when I first came through the village of Charing and telling me the lovely story of Queen Eleanor's statue? I would have my appeal to the good people of England fixed *there*, at the foot of the *Chère Reine* cross."

"Dragon will go on ahead and find means to fix it there against our coming," said Mortimer, having no wish to entrust such incriminating documents to anyone else. "It should rouse the Londoners to receive us with more assurance when we come."

But in the end they did not go to London. Her appeal must have elicited more sympathy than she had dared to hope. All along Mortimer had underestimated her popularity, but the Bishop of Hereford was shrewd enough to persuade him that it could, upon occasion, be a more potent weapon than his practised leadership. Adam Orleton's spies were everywhere and it was already known at Wallingford that King Edward had sent for the Sheriffs of London and charged them to defend the city, that he had taken his second son John into the Tower with him and was strengthening its defences. His masons were working feverishly from sunrise to sunset, and then by flares at night.

"Why does he not come out like a man to meet me?" demanded Mortimer. "He and the greedy Despenser rat who hides with him after gnawing at my lands."

"Why, indeed?" thought Isabel, sick with shame for the Plantagenet who was her husband. Yet she could not but be thankful for his pusillanimity suspecting as she did that had the rightful King of England risen up in the first place to defend his own from a horde of foreigners, half England would probably have risen with him instead of flocking to her aid.

All he had done, seemingly, was to send some soldiers to tear down her mocking offer of reward for the Despenser's head, but a band of mere 'prentice boys had taken upon themselves to encircle the Queen's cross to defend it. And just as Isabel and her hugely augmented army were about to march for London Dragon rode in with the news that King and favourite had fled, leaving young John of Eltham in the care of Lady Despenser and the kindly Bishop of Exeter, who had been Governor of the Tower since the disgrace of the unfortunate Sir Stephen Segrave.

"Now is the moment to take your capital city in the Queen's name!" cried Sir John, lifting his shining sword aloft. And to all present it must have seemed a moment for the successful culmination of an extremely chancy enterprise. But Isabel, already mounted, sat silent in her saddle. In this sudden unexpected division of objective she realized that even taking London, with all the inevitable flattering acclaim, would be but a sidetracking of her real intention—a disappointment to her deepest desire.

"The Londoners can be relied upon to hold their City against our return, milords," she said. "Let us rather ride westward after the Despensers."

"They have so long a start." "Once they get into the Welsh mountains they may well escape." "We should like to make sure of London first," her leaders counselled, in concerted disapproval.

"I, too, would find it easier to stay. I had hoped to see my children," she told them firmly. "But there are bigger things at stake, milords. Have we not set out to right the wrongs of this disordered country? And to cure a disease one must first find, and cut out, the canker."

"Her Grace is right there," said Bishop Orleton.

Roger Mortimer contributed no opinion. He knew that it was neither the King nor his capital that Isabel wanted with such driving intensity—but to get her hands on Hugh Despenser. Those little gloved hands now gripping the reins of her horse as firmly as if they were already about her enemy's neck. His own desire for revenge ran in the same direction, and he had no wish to gainsay her. "We are ready armed and the sutlers have the wagons laden. We will ride westward," he ordered.

To Sir John of Hainault it must have seemed like turning their backs upon a military objective of the first importance, and a deliberate disappointing of his troops. But if he had learned two things since the day he landed they were that the English with their strange feuds and friendships were inexplicable, and that the beauty of the lady he served was at times almost eclipsed by her courage. And when they halted for a night at Gloucester and a messenger overtook them with the news that London was entirely in the hands of her supporters he began to respect her wisdom as well.

"Is my son John safe?" she asked immediately.

"Safe and well, Madam. And the Sheriffs wish me to assure your Grace that they will keep him so until you return to us," the mud-bespattered man told her eagerly. "They have named him Warden of the City and do but act for you in his name."

"Then the Tower itself is in their hands?" said Mortimer.

"The Lady Despenser ordered the gates to be opened—in panic, after——"

"After what?" cut in Isabel. "And what right had that woman to interfere? I had supposed that the Bishop of Exeter——"

245

The messenger, a decent merchant, began to look less assured. "After the mob had murdered him," he said.

In the shocked silence that followed his words the Queen's grief and anger were patent. "They were maddened by misrule. They thought to please you, Madam," he stammered, turning to take a covered casket of some sort from his servant. "The Sheriffs have sent your Grace his head."

In mid hall he would have removed the cloth had not Isabel turned away with a horrified cry. Shocked beyond all caring for appearances, she clung to Mortimer. "No! No, I will not look," she protested. "He was a good old man, and often kind to me. I did not intend when I landed that such as Walter Stapleton should pay for it." Answering to Mortimer's warning pressure on her clinging hand, she made an effort to recover her composure and to speak civilly to the abashed messenger. "Take it— take your casket—on to Exeter with all reverence—to his own cathedral, where Devon priests will sing masses for the poor man's unhoused soul," she ordered. "And let no man say I had any part in this uncalled-for thing which was done in my name."

"A sad miscarriage of revenge, but now we have set ourselves to change our world you must steel yourself to accept such things," Mortimer warned her that night. "It is not only the culpable who pay."

"You will not find me so womanish when it comes to the culpable," she promised.

The King and the Despensers had taken refuge in Bristol castle, and most efficiently did John of Hainault and Roger Mortimer and purblind Lincoln lay siege to it. With their ever-increasing army, to which men from Somerset towns still flocked, the result was a foregone conclusion. Isabel lived with her army. It was one of those times in her life when intense preoccupation crowded out all need of luxury. She waited, strained and hard-faced, in her tent. And when the day of surrender came and a triumphant fanfare of trumpets proclaimed that the portcullis was being raised, she took Ned by the hand and walked across the war-flattened grass to the edge of the drawbridge. Already the boy was taller than she. Isabel could feel him tugging at her hand and saw the eagerness in his eyes, and knew that in a simpler world of his own, apart from all her poor torments and perplexities, he was looking only for his father. It was not Edward whom she, herself, had eyes for. But there should have been three men, and only one—an emaciated old man in armour—came forth through the gatehouse arch. And her momentary pity for the boy's disappointment was swallowed up in frustrated anger. The father of Hugh Despenser tried to bear himself upright, and she waited until the proud effort of his mailed feet had ceased to sound hollowly above the moat and he was only a few yards distant from her. "Where are the other two?" she called out to him.

He looked up at her then, thin as a wand and proud as Lucifer. "The King and my son are beyond your reach. They left two days ago by boat." Her question was answered with as stark a simplicity as it had been put.

"And you held out alone, to give them time." She turned away with a gesture of fury and frustration, leaving Mortimer to deal with him.

She scarcely knew whether Ned had followed her or not. She had forgotten his existence. She sat in the doorway of her tent, trembling all over and gazing across the wide mouth of the Severn. She did not speak until Mortimer came to tell her that they were going to hang the old man before the castle gates.

To Mortimer and Lancaster it was a usual practice of war, but because of his age they might have had pity. Sir John of Hainault even loitered about her tent as if waiting for her to intercede. And her half-brother, hearing the hammering on the rough-hewn scaffold, came and asked her outright to spare the elder Hugh Despenser. The man was nearly seventy and had held the town valiantly, he said.

But of all his words it was only the hated name she really heard. "Now we may never catch the younger one," she lamented. "Hang the obstinate old dotard in his armour." Her thoughts went back to the wretched days when he was for ever drawing the King's attention to her smallest extravagance and to the cruel way in which his daughter-in-law had controlled and baited her. "I will exterminate them all," she vowed.

The long thin body in armour was still dangling there when the son was caught. To Isabel's intense relief her husband had escaped. Their little craft, hidden near some back postern of the castle against the emergency of surrender, had set sail for Lundy Island. But contrary tides and winds had driven her back and forth, finally bringing her exhausted crew within sight of Bristol again, so that men on shore, after watching their failing efforts, had rowed out with a rescue party in a boat

belonging to a Knight called Beaumont. On finding the importance of the people whose lives they had undoubtedly saved,
Beaumont delivered Despenser up to the Queen. The news of
his capture so overrode all else that for a while few further
questions were asked. But listening to the garbled and evasive
accounts of Beaumont's men, Isabel suspected him of conniving
at the King's escape, for which she and Ned and Edmund of Kent
were secretly so grateful that no one pressed him further. It was
even rumoured that Edward, who was the better swimmer of the
two, had swum across to Wales where a loyal farmer, finding that
he could groom a horse and thatch as well as any of his own serfs,
had saved him from pursuit by setting him to work on his land,
and that he was now being cared for by the monks of Neath.

"Now we can go back and take possession of your capital,"
said Sir John, whose methodically trained military mind still
saw it as the main objective.

"And take our prisoner with us," agreed Isabel, with deep
satisfaction. She had no need to give instructions for his convey-
ance. Mortimer had seen to that. "Your marshal, Sir Thomas
Wager, has found the meanest mount in all Somersetshire," he
grinned. "Its bony ribs will gall him all the way. And Wager's
men have crowned him with filthy straw from the stables. As a
subtle reminder of how he tried to lord it over us all, no doubt."

"Tell them to add a tabard with the Clare arms so that his
lady wife may be associated in his shame," said Isabel.

The extent to which Hugh Despenser was hated was terrible.
Or was it, she wondered with that disconcerting streak of honesty,
that she herself had bewitched people into blindness to the
intimitant brilliancy of his statesmanship which would have protected both them and the Crown from the dangerous, over-wean-
ing power of the barons? They rushed out from shops and houses
and hovels to throw midden at his straw-crowned head and,
goaded by Bishop Orleton's sermons, followed him out of each
town blowing upon hunting horns and beating kitchen pots in
derision. They would have laid down their very coats for her
feet to tread on.

At the Bishop's request the royal party turned aside to Hereford to rest and refresh themselves in his episcopal palace. There
they kept the feast of All Saints with all the good cheer that helped
to swell the prelate's well-lined belly. And there Isabel found her
second son awaiting her, sent by the kindness of the Sheriffs of

London. It was good to see him again. He was growing up a studious, intelligent boy, though with little of his elder brother's strength and energy. He was able to give her a graphic account of all that had been going on in the Tower and, being a born mimic, to delight her and amuse the whole company with an excellent picture of his proud cousin Eleanor Despenser reduced to wheedling panic. With all the music and laughter, and having her sons and friends about her, it was easy to forget Eleanor's husband lying shackled in some cell beneath them.

"On such a holy Feast day should we entirely neglect our prisoner?" asked John of Hainault, whose chivalrous visions were beginning to be dimmed by disappointment so that his thoughts kept turning to a more mystic crusade in the Holy Land.

"Send him some of this excellent roast peacock, Orleton," said Mortimer good naturedly. His own face was flushed and moist with good fare and he lapsed into the English tongue embellished with a cheerful Welsh lilt. "Customary it is to give a man a good meal before he dies, look you."

Apparently he no longer bore his enemy much ill-will. It was easier for a man, Isabel supposed. He had caught him and would get back his land. But not even the Despenser's death could give her back her marriage—nor her clean, self-respecting soul.

She said nothing and the meat was carried to the prisoner, but he would not touch it. "He has refused all food since we took him," reported Sir Thomas Wager.

"Perhaps it is afraid he is lest the Queen has poisoned it?" suggested Mortimer, being more than a little drunk.

"Or hopes to cheat us of his death," said Lincoln, remembering the horror of his father's.

"He never was an athletic man, like the King or Gaveston," said Wager. Seeing his royal mistress's face redden with anger and becoming aware of the tactlessness of his allusion, he added hurriedly but earnestly, "The fact is, milords, I should warn you that in my opinion he may not reach London alive. There were those days and nights without food, tossing in that crazy boat. And the stunning blow to his pride. And even when my men bait him he scarcely seems to hear them now."

Isabel thought she detected pity in his voice, and saw it reflected in one or two faces about the festive table. She had set her heart on making Hugh Despenser suffer sharp insults of the crowds in

London, where she had suffered so much from him and his. But one could not have everything. "Then I pray you, milords, fix the hour of his trial for to-morrow," she said.

"Trial?" hiccoughed Mortimer.

"Why waste time on trying a dog?" muttered Lincoln.

"We must at least make some semblance of it," insisted Isabel coldly. "With milord Bishop's permission—to-morrow—here in Hereford."

And so next day in that same hall from which the festive tables had so recently been cleared a macabre sort of trial was held, with the prisoner slumped on a stool, too weak to stand or answer the long list of charges. Everything he had ever done seemed to be remembered and brought up against him, from weaning the King's natural affection from the Queen to being partly responsible for the death of Lancaster. Even the disaster of Bannockburn was heaped upon him. But he was dazed with hunger and did not seem even to hear when the dreaded sentence of "to be hanged, drawn and quartered" was passed upon him, or else he must have been emulating his father's stoic courage.

Only at the end as he was led from the hall did a flicker of life seem to return to him.

"I am sorry, Hugh Despenser, that you will not have time to come to London and see who reigns now at Westminster," she mocked, bending from the Bishop's borrowed throne as he passed.

At the sound of her familiar clear light voice his steps dragged to a standstill, so that his chains rattled against his suddenly halted guards. His dark eyes beneath their drooping lids seemed already to be looking at her from a great distance. His pale lips spat back her venom. Up to his last hour he was determined to be her most virulent enemy. With a last effort he managed to raise his voice sufficiently for those nearest to her to hear his cruel parting thrust. "Edward said—tossing out there in that boat— that if he had no weapon, he would willingly crush you with his bare teeth."

It was his final crow of victory, wiping out the impression of kindliness made by Edward's exclusion of her name from his proclamation of punishment, and killing any half-belief she might harbour that her husband still cared for her—if not as a wife, at least as the mother of his children. Isabel left the hall and went swiftly to her room. She was unconscious of how long or how short a time elapsed before Roger Mortimer came to her.

She looked up and saw that even he was whitish beneath his tan. "The first part of the sentence is finished," he said tersely. "Will you come and see that it has been done?"

"That too," she thought. It was as if he offered her some macabre kind of love offering, and that he would consider her a weak and inadequate partner if she did not accept it. She began to excuse herself. "I am too weary to go down there among all that crowd."

"There is no need. You wished him to be made an example of. I told Wager to have the scaffold built fifty feet high. You can see it from here."

He walked to the window and drew the curtain back with one hand and held out the other to her. There was nothing else for it but to go, or to know herself too cowardly to mate with him. She got up and walked slowly across the room and stared out across the courtyard and the sea of upturned faces to a tall platform surrounded by the glinting steel of soldiery. She saw the figure hanging from it, without armour but with a grotesquely crooked head. But for the strong warmth of her lover's hand she would have fallen.

"He is already insensible," he told her mercifully.

Then he would not know when they dragged his entrails from him. And when they came with a freshly sharpened butcher's knife to quarter his body, which the King had loved, he would be already dead.

Isabel sank down on the low stone window-seat, the rich stiff skirts of her gown billowing out around her. It was as if some long-striven-for object were at last achieved, as if no immediate purpose were left in life and as if all the strength had gone out of her.

CHAPTER 27

THAT night Isabel slept more soundly than she had slept for months. It was the sleep of exhaustion after achievement, of cessation from long-sustained effort. She felt as if some difficult chapter of her life were over, and hoped optimistically that the pages could be closed. On waking she resolutely put the past behind her and looked forward to the future. Success beckoned, and bound up with vain ambition was her sincere intention to shine as a benefactress to England. All the scraps of statecraft which she had gathered from her family and all her own natural ability were brought to bear upon the task. If the Constitution were to be altered so that power rested in her hands and Mortimer's, she wanted everything to be done decently and in order.

Before leaving Hereford she sent messengers on ahead summoning Parliament to meet at Westminster early in the New Year. As she did not know where the King was she summoned members in his name if he should be present, and failing his presence in the name of herself and of her elder son, whom she named Guardian of the Realm with the full consent of the lords with whom she travelled. It would be for Parliament to make the next move.

The journey back to London with the delirious delight of her subjects manifesting itself on all sides was another personal triumph, and her evenings, when her great cavalcade stopped to rest, were enlivened by the company of a fellow border lord of Mortimer's called Thomas Berkeley. One of her first acts on landing had been to free him from prison, at Mortimer's urgent request, since the young man had nearly died from gaol fever as the price of supporting him. "His castle is a few miles south of Gloucester on the English side of the Severn," Mortimer told her. "And although small compared with Caernarvon or Ludlow, it could be of the greatest strategic value. For which reason, coupled with the liking I have for him, I have given him my young daughter in marriage."

Isabel had taken an immediate liking for the courteous young man, and was sorry to see the ravages which the fever had set upon his lean, attractive face; and he on his side had displayed the most touching gratitude to her for delivering him from the prison where he had suffered so grievously. Since he was Mortimer's son-in-law she had even found time to ride out from Gloucester to Berkeley with them when he went to give some hasty instructions to his steward before throwing in his lot with theirs. It was an autumn day, aflame with russet and gold, and the comfortable domesticity of his castle pleased her, set as it was in flat sunlit fields and seeming to guard the peaceful little village at its gates. Although overwhelmed by her unexpected arrival, Glaunville, the steward, ordered an excellent meal, and

Isabel, coming from the hospitability of the hall, paused a while outside the guard room before going out into the courtyard where their horses waited. "I shall always remember Berkeley Castle as a pleasant, sunny place," she said politely.

"Yet it can look grim enough when the mists creep up over the river meadows," admitted its owner, with his sensitive smile, as they rode out of his courtyard. And when she looked back from the lane beyond the village the sun had gone in and the Severn mists were beginning to creep like grey ghosts towards the castle walls, and she shivered a little, seeing something of Berkeley's isolated sadness.

On the way to London they heard news of Edward. On learning of Hugh Despenser's death, he had come out of his safe retreat and deliberately given himself up, heedless of all consequences. "How foolish, and how characteristic of his clinging loyalty to the favourite of the moment," thought Isabel, realizing how much he must hate her now that he knew of his friend's ignominious journey and execution.

"Beaumont has him safely in Monmouth," Mortimer told her. "Shall we wait where we are until they come and bring the King with us into London?"

"And humiliate him as you humiliated the Despenser," thought Isabel. Not only was her instinct to protect Edward from physical harm, but she shrank from the thought of meeting him. She felt that she had too much to answer for, and that too many hurts had been exchanged between them. "I cannot bring myself to talk with him, and he has said that he never wishes to see me. If I am to continue knowing happiness with you, Roger, I must be allowed to forget all that unhappy past," she pleaded.

"Then we will persuade Lincoln to remain behind in charge of him," decided Mortimer. "Good fighter as he is, we can spare him better than some because of his blindness."

Isabel appreciated his deference to her wishes, knowing through the close fusing of intention which bound them that he himself was not one to put out of mind unpleasant realities, but would have preferred in his blunt way to bring the King before Parliament and make a quick decision. "The fact that Lincoln is a relative would make the arrangement more seemly in the eyes of the world," she said. "And I would have him fetch the King to Kenilworth for the greater comfort of both of them."

Mortimer saw to it that her wishes were carried out, and she and her son rode into London to receive a rapturous welcome. She was well aware that his youth and her forlorness made a most appealing picture, and could have wished at times that Roger Mortimer had not pricked his horse forward so frequently to ride beside them. It detracted from the aspect of loneliness with which she played upon their sympathies, and might confirm the rumour of her infidelity which, since their return to England, she had been striving so decorously to discourage.

One of her first concerns after arriving at Westminster was to make sure that the unfortunate Bishop of Exeter's body was retrieved from the muddy banks of the Thames where it had been thrown, and sent with all reverence to Exeter. And to punish the ringleaders of the mob who had murdered him.

"And what punishment will you mete out to Despenser's widow, who so cruelly spied on you and taunted you?" asked her lover.

Isabel had often looked forward to the time when she would be in a position to arraign Eleanor Despenser before her and return past humiliations, and strip from her every vestige of her proud Clare inheritance. But now that she had achieved Hugh Despenser's terrible death most of the desire seemed to be purged out of her, and a kind of surfeited weariness took its place. "Send the woman away where I shall never have to look upon her again," she besought Mortimer. "And from all the Despenser lands of which you will now take possession, you will surely be able to spare an estate or two for her to live upon."

The Queen sent for her small daughters and kept Christmas quietly with all four children around her. She sent gifts to Bringnette, whose first Christmas without her would be lonely in Ponthieu, and rewarded all who had helped her including Sir Eustace d'Ambreticourt and his kind lady in Hainault. Roger Mortimer she created Earl of the Marches. And she began to talk long and earnestly with Sir John of Hainault about the promised marriage between one of his inconspicuous nieces and her elder son, who might, it seemed, so soon be King of England.

In spite of snow-blocked roads the Parliament she had called was well attended, and tension mounted throughout the country. In one of his inflammatory speeches Bishop Orleton pointed out that if their captive king were to be released and returned to power it would undoubtedly mean the death or imprisonment of all who supported Queen Isabel. Events had now come to such a pass that they must choose between the two, he said, dwelling upon the danger to which they would all stand, as traitors, if the King returned. Edward of Caernarvon's failings were freely discussed. A bill was introduced accusing him of indolence, of weakly losing Scotland and of breaking his solemn Coronation oath. Even the crowds gathering at the doors of Westminster Hall shouted again and again that they would be rid of him, and that they would kill whosoever laid a hand upon their Queen and Prince. And the Archbishop of Canterbury set the seal of the Church upon their uproar by announcing solemnly that the voice of the people was the voice of God. Reverting to the fiercer authority of their Norman ancestors, the peers claimed the right to depose a king who had proved himself to be incapable of ruling. Almost faint with conflicting emotion, Isabel heard them preparing to depose her husband and to offer their allegiance to his son.

"So it is really done, this impossible-sounding scheme which Roger and I spoke of without pretence before we left France," she thought. A sense of unreality gripped her and in the intensity of her emotion, whether for joy or sorrow she scarcely knew, tears began to run unheeded down her cheeks. As if watching some dream she saw the beautifully proportioned hall lit by shafts of sunlight, the richly coloured tabards and houppelandes of men whose names were parts of England, whose badges blazoned a riot of heraldry against the stone walls and whose daggers were for once sheathed in agreement. She saw their faces, some young, some old, but all sharpened to intensity by the irrevocable importance of the thing they were doing. She saw Mortimer, who had ruled Wales without a crown and who would now rule England in like fashion, lead her fifteen-year-old son towards the throne with its canopy and backcloth of gold against which the three embroidered leopards *couchant* of England seemed to snarl in unaccustomed shame. She was glad that Mortimer motioned to him to mount the shallow steps to the dais alone and that, having done so, his glance met hers across the crowded hall. She knew by the proud lift of his head that he too was thinking "This daring thing which we two planned together is now as good as done."

And then she noticed that Ned was not seated but was standing rigidly beside the throne with a hand clutching one of the carved arms upon which his father's hand had so often rested. "He is overcome. He is so young and by nature shy," she thought, wishing that she could go to him and whisper reassurances, telling him that none of the real burden of ruling all these fierce-looking men and the famine-impoverished country would rest upon his shoulders—that she and Mortimer would be behind him, bearing it all. But when he spoke she was once again mortified to find how little she had ever understood him.

He was facing them all, frowning as he did in moments of stress. His voice seemed to have deepened to manhood and held no tremor. "When his Grace the King sent me to France I gave him my allegiance. And without his bidding nothing that you can say, milords, will induce me to wear the crown during his lifetime."

In the following silence someone's mailed glove, knocked accidentally to the stone floor, sounded sharply as a blast-fired arrow. His hearers were struck still in the midst of various movements so that they stood like so many suddenly arrested statues. "Bravely done!" Isabel's divided heart cried out to her son. But seeing Mortimer's angry start and the way the blood darkened his cheeks a cold thrust of fear went through her as she realized that all unwittingly, in loyalty and love, the boy might be signing his father's death warrant. The thought of such a consequence had never occurred to her before. To take from a man who had proved himself incompetent all power to harm the country further was all that she—and they, surely— could want. Even she, who had suffered most, had staked most of her desire for vengeance with Despenser's death. She brought herself back to warm, everyday reality when Ned returned to his chair of state beside her and members began to discuss a more legal form of deposal. After all, it would perhaps be more satisfactory in the end to have everything done legally, some of the peers was saying. There was the possible interference from the Pope or from France to be considered. Mortimer with all his hot urgency was irritated and impatient of the delay to his thrusting plans, but Ned, who had been trained to acquiescence on so many points, could not be coerced about this one thing. He could not, or would not, see that with the nation solidly at their back Parliament could force the King to agree to anything. "In any case, you can scarcely crown me without the regalia, and my brother John tells me that our father took it from the Jewel House when he fled from the Tower and has it safely bestowed somewhere up north. I would, Madam, you would let me go up to Kenilworth and see him!"

It was a cruelly bewildering situation for a lad of fifteen and clearly he wanted above everything to talk with his father first. But that was the last thing which his mentors wanted. It was Bishop Orleton, of course, who took it upon himself to go, saying that it needed a churchman to acquit the King of his Coronation vows. "Which were made to God, not to you, you fire-eating traitor!" Edmund of Kent was heard to mutter, having been led into deeper waters than he had ever imagined or desired.

In spite of Parliament's rare unanimity it was a decision which weighed heavily upon men's souls—to depose an anointed king. Only Edward's years of unpredictable folly and frivolous neglect and the blindness of his inordinate affections could have driven them to it. Of the three bishops who refused their oath of allegiance to his son, one was so badly mauled by the excited mob that his maimed condition served to silence any loyal waverers who might have joined them. Orleton travelled to Warwickshire with Sir William Trussel, the Proctor of Parliament and Sir Thomas Blount, who had been steward of the royal household; and the Palace of Westminster and the City of London settled down to wait with hopeful if conscience-stricken anxiety for their return. And when the uneasy days of waiting were over and the Parliamentary deputation rode back through Newgate and Cheapside they brought the regalia with them.

Their account of the few days they had spent at Kenilworth was disconnected and coloured by party prejudice. Each man's story was of the particular part which he had played. The supporting Bishops of Winchester and Lincoln, it seemed, had at first used arguments and persuasion. But Edward had been incredulous and dazed, and at sight of his bitter opponent Orleton and of Trussel, who had proclaimed the death sentence on Hugh Despenser at Hereford, he had fainted. His host and the other two bishops had been all concern, but almost before he was fully conscious again Orleton was preaching at him with all his customary fierceness, drawing up a denunciatory catalogue of all his sins and shortcomings since boyhood. Some of them utterly irrelevant and frivolous, the soft-hearted Bishop of Winchester reported sadly. Small, half-forgotten happenings within the privacy of his own palace for which only Blount could have scraped a perfidious steward's memory.

"Such foolish things!" exclaimed Isabel to Edmund of Kent. "Like the evening when he made that fat painter of his dance on the supper table, or the times when he and Gaveston used to scandalize the foreign envoys by playing pitch-and-toss or mimicking pot-bellied prelates like Orleton himself when they ought to have been attending to the grave bleatings of a Council meeting. Things which happened when he was young and which Piers Gaveston has already paid for. Do you remember, Edmund?"

But it was dangerous for either of them to remember because it brought back a sort of nostalgic tenderness for a time when the court had been young and gay and Edmund, at any rate, had received nothing from the King but an elder brother's indulgent kindness. Instead it was far safer to feel shame and disgust when the Bishop of Lincoln described how Edward had dressed himself dramatically all in black and how he, who could out-ride any of them, had sat weakly in floods of tears beneath the flaying of the self-indulgent prelate's final denunciations. "What could a woman like me want with such a womanish creature?" thought Isabel, her doting eyes upon Mortimer's virility and her mind upon the upstanding courage of her elder son.

Finally Edward had agreed to give up the crown on condition that it should be his own son who wore it, and even thanking them for having seen good to choose him. "He will do better than I," he had said, sending for the glittering regalia. And when the deputation described to Isabel how the Proctor had, in the name of England, renounced all oaths of allegiance ever made to him, and how Blount, his steward, had broken his staff of office there and then before him as if he were dead, the Court knew beyond doubt that Edward the Second was deposed.

"Do you suppose that he is kindly used at Kenilworth?" Isabel had asked, under cover of the wild shouting, plucking at the wise Bishop of Winchester's sleeve.

"Quite kindly, as a State prisoner. Or rather, Madam, as a guest in the house of a relative who has learned consideration from his own afflictions," the Bishop had assured her, adding some words which had puzzled her at the time. "Too kindly, perhaps, for Edward Plantagenet's ultimate good."

CHAPTER 28

THE roads leading into London were white for Christmas and warm braziers burned in the streets. The chandlers could not serve their wares quickly enough—tall wax candles to light before the Madonna and the Christ child in the churches, and stumpy tallow ones for family revelry in the home. The stalls in East-cheap were hung with holly, and carts and sledges kept rumbling in from the country with turkeys and fat geese. Husbands and sons were home from the everlasting wars, and people laughed again. After years of muddled government and baronial bicker-ing, it seemed as if a new and hopeful era had dawned at last. And it was a woman who had brought it about. A woman with a strong man beside her to carry out her commands.

It was this unsuspected side of their Queen's nature, so long and so cleverly hidden beneath an appealing air of ill-used fragility, which amazed the people and commanded their respect. She had only to ride out from the palace to be surrounded by deliriously cheering crowds. She was in her early thirties but success lent her a spurious air of youth. And when she smiled at them with eyes sparkling like the Nativity star, with the frosty air whipping colour into her cheeks, and her children gathered about her, the simpler of her subjects were almost ready to believe that the Madonna herself had come among them to im-prove the hard poverty of their lives. Isabel the Fair could have done anything with them then.

There was someone now who attended to affairs of state, they felt, and who seemed to have a firm hand on every necessary matter at once. It was French Queen Isabel who, soon after her return, had thought to grant leave of absence to most members of her household to enable them to visit their homes, and who had taken the trouble to understand ordinary people's English, and who even had the insight to know that foreign soldiers, however useful they might have been in bringing about this happy state of affairs, were never really welcome for long in this insular land. There were to be special festivities in their honour this Christmas, and then they were to go back to Hainault.

Thomas Plantagenet, Earl of Lincoln, now succeeding to his

father's Lancastrian title, had come to London for the Coronation and to bestow knighthood on the young king prior to the ceremony, and it was Isabel who honoured Sir John of Hainault by asking him to assist at the investiture. How dearly Edward of Caernarvon would have loved to knight his own son no one stopped to think. In all that blaze of excitement and preparation he seemed to be deliberately forgotten, except by the inarticulate lad who was the centre of it all.

Isabel had proof of this when, weary of dressmakers and tailors and coiffeurs, she went out into the thin wintry sunshine for a breath of air before the midday meal on Christmas Eve. The snow had been swept from the Palace yard and the splendid Flemish gelding which Sir John had presented to his cousin, the new young King, had been brought round from the stables that its trappings might be approved for the morrow's procession. At the head groom's humble request Ned had mounted to make sure that every piece of harness and scolloped velvet horsecloth was as it should be. He was riding the high-spirited creature round in circles for the inspection and comments of a group of knowledgeable friends and squires and grooms. And Lord Berkeley, to whom Ned had taken a liking, stepped forward courteously from among them as the Queen and a few of her ladies joined them. "It is true the horse stands nearly sixteen hands, Madam, and is but newly broken in; but I am sure his Grace will be able to control him even in a cheering crowd," he assured her, perceiving that she was worried lest the gift horse should prove too powerful a mount for her stripling son.

Too occupied to speak to her, Ned rode once more round the courtyard before dismounting, then turned to pat the gelding's glossy neck. "What are you going to call him?" Isabel asked, with several tactful Flemish suggestions on the tip of her tongue.

But Ned turned round to look at her in grave and pained surprise. "What else but 'Cher Ami', Madam?" he asked. And Isabel, feeling rather as if someone had unexpectedly doused her face with cold water, recalled the homely picture of a small stocky boy tending a beloved wooden horse made for him by his father. Annoyed by the lad's undeviating tenacity of mind, she suspected that all favourite horses would always be "Cher Ami" to him, and realized that even in all this last minute rehearsing for to-morrow's Coronation the lonely man at Kenilworth who had been through it all a score of years ago was very far from being forgotten. In a kind of helpless panic she hoped that, as they all rode through the decked and garlanded streets and the Abbey bells rang out for joy, most of the older citizens would not be thinking of him pityingly, too.

But if they were, there was no sign of it when young Edward the Third went to his crowning that Christmas Day. Only Isabel herself sat through the ceremony shedding tears she could not hide because she was naturally emotional; because although this crowning set the seal upon the new life which she had schemed for, it was at best only a substitute for the honourable life she had originally dreamed of, and because—on this day of family reunions—she had hidden in the bosom of her glittering robes a letter from her husband beseeching that he might return to be with his children on Christmas Day. A small thing for a deposed king to ask for, whose lightest whim had always been so instantly obeyed. And a desperately desired thing, seemingly, since it must be begged of a faithless wife whom he had said that he would kill, if necessary, with bared teeth.

Isabel had composed a gentle reply to be carried back to Kenilworth by one of Lincoln's men, sending Edward news of the children and saying with half-pitying mendacity that she herself would have brought them to see him but that Parliament had forbidden her to do so. And to blot out the memory of him she saw to it that the feasting and revelling ran high at Westminster from Christmas to Twelfth Night, and that during the general festivities the feeding and merriment of the people outside the palace were well catered for. For mixed motives of gratitude and policy she advised the young king to grant her chivalrous Sir John an annuity, and to shower gifts upon his followers—particularly upon the ladies who had accompanied her from Valenciennes and who could be counted upon to give a good report of the English Court to Philippa's parents. That the gifts were paid for out of the last remains of the girl's dowry no one but the confidential clerk of her Exchequer need know.

As soon as the Flemish supporters had departed Parliament appointed a council of regency presided over by her second-cousin Lincoln and composed of twelve bishops and twelve peers, among whom were Thomas of Brotherton, now Earl Marshal of England, and Edmund of Kent. It gave Isabel a feeling of security to have her blood relations so represented. Plantagenets as they were, the French ancestry which they had shared with her and the May Queen seemed to bind them as closely with herself as with Edward. The easy comments which they made in the idiom of the family circle had always been very different from the more guarded ones which they contributed in English council chambers. And Isabel was quite content for the conduct of the regency to lie officially in the hands of men chosen by Parliament, knowing as she did that the real power would lie with her and with Roger Mortimer. But Mortimer was primarily a soldier and as the weeks passed she found herself more and more frequently relying upon the advice of Bishop Orleton of Hereford, although she had none of that personal liking for the man which she had felt for Aymer de Valence of Pembroke. When the last of William of Hainault's money had been spent, it was Orleton who helped her to appropriate to her own uses more than half of the country's revenue. Her dowry, he called it; unctuously explaining to any who dared to criticize that restitution should be made for all the privation which the Queen had suffered under the Despensers' sway, and that it was now offered in grateful recognition of all that she had done to bring back tranquillity to the nation.

But tranquillity was short-lived. Before Easter Robert Bruce had begun harrying the northern border again, and Mortimer was wanting to move Edward from Kenilworth. "Suppose the Scots were to swoop down secretly, as the Black Douglas did when you were at Brotherton, and abduct him?" he said, bringing Orleton to her apartments after a council meeting as he so often did of late.

Isabel looked up in surprise from her steward's account book which, with a Frenchwoman's native shrewdness, she always insisted upon checking. "As far south as Warwickshire?" she demurred. "And of what hostage value would he be to them, now that he is deposed?"

"Of little, Madam, as you say," agreed Orleton. "But they might well use him as a figurehead to raise sympathy among his former subjects. 'Behold my dear ill-used brother of England' and so forth. There are still quite a number of people who are not wholly with us in this matter of his deposition."

Isabel set a marker in the book and turned from the table to give them her full attention. "My dear lord Bishop, are you not daily deafened by their cheering every time my son or I ride abroad?" she asked, with smiling indulgence.

"I admit, your Grace, that I speak only of parts remote from

London," he hastened to assure her. "But there is another point to be considered, which is that the new Earl of Lancaster is now President of the Council. A position which necessitates his being so frequently at court that he can seldom be in charge of his—er—guest elsewhere."

"He is half blind in any case," pointed out Mortimer moodily, poking at a fallen log with the point of his shoe. "And when he *is* at Kenilworth he allows Edward Plantagenet to go hunting and hawking with him, and the tenants all doff their hats and the Warwickshire women gape admiringly. Your husband, my dear Isabel, makes far too fine a figure on a horse, besides being able to ride twice as fast as any of his so-called guards."

"What you mean is that cousin Lincoln is too kind," interrupted Isabel with rising acerbity.

"He certainly allows him too much liberty for your safety. If Edward were to escape and form a party——"

It was the masterful man caring for her, for which she had always craved. "Where would you send him?" she asked almost meekly.

"Further west. Across the Severn if possible. Somewhere in my own domains, where men obey me as spontaneously as they breathe."

"We cannot afford to offend Lincoln," Orleton reminded them.

"If we make any change he or Edmund would be sure to speak of it to Ned," objected Isabel, feeling strangely loath to let Edward disappear from her ken somewhere into the wilds of Wales.

"There may be no need for him to know," said Mortimer. "I shall organize a force to put down this trouble on the Scottish border and it will be just the moment for a well-grown young princeling to go north and win his spurs campaigning."

"I doubt if you could hold him back," said Isabel, feeling that some of her past shame for her husband was being healed by the manliness of her son.

"Ned should make a fine enough soldier," allowed Mortimer, coming to sit near her when the Bishop was gone.

Always glad of his company, Isabel pushed aside her neglected accounts. "I love you both," she sighed. "How I wish you liked each other better!"

"He scarcely ever speaks to me unless he is obliged," burst out Mortimer, who had set him on the throne.

Isabel leaned forward with a caressing gesture to lay her hand on his. "What can you expect when you have taken his father's place?" she asked softly. "Perhaps if you were to—to respect his young dignity a little more. Several times lately I have seen you walk in public beside him, and others have noted it. Even I, his mother, walk a pace or two behind him now."

Mortimer moved rebelliously beneath her restraining hand. "Do you expect me to come to heel like a little dog? I, without whom he would not have become king for years. As you yourself just said, I *have* taken his father's place. And in any case your precious son is only a gangling boy."

Isabel withdrew her fondling hand and sat back in her chair, her head held high. "But a Capet and a Plantagenet," she snapped haughtily.

"As I am a Mortimer, with blood from the old British kings. All north Wales obeyed me, and now it is England's turn," stormed Mortimer, springing up and kicking aside his chair. But the next minute he had crushed her in his arms. "We must always fight, we two," he was whispering laughingly between his passionate kisses. "It is the fiendish pride which is in us both. But I told you long ago I want no mouse of a woman, did I not, my sweet? And your spitfire thrusts but make our love-making the fiercer."

Overborne by the undiminished mastery of his embrace, Isabel capitulated as usual. "If not Lincoln, then whom had you thought of to take charge of Edward?" she asked, when the passion of the moment was past.

"Sir Thomas Gourney, perhaps, or Sir John Maltravers of Dorset who was with us in exile," suggested Mortimer. His tone was negligent but Isabel felt intuitively that the whole matter had long been arranged in his own mind.

"I do not like the faces of either of them," she said. "And Maltravers, having fought for my uncle of Lancaster at Borough-bridge and been forced to fly the country, would certainly bear a sore grudge against Edward. Perhaps that is why you have chosen him?"

He did not answer directly but pulled a roll of parchment from the leather pouch hanging from his belt. It appeared to be an order of some kind upon which she caught sight of Gourney's name. Mortimer laid it before her as if he would have had her sign it but she shook her head, walking away towards the window as though she would none of it. "I am the last person——" she began unsteadily. "It is for Ned, the King, to sign. And if he too dislikes these two men I doubt if he will."

"He can be as obstinate as a mule," agreed Mortimer, remembering how steadfastly he had refused to wear the crown in his father's lifetime.

The thoughts of both of them pursued the subject in the silent room. Mortimer knew that once Isabel had capitulated to his wishes she would work with him, whatever the opposing drag of personal feelings. And presently she turned from the window. "I think I can persuade Ned," she said, in that pleased silky tone which so often now clothed her cleverly-thought-out designs. And meeting her lover's questioning gaze, she smiled reassuringly. "There is that girl Philippa whom he has set his heart on. Left to himself William of Hainault would certainly give him the eldest daughter and they are all much the same to us. But I could promise to drop a hint to Joanna, my sentimental Valois cousin, to persuade him. And if I win Ned's gratitude he may prove more amenable."

Mortimer's admiring grin was reward enough. Isabel returned to her chair and picked up the document distastefully. " 'Sir Thomas Gourney and Sir John Maltravers to conduct the said Sir Edward Plantagenet to Corfe Castle in Dorset,' " she read. "Why Corfe?"

"It belongs to Maltravers. It will give me time. Until Gourney—or both of them—can take him farther westward."

Isabel laid it down again. A part of her was still fighting, however feebly, on her husband's side. "Roger," she said, on a sudden inspiration, "why not Berkeley eventually?"

"Berkeley?"

"That charming castle you took me to from Gloucester. Oh, I know it is on this side of the Severn, but they are all your good friends and neighbours there. And Thomas Berkeley is your son-in-law. It will be a way in which he can serve you, since I imagine that wretched fever he caught will scarcely allow him to go fighting the Scots. And Ned likes and trusts him. He would willingly sign an order for putting his father in *his* care."

Mortimer, with his slower mind, stood absorbing the new idea. "No man ever had such a partner," he said. But he pulled her to her feet and looked searchingly into her eyes. "Your suggestion is wholly to satisfy Ned, I hope," he said. "You are not still a little in love with that handsome husband of yours?"

His uncharacteristic spark of intuition and the shred of truth it held shocked her. But she gave him back gaze for level gaze. "What love I had for him was killed when he ran away at Pannockburn," she answered.

Yet the pleading letters which Edward managed to send her from time to time still wrung her heart. Once he had reached Corfe they became much less frequent, mere smudged notes on the back of used pieces of parchment, or a page torn from a book, for which she judged he must have found difficulty in finding a messenger. They were usually handed to her secretly, so that she seldom mentioned them, not wanting to close her last means of contact with him. But there came a time when she felt impelled to speak for him. "Edward writes to tell me how much he yearns to ride in God's free air again," she once told Mortimer, during the deposed king's imprisonment at Corfe.

"A yearning for which he condemned me to many months in the Tower," he retorted grimly. "Besides, Orleton was right when he said that the people in country districts are inclined to forget his follies and press about him too sympathetically when he rides abroad."

"Perhaps if he were to change clothes with his groom——"

Mortimer stared at her in surprise. Obviously she still pictured him with some of his own servants about him. But he did not disillusion her. "My dear Isabel, is he easy to disguise—with his height and his trimly curled brown hair and beard?"

She was thinking now more of the dangerous sympathy than of Edward's desire for fresh air. "If someone could persuade him to shave off the beard——"

"I am sure Gourney could persuade him. And it would make it safer moving him about."

Isabel looked up too quickly, catching the fleeting ruthlessness of his smile, and wished she had not pressed the matter. A sense of inexplicable foreboding seized her. "You used to like him once. I remember how he greeted you that day before Bannockburn when we first met."

"I was *loyal* to him. I do not *like* incapable perverts. But do not worry. He will have all the riding in God's free air he wants next week, when Gourney and Maltravers will be escorting him to Bristol."

"Bristol is a long way round to Berkeley. Why do you keep moving him from castle to castle—and in such misfortunate weather?"

"It could be fortunate for us. Particularly as I now think of having him moved by night."

Isabel saw the sinister smile still on his lips and recoiled. "If you hope to rid yourself of him that way you will not succeed. It is useless to ill-use him, Roger. He is sound and hardy as a horse."

But even Edward was only human, and never had there been such a wet and blustering April. The roads near London were quagmires, so that one could scarcely imagine what the tracks and lanes in the west must be like. All day as rain and wind beat against the palace windows Isabel's thoughts kept turning unwillingly to her husband. If she sat quiet for a moment or closed her eyes in chapel she found herself picturing him riding sodden, weary and shivering through the darkness. That evening she sent for her favourite French musicians and the best troop of players in London because she did not want to think of him, but before nightfall she had called Ghislaine to accompany her along endless passages to the deposed King's wardrobe. With a few of her women and a single page holding a torch she looked through such of his possessions as were left. Although all his jewels and valuable robes had been removed at the time of their son's coronation many of his familiar garments were still folded away in the great oak chests or hanging from the tenter pegs in his closet. As the women took them down and shook them out the scent of musk which he affected filled the stagnant air so that Isabel was almost fearful of turning about too suddenly lest she should see him staring at her accusingly from the shadows. Hurriedly she chose his warmest riding cloak and a favourite fur-lined, rose-embroidered houppelande of tawny velvet and his riding boots of crimson Cordova leather, and had them bundled into saddlebags for a messenger to take to him for his journey to Bristol, and when her women kept looking at her curiously and wondering for whom the fine things were destined, she said negligently and audibly to Ghislaine, "God knows we should think of the poor and needy during this cruel weather!"

The poor and the needy—who had been King of England, she thought. And remembering that he had a passion for honeyed marchpanes she sent the page to beg a basketful from his young sweet-toothed successor, knowing how much Ned would wish to contribute them to her parcels. Warmed by her forethought, she hoped, Edward arrived in Bristol. But she learned from Mortimer that it had been impossible to keep him there for long owing to an unexpected rising of the citizens in his favour. Why, oh why, she thought, could people not see how their well-meant sympathy only made things harder for him? And a week or two after he had arrived at Berkeley she returned from evensong to find Ned waiting for her in her private apartments. He was standing without ceremony before the hearth, the firelight sparkling on his golden circlet and his red-gold hair and on a sheet of paper which he held. Reading suppressed excitement in the abrupt way in which he turned to her, Isabel dismissed all her attendants from the room.

"It is from the K—from my father," he said, holding out the piece of parchment. "One of Glaunville's grooms brought it."

"And who is Glaunville?"

"Milord Berkeley's steward, Madam."

"Ah, yes, I remember him." Isabel wondered anxiously what Edward could have told their son, but looking down at the paper she saw that it was nothing more innocuous than a poem of some kind.

"See, Madam, it is undoubtedly in his own hand. The niggly little letters and the tall looped l's," Ned was saying, excitedly. "And the man said that milord Berkeley specially wanted *me* to have it."

Between the effect of his agitation and her own limited scholarship the verse seemed meaningless. "It is in Latin, Ned. I pray you translate it for me into French."

Being now taller than she, he read it over her shoulder as she held it. " ' Mamnum mihi contulit tempore brumali——' My tutor will tell you that my Latin limps like a spavined horse. But it goes something like this.

> "On my devoted head
> Her bitterest showers,
> All from a wintry cloud,
> Stern Fortune pours.
> View here her favourite
> Graced with fair comeliness!
> As fortune worsens
> Each grace has vanished,
> Wisdom and wit depart
> Beauty is banished."

"Without the least trace of vanity he must always have been aware of his comeliness," smiled Isabel, relieved that Edward had made no specific appeal to his son. "And though I doubt if there was ever much wisdom it would take a great deal of misfortune to banish his beauty!"

"But he speaks of fortune *worsening*. Why was he ever moved from Kenilworth? How can you and that devil Mortimer do this to him?" The words burst from Ned with boyish impetuosity, and then he stood abashed. His kingship was too new and too circumscribed for him to dare to speak to her so. But because she secretly shared some of his anxiety Isabel was gentle with him. "You know that my cousin Lincoln is too much occupied with affairs of State in London to care for him. And you trust Thomas of Berkeley, do you not?"

"With all my heart, Madam. But he is not there. Glaunville's man said that Thomas Berkeley was taken ill at Bradelye or some such place while making a tour of his estates. And that for some reason or other he particularly wanted me to have my father's verse."

"It must be a recurrence of that vicious fever Berkeley caught when your father and Despenser had him gaoled, yet he sends you the poem." Isabel spoke half to herself, gaining time to think. Young Berkeley was Mortimer's friend, he could have little love for Edward, but he had shown himself a man of humane gentleness and honour. Could the verses be some kind of warning, sent desperately to the highest quarter of all, because he himself was powerless to move? But of course that was absurd. She must have become fanciful of late. And she recalled how often she had seen Edward and Piers Gaveston with their heads together composing frivolously artistic odes to a broken heart or a dying swan. "Do not take your father's durance so seriously, Ned," she said. "I myself have sometimes received letters from him which were far more wretched than this, and I have more than once written to him of you children and sent him warm clothing. But now he is in Berkeley Castle all will be well with him. You have only to look at this verse, my son. Exquisitely written and carefully composed. And in Latin, which does not come too easily to him. I have been in Berkeley Castle and I can imagine him sitting before the fire in Thomas's comfortable hall, with the musicians playing softly in the gallery and a fine hound or two at his feet." As she drew the reassuring picture, her own momentary doubts vanished. With a gay flip of her jewelled fingers and a cynical smile she handed the paper back to him. "No, no, Ned. It is only the man who had my dear uncle of Lancaster put to death being dramatically sorry for himself."

CHAPTER 29

ALL through the long hot day people had been roaming restlessly about the streets, cheering and laughing, weeping and waving. Baggage wagons had been rumbling over London bridge from the newly acquired borough of Southwark on the Surrey side of the river and bands of soldiers were making for some assembly point among the open fields of Aldersgate. The tranquillity they had hoped for with the Queen's return had been short-lived, and now they were off again to drive the persistent Scots back over the oft-harassed border. But at last the round red September sun went down, curfew sounded and within the palace of Westminster the Queen's women withdrew from her bedchamber. They knew that her lover would come. Mortimer, in his arrogance, made no secret of it now. After being separated since morning by various public engagements he and Isabel faced each other anxiously at the foot of her bed, released at last from the necessity of public graciousness. "You have heard that Edward has managed to send an appeal to the Pope?" he said, having waited all day to discuss this thing.

It was clear from the drawn look of her face that she had. "Bishop Orleton whispered it to me as I was on my way to the review," she said.

"And he should know, having just returned from a visit to his Holiness at Avignon."

"Edward must have contrived to send his petition weeks ago."

"From Kenilworth probably. We did well to move him."

"And to think that I tried to dissuade you from it." The Pope's intervention was the one thing which Isabel had been secretly dreading, and which she would do anything to avert. "And now the damage is done."

"Orleton thinks his Holiness will tell you to go back to your husband."

270

"I can't! Oh, I can't!" In her distress, she began to pace the floor, clasped hands pressed to her mouth and the silken hem of her bedgown swishing back and forth after her.

Mortimer watched her half-calculatingly, half-pityingly. "He *is* still your husband—as long as he lives," he said.

"And if the Church drives me back to him it will mean leaving you."

"True, you cannot have us both in your bed." Mortimer smiled and stopped her agitated pacing by taking her hand and kissing it. "Could you face excommunication even for me?" he asked, regarding her over their joined hands which were still at his lips. "Or could I, for our bodily joy, condemn your soul to eternal damnation?"

"Oh, Roger, must you so torment me?" She pulled away her hand with an agonized gesture. "And even in this world it would mean throwing away all that we have striven for—the success and the power. The chance to use one's talents, the complete partnership, the perfect mating. And all for a marriage which was rotten from the start. It is a cruel decision the Church would thrust upon me."

"But one which must hang over us as long as Edward lives."

" 'As long as he lives! As long as he lives!' Why must you keep saying that?" she cried. Suddenly her control snapped, and she beat upon his breast with clenched fists then flung herself upon him, weeping passionately, and crying out that she wished she had never seen him. But Mortimer knew that it was only the strain she had been living under for months taking toll of a strongly emotional woman. He held her close and was patient with her, still working towards his end. "You are not usually unintelligent—or obstinately blind—my sweet," he said with gentle relentlessness. "You must realize that it is not only the Pope. Edward's precious half-brothers—and Lincoln—and hypocritical public opinion are all beginning to mutter about us. And the muttering is growing dangerous. And the people are already forgetting Edward's wrongdoings and growing pitiful for his misfortunes. One day it may well be their deposed Plantagenet or us. So he must die."

She drew herself away from him sharply. She knew that he was exaggerating the situation—trying to coerce her to his will. "The people still cheer me. I can still twist most of the counsellors round my little finger," she reminded him defiantly. "What harm can poor Edward of Caernarvon do composing sad poems in some lonely Gloucestershire castle?"

"Nothing, except breathe. But even that is enough because, deposed or not, he is still Sir Edward Plantagenet. No one can take away either his knighthood or his name." Mortimer unbuckled his belt and threw it down upon the bed as if to breathe more freely himself. "Ask Orleton how dangerous he still is, if you doubt me."

"Orleton? Who is he to advise upon so private and terrible a thing as you suggest?"

"He could at least convince you of his Holiness's intentions." Mortimer sprawled across the foot of the bed, his face shadowed by the half-drawn curtains, his voice hurried, shamed and urgent. "Listen, Isabel. We must decide how to act in this matter—and decide quickly. You yourself told me that Thomas Berkeley is away from home. And I have set Maltravers and Gourney in charge there in his place. And Gourney is awaiting his instructions. He has sent a man to me to warn me that my incorruptible son-in-law may soon be well enough to travel home."

"Then some of you have already discussed this thing." Isabel stood white and tragic-eyed against the uncurtained window, with a rising moon making a silvery radiance behind her unbound hair. "And you expect *me* to decide, to give that vulturine-looking man his orders?" she gasped.

Mortimer jabbed thoughtfully with his sheathed hunting knife at an inoffensive peacock embroidered on the bedcover. "It might be safer if neither of us gave them," he said. And almost immediately suggested that she should grant audience to Orleton, and abide by his counsel.

"Now? So long after curfew?" she exclaimed. "Surely after his return voyage the poor man must be abed."

"When I came through the ante-room he was still there—alone—trying to finish some urgent despatches. And Gourney's man will be leaving soon after sunrise."

Isabel guessed that the urgent despatches might be only a pre-arranged excuse for the prelate to be at hand. After a moment or two of uncertainty she fastened her bedgown more closely about her and walked to the door. "You will be content to abide by what he says?" she asked, with her fingers on the bolt.

"*He* can write the message if it will ease your conscience," said Mortimer almost negligently.

"And as a churchman he cannot condone murder," she told him triumphantly.

In the ante-room the Lord Bishop of Hereford rose from a table littered with important-looking documents. If his surprise at seeing his Queen was not genuine, it was at least well simulated. "Arrears of work and letters to Papal officials," he apologized, rising with a flurry of scarlet robes to set a chair for her. "And I supposed your Grace to be long since asleep."

"I sleep ill of late, milord, and would have your immediate advice," she told him without subterfuge. "Late as it is, I pray you be seated again and spare me a little of your time."

"It is about this misfortunate husband of yours that you seek help, my daughter?" he asked, in the suave encouraging tones he usually kept for the Confessional.

"Is it true that his Holiness the Pope will offer me the choice between excommunication from Holy Church and going back to him?" she asked bluntly.

"He is still your husband, and when I left Avignon the document was being prepared."

"And you know milord Mortimer's mind in this?"

The corpulent prelate bowed his head in assent.

Stark honesty poured from Isabel's lips. "God knows I have suffered much from Edward. And that for my own sin's sake I would be free of him. For my son's sake, too, who now wears the crown. And for milord Mortimer's, who would assuredly die if Edward were to come to power again," she confessed. "But I cannot take part in this desperate thing which is in my lover's mind."

"It is not meet that any of us should ask you to, my child," soothed Adam Orleton. "If Sir Edward were to die naturally— and soon—by some fever or by the rigours of imprisonment as old Lord Mortimer of Chirk did—well, we are surely sufficiently worldly-wise to admit that it would be—er, convenient—for you both. But beyond that we cannot in good conscience go."

Isabel saw his fleshy red face and shiny tonsured head as a warm round beacon of comfort, and let out an audible sigh. "I felt sure that you would say so, milord, but I have to know to-night because, as you are probably aware, a messenger will be leaving for Berkeley in the morning. And I was afraid that my—that Roger Mortimer would——" Faint with relief and with terror of the price which she might have to pay for that relief, Isabel found herself beyond speech.

"To save you pain, Madam, and with your Grace's permission, I will myself write accordingly to Sir Thomas Gourney," the Bishop was saying. He settled himself more comfortably at the table and turned back his flowing sleeves. Pen and paper were already before him. She could only sit quiet opposite to him, watching the candlelight gleam like blood on the ruby of his great episcopal ring and striving to control the trembling of her limbs. For a long time, it seemed, the only sound in the room was the scratching of his goose quill, so that when he laid the piece of parchment before her she was surprised at the shortness of his message. The delicately formed letters danced before her eyes. She wished that he had written in homely unequivocal French or English, but ecclesiastic minds moved in Latin, she supposed. "*Edwardum occidere nolite, timere bonum est,*" he read, leaning forward to point carefully at each word with the feathered end of the quill. "Literally construed, 'Edward kill not, to fear the deed is good.'"

The words lay before her, quite intelligible now and bringing —in spite of all future fears and difficulties—immeasurable spiritual relief. "You will be sure that Sir Thomas gets it?" she insisted anxiously, wishing the message already in harsh Gourney's hands.

"I will have his man roused at once and you shall see the paper given into his keeping with your own eyes," Orleton assured her, with the paternal patience which he might have shown to some over-wrought child.

Isabel smiled apologetically for her nervous stupidity and laid a grateful hand on his, but he waved aside her thanks with the ponderous bonhomie of the obese and, while waiting for his servant to bring the messenger, busied himself with the final preparations of his parchment. Although the rich fullness of his sleeve lay like a scarlet barrier between them she saw him take up his pen again to sign it, to add some stop or comma, and then to address it. And then he was rolling it, tying it meticulously with red ribbon and setting his seal upon it. And so the thing was done which would save her from being a party to murder. Her eyes never left the rolled parchment until she had seen it pass from the Bishop's plump white hand to the rough weather-beaten hand of Gourney's man, and had heard Orleton's clear instructions to ride with it immediately to Berkeley. And then, gratefully, she knew that she would sleep that night. Beyond that she dared not look.

By the morning most of her fears were calmed. Roger Mortimer neither questioned nor gainsaid her, allowing the Bishop's order to go unintercepted as he had promised. And both of them suggested that it was now the moment to send to Hainault for Ned's bride and to make arrangements for the wedding.

"It will keep the Queen from worrying," said Orleton.

"And the puppet king from poking his nose into our affairs," muttered Mortimer, incensed because Ned had questioned him in open Council about the extraordinary augmentation of the Queen's dowry.

And so Isabel's flair for arranging things was called into play again, and her mind kept far too fully occupied to think often of her imprisoned husband. With her own hand she wrote to invite Sir John of Hainault to accompany his niece as England's principal guest. She rewarded Orleton by sending him as royal envoy to Valenciennes, and kept Ned in a state of grateful good humour by backing up his request that Philippa should be chosen.

"I see the matter was loosely worded," pointed out Orleton, consulting the original betrothal contract. "It says here '*a* daughter of William Count of Hainault, Holland and Zealand', and since I understand there are four he may well wish to send us the eldest."

"In that case appeal to my cousin, his wife, to persuade him," Isabel urged him, knowing that Ned's long memory would never forget that she had done this for him.

"To me they looked all alike," remarked Mortimer, when he and Isabel were alone. "Why make possible difficulties by pandering to his calf love?"

Isabel, looking down from her window, watched her elder son mounting *Cher Ami* and riding off with a company of robust young men for a day's hunting. "I do not think it is calf love," she said reflectively. "Nor, perhaps, love at all—as we know it. But rather the relief of a reserved, woman-shy youth at finding one girl with whom he is at ease and to whom he can speak his mind. Even about us, probably. Has it never occurred to you, Roger, that apart from all his military companions and his tournament opponents and his adoring grooms, Ned must be a very lonely person?"

And before his marriage could be arranged Ned was to become yet lonelier. No word had come from the Pope, and Isabel was beginning to wonder, with a mixture of resentment and relief, whether her lover and Orleton had been playing on her fears for their own ends. And then, quite suddenly, all fear of what the Pope might say was groundless. During the last week of September news reached London that Edward, her husband, was dead.

Her mind had been so full of festive affairs—she had pictured him so clearly moving about the hall and battlements of Berkeley Castle—that the news shocked her profoundly. It shocked the whole nation. "How did he die?" she asked, as she knew only too well every man and woman in England and Wales must be asking. As Parliament would be asking on the morrow.

"I know no more than you, milords. I was not there," she heard Mortimer answer coldly before an aghast Privy Council. "All I can tell you is that my son-in-law, the Lord of Berkeley, is still sick at Bradelye, and that his steward, Glaunville, sent a messenger to tell the Queen that Edward of Caernarvon died during the night of the twenty-second of this month, and that this Glaunville was asking for instructions about his burial."

Averting his eyes from his royal nephew's grief, Thomas of Brotherton broke the uneasy silence. "Does the man not say of what sickness my brother died?" he asked, in a curiously threatening voice. Edmund of Kent was weeping unashamedly. And blind Lincoln leapt to his feet and cried out that there must have been foul play. Pandemonium broke out, only to be silenced when the sixteen-year-old King rapped out an order that the murderer should be found. To the older men present the authoritative ring in his voice was singularly reminiscent of his grandfather's, and many must suddenly have realised that he was now King beyond all question.

But Mortimer was quick to nip such new and regal self-assertion in the bud. "I pray you have a care whom you accuse, Sir," he warned. "Had there been foul play would the murderers have been such fools as to leave the body unburied?"

"And it may comfort your Grace to know," added Orleton, "that I have this morning received a letter from Abbot Thokey of St. Peter's in Gloucester, telling me that he rode immediately to Berkeley to see if there was any service he could perform, and that he said prayers over the dead body of your father and was greatly relieved to find that there was no sign of violence upon it."

The letter he produced was passed from hand to hand, and although some members of the Council still muttered among themselves there was no immediate accusation they could make. Several of them cast covert glances at Mortimer, but he stood near the Queen, apparently unconcerned, staring them down. "Why not satisfy yourselves and the whole country by sending a party of physicians to confirm what this Abbot of Gloucester says?" he suggested.

"I myself will go with them, if only to look upon his face once more," began the third Edward. But even his relatives saw how unwise this would be in the circumstances and dissuaded him, and his brief flash of authority was gone. Some looked towards the popular Queen to see whom she would suggest sending; but they looked sheepishly, as if seeing her with new eyes—as if realizing for the first time that she, with grave marital wrongs in her memory and a lover beside her, had more cause than most to wish Edward of Caernarvon dead.

She knew what was in their minds. "Send someone of your own choosing, milords," she said haughtily, secure in the knowledge of Orleton's message. "Someone whose word is above suspicion, and who has no axe to grind. If, in these turn-coat days, you can find such a being! And lest there should remain any scruple of doubt in people's minds, for my sake and for my son's, have my husband's body embalmed and left exposed for all who wish to see. I pray you let it remain unburied until either foul play is proven or such hideous suspicion dispelled."

She saw the quickly concealed flicker of admiration in Mortimer's strange eyes. The tongues of the Council were effectively stilled, even if their thoughts were not. She walked slowly back to her apartments, unaccountably weary, followed by her silent women. She sent for old Stephen Taloise, who in his hey-day had fashioned her wedding gown, and bade him make her trailing black mourning garments. With her own hands she discarded the gorgeous metal wings of her headdress and had her tiring women replace it with nunlike wimple and swathe her little pointed chin in the widow's barbe of soft linen to which she must now grow accustomed. "I am a widow," she kept telling herself, trying to compose her face to sadness and to fight down the rush of relief that made the very air seem lighter. "I shall never have to look Edward in the face again. The Pope will not threaten to excommunicate me. I shall never have to leave Roger."

When they had finished dressing her in her becoming weeds a page came to tell her that the King wished to see her. It was the first time that he had ever sent for her. Even since his coronation he had still come to her dutifully, as a son. "But now he feels himself King indeed and he is going to try to have his father buried in Westminster Abbey," she thought, with that deadly intuition she had of other people's minds. "And, weary as I am, I shall have to persuade him that it would make trouble among the people, without letting him see that it would be suicidal for Roger and for me."

Her surmise was right and Ned went on protesting about it intermittently for days. "What has he ever done that he should not be laid to rest in Westminster or Winchester with all our other kings?"

"You must be content with St. Peter's Abbey in Gloucester, where he can be taken privately," Isabel told him for the tenth time. "Your father thought it very beautiful and was one of its benefactors, and this Abbot Thokey has recently had it enlarged. Although it is now in the See of Worcester it may one day become a cathedral. And Abbot Thokey is willing to give the deposed king suitable burial which, you should remember, many other communities are afraid to do."

"I shall see that he is recompensed and that every possible privilege is granted to Gloucester. And I shall have my cleverest masons make my father the loveliest canopied shrine in all England. A single tomb where he will lie alone, as he died alone."

"That will be for you to decide, my son," agreed Isabel, who had no desire to lie beside her husband either in the flesh or in stone.

Ned's temper was rising, and of late it had shown promise of growing to true Plantagenet proportion. "And if Mortimer tries to interfere with the funeral ceremony or the daily Masses I shall have sung," he raged, "I shall accuse him openly!"

But there was nothing to accuse Mortimer of. The carefully picked party of renowned physicians and disinterested public officials sent by Parliament confirmed the Abbot of St. Peter's statement. There was no sign of foul play and there was nothing in the stomach to suggest poison. They reported that the late

King's body lay reverently exposed to public view, between tall candles, in the chapel of Berkeley Castle. When pressed further they admitted that his athletic slenderness was perhaps a shade more pronounced than in lifetime, and that his face bore signs of strain or pain, though no more than was consonant with the grave troubles that had befallen him and months of imprisonment. Even the burghers of Bristol, who had raised so much tumult on his behalf, had been invited to see him and admitted that there was no single mark of violence upon him.

Edward's corpse lay there for three months and though his cousin and half-brothers left the Council and other supporters drifted away, not even Mortimer's most jealous enemies could bring any accusation against him. Thanks to Isabel's quick wit in delaying the burial, people began to tire of the subject and conjecture died down. And soon she was able to busy herself about the provision of a rich pall and the painting of the arms of England on a funeral chariot to be sent to Berkeley, and with letters to Glaunville telling him to have the best chandler in Gloucester come out to make the wax effigy to be borne before it, and then to fix the date when the Abbot and whole community were to come with sad chanting to form the cortège. She was glad to be occupied, for whenever she was sitting alone, which she contrived to do as seldom as possible, the words "no single mark of violence" ran through her mind, replacing and refuting those other words "as long as he lives" which had been so often on her lover's lips. They became a kind of slogan such as the Scots used to gather their forces for battle. And every time she caught herself looking searchingly at Roger Mortimer, she dealt with her own doubts by making her mind repeat monotonously "Not a single mark of violence".

CHAPTER 30

BISHOP ORLETON was successful in getting the bride whom young Edward the Third wanted. But by the time she landed at Dover the prospective bridegroom was away up north winning his spurs in a desperate if not very successful effort to push the Scots back over the Border. Even in the midst of the fighting he sent emphatic orders for her reception, telling the Governor of Dover Castle to provide for the comfort of her retinue and urging the chief citizens of every town through which she would pass to extend to her the warmest possible welcome. It was noticeable how little urging they needed, for Philippa's fresh young simplicity made ready appeal to minds confused by so much scheming, and many of them were beginning to transfer their hopes from Isabel to the young king, if only he could free himself from the over-weening mastery of Mortimer and the fondly expressed domination of his mother. The Londoners entertained the Flemish princess during Christmas, sparing no expense to give her pleasure, but she was a shy, reserved girl and clearly her only desire was to join her betrothed, so as soon as Ned had time to take up permanent quarters in York she was escorted there for their wedding.

Isabel and Mortimer were already in the north, doing their utmost to conclude a peace treaty with Robert Bruce. And Isabel had taken her five-year-old daughter Joan with her to set the seal upon it by betrothing her to Bruce's son David. She knew that the marriage would be unpopular with the English, but had the good sense to see that her son's kingdom could never be secure or strong enough to keep his continental possessions unless these everlasting border frays ceased. "Years ago when I left for France with so much unhappiness in my heart and so much uncertainty before me, I promised that I would make you a queen, my sweet Joan," she said, caressing the dearest of her children. "And now that your brother's marriage is being discussed, and I am hoping to keep a stake in the French succession by betrothing your sister to one of the Valois cousins, why should you not be Queen of Scotland? Particularly as, with no sea flowing between us, we may be able to meet sometimes, when you grow up."

She had gone with Mortimer to Berwick for the child's wedding, soon after the young King and Philippa were married in York. It had been a breathlessly busy winter and two of her favourite schemes had been brought to fruition. Joan was being brought up in Scotland and Ned was safely occupied enjoying his bride at Woodstock. Mortimer was still up north speeding their Scottish guests and driving as hard a bargain as he could for the peace treaty. And she herself was travelling leisurely back to London where, although now merely the Queen Mother, she would in reality reign again. But a late and unexpected snow storm had made the roads impassable and, to her intense annoyance, she had been obliged to break her journey at Nottingham. "At Nottingham Castle, of all places, which I hate," she had complained, shivering in spite of the roaring fires which Sir Robert Eland, the Constable, had made.

"And it looks as if the sky is still full of snow, so that we may be held up here for days," said Ghislaine, who was returning with her from their beloved little Joan's wedding.

"Well, at least I can well occupy the time," said Isabel. "There has been so much going on that I have not found a moment in which to check even my own household accounts since—I was widowed. So after supper, dear Ghislaine, tell the others they can go to bed and send Fontenoy to me here and tell him to bring all his books."

When the castle was quiet and the curtains drawn against the bitter howling wind she sat alone before the fire ready to receive her confidential clerk. "Why does this place always depress me so?" she wondered, glancing round uneasily at the life-size figures on the tapestries as they stirred eerily in some sudden draught. "It is not just because Roger is not with me. Nor because I am a widow and past my first youth. Nor because I am no longer Queen." Her thoughts went to Count William and her cousin of Valois' child who had so recently been fêted through the streets, and who seemed to have inherited so much more Flemish blood than French. "How different she is from myself, when I came as a new young bride!" she thought, contrasting Philippa's undramatic goodness with her own vivacious, sex-conscious beauty at that age. "She has the freshness of youth but after a confinement or two she will probably grow clumsy, whereas even now, in my thirties, I am still beautiful." She drew towards her the mirror which was never far away, and setting it beneath the candlelight, looked critically at the carefully painted reflection that it gave. "Still beautiful—but so strained and hard that Marguerite would scarcely recognize me now," she decided honestly, as though conferring with that former vision of gay, generous youth which she sometimes caught herself regretting so nostalgically in her more unguarded moments. "No, there are some things one cannot do, *ma belle Isabel*, without accounting for them in one's face even if they are not entered in one's household books."

The door opened and Fontenoy, who had been in her service

all her married life, was bowing at her side as respectfully as he could with both long arms clutching a pile of dull-looking leather-bound volumes. "Ah, well," she thought, as he laid the first of them before her, "with all my sins at least no one can accuse me of sloth."

Since she had taken over the government it seemed that she must keep her finger upon a dozen things at once. She realized how much Edward, with his pleasure-loving indolence, must have hated it all, and of late there had been so many matters which she and Mortimer must keep locked privately in their own minds. "The accounts in that other book, Fontenoy? The locked one with the precise amounts of how the Flemish dowry was spent. You have never left the hasp for a moment unlocked?"

"Your Grace will see that no other hand but mine has ever written in it. And here, Madam, is the key."

"Thank you for your pains, good friend." With a sigh of relief she slipped the key into the bosom of her gown, free to turn her attention to more ordinary and open matters. "And where do we begin tonight?"

With long, scholarly fingers he turned the pages of the open household book before her, and set a golden candlestick so that the light shone down upon his neat entries. "Here. Early in October, Madam. These are the accounts sent by milord Berkeley's steward, Glaunville. An honest and capable man, seemingly."

"*Must* we begin with these?" she asked, seeing at a glance what kind of entries they would be.

"Perhaps if your Grace finds them too painful——"

But Isabel overcame her momentary weakness and laid a firm guiding finger on each clearly dated item. As Fontenoy had suggested, Berkeley's man Glaunville appeared to be a most businesslike individual, capable of reducing to a few stark phrases the whole tragedy of a king's death.

"'Paid to Beaukaire, the officer sent from Westminster to guard the late King's corpse, for three months,'" she read aloud. "'Paid to milord Berkeley's men-at-arms for same. Paid to carpenter of Berkeley for making barriers to keep back the press of people.' And here again 'To mending the said barriers.' *Could* there have been so many people, Fontenoy?"

"When Glaunville met me in York he said that they came from as far as Oxford and Caernarvon."

Isabel felt the cold hand of fear grip at her stomach, but went on with the lugubrious details before her.

"'To priest for oblations in Berkeley chapel. To the best chandler in Gloucester for the making of a wax effigy of the late King'"—Isabel's voice faltered for a moment—"'to be carried before the funeral chariot—forty shillings. For a gilt crown for same.'" And all that time she had been picturing him sitting before the fire at Berkeley with book or lute. She tried not to picture instead the purple-robed, counterfeit thing lying mutely on a black-draped bier with all the torches and carved angels and Plantagenet heraldry about it. That still insensate thing with Edward's shape and features, but no knowledge of his pleasant voice or of his lithe movements. She hurried on to the next item. "'Travelling expenses for Sir Thomas Berkeley's steward to York. And for the woman Druscilla from Berkeley.' God's grace!" cried Isabel, with nerves on edge. "Is the royal Exchequer expected to pay for his pleasures as well?"

When her clerk did not answer, she looked up sharply. "She is not that kind of woman, Madam," he said, with slow reluctance.

"Then a relative, perhaps, having a free jaunt at my expense?" She was far from mean towards those who served her, and normally might not have questioned so small an item, but already she had borne enough. Fontenoy leaned forward to point to a line below where her own finger still kept the place, where she saw an entry, stark and undetailed, for the embalming of the late King. "She is the woman who did it," he said.

"The *woman!*" repeated Isabel. Her hands slid from the book, which had unexpectedly opened up so much information for her. She sat back in her chair and stared at him incredulously.

"I understand that no physician was available."

"No physician—in all Gloucester, Hereford or Worcester?"

"Glaunville says that Sir Thomas Gourney wanted it done quickly."

"I can well believe that!" The Queen's voice was low with fury and she pushed back her chair so suddenly that an inkhorn went flying, spilling its contents in an ugly black flood spreading across the table. "Where *is* this woman?" she demanded. "Find her. Have her sent for."

"Madam, there is no need," said Fontenoy, springing forward to save his precious papers from harm. "She is here."

"Here, in Nottingham?"

"She must have followed us from York after Glaunville returned. She tugged at my sleeve this forenoon as I rode in from the town. She said that she must speak with your Grace, and begged to be allowed into the castle."

"And you, like a fool, said it was impossible and sent her away, I suppose? Go instantly and find her if you have to drag everybody in the town from their beds. No, leave the ink and your books and bring her here even if it be past midnight. And tell no one why I want her, Fontenoy."

The woman could not have gone far, but the embers were dying on the hearth by the time Fontenoy had brought her and gone away again. In spite of all her impatience Isabel had become so deeply wrapped in thought that she did not realize how cold her limbs were, nor hear the heavy oak door open and shut, but when she looked up the woman was standing there. A small, grey-haired wren of a woman, with eyes as alert and intelligent as her own. Clearly she was no light-of-love whom the worthy Glaunville had picked up to enliven his travels, but the respectably dressed wife of a reasonably well-to-do tradesman. Nobody in particular in the eyes of the world, but to Isabel's searching gaze the only person besides Gourney, who was gone overseas, who could tell her the truth about her husband's death. "What is your name?" she asked, motioning to her to come into the circle of candlelight and take off her snow-flecked cloak.

"Druscilla Dunheved." The woman answered clearly, and although she could never have been in the presence of a queen before she seemed to be in no wise over-awed. The macabre thought occurred to Isabel that perhaps the reason lay in the fact that she had so recently had the intimate handling of a king. "Why did Master Glaunville bring you?" she asked.

"He brought me only as far as York." The woman's words were so calm and matter-of-fact that Isabel scarcely noticed that they were an evasion.

"And can it possibly be true that you embalmed the body of the late King?"

"On the twenty-second night of September I was sent for to the castle to do it," agreed Druscilla. Her speech was not uncouth, though leavened with the faint suspicion of a Welsh lilt to be found so often in the border counties.

"Your phlegm amazes me. Does it not seem strange to you

that you—a woman—should have been called upon to perform such an office?"

"My husband was the chandler in Berkeley. He often embalmed the local gentry when they died."

"Then why was he not sent for?"

"Madam, he has been dead these six months." For the first time Isabel noticed the little woman's white linen barbe and black dress. "I knew something of his trade, having helped him at times. And I am used to handling bodies, being the village midwife, and folks always wanting me to lay out their dead. Likely enough that is why Sir Thomas Gourney sent one of my sons for me in the middle of the night."

"Your sons? Were *they* not in their father's trade?"

"They both served milord Berkeley as men-at-arms up at the castle."

"Then Sir Thomas Gourney sent for you—as soon as it happened?"

"Before the corpse was well cold."

Isabel shuddered with cold herself. She supposed that it was the woman's calling which had gradually deprived her of all imaginative human feeling. "And you saw no mark of violence upon it?" she asked. But for once the woman's almost irritatingly quick tongue failed to respond immediately. "Well, did you?" Isabel insisted, conscious that her voice was rising sharply.

"No, Madam."

"Then why stand there like a dumb, unfeeling block of wood? If your sons are in Sir Thomas Berkeley's service," she added questioningly, "I suppose they must have seen something of the late King's life there?"

"As much as any man, Madam. They were both among the escort that fetched him from Corfe to Bristol, and then—when the burghers there protested at the way he was treated—they brought him on to Berkeley. At first they baited him—like the rest——"

Isabel found her hands clutching at the table edge. "Baited him?"

"Jeered at him, like. When they were getting the horses out of the stable of a morning they'd plait a crown of filthy straw and stick it on his head when they waked him, and bellow out 'Come forth, Sir King!' Or pretend that a messenger was coming from his son to set him free. Oh, nothing to injure him, Madam! Nothing more than milord Mortimer's orders."

"And what exactly were milord Mortimer's orders?" asked Isabel, blaming herself because she had so often of late deliberately spared herself the pain of finding out.

Druscilla Dunheved looked puzzled. "How could I be knowing that one-half so well as your Grace?" she countered, taking it for granted that the Queen must know their entirety. "All I know is that Gourney's men were told to move him after dark from one castle to another, and that the nights were cold and they were forbidden to lend him their cloaks to put over his threadbare hose and thin shirt."

"But I sent him his warmest riding cloak. And a houppelarde made of figured Utrecht velvet lined with miniver."

"Would it have been a kind of tawny colour with great crimson flowers embossed on it?" asked Druscilla, seeing the Queen's agitation.

"Then my—Sir Edward Plantagenet *did* receive it?"

"Not to my knowledge. But I once saw the Captain of the Guard peacocking about in one like that the Sabbath after milord Berkeley went away, and an ungainly fool he looked in it!"

Isabel rose, walking with stiffened limbs to the hearth to induce a small last blaze with a poke from her own satin slipper. "What else do you know? What else did those sons of yours tell you?" she demanded.

"Towards the end they seemed reluctant to talk about him much. But I remember a man called William Bischop telling how Gourney'd given orders to shave the prisoner's beard off. Queen's orders he said it was, saving your Grace, because of the way folks would call 'God have pity!' when they recognized him. And a fine play those young blades made of the barbering, bringing him dirty water from a ditch in an old broken helmet and making him sit on an ant heap."

Isabel seemed to shrink away from her. "They did *that* to him—by *my* orders?"

"And he was so cold and humiliated he wept like a child. 'At least my tears may warm the water,' he said, half jesting and half pathetic like. 'Twas after that that my lads Steve and Tom came over all pitiful about him."

"Dear Mother of God, was it not time someone did?" muttered his wife brokenly, going back to her chair.

"They used to come home some evenings and say it touched their hearts the way he'd sit for hours singing softly to himself.

French love songs, mostly. And it seems that even Master Glaunville would slip a hunk of bread and meat into the guardroom for him."

"Into the *guardroom*?" repeated Isabel, thinking that she could not have heard aright.

"That's where they kept him after milord Berkeley left."

"And to think that I once stood there—outside the door, talking to Thomas Berkeley. Little did I ever think——"

"Milord Berkeley would never have allowed it. And when we heard that he was getting better and might soon be coming home Gourney sent a messenger to London. Everyone was saying that the poor King's time would be short. My sons were fair besotted about him by then. They even risked their lives helping him to escape. One evening when it was getting dusk they gave him the signal when to get out and threw a bundle of faggots on to his shoulders so that he should look like one of the servants going home with his pickings from the log pile. They do say King Edward killed the guard at his door with his bare hands, easy as choking a coney, and it's God's truth he got away. For more than an hour he must have been free, but it was getting dark and the mist came swirling up over the meadows from the Severn and he could have been walking round in circles, not knowing the place. And as soon as he was missed they set the bloodhounds on him."

"And after that?" Isabel's voice was no more than a hoarse whisper. It seemed incredible that the woman's bright tone could go on so dispassionately when she herself could imagine so vividly what it must have felt like to have got free, and then be dragged back again.

"After that? Well, it's not what a delicately nurtured lady like your Grace would want to be hearing about. They made him sit for hours above the castle cess pit, hoping the stench would do what cold and starvation hadn't. Until word came from London."

"I saw the message. I know what it said. Edward kill not."

"And that was the night he died," went on the chandler's wife, as though she had not spoken.

Isabel rose and confronted her. "But you said there was no mark on him. How can you dare to infer——"

"Nor was there. Gourney dared not run that risk. They say he offered a hundred pounds to anyone who could think of some safe way to be rid of him, and a man called Ocle who had been in charge of the escort thought of a way. A way that Satan in hell wouldn't have thought of. And I, God help me, had to be the person to find out about it." For the first time the capable little woman showed signs of personal emotion.

Isabel stood waiting, both hands clutching her chair back. The last log fell in a soft shower of red ash to the hearth, and two of the three candles were guttering out. In the gloom it was easy to imagine that Druscilla Dunheved was back in Berkeley Castle, seeing again what she described. "They told me to bring my husband's things—the surgeon's knife, the herbs, the wax, the flaxen cloths, the needle and thread and all. Gourney himself was in the courtyard at the foot of the guardroom stairs. He knew my husband had died, but told me to do the best I could. The lower room was full of soldiers, some of them men I knew. But they looked away and not one of them spoke to me as I passed. And they weren't talking among themselves either. In the warm light from a brazier they looked scared and white, and one youngish fellow was vomiting in a corner. Serjeant had a curious long pipe made of horn in his hand, and a couple of iron rods were still stuck heating into the hot coals. And about all there was a sickening smell of scorching flesh like you catch on the breeze at the end of a hunt when they burn the stag's umbles. The serjeant put down the horn pipe and led me up the stairs, and called to a couple of his men to bring torches. As the light and shadows wound up round and round the stair walls, the stench grew worse. And as soon as my eyes came level with the top, I saw him. He was lying on his back on the bed with his knees up. The guard-room table lay upside down beside him as if they'd used it to hold him down. He must have been still strong when he came to die. They held the torches aloft for me though there wasn't much left for me to do really. I was only a village woman, not one of these prying physicians who might have talked. And it would have been useless, anyway, trying to hide from me what they'd done. They'd passed the hot irons up through the pipe to burn his bowels out."

Druscilla did not seem to hear the moaning sound the Queen made, nor to notice that she had slumped across the table with her head on her extended arms. In the semi-darkness she was still seeing what she had seen back in the guardroom at Berkeley Castle. For the first time there was pity in her voice. "His face was twisted with pain, poor soul. And several of us had heard his screams down in the village. But neither those folks who came crowding from Bristol nor the physicians sent by Parliament could have guessed a thing. There wasn't a mark on him. May I go now, Madam?" she added after a long silence.

With an almost superhuman effort Isabel dragged herself back from the brink of unconsciousness. Fear made her keep her wits. For Mortimer's sake she forced her thoughts forward. She even managed to pull herself upright. "You do not suppose, do you, that I will let you go with that tale on your tongue?" she said, and even to her own ears the words sounded like the hissing of a startled serpent.

She would call Fontenoy. Send for Robert Eland. Have her put to death or incarcerated somewhere down in the dungeons for the rest of her life. Some early remembrance flashed across her mind of how earlier French kings had dealt with people who knew too much by having their tongues cut out. She had no personal hatred for the woman. It was only that she dared not let her go. But even now, to her amazement, Druscilla did not seem afraid. She drew a crumpled paper from the pouch hanging from her belt and laid it down beneath the light of the one remaining candle. "That is a copy of the message Gourney had. Master Glaunville saw it and made a copy of it, lest he and the rest of milord Berkeley's men should be blamed."

Isabel passed a trembling hand across her eyes before she could read, and then she knew the extent of Orleton's cunning infamy. It was the same single line of Latin words that she had seen before. Only the placing of a single comma had been altered. And that had altered everything. "*Edwardum occidere nolite timere, bonum est,*" she read. And even her superficial knowledge of Latin told her how she had been tricked. The single comma completely changed the meaning. "Edward to kill fear not, the deed is good."

And Roger Mortimer, almost certainly, must have known of it and approved.

"Why did Glaunville send you to torture me?" she cried.

"He did not. He but took me to York to show that message to the King and to have me tell him what I have told you, so as to clear our beloved lord of Berkeley," repeated the woman obstinately. "And it is not *you* who are tortured, Madam. I, who embalmed the late King's body, should know."

Isabel was staring at her with far more fear than she could ever hope to instil. "Then—my son—knows?" For all her effort, she was only mouthing the words. She recognized this as the end of filial love, of her own security, of her lover's day-to-day safety.

"It was the young King himself who sent me to your Grace."

All power of practical thought was beyond Isabel. "At least he knows that I was tricked," she kept whispering over and over again. And when the trance of horror cleared, dawn was breaking palely behind the curtains and the woman was gone.

CHAPTER 31

"HE KNOWS what you have done," said Isabel, still white and exhausted, when Roger Mortimer rejoined her at Westminster.

"What *I* have done?"

"Otherwise he would not have sent the woman who did the embalming."

"And you were crazy enough to let her go!" Mortimer, who so seldom showed agitation, walked restlessly about her room between hearth and bed.

"I think I must have fainted."

He stood looking at her, gnawing at his finger nails as he did in moments of uncertainty. "You do not suppose that I planned this horrible thing? I left the details to Gourney. All I stipulated was that his captive should die—or seem to die—naturally."

"Naturally!" She put her hands to cover her ears as though she could still hear in imagination Edward's screams. "So you meant to murder him? You and Orleton. That Latin message of his was a shoddy trick to keep me acquiescent."

It seemed unnecessary to Mortimer either to deny or to admit her accusation. Since the deed had been accomplished there were more urgent considerations. "You think that this woman talked? That it is generally known around Berkeley?"

Isabel shrugged her uncertainty. "In any case there were the soldiers. Though they were well paid no doubt to keep their mouths shut."

"And afraid to speak for the sake of their own skins," he agreed with some degree of relief.

"All the same, one knows how these rumours spread."

He nodded. "There is a new one growing up now. The usual thing. That Edward is still alive. That he is back in Corfe."

"You mean that people *believe* it three months after Thokey gave him burial in his Abbey at Gloucester?"

"You know how such things are spread by travelling friars and pedlars. And how credulous the common people are."

"Better that they *should* believe *this* fantasy than—suspect murder."

"The devil of it is that your son knows the truth."

Isabel sank wearily into a chair, and sat turning the rings on her fingers. "I have been devising all manner of entertainments for him and his bride so as to keep his mind from dwelling on it—or on us."

"The most important thing is that he should have no chance to talk to Lincoln—or his uncles."

"Lincoln is his guardian and it will but add to his discontent and his growing distrust of us if we seem to prevent him from having any opportunity to speak to Ned alone."

"A guardianship which would have been more safely bestowed on me," muttered Mortimer. "Already Lincoln and Norfolk and Kent are secretly raising and arming their retainers, Dragon tells me."

"He acts as your spy everywhere these days, does he not?"

"Ever since he managed to follow me to France. And I have need of one," said Mortimer harshly, "with your turn-coat brother-in-law of Kent and his double-dealing. It is he who is spreading it abroad that Edward was murdered. And now young Ned knows. How convenient it would be if he could go abroad for a few months until things have simmered down!"

Ned as a boy king had been a useful prop for his plans, but Ned the very young married man, nearing his majority and knowing too much, had become a problem. Every time Isabel saw him, tall as Mortimer and almost as martial looking, she wondered how much longer England could hold them both.

But events were happening in France just then which were of great personal moment to her, so that local anxieties and for a time even the horror of Edward's end could be pushed to the back of her mind. She had been widowed only a few months before her brother Charles died, leaving no son. This was the situation of which he had once spoken to her, and Isabel became obsessed by the consciousness that she was the only remaining child of *Philip le Bel*. "If only I had not been born a girl I should now be the rightful King of France!" she boasted. And ambition flamed in her for her elder son. "Charles himself once said to me that Ned might one day be more important than he knew, and he liked Ned far better than this Valois cousin the French nobles are choosing for their King. Young Edward Plantagenet on the throne of France would have united our two countries and kept the Capet line alive."

"It is the old vexed question of the direct line descended through a woman or being set aside for the son of a younger son, which your Salic law sanctions," observed Mortimer, who had the more immediate matter of personal security on his mind. "Though I admit that, to our eyes at any rate, the matter looks as though it might bring strife between England and France for a hundred years or more."

The realization of her blood claim to the throne of France made her inward regard for England more arrogant than ever. By the light of this new interest in events across the Channel her bright plans for the country of which she *was* Queen grew less and less important, so that she was apt to act less warily, often doing things which she knew must offend the people and making no particular effort to hide her relationship with Mortimer.

Ned himself she found more easy to inflame than Mortimer on the subject of the French succession. "To think of the son of a Capet bending the knee in homage to a Valois!" she would say, torn between personal indignation and relief that a new and vital interest had cropped up at the right moment to get him out of England and turn his mind from his father's death.

Unwillingly, the young man who, besides being King of England, was Duke of Guienne crossed the Channel again to do homage for it, but this time not to a pleasant, indulgent uncle but to a cousin of a younger branch whom he considered an usurper. He hated what he had to do. "Wait until I am of age and can get a well-trained army together!" he said openly to his entourage before he left.

"He very soon *will* be of age," Mortimer would mutter uneasily.

"And a father, by what Philippa's women say," said Isabel, reluctantly picturing herself as a grandmother.

"It should all help to make him forget about Berkeley," said Mortimer, hoping that Ned would stay abroad until he himself

had had time to deal with a secret rising which Lincoln was pro-
moting among the people.

"I doubt if he ever forgets anything!" sighed Isabel, wishing
that Ned were still a boy and not growing into a man whom her
ruthless lover might consider it necessary to deal with too.

With his usual efficiency Mortimer speedily snuffed out
Lincoln's rather feeble effort at rebellion by ravaging his lands
before half his retainers could be raised. An insatiable greed for
power seemed to possess him, but Isabel realised that as dislike for
him grew he was, in fact, more concerned with holding what he had
already gained. "I wish I could settle Kent's underhand interference as easily," he said, returning more grimly than usual from
the campaign. "He is one of those bland people whom it is difficult to accuse. A two-party man. But I know that he is trying to
persuade Norfolk to join him in raising a party who will oust us
as murderers and make Ned King indeed."

"If only *he* could be persuaded into believing this crazy rumour
that Edward is still alive!" she said, with a laugh which held little
amusement. "It could keep him quiet, and he is just the sort of
lovable young fool who *might* believe it."

"You really think so?"

"We always used to tease him for being so gullible. And
have I not told you that he is a visionary, like John of Hainault?"

"Orleton said something of the kind to me only yesterday. He
thinks that if Kent could be persuaded of it we could trick him
into betraying his intentions."

"Orleton! Orleton's mind must be a mass of trickery," scoffed
Isabel. Although that crafty prelate now held the richer See of
Winchester as reward for services rendered, she had never really
forgiven him for duping her with an altered comma, and it was
the mastery of his superior scheming which she resented. most.
"If you feel that there are still too many Plantagenets breathing,
and it is to be either my son or my brother-in-law whom you must
suppress, then it must be my poor brother-in-law," she said
tartly. "And I will show you that my wit is quite keen enough to
do it without my lord Bishop's help. *Show* him Edward at Corfe
—oh, at a distance and well guarded of course—and if I know
Edmund he will soon be passing in to him letters full of loving
offers of help."

Even Mortimer the fierce border lord regarded her with fearful
horror. "*Show* him Edward?" he repeated.

In order to irritate him and to show him how easily a woman's wits outpaced a man's, Isabel went to her mirror and began deftly brushing a touch of smudged charcoal beneath her eyes. "There is the effigy that was made to carry before his coffin," she said almost nonchalantly, so that he could not guess with what equal horror she had thought of it at the time. "Such things are usually kept. After all, I paid the chandler forty shillings for it. Probably the Gloucester monks still have it down in some crypt."

"You mean—pretend it is Edward himself—asleep?"

Isabel laid down the charcoal pot and crossed the room as lightly as a girl to kiss him on the cheek. "No, foolish one. Have you *no* imagination? Sit it in a chair—before the fire. At supper or chess board."

And so it was arranged that a preaching friar—a creature of Orleton's—should report to Edmund of Kent that he had actually seen the late King walking on the battlements of Corfe Castle. And that Kent's credulity should be so worked upon that he himself should go to Corfe. There he was received secretly by the castle porter, who for a bribe and in pretended fear of the conniving Constable, Sir John Daverill, allowed him to dress as one of the servants and look briefly from the serving screens upon the supper table at the other end of the hall, where in the flickering torchlight he beheld his half-brother, clad in a kingly red mantle, sitting pensively among the others at his meal. It was true that during those few minutes he neither smiled nor spoke, but Kent would know those beloved familiar features anywhere, and was the more moved by his understandably silent abstraction. Whereupon he had impulsively written to Edward, as Isabel had foreseen, offering brotherly allegiance and comfort, with a promise to bring him out of prison and make him king again. And he had rashly added an assurance that most of the great men of England were already sworn with him to accomplish this. As instructed, the bribed porter had handed the letter to Daverill, who had immediately forwarded it to Mortimer. And that was evidence enough. The letter was in Kent's own handwriting. Five thousand men, he claimed to have, ready to put the deposed King he supposed to be living in the place of the reigning son. A charge of treason was brought against him at Winchester and he was condemned to death. It had been as easy as that.

By her ready wit the Queen had out-moved the Bishop.

But it had not been easy to find an executioner. The tide of public opinion was beginning to turn. All the progress and improvement which the Queen's return had promised had never come to pass. Still darker and more inexplicable things than ever had occurred. And then again, the insular English were ever wary of foreigners. French Capet and Welsh Mortimer had held power for only a few short months, but Plantagenets had ruled England for years. And the Earl of Kent, however bad a landlord he had been, was a son of the great first Edward. So the public executioner of Winchester had slipped furtively away and no one could be persuaded to take his place. The city, once the capital of England, had grown silent and sullen. Pitiful Hampshire folk stood about in groups looking up at the lonely, guarded figure waiting on the scaffold with a patient variety of Plantagenet courage for someone to end his gentle life. "The young King will come and save him," they told each other. "Mark my words, he will come riding in through the city gate and shout up to Mortimer's butchers to free his favourite uncle."

But they had chosen a Sunday when the King was hovering anxiously over his beloved Philippa at Woodstock, waiting for the birth of their son, when they knew he would have thought for no one else. And just as the sun was sinking below the city wall a man freed from the gaol, to save his own filthy skin, made a botched and brutal business of cutting off the Plantagenet earl's head.

"And he the most lovable of them all! And I began it all, out of vanity, like some game of wits," lamented Isabel, when they brought her the news. Her lover's life would be safe, but she was thankful that Marguerite, the beloved, was no longer alive. Marguerite, who had always worried about her younger son's gullible weakness. Marguerite who, had she lived, might have kept her from so much evil.

"And Ned is safe, too," she thought that night, daring to listen to that voice of fear which had lain of late in her heart. The fear that if any fresh revolt should bring her son to full power, Mortimer would see to it that he went the way of his father. Roger Mortimer had sworn that he did not want the actual crown for himself, but two grown men could not share the ruling.

The score against Mortimer had been mounting up, and now the execution of Edmund Plantagenet counted heavily. Isabel, with her interest and intuition rudely drawn back again from France, knew what they said about him. Who was this Welshman to destroy their royalty? And to sell the kingship of Scotland for twenty thousand pounds? And into whose coffers had the twenty thousand pounds gone? And when he seized Edmund's good Kentish lands and gave them to his son Geoffrey, even she herself protested. She thought of Ned and Philippa's new-born son, another Edward, and was determined that he should have no rival in the son of Roger's wife. "That night in Paris when we talked with heart's candour of the things we each intended to do, you swore that our ruling would be in Ned's name," she reminded Mortimer sombrely, believing that whatever he set out to do would be accomplished. "Your ambition has not widened since then? You do not now mean to get the crown for yourself?"

He still swore that he did not, that one day he meant to go back to Wales and make that his kingdom, but though he seldom lied to her she still had doubts. Just as one evil deed led to another, she thought, so a man could have ambitions which grew bolder without his being aware of it. And that any tittle of land or power should pass to Lady Mortimer's son from her own, who should be King of France, was more than she could stomach.

Isabel had taken no joy in his loving since Druscilla Dunheved had been sent to her. That her son should have deliberately sent the woman to her to show that he knew she lay with his father's murderer, seemed to Isabel sufficient punishment for all her sins. As long as she lived that night in Nottingham Castle when she had sat and listened to the fiendish tale would seem like a foretaste of hell. Sometimes when other people were telling her some frivolous story or discussing serious affairs of state she would suddenly sit rigid, staring blindly before her. Through and beyond their various voices she would hear Druscilla's, toneless and pitiless, saying, "They made him sit for hours above the castle cess pit . . . A couple of red-hot irons stuck into the brazier . . . There wasn't much left for me to do, really . . . No, not a mark on him." And then at other times she would be able to persuade herself that the whole thing had never happened, that it was some nightmare which she had had, too terrible to be true.

"And now they want me to go north to Nottingham again," she complained, when Mortimer had urged in Council that the coming Parliament should be called there. "Why cannot members come to Westminster as usual?"

"Because the face of London is much changed towards us these days. You have not been in the streets lately."

"You mean because Philippa is now Queen, and the city is full of bonfires and banners for her new-born child instead of for me?"

"I mean more than that. Edward seems to have proved more dangerous dead than living. And Nottingham is in the very middle of England. With a remarkably well-disciplined garrison and walls strategically sound."

"Oh, come, my love, you too must be beginning to feel the strain," soothed Isabel. "Have you not dealt with most of our enemies? And Ned himself seems to be bearing us no rancour. Philippa, or marriage, has made him more lively. He is becoming almost as frivolous as his father was in Gaveston's time—dancing and feasting and junketing."

"It should please your roystering, romantic English to have a young couple as King and Queen."

"A young couple in love," agreed Isabel with an envious sigh.

At the thought of it an almost forgotten holiday mood rose in her. How good it would feel to be gay and beautiful and carefree again! Even though she was so deadly weary and only the Queen Mother now, she could still make this pleasant-faced Flemish girl, good as she was for Ned, look like a pink and white milkmaid. Everyone would soon be gathering in the town of Nottingham for the Parliament. There would be the usual arguing and snarling against her lover, and his high-handed over-ruling of the King and shouting them all down. The plan to snatch a little pleasure for herself first was forming in her mind even while Mortimer was holding forth to his officers about where the various members were to be accommodated and insisting that no more than two of the King's personal friends should be admitted within the castle itself.

"Do you go on ahead, milord, and see to all your affairs," she urged him. "And I will follow next day with my women. I shall enjoy a leisurely journey."

She was sending him on ahead because she needed a rest from his company, and from his fierce love-making. And because she wanted to ride through the towns and villages alone, to take to herself the balm of the people's love, to hear them cheering and to restore her self-esteem by feeling the power of her charm. And now while Ned and the new young Queen were out of the capital would be the time to do it. The day after tomorrow would be Michaelmas when everybody would be in the streets. Roger had been right. It was so long since she had ridden abroad, and if she must go to Nottingham she would give herself this pleasure first. He would already have left and Ned would be following later to open Parliament.

With a warm thrill of anticipation she had herself made specially beautiful on Michaelmas morning. But now it took longer. She spent hours before her mirror and reduced several of her tiring women to tears. She chose a russet and gold brocade which enhanced the creamy pallor of her skin, and used crushed rose petals to revive a glow of youth in her cheeks. She had her women pluck her brows and redden her mouth and cover the tired little lines beside her carefully painted eyes with pomade. She rubbed a touch of hyacinth juice on the palms of her hands and behind her ears. And if the reflection which looked back at her was a little harder, a little more artificial, it was still arrestingly beautiful. More arrestingly beautiful than ever perhaps, within the nun-like mockery of her widow's barbe.

But by the time she was ready to start she was already a trifle tired and her mind was exercised with the problem of how, to please Mortimer, she could persuade the young King to bring no more than two of his nobles into the castle, and whom it would be safest to have. Lord Montague of Salisbury, perhaps, for one, since he was pleasant company and always seemed harmless enough, with his love of music and his passion for hunting. As she rode forth at the head of her retinue, half her mind was already in Nottingham, so that she did not at first notice the strange silence. It was not that the people were not there to see her pass. She had been right about the streets being crowded. But they had had a great deal to think about since she had last ridden through London. There had been all the ugly rumours about their late King. They had seen the regalia of Scotland being taken from the Jewel House and borne away back to the Bruce. And although the crowning stone of Scone had not been returned the famous Black Cross of St. Margaret had been sent instead, which they found it hard to forgive. And then there had been the cruel end of Edmund of Kent.

Just as she passed through the Palace gate she heard a woman's voice call shrilly, "Look, there she goes, the she-wolf!" And her voice was so shrill that Isabel, still half-wrapped in her own calculations, looked back over her shoulder to see whom the woman was speaking of with so much venom. It was then that she first began to notice the ominous silence, and to feel uneasy. She looked down upon the rows of still, upturned faces. *Why* were they so still? Why was there none of the usual waving and cap-throwing and good-natured pushing. There was certainly no thrill or pleasure to be had in riding through this expressionless sort of throng. But were their faces really expressionless, or merely sullen? Isabel wondered uncomfortably whether her beauty were really fading and they were disappointed. It was a thought which had been nagging at her of late. She put an anxious finger to the corner of her eye. Too much paint, perhaps. And then she heard it again. A man's voice this time. "There she goes, the she-wolf who eats men's lives!" Again she turned to look. Whoever it was whom they hated so much must be following her closely among the crowd because her cavalcade had now turned the corner into the Strand. And then as they rode through Charing Village a group of 'prentice lads took up the cry and chanted it from the steps of Queen Eleanor's cross where once they had gathered to protect the offer of reward for Hugh Despenser's head. "She-wolf! She-wolf!" And as they neared the City gates drabs from Cock Lane came running out in their yellow cloaks. "She-wolf! French harlot!" they laughed with cruel ribald gestures. And then Isabel realized that it was she herself whom they were all staring and pointing at. At herself, Isabel the Fair, whom they had always adored—who had always been able to make them do anything she pleased. It was incredible. But it was true. What a fool she had been to ride alone! Had Roger Mortimer been there they would never have dared. He would have had his men-at-arms ride them down.

With set face Isabel spurred her horse forward. She tried to cover her ears. Anything, anything to get away from that hating cry. "She-wolf! She-wolf of France!" So that was what they called her now.

As she hurried through the City past St. Paul's and out through Aldgate, with all her company clattering after her, and gained the merciful quiet of the Great North Road it seemed as if all the vengeful shouting had died down into Marguerite's gentle voice saying, "As long as you have the protection of the people's love you will be safe."

And now, Heaven help her, she had lost that love.

CHAPTER 32

SIR ROBERT ELAND, Constable of Nottingham Castle, was waiting to receive Isabel at the end of her journey, and to escort her up the winding stair from the banqueting hall of the keep to her apartments. "It is the same bedchamber which your Grace occupied before," he said, throwing open the door which separated it from the ante-room. "I trust my people have thought of everything for your Grace's comfort."

"Yes, it is the same room," she agreed. "But for all your pains, Sir Robert, I doubt if I shall find much comfort in it."

As she sank down into the high-backed chair which had been set before a cheerfully blazing fire her palms slid along the familiar carving of its arms. It was the same chair, too, in which she had sat and listened in the gloom to the hideous tale of her husband's murder.

Druscilla's flat, expressionless voice and those other more shrill and recent voices that had execrated her in the streets were already mingling in her memory. All she wanted was to shut them out, and with them all the enemies whom she and Mortimer had made. There must be hundreds of them, she supposed, scattered all over England. Some of them might even be encamped outside this midland castle. The October nights set in early and Curfew had already sounded. Down in the town all was darkness so that anyone could approach close up to the rampart walls without being seen. "You had all the locks changed before we came, as milord Mortimer ordered?" she asked.

"And the bolts strengthened," Robert Eland assured her.

Isabel relaxed and leaned back with closed eyes. She had been shaken to the soul by those cries of "She-wolf!" but now she was safe. "And the drawbridge is up and the portcullis lowered for the night?"

"And the postern gate barred and guarded."

"And your men are keeping a good look-out from the battlements?"

If the experienced constable were amused or offended by her womanish insistence he was too polite to show it. "Milord

Mortimer himself made the rounds with me and, expert as he is, found nothing amiss," he told her gravely.

Isabel touched his arm with a charming little gesture of apology as he bent down to push a footstool beneath her feet. "I know, I know, my good Eland. He considers you one of the best Constables of any of our castles. It is only that I have had a——" Before her women she would not admit to having sustained a shock. "A horrible journey," she concluded wearily.

All that night she lay awake wrestling with her fears. "You are sick, or over-tired?" suggested Mortimer, when she fended off his embrace. But she could not bring herself to tell him of her humiliation, only mentioning that some low types of people had shouted at her. "I told you the face of London was changed," he reminded her, half his mind on what he would say on the morrow when Parliament assembled. And when morning came she was comforted a little by the sight of her son riding in, looking the picture of health, accompanied by the ever-cheerful Montague.

It was a stormy Parliament with Mortimer at his most domineering. He sat in the presence of the King and insisted that all men should address him as the Earl of March. He shouted all his critics down and demanded of blind Lincoln and of Bohun, Earl of Hereford, how they had dared to take up lodgings so near the castle and the Queen, with the result that an embarrassed Eland was obliged to find lodgings for the noble lords outside the city walls. So that by the end of the week little had been achieved except a deal of quarrelling. "We make more and more enemies," thought Isabel, seeing men standing about in separate groups talking angrily among themselves.

"The King will surely object to his cousin Lincoln being so summarily treated," she warned Mortimer.

"The King!" he scoffed carelessly. "All he thinks about are masques and tournaments like his father before him!"

"I hope you are right, but you remember how earnestly he out-faced everyone at that other Parliament, refusing to wear the crown in his father's lifetime. I saw him with Montague this morning from my window, both of them talking seriously with Eland in the seclusion of the chapel garden. Protesting about the rest of his followers not being allowed to lodge in the castle, no doubt. You do not suppose, Roger, that our efficient Constable——"

"My dear Isabel, your nerves are in such a state that you see danger if a cat jumps!'' he protested testily. "The King and Montague are far more interested in finding out what sort of hunting there is around here than in whether Lincoln and de Bohun had comfortable beds. And Eland hasn't a thought beyond balisters and battering-rams. His defences are in such good order that I can assure you an army of Saracens could not get in either by wall or gate. But if you mistrust his loyalty and my judgment I will have him bring you the keys of the castle each night and you can keep them yourself."

"I have no reason to distrust him, neither do I know whom or what I fear," she confessed—with rare tears in her eyes. "And it is true that my nerves are badly jangled. I have not slept properly since—since I was here before."

He kissed her and set his new greyhound pup in her lap to cheer her. "What you need is some of that sleeping potion which Doctor Bramtoft prescribed for you in the Tower and with which you helped me to drug my gaolers," he said, with a grin which made her envy his confident composure.

And from that day the keys of Nottingham Castle were handed over to her as soon as the great gates had been shut for the night. Foolish as it was, she felt happier so. For all his suave efficiency, she did not quite trust Robert Eland.

It added to her growing ease that her son had accepted all the quarrelling and unpleasantness good-naturedly, although he was clearly anxious to get away from it all. As soon as Parliament rose he came to her room to wish her good-bye. He and William Montague had been planning a few days hunting in Sherwood forest, and the Constable had been most helpful in sending one of his men as a guide. It was only natural that her son should be so keen to get away from his quarrelsome elders for a while, she supposed. He would come back and see her, he said, before rejoining Philippa, who was already on her way northwards. Both she and Mortimer did everything to facilitate his project, preferring to have the castle to themselves. But for Isabel it was still full of unhappy memories and foreboding, so that she kept moving restlessly from room to room.

"Sir Robert is late," she complained, the evening after her son and Montague had left.

"I have but now heard the clang of the gates and he is the soul of punctuality," soothed one of her women.

He was indeed. One should feel safe with such a custodian.

A few moments later he was bowing at the Queen Dowager's elbow, in his armour as usual, holding out the great iron keys. The key of the barbican, the key of the inner gateway and the smaller key of the postern gate. Never before, probably, had he been expected to give up his precious keys to a woman, and she tried not to see his sardonic smile. She knew that she was behaving crazily, but then she had *felt* crazy—ever since the London crowd had shrilled their hatred at her.

As soon as the Constable had bowed himself out she crossed swiftly to her bed and slipped the keys beneath her pillow, ordering her women to draw the tapestries close and not for a moment to leave the bedchamber until she came to bed. She could hear Mortimer talking and laughing with his friends in the ante-room and restlessly she signed to a page to open the door and went through to join them, searching for gaiety to distract her sombre thoughts.

Mortimer and the Bishop of Lincoln were sitting by the brazier and Sir John Daverill, who had come up from Corfe to attend Parliament, was describing to them how he and the household had sat at supper with an effigy to trick the late Earl of Kent. Oddly for a man of God the Bishop seemed to find the story quite amusing, judging by the way the candlelight kept sparkling on the jewelled cross on his breast as he laughed. Two other adherents of Mortimer's, Sir John Neville and Sir Hugh Turpinton, were sitting at a table at the other end of the room playing chess, while Dragon, as usual, was standing guard by the outer door. Daverill, who was standing, broke off his macabre story at sight of her and Mortimer rose to offer her his chair. "His Grace and milord Montague should enjoy good hunting," he remarked, embarrassed by the recollection that Edmund of Kent had been both her cousin and her brother-in-law, and hastening to change the unfortunate subject.

To cover his own embarrassment, he strolled to the window, pushed open a casement and looked out. "Although the night is singularly dark and starless, there is no sign of a frost, so hounds should find," he reported, drawing in his sleek dark head.

He would have closed the casement but Isabel put up a restraining hand. "I find this room so oppressive," she explained, with a small apologetic laugh.

"Her Grace has ever disliked this castle," explained Mortimer, noting how the Bishop moved from the chill night air towards the warmth of the brazier. "For myself," he added, tossing off the contents of his tankard and refilling it, "I find it almost as well run as Ludlow or Raglan or any of my own border fortresses."

He was always inclined to be boastful when warmed by good wine, but the Bishop of Lincoln was the soul of tact. "How well our young King is looking, Madam. He has gained much in manly poise and a more sophisticated tolerance if I may say so," he remarked, turning affably to Isabel.

"Marriage and fatherhood seem to suit him, milord," agreed Isabel, with a pleased smile. "He rides life more easily, I think. Did you hear him the other night at supper telling us about the magnificent tournament he gave in London in honour of Queen Philippa and our infant Prince?"

"Unfortunately I had not arrived, Madam. Where did it take place?"

"In Cheapside, with straw laid down from Wood Street to Queen Street to prevent the heavily barbed horses from slipping. And a tower specially built to accommodate Queen Philippa and her ladies, and thirteen combatants on either side."

"An unlucky number, one would be inclined to think, since all the seating in the tower collapsed," vouchsafed Daverill, who had passed through London at that time on his way from Corfe.

"Collapsed? The King did not tell us about *that*," exclaimed Mortimer.

The Constable of Corfe, who had an eye for the dramatic, enjoyed remedying the omission. "The incident completely stole the combatants' thunder. As you can all imagine, the whole of Cheapside was ablaze with banners and quarterings. The squires had handed up the lances, and vizors were being lowered. The young Queen had been escorted to her flower-decked seat immediately above the lists as Queen of Beauty, with all her visitors and ladies around her. The Marshal had raised his baton and the King's heralds were sounding a fine fanfare, when suddenly the silvery sound of their trumpets was almost drowned by the most appalling rending and crashing of wood and by women's terrified screams. Almost the whole of the scaffolding supporting the tiers of seating had given way and spectators were thrown this way and that among the debris."

"And was the Queen hurt?" asked Isabel quickly.

"No one was hurt, mercifully, Madam, though many were badly shaken. Every man within sight rushed to the Queen's assistance, but although white as her whimple her Grace picked herself up quickly and tried to make light of it. But milord the King was furious. He called to the Earl Marshal to hold up the jousting till the morrow and in a royal rage ordered the unfortunate carpenter responsible for the seating to be hanged on the spot."

"Merciful Heaven! Even a King, surely, could not do that!" cried Isabel involuntarily.

"Yet another exhibition of ungovernable Plantagenet temper," observed Mortimer, realizing how much such arbitrary action would offend the Londoners. "No wonder he did not mention that part of his lavish entertainment."

"But the poor wretch did not hang," Daverill hastened to reassure them. "Our Flemish Queen went down on her knees on the cobbles of Cheapside before them all and interceded for the unfortunate man's life, and what could King Edward do but pardon him!"

"That should make her exceedingly popular with the people," observed the Bishop of Lincoln.

Isabel, with her vivid imagination, could picture the dramatic scene, which was precisely the sort of thing which she herself had so often turned to her own personal profit, and a hot spurt of jealousy shot through her. "Henceforward she will always have their love and protection," she said. "Although probably she lacked the wit to make her effective gesture for that reason."

"Just natural goodness," murmured the Bishop.

"Because she insists upon feeding her son from her own breasts like any peasant?" enquired Isabel. "A performance which for some reason is always synonymous in the male mind with goodness. I am afraid if she proves prolific poor Philippa will soon loose her figure, but at the moment all the foremost painters are falling over each other to paint her as the Madonna on some altar diptych."

"Whether she encourages the arts or not she is certainly helping trade," said Mortimer. "Inviting over experts in wool combing from her own country to establish a cloth industry with the wool from our own sheep. Which is one of the few intelligent things your husband always wanted. A merchant from Norwich was holding forth on the subject only yesterday. He declares that, given skilled dyers and fullers, East Anglia could make twice as much profit from the woven cloth as it gets now from shipping the raw wool.''

Having no wish to discuss either the price of wool or the virtues of her daughter-in-law, Isabel rose and bade them all good night. They sprang to their feet and Daverill pushed open the door of her bedchamber, so that she might pass through. Mortimer had poured himself another tankard of wine and held it aloft as she passed him. He was by no means drunk but his brown-flecked eyes looked boldly and possessively into hers as she passed, telling her as clearly as words that it would not be long before he got rid of the rest of them and followed her. "To Isabel the Fair," he said, toasting her beauty. And those were the last words she ever heard him say.

Her bed covers were turned down invitingly and her two women were waiting sleepily to undress her. The friendly laughter of her lover and his friends followed her from the ante-room. But when she had taken only a few steps into her bedchamber and while the door still stood wide she became aware of another sound over-riding and stilling their lively voices. It sounded like a scuffling of mailed feet, followed by a battering and splitting of wood. It came from the far side of the ante-room and, turning to look back, she saw Dragon holding fast the bolt of the outer door—pushing against it with all his weight—until an axe clove right though an oak panel and his neck, pinioning him to the splintered wood.

Her hand flew to her throat and she heard her women scream. The door burst open and the round ante-room was suddenly full of armed men, among them William Montague and her son. "Take him who had my father murdered," she heard the young King order. "He has stood in my way too long." Turpinton and Neville rose to defend their friend, but had barely time to draw their swords before they were struck down among their scattered chessmen. She saw Mortimer, with his back to her, dash the metal tankard at his assailant's face. He whipped the dagger from his belt and plunged it into another man's throat, but he had no other weapon and before he could withdraw it half a dozen others had overpowered him. When Daverill tried to protest that all he had done at Corfe had been by the Queen's suggestion, Ned himself strode forward and silenced him with a blow across the mouth. "Bind them and bring them both to London," he ordered curtly.

The scream that Isabel had stifled croaked to a sob in her constricted throat. "Sweet son, have pity on Roger Mortimer!" she heard herself crying over and over again. But he, who had always been so politely dutiful, merely hurried his men away, with Mortimer and Daverill bound in the midst of them. With a shock as sharp as when the people had called her a she-wolf, Isabel realized that the power which she and her lover had held for so long had suddenly been stripped from them and had passed to the young man to whom it legally belonged.

The shattered door hung drunkenly on broken hinges. Still transfixed against it hung Dragon's dead body, and as she ran after them her silkshod feet slipped in the dark, spreading pool of his blood. Somehow she groped her way down the dark spiral of the stairs and out into the scarcely lighter mildness of the late October night. Forgetful of all dignity, incapable of all thought save that her lover was being taken from her, she ran across the deserted courtyard towards a group of bobbing torches by the castle gates. Grooms were bringing horses and men of the King's party were springing into saddles. "My son, my son, spare Mortimer!" she was panting all the way.

But no one heeded her. The scraping of hoofs, the shouting of orders, the creaking of the windlass in the portcullis chamber above the gates, all drowned her thin and frantic cries. They hung in the air with the sad impotence of those wraiths of mist which must have hung above the Berkeley meadows that night when her husband screamed for mercy. For a shattered moment Isabel caught sight of Ned, tall as his murdered father, on *Cher Ami*, with a bunch of horsemen crowding after him onto the narrow drawbridge. She thought that she saw the proud green and gold of Mortimer's coat. But before she could reach them the bridge was slowly rising, black and menacing in the glow of lanterns, and with a grinding sound the cruel iron teeth of the portcullis were coming down. Like prison bars they shut her in from the whole world of love and adventure and outside life. And no orders of hers would ever raise the portcullis into its strong stone grooves again.

She saw the Constable coming back into the courtyard. "Bring a couple of your men to close the passage, Jevan," he called to the fair-haired young captain of the guard. The four of them walked leisurely to a spot just within the castle wall not far from where she was standing. One of the men-at-arms held aloft a lantern and to her amazement she saw the yawning gulf of a passage-way which appeared to burrow down beneath it. The captain took the lantern while his men bent to replace the heavy flagstone which had concealed it. "No more visitors to-night! But the old tunnel has served its turn," he said laughingly. "How long has it been there, Sir?"

"Ever since the Danish invasions in the tenth century, the local people say. So that Saxon garrisons could escape or bring in food. It comes up in a kind of cave hidden by briar bushes outside. Truth to tell, I had almost forgotten about it until the King and milord Montague began sounding me before they went off on that so-called hunting expedition," Isabel heard Eland say with a chuckle.

The men had lowered the flagstone and been dismissed. In the downcast circle of yellow lantern-light she could see the captain pressing at the edges of it with his mailed foot, and shoving a powder of dust across it so that it should look no different from any other stone. "It is good to have a King— who is a man—again," he was saying, between his exertions.

"Welsh Mortimer, for all the trouble he has caused, is a man," conceded the Constable of Nottingham Castle.

"And self-confident as a cockerel. He was so satisfied about our fortifications. Well, of course, he wasn't to know about the tunnel——"

"But the French Queen, somehow she mistrusted this place. Some kind of intuition women have——"

"What will the King do with him, do you suppose?" the young captain was asking with a yawn as the two of them turned away.

"Do? With Roger Mortimer? Serve him the same as *he* served Hugh Despenser, I suppose." The Constable's answer seemed to come from a long way off as Isabel fell fainting to the ground.

CHAPTER 33

A SMALL white unicorn with a mild surprised face was stepping daintily through a flower-strewn meadow at the edge of a dark wood. Isabel lay staring at it from beneath her long lashes, although her eyelids felt too heavy to keep open for long. The sun was shining and birds were singing in the meadow, and there was a stream of cool water to assuage her burning thirst. The sunny meadow seemed full of the peace of Heaven after coming out from the wood, which had been full of hidden dragons and half-seen violence. She stretched out a shaking hand and made a little moaning sound for the water, and the white unicorn turned into Ghislaine, bending over her and holding a cup to her lips.

Isabel began drinking thirstily, but the cup and Ghislaine soon dissolved away and they were dragging her back among the dark trees again—pleasure-loving Gaveston and jibing Eleanor of Clare and clever, grasping Despenser. And Edward, her husband, was standing just inside the shadow of the trees, fondling a hound and laughing carelessly at her struggles to keep in the serene sunlight. Marguerite was lovingly rebuking him and would have helped her, but a strongly-built knight in yellow and green came striding firmly down a straight path towards her. He, of all of them, seemed purposeful and to know where he was going, and the moment Isabel saw him she knew that she wanted a strong man like him for a lover, and so she forgot Marguerite's advice and her husband's ineffectual laughter and followed the newcomer deeper and deeper into the wood. And the dragons came out from their unforeseen lairs, one by one, and pounced on her. Clawing and mauling and scratching, they changed her from a beautiful gay princess into a hideous fanged she-wolf. They did nothing to change the strong man she was following, but suddenly reached out and killed him. And just as she screamed aloud Piers Gaveston broke off from some ridiculous story he was telling Edward and, with unexpected efficiency, pushed the dragons away. Although he was gorgeous with her jewels she noticed that he, too, had at some time been marred by their brutal scratches. He smiled at her understandingly and held out a steadying hand, negligently telling the dragons of the wood and anybody else who cared to listen that she really belonged back in the sunny meadow.

In some half-world of returning sanity, Isabel began to understand that meadow and wood represented her married life, and so when she had gone back to the beginning of it all, and through it and over it for the hundredth time, she opened her eyes again and found herself lying in her bed in Nottingham Castle. The little white unicorn and the dark trees were embroidered on the familiar tapestry of the half-drawn hangings, outside in the bailey a belated blackbird really was singing, and Ghislaine was there beside her with a cup in her hand and her sweet fair face full of anxiety.

"I hoped I had died," Isabel heard herself saying, out of the pool of stillness in which all the vivacious activity of her former life seemed to have foundered.

"You have been lying here for days—ever since the Constable picked you up by the outer wall. You must have been trying to follow milord Mortimer. Quite wandering from your senses, you have been, poor sweet. So the King sent his personal physician and allowed me to come with him."

"From London?"

"Yes," said Ghislaine, perceiving that her mistress's senses were indeed coming back to her with cruel sharpness.

Isabel closed her eyes, but clutched Ghislaine's hand tightly. "Then you must know," she whispered huskily. "Is it all over—for Roger?"

Ghislaine bowed her head. "All over. With merciful quickness."

"Tell me," said Isabel, lying rigid.

"They took him to the Tower——"

"How hard to be dragged back there when one had once had the courage and ingenuity to escape!"

"But only for a few hours. All men agreed that he had made discord between the late King and yourself, and was guilty of doing grave damage to the whole realm. Your son would not allow him to speak—lest he might say something to incriminate your Grace, it is thought."

"Roger was not the kind to betray a partner, even though they might serve him as we served the Despensers. Did they do that, Ghislaine?"

"Yes. And Daverill too, because of milord of Kent."

There was a long silence in the much-hated room. Isabel looked towards the door of the ante-room where they had been arrested. The dark wood seemed to be closing about her again. The shock of seeing that sudden shambles still had power to nauseate her. "Where did they do it?" she asked sharply. "I must know—so that I may add it to the other—terrible pictures—which I must always carry in my memory."

"It was at a place called Tyburn, just beyond Westminster. There is a little stream there, and a group of elm trees. But your Grace would scarcely remember it. Robert says no one was ever executed there before. Oh, my poor lady!" Ghislaine, fearing that she would faint away again, called to one of her ladies to raise her up, and held some medicinal draught to her pale lips. "The doctor says you are to drink this. It will quieten your nerves. And if only your Grace can gather strength to receive a visitor——"

"A visitor? But the gates are locked against me. I seem to remember the portcullis coming down, down, shutting out the world." The shadows were closing in on her but she made a great effort to do as they asked and gradually some colour came back into her face, and curiosity prevailed. "Who would come to see me—now—in the hour of my disgrace?"

"None other than the Queen. Queen Philippa. By her own request."

"But without the King's knowledge?"

"It may well be so," admitted Ghislaine. "She was in the Midlands and asked to join my humble cavalcade."

"To mock me?"

"She is not that kind of person, I think. Rather to reassure your Grace on certain matters for the future, I gathered."

Nothing could so surely have aroused the Queen Dowager's resources. "For whatever reason she comes I will not be seen at such a disadvantage," she declared, gathering all her will-power and beckoning to her tiring women to bring comb and ewer and rose-water. "I must have been crazed indeed, judging by the fearful looks they still have at coming near me," she remarked with the semblance of a chuckle. "But you, my dear Ghislaine, will not completely desert me?"

"I will visit you whenever you are lonely and my duties to my family permit."

"Then the King, my son, will not punish me with imprisonment?"

"Not too rigorously, I think. But the young Queen knows more of that than I."

"Out of all the glittering pageantry of the past, you are all I have left," whispered Isabel, clinging to her with tears.

Helped by the releasing balm of weeping as much as by the potion Isabel fell into a brief, healing sleep; and when she awoke her daughter-in-law was there, alone, regarding her from between the drawn curtains at the foot of the bed. The last person whom she had wanted to see. The new young Queen who had taken her place, who had a loving husband and a son born without all the tattle of humiliating delay, and who had even without any particular intent won the people's enthusiastic cheers by begging for a careless carpenter's life. Yet only a modestly trained daughter of so good a mother as Joanna de Valois would have come with so little ostentation. "I cannot rise," said Isabel. "I pray you be seated, Madam, and tell me why you have come. For amusement, curiosity or condemnation?"

The morning sunlight shone on the Flemish girl's tall, well-built body, on her kind grave eyes, and on the distressed pucker of perplexity on her wide forehead. "For none of those reasons," she said, seating herself with unstudied young dignity beside the bed. "But in hope that I could comfort you a little."

"Out of your native goodness!" jeered Isabel, eaten with envy for the thing she had lost.

Philippa, young and vulnerable, reddened uncomfortably. "I do not understand——"

"I do but quote from one of our Bishops who, with all the rest of the English, admires you," explained Isabel more lightly. "For myself, I, too, in all sincerity do not understand. Why you should travel miles, I mean, and perhaps enrage your husband by wishing to comfort a woman whom you dislike."

"We scarcely know each other, Madam. Save for formal occasions in public and once when you came and danced in our garden at home, and my sisters and I were so stupidly overawed by your beauty, I have never been close to you as I am now. Of course, I am afraid of you. But why should you suppose that I dislike you?"

Isabel's shrug was entirely and expressively French. "Is not every woman suspect from the unsought moment when she becomes a mother-in-law? Besides, what you do not know personally of my vanity and cruelty and immorality has probably been very thoroughly poured into your innocent ears by my enemies."

"There are unpleasant persons who try. But the King tries to keep such slanders from me."

"For very shame. But at least I am not pretending to you that they are not true."

To her surprise, instead of looking shocked, Philippa regarded her with candid curiosity. "I think you are more interesting than anyone else whom I have met in this country. When you first came as a bride you must have been much as I am—except that you were far more beautiful and clever. And now you are so—different. Do you suppose that in the years to come I, too, shall change so much?"

Her naïveté, while it hurt, was touching. "Why should you?" asked Isabel with a kind of bitter generosity. "You, with your native goodness and your devoted husband. And let me tell you, Philippa, that even if you grow fat and lose the fresh sweetness of your youth you will *keep* his love. My son is like that. He is tenacious. All through the years you will be the adored Queen and wife and mother. You will have the one crowning thing I wanted."

She turned her head away that she might not see the glow of happiness suffusing Philippa's face. "Every night and morning I thank God that my husband is so kind," she was saying softly.

"Thank Him, rather, that he is strong and normal," advised her mother-in-law. "What does my son intend to do with me?"

Philippa roused herself from such rare unreserve to her usual practical kindness. "I heard him telling his cousin Lincoln that your household should be removed to a place called Castle Rising—in Norfolk, is it not?"

"As a prisoner?"

"Indeed, I do not think so, Madam, since other estates will be left you. In case you should need some change of air, the King said. And he himself will come sometimes to visit you and bring you news of your family."

"Which means that I am not to come to court. Oddly," said Isabel ruminatively, "I do not want to come to court. How could I bear it now? And what of my money?" she asked more sharply.

"That, I am afraid, will anger you. An allowance. Sufficient for your household expenses and reasonable state, or occasional travelling. Oh, do not look so angry, Madam! Because there is something so much more important which Edward is doing for you—so much more important to your *safety*——"

"Beshrew you, child, I care little enough for that now that they have killed my lover. But what is it?"

"Orders have gone out that no one will be allowed to give evidence against you. Oh, I do not exactly know about what. But there were people like Daverill and Maltravers who tried, and were forbidden."

Isabel's thoughts were wandering back to the dark wood. "There was a woman called Druscilla——" she murmured.

"I know nothing of her, Madam."

A faint sigh escaped the Queen Dowager's lips. "Except that the expenses of her journey will always be written there in the state papers, I suppose she must have sunk back into her dull obscurity—with the soldiers——"

"There was a man called Gourney. Sir Thomas Gourney."

Isabel sat up straight in the bed. Fear stared from her eyes. "What of him? Has he spoken?" she demanded shrilly, although nothing could hurt Roger now.

"No, he never will. Edward is having him chased from country to country and if he takes ship he will be killed at sea. Because he holds him responsible for his father's murder and fears that, to save himself, the wretch may try to incriminate your Grace."

Isabel sank back against her pillows with a sigh of relief. "I was not guilty of this terrible thing, except in so far as I and my sins unconsciously paved the way for it to happen," she said slowly, although she had never sought to justify herself to anyone else. "My son is acting generously towards me and it was charitable of you to come."

"Edward, I feel, would have done the same in any case," said Philippa. "But I think my devout parents would like you to know that his Holiness the Pope wrote to him immediately, pleading on your behalf that in all that happened you were influenced by the late Lord Mortimer and counselling him to keep your name from all dishonour."

Tears of weakness welled into Isabel's eyes. "His Holiness did that for me?" she murmured, wondering at the undeserved kindness shown her on all sides. And presently her daughter-in-law leant forward with a tentatively out-stretched hand. "I have been wondering," she suggested humbly, "would it not be easier for your Grace to enter some Convent than to live this—lonely—secluded life at Castle Rising?"

Isabel touched her hand with her own, all distrust and antipathy gone. "I have had the same thought in mind," she said. "Easier it certainly would be, but alas! I have no vocation. I have ever been a worldly woman, Philippa. Ah, well. Instead, I will go on a pilgrimage, perhaps, as I once intended to—but fell to quarrelling instead."

"Quarrelling—on a pilgrimage?" smiled Philippa.

For the first time for days Isabel smiled too. "With a vixen of a woman who for no reason at all shut me out of one of my own castles. In faith, even your gentle heart would have admitted that I had great provocation. It was, as far as I can recall, the only time when my husband stood up for me."

Philippa watched the sudden bewitching attraction of the lined and ravaged face when moved to laughter, and sighed for her own dullness. "By all people tell me, you must have lived most—excitingly, Madam, when you were young."

"Beyond belief," agreed Isabel, who was not yet forty. "Everything that could possibly have happened to a woman seemed to happen to me. I have been swindled out of all my jewels—and my husband's heart. Made love to by my handsome master-of-horse. Abandoned in a horrible castle while my husband and his friend took the only boat. Driven suddenly in the middle of the night out of my native country with scarcely a penny. I have even led an invasion. And when I was *very* young like you, Philippa, the court was much gayer than it is now. Why, I can remember my husband helping to toss his fat little jester up to the ceiling in one of my aunt's best table-cloths and——" Abruptly, Isabel stopped speaking and all the fun and sparkle died out of her face. She had come to that memory of Edward, warm and handsome and laughing, in the days when she had loved him, fooling with Piers Gaveston that Christmas at Eltham. And now he was cold and dead in Gloucester Abbey, which surely he had never deserved to be, feckless and incapable as he was. "It was not really very amusing, most of it," she said soberly. "And not one hour of the ecstasy of physical love I sold my soul for afterwards was worth the sinning——" She had forgotten Philippa, and was away in the agonizing self-reproach of her own thoughts. She knew that she was still over-wrought by shock—that as time went on she would get better, and have courage to make something of her new, secluded life. But for the moment she was too tired and weak to talk coherently. It was an effort, but she rather liked the girl and in common civility she must try. But the everyday pleasantries of life eluded her. They had been too drastically cut away, so that her thoughts could only move inwardly. "I may never expiate my sins, but a man who had wronged me once said that whatever I might become or do would to any thinking mind be justified. 'Because of two worthless fools,' he said, 'an eager, generous girl, exquisitely moulded for high destiny, grows bitter with good cause, harbouring the seeds of cruelty.'"

Isabel was picking the words carefully from her memory, and Philippa supposed her to be wandering again. "What became of him?" she asked, humouring her and preparing to depart.

"What became of him?" Isabel's voice quavered like an old woman's, her mind was too weary to concentrate. "Oh, young and loving life excessively, he went to his death on a sunny hillside overlooking the Black Dog of Warwick's town. I forgave him. Because he once let me see his soul beneath his facile charm—or perhaps because I was half in love with him? Who knows? God knows I forgave him. But it all happened again. With another man who cruelly, deliberately destroyed all that I had rebuilt. And how often must one forgive? 'Unto seventy times seven', the Book says . . ."

With one last pitying glance the new Queen of England had moved towards the door, but while someone on the other side sprang to fling it wide for her she could still hear Isabel the Fair murmuring, first in French and then in English, "*Notre Père qui es aux cieux, pardonne-nous nos offenses, comme aussi nous les pardonnons* . . . Oh, compassionate Christ, forgive us our trespasses, as we must somehow learn to forgive those who trespass against us!"